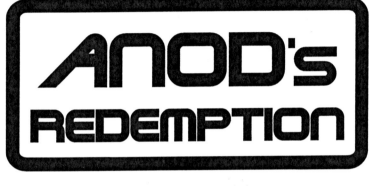

CAP PARLIER

CAP PARLIER

SAINT GAUDENS PRESS
Wichita, Kansas & Santa Barbara, California

Books by Cap Parlier:
Anod's Seduction
Sacrifice
Anod's Redemption

and with Kevin E. Ready:
TWA 800 - Accident or Incident?

These and other great books available from Saint Gaudens Press
http://www.saintgaudenspress.com or call toll-free 1-(800) 281-5170

Visit Cap Parlier's Web Site at http://www.parlier.com

Saint Gaudens Press
Post Office Box 91847
Santa Barbara, CA 93190-1847

Saint Gaudens, Saint Gaudens Press and the Winged Liberty
colophon are trademarks of Saint Gaudens Press

ISBN: 0-943039-04-5
Library of Congress Control Number: 2004096707

Printed in the United States of America

DEDICATION

To Jeanne, Jacy, Courtney, Tyson and Taylor.

Thank you for your unwavering support.

Special appreciation is offered to Greta Robertson, Leta Buresh and John Richard for their generous time, criticism, advice and friendship. Criticism, like a mirror, shows us how others see you. Their honest contribution was of considerable value.

Chapter 1

The consequences of banishment sank deeply into her consciousness. Anod felt the humiliation of her ejection from the Society, and yet her attachment to Zoltentok, the son born of her body and the product of her love for his father – Bradley James SanGiocomo – made the sting dissipate more quickly than she imagined it would. Anod continued to learn and marvel at the dimensions of life that had been held beyond her vision or grasp. Life was good despite banishment. Her salvation and strength rested in those closest to her – Zoltentok, Bradley, Nick, Mysasha, Otis and Guyasaga.

Zoltentok was growing quickly, more quickly than Betan norms according to Nick. The little boy was approaching his first birthday and was walking and beginning to form his first words. Anod derived considerable pleasure from just watching the changes in her son.

The other men in her life now added the remainder of her contentment. Otis Greenstreet, despite their early relationship, now took on all the characteristics of her protector, what the Betans called her brother. A different sort of closeness had developed between the two former lovers when the previous tension vanished from their relationship. Nick provided the guidance – the soft, gentle hand with words of advice and reflection. There were no subjects too sensitive or too private for them to discuss. She was very thankful for the care and nurturing the elder SanGiocomo freely gave to his adopted daughter. The relationship between Anod and Bradley continued to grow stronger and bigger with every day. The topic of marriage under Betan custom had not come up for sometime. Bradley seemed to be content to wait for the time to be right with Anod. Their relationship did not need the consent of society although Bradley and Nick still held their desires to themselves.

Anod chose to remain out of the negotiations with the Society, represented by Colonel Zontramani. Prime Minister Bradley SanGiocomo performed his tasks and functions in an exemplary manner befitting a head of state. The agreement reached after a month of discussions, compromise and development formed a loose alliance between the Society and the simple government of θ27β.

The θ27 star system would come under the protective umbrella of the Society. Starships would patrol this region of the galaxy to ensure neither the Yorax nor any other aggressive faction would subjugate the Betan people and their passive culture.

The three starships remained in the vicinity for another month after the agreement. The crews of the three vessels rotated standdown periods to allow for some rest and relaxation on the surface of Beta. The inhabitants accepted the visitors as guests, and a mutual respect and relationship blossomed.

As with Anod, most of the starship crewmembers had never set foot upon the surface of Earth. Those few who retained memories of Earth made the comparisons between Beta and their mother planet. The environment as well as the people brought a genuine tranquility. The burgeoning union was further enhanced with the direct assistance of the starship crews and the technology of the vessels to repair and rebuild the damage done by the Yorax.

The uniform of the starship crew was more than Anod could bear to see. The simple but functional uniforms reminded Anod of her punishment for the transgression she no longer saw as wrong. She avoided all the places frequented by the visitors, confining her journeys to the forest around SanGiocomo with an occasional return to High Cave. Zoltentok accompanied his mother during her outings, riding in a native harness on her back or positioned facing forward on her chest. The two were inseparable. Anod accepted her role as teacher as she drew pleasure from telling her son about the many wonders they saw during their walks. On a few rare occasions, Bradley joined them for a couple days, together as a family at High Cave.

An uneasiness lay not far beneath the surface of Anod's consciousness. The quiet, private rage of intolerance intertwined within her situation was abated somewhat once the rail system was repaired and operating. Anod began to make regular excursions to Astral, at first just to see the interceptor and to show Zoltentok an object that he could not yet comprehend. The transition process did not take long. Anod fashioned a new harness for her son to secure him to the standard harness and fit him in the small cockpit with her 180 centimeter, 64 kilogram body. She found ways to work around his sometimes fidgeting body. Mother and son went flying.

Zoltentok took to the change in his environment like it was meant to be. Anod used the interceptor for her own enjoyment as well as their personal tour vehicle. Most of her flight time was in the atmosphere and was masked to avoid frightening or disturbing the citizens after the trauma of battle with the traitor, Zitger, and his Yorax brethren. There were also a couple of trips to circle an orbiting starship with proper prior approval so as not to alarm the vastly superior spacecraft's crew. Once beyond the visual range of the Betans, Anod would unmask to preserve power and take an occasional hyperlight dash.

The flight sorties were a unique anesthetic helping to ease the pain. The momentary periods of freedom were small islands of refuge in an otherwise turbulent and stormy sea that existed only within her mind. The thoughts rumbling through her consciousness were no different from the myriad of other contrasts that had entered her life since her arrival on Beta. Anod was happy and sad, elated and dejected, content and restless. There were too many elements of her current situation that were not right – not acceptable – and there was too much fight left within her to acquiesce.

Anod waited for the tensions of leadership to loosen their grip on Bradley before she let the subject of her discontent arise. The desired opportunity was a habitual walk after a leisurely and warm family meal. Nick was content working on one of his many projects in his laboratory, Anod's former room, and Zoltentok was safely and quietly sleeping. A solo cloud moving slowly across the night sky occasionally obscured the blanket of stars above it.

They walked from the cave to the edge of the forest on the far side of the clearing without a word. Anod stopped to face Bradley and looked into his eyes. "This is not going to work," she said with a clear image of what this was.

The clarity of imagery was not afforded her mate. "I'm not sure I understand what you mean."

"I feel like a caged animal."

An empathy as well as understanding welled up within the Betan prime minister. He had often wondered if he would ever participate in this discussion. He hoped he never would. The arrival of the topic was undeniable. "Anod, you are free. There are no restrictions on your movements, your travels, or your desires. You are free to do what you want."

"Yes, yes, but I am not free to enjoy all the things I do enjoy. I have been denied things that have been part of my life. I suppose I am having trouble with the fact I have been told I cannot have something." The soft, melodious tone of her voice did not lessen the serious, strong and determined words she spoke.

Bradley did not like the direction of the conversation although he fully recognized he was impotent to alter its course. "What do you want to do?"

"I don't know."

The words floated in the air for some few moments as Bradley considered what he should say to soothe the trouble in the woman he loved. The words did not come easily. It was difficult for him to comprehend the turmoil within her, however there was no problem detecting its existence. A thought did occur to him that he might try to let the disturbance dampen out somewhat, but he knew deep down it would not. He knew the question he must ask. It was the answer he really did not want to hear. "Do you want to leave?"

The cool response to his inquiry as well as the considered pause in responding told Bradley, she had asked herself the question many times before the words were actually spoken. He grimaced within, bracing himself for the horror of the answer he would surely receive.

"I have thought about it," Anod finally answered.

The words hit Bradley like a sharp spike plunged into his chest.

"I don't know where I could go," she continued. "I am not sure there is any place in the universe that can give me what I have been denied. I want many of the elements of my life in service to the Society, and yet I cannot relinquish what I have gained here with you."

"Do you see yourself within a paradox that has no solution?"

"In some ways, yes, I do."

"Why can't you adjust to life on Beta, to the ways we have chosen to live?"

Anod smiled with the warmth of their bond in her eyes and ruffled her short, auburn hair. "It is not that I am disappointed or resentful of my life since fate brought me to this planet and to you. I want the pleasures and enjoyment I have found with you, with your father and with the birth of Zoltentok. You are important to me, so I know I cannot go back to the laws of the Society. The option simply does not exist. However, I could do so much more as a pilot in the Kartog Guards. There was excitement, adventure, discovery and exploration. It is a difficult thing to describe."

"You have the interceptor. Although it is not something my people, as a whole, would want on their planet, we have allowed its presence for your benefit," Bradley said with gentleness.

"Yes, and I suppose that is also part of the problem." The puzzled expression on Bradley's face was testimony to the excessive jump she had just made. "I know the interceptor is against the desires of your people. A capability which is important to me is a serious irritant, if not an outright offense, to your people."

The waves of frustration were evident in Bradley's eyes as the Betan leader absorbed Anod's words. The dichotomy was no longer one to be ignored.

The ensuing weeks brought pulsating discussions and eventually debates among a small group of Betans. Bradley and Anod could not avoid the conflict associated with the central topic. What direction should the future go? Should they embrace the burden and responsibility of technology? Should they become a merchant nation trading with other peoples scattered across the galaxy although they possessed no vessels for transport? Issues their ancestors had faced and resolved were once more being brought out into the light of day. Not everyone was pleased with the turn of events. The discussions were initially kept to a small number of trusted people – friends – most of whom knew or were aware of Anod.

The participation of the former Kartog Guards pilot was certainly a stimulus. Anod bore witness to emotions she had never seen displayed by the humans of her culture. Words assembled into precision cutting instruments were drawn from the scabbards of fertile minds to ensure nothing was left out of view. The discussions seemed to take on an existence of their own with increasing fervor, commitment and resolve as they struggled with the future.

One day, after many sessions in the debate surrounding Anod and the future, she was able to gain some distance from the fray to become an intellectual observer. Her emotions took broad swings, from revulsion to excitement, as she listened and watched the animated performances of various individuals. There were no parallels in her catalog of experiences. There were no similarities. This was the freedom of debate, the freedom of expression and the delicate workings of democracy at work before her.

Anod had always considered herself free. There were no topics that could not be discussed among the other pilots, however she could not recall any topics of a philosophical nature about themselves and their relationships. The Kartog Guards pilots as well as other officers of the warrior class always talked about space, flight, tactics and martial history. They were professional discussions, not personal.

The discussions of the future were the latest and most graphic demonstrations of the passion for life that existed beyond her previous environment. Passion was not a word she had ever spoken or needed to speak as a Kartog Guards pilot and warrior. It was a word that she had learned on Beta and seemed to surface within conversations often among the Betans. Passion was a word used by the Betans, and now Anod, to share various occurrences filled with a spectrum of emotions. It was also a word Anod had learned to relish, to absorb, to wrap around her. There was a unique energy associated with events described as passionate.

The conversation that would alter the course of history occurred one evening after a particularly volatile day of debate within the Betan Council. Bradley had never seen such intransigence in his people. Anod had no basis to judge. The meal was complete. Zoltentok was asleep in his small bed. Nick, Bradley and Anod sat around the dining table talking about the events of the day.

"My frustration with these particular negotiations has essentially reached a limit," Bradley said. The deeply furrowed brow and a pained expression spread across Bradley's face punctuated his statement. "We seem to be more divided than when we started this debate. Plus, I am beginning to think there may not be a solution."

"There is always a solution, son. We simply have not found the catalytic compromise, yet."

"I have tried everything I am able to imagine, and there is always at least one more point of impasse."

"We have been through hard times before, and our ancestors have been through much worse. There is a solution," Nick stated with a calm confidence that was his character. It was also easier to offer wisdom when you are not embroiled in the debate.

"That may be, but I have not found it."

Anod considered the words in the perspective of event chronology. "I must leave," she said with a firm conviction of a determined woman who had made up her mind.

"Anod, please. Running away from a problem does not solve it," Bradley said with even more frustration.

"I am not running away," responded Anod with some degree of offense. "It is not my nature to run away." Both men knew this to be true as several episodes displaying her courage came to mind. After all, she had single-handedly defended the planet against unconscionable odds. "However, the sign of a good leader is knowing when to alter his approach, or direction. This is such a time."

Bradley wanted to relieve the tension continuing to multiply within him. "There are no other suitable habitats in this sector of the galaxy. In fact, I do not know and have not heard of any virgin environments, period."

Nick ignored his son's pronouncement.

"There is a solution, Anod," Bradley added speaking to her and trying to calm the growing emotions within his son. "We will find the answer. We always have."

"I continue to be the cause of all this turmoil. It is a heavy burden to bear especially with respect to such a kind and gentle people."

Both Nick and Bradley acknowledged the compliment but did not respond verbally. Neither man wanted to disagree with Anod, nor did they want to accept her conclusion.

"We have not asked the Society to assist us in finding a virgin environment, as you call it, or even a suitable place," added Anod.

Nick and Bradley thought about the implied suggestion. "Even if we did find something, furthering your banishment to such a place would serve no purpose and is totally unreasonable," Nick answered for both of them.

"We cannot know that until we have exhausted all possibilities. I do not believe we have reached that point, yet." Anod felt a slight sense of renewal with the added option although the likelihood of success was remote.

A noticeable change washed across Bradley's face. "What if, there is another world?"

"Bradley, stop talking about that option!" Nick pointed his right index finger at his son to emphasize his exclamation. "We cannot ask Anod to go anywhere alone."

"Father, I was not thinking of Anod being alone."

The other two participants in the discussion looked puzzled after hearing the words and considering the implication. Each of them thought of something different although the consequences were the same. Neither of them wanted to ask the obvious question.

Bradley continued, "What if, we started a new community, a new culture, leaving Beta as we intended it to remain?"

"You said, we. Who are you referring to when you say, we?" Nick asked with an irritated jaggedness to his words.

"I suppose I mean those of us who may be willing to start a new nation, given the assumption there is a suitable planet somewhere."

Anod jumped in with a spark of enlightenment. "We could combine the best of both cultures, take advantage of the good in both communities." Anod thought about saying something to the effect of discarding the worst, but the thought was too negative for the flavor of the moment.

The response was not what she expected, at first. Anod's revelation was a poke with a sharp stick to Nick and Bradley. Until Anod's arrival on their planet, both men were quite content with the structure of their lives and the nature of their adopted environment. Neither of them held any thoughts that their culture was less than ideal. Anod's idea implicitly stated there were bad things, or at least less desirable things, about the life they considered somewhat idyllic.

The reaction to her comments did not fail to register on the speaker. "Never mind, it was a bad idea," said Anod with her disappointment not far from the surface. She rose from the table and began to walk out of the room. All of a sudden, she needed some fresh air.

"Wait, Anod. Let's discuss your suggestion," requested Bradley.

She continued to walk away and did not turn to respond. She simply said, "No, it was a bad idea."

"We discuss all ideas regardless of their merit. It is a price of freedom," Bradley said with the strength of a leader. Anod stopped and turned without expression. "I admit I did not respond well to your suggestion, at first, however we should examine it more closely before we discard it." He paused to let his words sink in. They had the desired effect. "Come back and sit down. Let's look at your idea."

Another spark rekindled a smoldering ember. Anod did return to the conversation that eventually extended without concern or realization into the following morning. All three of them began to contribute to the synergistic reaction of powerful minds on a galvanizing topic. The more aspects they discussed, the more attractive Anod's suggestion was becoming. She drew upon some of her newly stimulated emotions, long dormant in her being, to articulate her observations and to describe the essence of what had been, for some time, an immaturely formed, conglomeration of concepts.

By the time fatigue finally began to dull their senses, a viable basis for a new culture had begun to take shape. There were numerous precarious assumptions involved in the formation portion of the concept. Bradley felt a latent segment of the Betan population would be attracted to an evolutionary metamorphosis which was possible from the union of the two cultures, the technologist Society and the agrarian Beta.

Nick was less quick and enthusiastic about embracing such a drastic change, although certain aspects of the concept did tickle his imagination. The basis of the new culture was the humanization of the Society's technologic strength and the amplification of the Betan philosophical freedom. The idea hinged on an appropriate environment for such a community. Bradley and Nick were both convinced the majority of the Betan population would want to remain, and maintain the slow paced, comfortable life they and their ancestors had sought for so long and finally achieved.

The germination of the idea was successful. The fertilization and nurturing of the developing concept took longer and began to involve more people. Some of those exposed to the discussions were repelled by the thought of another major change and were reassured there would be no attempt to restructure the Betan culture, customs or community.

With several hundred Betans in general agreement with the direction the new society was heading, it was time to address the largest assumption. Bradley, as Prime Minister of Beta, initiated the call to the Society for another meeting. The response took more than a week to return. The Starship *Karamaki*, the closest of the Society's intragalactic emissaries, intercepted the communication on the subspace radio channel and relayed the request to Central Command via a hyperspace communications link. The Starship *Endeavour* would be directed to return to Beta for further discussions. The estimated time of arrival within other constraints was nine days away.

The intervening time was spent continuing to develop a plan. Bradley was so attracted to a scheme where he could maintain the pleasurable features of his Betan life as well as the companionship of his lover and mother of his child, he passed leadership of the Betan people temporarily to his deputy who was all too happy to accept. The basis of the new culture was coalescing quite nicely when the *Endeavour* arrived.

Colonel Zontramani and Bradley SanGiocomo, no longer prime minister of Beta, met again in the *Endeavour* captain's command conference room. The initial talks were general in nature with an update of the status in this sector of the galaxy. Zontramani described the actions the Society was taking with respect to the Yorax in an effort to preclude any future confrontations similar to the θ027 incident. They confirmed the betrayal and defection of Zitger, and were still negotiating with the Yorax for his extradition. Zontramani remained guardedly optimistic an agreement – a treaty – could be achieved with the Yorax, although there was not much chance of Zitger being returned to face his crimes. Bradley again thanked the starship captain for their protection and security that had been returned to Beta through their efforts.

"Colonel Zontramani," Bradley began then paused to indicate a change in subjects. "I asked for this meeting to seek the assistance of the Society. We are considering the possibility of forming a new nation."

"I am not sure what assistance we can be to such an activity. What is your proposal?"

"We want to start a new community that combines the best of the Society and Beta. We want to take advantage of the Society's technology and yet retain the freedoms and pleasures of Beta."

The telltale tingling of a threat instantly jumped into Zontramani's consciousness. The nature of the threat was not readily apparent and certainly not obvious to the starship captain, but it was present nonetheless. The proposal seemed innocuous and yet sometimes the most innocent of individuals or events were the most dangerous and deadly. He sensed the underlying influence of the former Kartog Guards lieutenant – Anod.

Zontramani wanted to maintain some distance from the proposal and any explicit or implicit commitment of assistance. "How do you think we can help you?"

"We want to leave Beta as it is. We want to find another suitable virgin planet to begin anew."

The short laugh was certainly an indicator of the likelihood. "You are asking for too much. Class E planets are not commonplace in this portion of the home galaxy, and the closest galaxy beyond our own is too far for our current propulsion systems. There are no pristine planets to the best of my knowledge."

The disappointment of his words was expected and prepared for. None of the new colonists thought the search process would be quick, but the exploratory nature of the Society starships as well as the wide range of the vessels made them the best hope.

"Can we discuss possible compromise options?" asked Bradley.

"Certainly. We have no reason to withhold fundamental information from you," Zontramani answered. "Mostron," he spoke to the unseen third party, "search your records and those of Central Command for any uninhabited Class E planets."

"As you wish," responded Mostron, the starship's central computer system.

"You should expand your search to class D and F planets as well."

"As you wish."

Zontramani's eyes returned to Bradley. "While Mostron searches the records, I thought we should expand the search to all planets that are inhabitable by humans."

"What are class D and F planets?"

"Class D bodies are similar to Class E planets, however they have insufficient oxygen to sustain human life. A supplemental breathing device of some type is required in the atmosphere although there are no toxic elements. Class F planets have insufficient water to support a population. Hydro-production equipment is required assuming the elements are present."

"They do not sound like very hospitable places," responded Bradley.

"As I said, there are not very many Class E planets in this galaxy. Your ancestors have been to most of them and discovered the last planet. Beta was not in our records until Anod called during the confrontation with the Yorax. There may be other Class E planets out there somewhere, and there probably are. We simply have not found any more, and there are none that are not already inhabited. However, we also have not searched and charted the entire galaxy, only a relatively small portion."

"Thank you for your efforts. We will await the results." Bradley rose to depart.

"May I ask you a question or two?"

Bradley nodded his head in the affirmative.

"How is Anod doing?"

Bradley recognized instantly the caring of a man who empathized with Anod's plight even though it was he who sentenced her. "She is doing as well as can be expected," he answered succinctly.

"Is she the instigator of this change you seek?"

"In large part, yes. The combination concept was her idea. She was hurt by her banishment, and she wants to retrieve some of what she lost," he paused then added, "and retain what she has gained on Beta."

"Good. She is a very good person. I deeply regret, and probably always will, terminating her citizenship. She has such great potential. It is a shame the Society lost her."

"Your loss is our gain, I should think."

"Indeed." Zontramani looked deeply into Bradley's eyes to touch some of the commitment in his voice. "I will let you know as soon as

Mostron has completed his search."

"Thank you."

Bradley returned to the surface to convey the content of their talks. There was an undercurrent of optimism moving among the small group. Anod listened with interest as Bradley told her about the continuing negotiations with the Yorax and the move to extradite the traitor, Zitger.

The search process took nearly four hours, which for a computer with the speed and power of Mostron meant an incredibly extensive effort. Zontramani decided to deliver the results in person arriving via transporter near midday.

Nick welcomed their guest and provided a short tour of his abode. He was, as always, proud of his laboratory, and this occasion was no different. Zontramani was impressed and intrigued by the use of the natural antratite as a protective shield against probes of the interior. The material explained the difficulty the *Endeavour* had trying to locate Bradley. The starship's sensors found the biological tracers that comprised Anod when she left the protection of the cave walking into the forest. Neither she nor Zoltentok were present when Zontramani arrived.

"What have you found for us?" asked Bradley finally too impatient to wait any longer.

"Let's sit at the table first," Nick interjected. "I have made some tea and biscuits for our midday meal."

The three of them sat at the table, each taking a few biscuits. Zontramani followed the lead of his host dipping his biscuit into to a communal bowl of fruit jelly.

"The search was more extensive than I had figured. I believe we have exhausted all known data regarding this section of our galaxy. Mostron found three potential Class D planets and seven Class F planets."

Bradley wondered if Zontramani was toying with their anticipation by withholding the information about the Class E planets, planets similar to Earth and Beta. "What about the Class E planets?" he finally asked.

The answer was candid and blunt. "There were none found."

"None," Bradley nearly shouted. "There are none in the entire galaxy," he said half as an exclamation and half as a continued interrogative.

"In the seven thousand plus years of human astronomy and space exploration, we have charted and catalogued only a mere fraction of a percent of the home galaxy, let alone the known universe. There is much more out there than we are aware of at this moment."

Bradley wanted to approach the question from another direction. "How many Class E planets are known?" His voice was more controlled and determined.

"If I can remember Mostron's report, there are seven Class E planets with the correct ranges and combination of atmospheric gases, water and alternate life."

"That is seven out of how many charted planets?"

"I am sure I cannot remember the totals, but as I recall, Mostron mentioned something about point zero six percent, if my memory serves me correctly," answered Zontramani.

At that moment, Anod walked into the dining room and froze upon seeing Zontramani. Zoltentok was soundly asleep in his harness on her back. "Colonel Zontramani," was all she said.

"Anod, it is good to see you again," he responded with genuine happiness. A nod was all she wished to muster as an acknowledgment. "Is that your infant child?"

"Yes."

"May I see him?" Zontramani was interested as a visitor, but he was also curious since ancient human reproduction was non-existent in his world.

Anod carefully removed him from his position on her back cradling him in her arms. Zontramani looked down at the child with a broad smile on his face reaching to touch his soft, rosy cheek. Being close to an infant child was also not something Zontramani had experienced in many years. Progress through the Society's education process precluded much contact with other human age groups until they were complete and adults.

"He is a beautiful child," stated Zontramani. "What is his name?"

"Zoltentok James SanGiocomo."

"Zoltentok, huh?" The starship captain looked directly into Anod's eyes with a smile. "You named him in honor of Admiral Zolten?"

"Yes."

"He was your mentor?"

"Yes."

"No wonder you are so strong," he said. "What are the other names?"

Anod did not want to get into this particular discussion with Zontramani, however she was not ashamed of what Zoltentok represented either. "The name combination reflects Betan custom. He bears the family name of his father."

The words coming from a Kartog Guards pilot were strange and foreign to his ears. Somehow they just did not fit together. The explanation also completed his understanding of what had happened to Anod while she was on Beta.

"With that percentage of Class E planets," Bradley said to recover the topic being discussed prior to Anod's return, "there is a possibility other Class E planets might exist in the unexplored portion of the galaxy?"

Zontramani returned to the table offering another chair to Anod. She left the room to put Zoltentok in his bed then returned to the table to listen.

"There is always that possibility," Zontramani answered.

"Does your computer know of any good prospects?"

"Yes. There are several systems with potential Class E planets."

"Can you explore them for us?"

Zontramani thought about the options available to him within his standing and current orders. The Yorax negotiations were the number one priority. He also had other directives that did not include the systems identified by Mostron. His authority only went so far. Alteration of his current orders would be required.

"I do not have the authority to initiate the necessary search," answered the captain of the Society Starship *Endeavour*.

The disappointment was clearly marked on Bradley's face. Numerous doors began to close with Zontramani's response. "Is there another starship that could conduct the search?"

"They would have the same problem I have."

"Do you have any suggestions?"

"The likelihood of finding a suitable Class E planet is remote. I think you should consider working out some compromise here on Beta, or consider one of the Class D or F planets."

Each of Zontramani's suggestions was less than desirable. Remaining on Beta would probably cause an irreconcilable rift between the two factions. The idea of living in conditions where some form of supplemental assistance was required just for survival was not an acceptable alternative either.

"Would you ask Central Command for a modification to your orders?" asked Anod participating in the discussion for the first time.

Zontramani looked at her with the resentment of being asked a question he did not want asked. Despite his objections, he knew it was a question that had to be asked by a small group in need of additional assistance. "I will convey your request."

"We can ask no more," Bradley added with a slight smile.

"I must be going. I will let you know when I get a response from Central. We will remain in orbit until we conclude this discussion."

"You are most welcome. We will extend an invitation for your crew to enjoy a rest on our planet."

"Thank you. I am certain they shall appreciate the opportunity as much as they did on our last visit."

Colonel Zontramani departed the same way he arrived as the scintillation of his conversion from matter to energy initiated his transport to the starship passing above. Nick, Bradley and Anod watched him disappear into the ether.

"What do you think will happen?" asked Bradley turning to Anod.

"It is hard to say. I do not have much experience on starships. I do not know how flexible their orders are. I think it will actually come down to whether the Society wants to support us and maintain good relations. It also depends somewhat on how Colonel Zontramani presents the question. Fifty-fifty. Our chances are probably fifty-fifty."

"That is better than nothing," Nick added.

Neither Bradley nor Anod responded to Nick's assessment. All three of them looked at the spot Zontramani last stood on Beta as if he might reappear at any moment.

"Zoltentok should be asleep for another hour. I want to take a walk to think some more," said Anod with a nearly quiescent voice.

"I will go with you," Bradley offered.

"No," answered Anod looking back at her companion. "I would rather be alone, if you don't mind." He shook his head to indicate his lack of objection and acceptance of her wishes.

Anod walked casually through the forest shuffling her feet to hear the fallen leaves rustle and crackle as she stepped. The moving spots of light and shadows shimmered on the forest floor as the wind moved the trees above her head. The soft sounds the leaves made in the wind added a touch of serenity to the puzzling thoughts roaring through her brain.

Life had instantly become more complicated with Zitger's betrayal. His selfish motivation, or whatever drove him to do such a heinous deed, had set a chain of events in motion that led to the moment in time she now occupied. So many things might have been different, but they were not. She could not rewrite the past although the thought was tempting, however impossible it might be. Certainly, there were pleasures and expanding experiences. It was the turmoil and trauma that came with them that made Anod consider the past and what might have been.

A member of the elite Kartog Guards was what Anod used to be. Her skills, knowledge and instincts had not changed, simply her affiliation. She missed those days. By her current metrics, they were less complicated times, where reality tended to be black and white without many shades of gray. Now, there was an aurora of brilliant colors that was often difficult to assess or to understand. Each life had its attractors and detractors, its benefits and costs. With the experiences she now possessed, Anod knew she could never be truly happy in either system. The process of rationalization was working its relentless tentacles throughout her reasoning. The seduction of Anod was nearly complete as she made her way back to the cave. The combination of the two cultures was the only way to satisfy her newly formed desires. Anod could only hope the others were equally convinced. Maybe even current members of the Society would eventually join their small group, if an acceptable and appropriate home could ever be found.

The afternoon was waning as she reentered the cave home of Sebastian Nicholas SanGiocomo, father to Bradley and grandfather to Zoltentok. A refreshing contentment pervaded her thoughts, now. No matter how long it took, Anod knew what the outcome must be. She was wise enough to maintain her patience.

Nick and Bradley had prepared an early meal. The table was full of a variety of natural and prepared foods common to the Betan culture. Bradley was holding Zoltentok who had become somewhat restless and was beginning to freely display his displeasure.

They sat down to eat. Anod fed the infant.

Their words, however, were of the day's events and the prospects for the future. There was a growing vein of optimism among them. Optimism in an acceptable solution no matter what was determined by the Society. Even Nick, despite his years and earlier reluctance, was talking of a new beginning, an evolutionary change in the human condition. Each of them drew energy from the others.

Toward the end of the following day, the response to their request for assistance came in the form of an emissary – Colonel Astrok, the first officer. She asked Bradley and Anod to return to the *Endeavour* with her for a conference meeting with Colonel Zontramani. An invitation was also extended for them to attend an official meal with the captain. Anod thought about taking Zoltentok with her, but convinced herself to the contrary. They departed the way Astrok arrived.

Colonel Zontramani was waiting for them. "Welcome aboard *Endeavour*, again," he said as they completed the transfer.

"Thank you," responded Bradley for them both.

This was Anod's first visit to a starship after her banishment and the feelings were not as she expected. Her confidence and pride had returned. She was now a *de facto* leader of the new faction standing beside her cohort, companion and lover. There was a blossoming satisfaction among the other feelings she possessed. Anod liked the freedom she was unaware existed in her earlier life. It felt good.

Major Astridag, the science officer, and Captain Zalemon, the security officer, joined the four of them for the discussions. The talks lasted roughly two hours and covered a comprehensive background briefing by Astridag regarding the substance of Bradley's request and the potential search areas identified by Mostron and his brethren. The conclusion was a proposed agreement between the new community wherever it might be located and the Society. The proposal was general in nature, and not restrictive nor constraining. Bradley tentatively accepted the offer contingent upon approval by the other members of their small group.

With the discussions concluded, the group moved to a unique room for their celebration meal. The table was set in the traditional manner. Anod was convinced it was to impress Bradley, situated in a room whose walls were a perpetual scene wall, a complex holographic projection system that could replicate any scene. The scene chosen by Colonel Zontramani, or one of his officers, was a bountiful forest complete with the appropriate sounds and smells. It was as if they were dining in a new portion of forest on Beta. Anod found some satisfaction in the fact the representation was not as good as the real forest. Nonetheless, the forest scene was better than the sterile walls of the starship.

Anod knew the food was from the replicator although Bradley did not even consider the source. The food was delightful and perfectly prepared as would be expected from a replicator, and the talk was light and lively. Observations of the flora and fauna of the surrounding scene occupied a respectable portion of the conversation. Everyone including Colonel Zontramani and the former lieutenant, Anod, were pleased and privately impressed by the meal, the company and the outcome.

Anod and Bradley disembarked *Endeavour* after four hours. It was nearly midnight when they were deposited in the clearing in front of the SanGiocomo cave. The couple stood arm in arm without speaking, outside under the crystal clear sky looking up at the glorious blanket of stars. Bradley reached across to cradle Anod's face in his hands and gently kissed her. Anod responded with her acquired physical expression. She had learned and Bradley already knew the name that described what they both felt . . . love.

"Do you think they will be successful?" asked Bradley in almost a whisper.

Although the non-specific third person, they, could be anybody, Anod knew precisely what Bradley was asking. She was a warrior, and not an explorer. Her professional life had been close to the exploration segment of her profession, and she was aware of events as they occurred around her, but she knew she could not answer the question authoritatively. It was also not a question of precision. "It may take a longer time than we would like, but I do think they will be successful."

"Look," Bradley said pointing above them. "Zontramani isn't wasting any time getting started." The starship rapidly changed size and direction as the Society vessel departed its orbit around Beta for the journey ahead.

"Godspeed and following winds," Anod muttered the mariner's good luck wish to the departing starship. "Maybe we should go in," she suggested to Bradley.

Without a verbal response, Bradley moved toward the cave holding Anod close to him. There was a dim light inside which made the entry easier. As they entered the lighted room, they were no longer alone.

"You waited up for us," Bradley said with some frivolity.

Nick had been reading several of his journals and still appeared to be wide-awake and fully alert. "This was an important visit. I wanted to hear the results immediately."

"Well, Father, we have an agreement. Colonel Zontramani and his crew have identified several potential regions where a suitable planet might be found. They will search for us. Anod thinks it may take a long time, so we will have to be patient."

"Then, it sounds like good news."

"I would say, yes."

Anod left the two men. She wanted to see her sleeping child and touch his warm, soft cheek.

"What do we have to do in return for assistance from the Society?"

"The agreement is rather general. We would become a member of the Confederation of Planets and participate in that organization."

"We will have to get the approval of the others," Nick added.

"Yes. I told Zontramani the agreement was contingent upon approval by the others who wish to participate."

"Do you intend to start the approval process tomorrow?" asked Nick.

"In a day or so." Bradley reached for a small table biscuit. The single bite was taken in slow motion as if rapid movement might damage a delicate pastry. "I think I would like to take a few days with Anod and ZJ up at High Cave."

"As you wish . . . ."

The short remainder of the night was spent in restful embrace. Anod and Bradley were awakened by the sweet smell of fresh bread. Nick had risen early to send off his family in the best way.

The new family of three departed for High Cave later that morning. Zoltentok was excited by the unmistakable prospect of another journey into the forest with his mother, and this time a special treat, his father joined them as well.

High Cave was now the most treasured place for Anod. The quiet, natural environment brought an incomparable serenity to her, and yet it was the most energizing location she had ever been. After the two most recent visits, Anod had begun referring to High Cave as her place in a commendatory manner rather than as a possessive statement. Despite all the previous trips to High Cave, even Bradley felt a new closeness to the area.

The days spent at the mountain hide-away were leisurely and peaceful, filled with the union of their three souls. There was a freedom of life without bounds, without constraints, among the majestic trees, the crystal clear, sweet water and the idyllic chirping, whistling and clicking sounds of the forest.

The words between Anod and Bradley were mostly of love and the still growing emotions that bound them to each other. Anod was continuing to learn the true dimensions of love, of sharing, of giving. Occasionally, she wondered how she had been able to live life without those emotions, without the intimate contact of another human being. The blossoming of her personality and character was the vindication – the living proof – she had made the correct choices, even though some of those choices did not present themselves in such a manner. The past was now behind her and her eyes were firmly on the future.

Chapter 2

Life on Beta was a study in compromise with the seemingly constant pressure of annoying dissatisfaction associated with the molding influence of local custom. Every time Anod ventured away from the forest region of SanGiocomo, there were different elements that reminded her of the perceived confinement she was relegated to live.

Anod was becoming more recognized by the Betan population, some of whom were not reserved in their display of dissatisfaction over what she represented. Stress on the fabric of Betan society was what her persona had become to many citizens. During excursions to Providence and other towns, with or without Bradley, Anod usually saw the full spectrum of reaction. She was nearly worshipped by some of the people for her exploits in their defense and the potential new life she symbolized. It was the revulsion and disrespect of those who felt threatened and vulnerable that had the most impact on her psyche. Until her arrival on Beta, Anod had never known love, but she had also never experienced hate.

"Bradley, why do some people seem to hate me?" she asked at the end of a particular negative excursion.

He first looked to his father, who could only shrug his shoulders, and then searched her eyes for several seconds as he tried to measure the seriousness of her question. "I don't think it is truly hate. For the most part, we led a rather peaceful life on Beta. Our people enjoyed the pleasures of life without all the other pressures we worked so hard to discard. Your arrival changed that."

"Why? It was not my fault. I did not impose myself on Beta or anyone else."

"True. But, as happenstance would have it, you brought evil with you."

"Not of my doing. I did not even know where I was."

"Yes, but, it was the trauma of the Yorax incursion they remember, and unfortunately they see you as the representation of that inflicted horror."

Anod recognized the truth and candor in Bradley's words. They did nothing to make her feel better. Zoltentok began his characteristic soft whimpering sounds Anod learned meant he was hungry. She lifted him from his crib, sat in an old wooden rocking chair, cradled him in her left arm and opened her shirt.

She remained fixated on her son, now attached to her, and she privately reveled in the deep sensations of his suckling. The simple act of mother and child nourishing each other took the emotional pain of the day's journey completely away. He finished at one. She shifted him to give him her other breast. The bonding, emotions, commitment and energy this little tiny child evoked in her added a dimension to her life beyond her wildest imagination.

Bradley did not wait for her to finish. "What happened today?"

Anod did not alter her attention for several moments as she considered whether to continue the discussion. Zoltentok made her forget the tribulations. Bradley, in his innocent concern, was bringing her back. "Just the usual," she answered without taking her eyes off her son.

"What does that mean?"

"Nothing."

"Anod, it is something. Whatever happened today, it has certainly given you a touch of melancholy."

She finally raised her head and eyes to capture his stare. "There are people who blame me for all the destruction of the Yorax assault."

"There will always be those people."

"Yes, I suppose. However, if my presence elicits such a response, then I should leave you in peace."

"No," interjected Nick. They both looked at Bradley's father. "You can never please everyone. There will always be those people who want somebody to blame for the misery in their lives. You must ignore these . . . these . . . these ridiculous insults."

"They bother me."

"I am sure they do. They would bother me as well, especially by their senselessness."

"Leaving will not solve anything," said Bradley.

"It would remove the reminder of their suffering and loss."

"Perhaps," Bradley answered and paused. "But, it would also take away the greatness you have given us."

Anod only nodded her head and returned her attention to her son who seemed to be nearly at the end of his larger than normal intake. She tended to Zoltentok preparing him for his morning adventures. Nick had rigged an array of objects above his crib. The variety of textures, colors, shapes and sizes kept his attention, intermittently, for long periods of time.

The baby started swinging at the objects before Anod could lay him on his back underneath them.

"There is something else bothering you," said Bradley.

Anod stared at him then glanced at Nick. The older man must have read her mind.

"I will watch ZJ. You two need some time to talk," Nick offered.

Anod nodded her head again then walked toward the cave entrance. It was a bright, clear day with a moderate breeze rustling the trees and carrying the scents of the forest. Small, white puffy clouds dotted the sky. She walked over to their favorite gathering spot, a group of large rocks and tree sections roughly arranged for conversation. Shade from a large, deciduous tree covered part of the rocks and stumps. The wind in the leaves added a peaceful, almost melodic background sound. Anod chose a stump then waited for Bradley to sit.

"Yes, Bradley, there are many things bothering me." It was his turn to nod his head to let her continue. "Try to put yourself in my position. I violated several of the most fundamental precepts of the Society. I had intimate contact with you and Otis. I even gave birth to our child. I do not think natural reproduction has occurred within the Society in centuries. Humans from Earth just do not do that."

"We are humans from Earth," Bradley interjected.

"Yes, banished, in a form, for wanting to preserve the ancient ways."

"What is wrong with that? You have seen what pleasure means. You have experienced the pain and elation of childbirth. I know you feel pleasure when you feed ZJ in the old way."

"Yes, all true and all forbidden in the Society."

"So, you have joined us."

Anod turned pensive and shifted her gaze to the blades of grass moving in the wind below her. She looked back to Bradley. "I am chronologically ten years older than you, and I am also 10 to 15 years genetically or biologically younger than you. Have you asked yourself, why?" He only shook his head, no. "Once our genetic print is established, the bioscanner maintains the print, increasing productive life span by two to three times, in some cases more."

"Now, doesn't that sound pleasurable?" Bradley answered with a broad grin.

"Life is everything."

"Perhaps, but enjoyment of life is the sweetener."

Anod ignored Bradley's remark and returned to the grass. The words she wanted to say were not coming out. "I feel naked," she murmured.

A deep, guttural laugh bellowed from Bradley. "Now isn't that a statement – the only woman on this planet who feels no shame, no inhibition, to being seen stark naked by the whole planet."

True enough, Anod said to herself, but the intonation did not feel good. "It is not my body I am talking about. Just as I wear clothing for protection or utility, the people and technology of the Society protected me."

"I really don't think you need protection."

"What do you mean?"

"Anod, you were a lone woman, and you took on the entire Yorax battle force . . . and won," he added for emphasis. "Does that sound like a woman who needs protection?"

"That is not what I mean either."

"Then, what do you mean?"

"Everyone within the Society has a shared set of values, a shared destiny. Here, on Beta, everyone seems to do whatever they want."

"Within limits."

"Yes, within limits, but some people seem to revere me and some people hate me for events only meant to save them."

"It is called freedom, Anod. It is that principal that makes us human."

"Then, I am not human," she protested, standing straight to her 1.8 meter height. The wind barely rustled her short auburn hair. Her emerald green eyes broadcast her strength.

"No, no, that is not what I meant. You are human, biologically," he said admiring her slender, muscular body and imposing figure. "You have the anatomy, the appearance of a human woman . . . a very beautiful specimen, I might add," he said with a wink. "But, you are not a complete woman . . . well, you are becoming complete. You have the body of woman, but until you came here, you had no emotions, no feelings, no fluctuation or variation in your personality. You were a mere child, emotionally."

"Why are emotions so important to you? They do not appear to accomplish anything. They do no work. They do not solve problems. If anything, at least from what I have seen, they interfere with accomplishment."

"Now isn't that a profound statement. I suppose you are correct, but life is not just about accomplishment. Life is smelling the forest," he said raising his nose and taking a very deep breath. "Life is feeling the warmth of another person, the ecstasy of human union, and the mountains and valleys. Life is having that baby," he said motioning with his head toward the cave, "suckling at your breast. It is the uncertainty of human relations in all their glory, impetuousness and enormous . . . what should I say . . . enormous spectrum of colors," he said waving his arms wildly as he stood and turned several times.

Anod stared at Bradley as he stood in front of her with his arms held straight out to either side at shoulder height and palms turned up. A smile slowly grew across her face. "I have experienced those feelings."

"Yes, and aren't they great," he shouted as if there was some huge audience to hear.

"Yes, they are."

"Then, what is the problem here?"

Anod's smile disappeared. "It is hard for me to explain. Perhaps it is solidarity, or *esprit de corps*, or something that gives you a sensation of strength far beyond your own musculature or mind."

"We have a larger community. We share the same basic values, just as you do."

"Yes, but you are individuals in a group. The Society is a true collective in the strongest, most powerful terms."

"In a frame, I think we are too."

"Perhaps."

"With the correct leadership, we can be just as strong. We are certainly not as big or expansive as the Society apparently is, but we can be a stronger collective."

"But, you have resigned your post."

"Then, you should lead us."

Now, it was Anod's turn to laugh, an action she had never done until her transformation on Beta. "I should not lead you."

"Why not?"

"I am not one of you."

"You are now."

She stared back at him as though he was an obstacle to be overcome. A chill shook her body. "It was not of my intention."

"Maybe not, but nonetheless, you are here. You cannot go back to the Society. You have borne one of our newest citizens. It is now our task to raise the future leader of our people."

"Our people."

"Yes, our people. As I said, you are one of us, now."

"But, I miss the bioscanner and the certainty of health and longevity. I miss the isopod and the rejuvenation it brings each day; I must sleep almost double the length of what I do with an isopod just to recover my strength. I miss that access to knowledge and information carried, protected and offered by our central computers."

"The technology."

"Yes, the technology, but more than that. I have spent my whole life in space, among the stars and planets of this most bountiful universe. I have explored new worlds. I have met new beings . . . some good, some not so good . . . and, seen life in all stages of development. That technology enables the adventure of space in all its wonder."

It was Bradley's turn to become inwardly thoughtful.

Anod rose from her stump again and began to pace back and forth, weaving among the rocks and stumps. "It is hard to explain unless you have seen it, experienced it, and lived it."

Bradley's eyes shot back to her and captured her attention. "Cannot the same be said about the human experience you have felt on Beta? Is there anything more wondrous than feeling a child growing within you, suffering the pain of childbirth, and then to feel the sensations of ecstasy and bonding with that young child? I wish I could experience those feelings, but I can only watch. You have felt them. Tell me they are not just as wondrous as space."

Oddly, tears welled up in her eyes, and then descended her cheeks. The feelings Bradley cited were indeed the most wondrous she had ever experienced. That small boy made her banishment from the Society less painful. She knew Bradley was correct.

Bradley reached for her and grasped her cheeks in his hands then used his thumbs to wipe away the stream of tears. She could see and feel the empathy in his eyes.

"You are correct."

"Yes, I am."

"They are more wondrous than space."

"There, you see." He leaned forward to kiss her. She embraced him and returned the kiss. They held each other for several minutes, and then Bradley drew back just enough to see her eyes. "I will never experience childbirth, but I can experience space," he said. Anod nodded. "We talked about combining the human dimensions of Betan society we have worked so hard to maintain and the technology of your former culture. That will work."

"Yes, but not on Beta."

"Maybe . . . maybe not. If Colonel Zontramani is successful, then we simply migrate to the new planet."

Anod searched his eyes. "I know you have said that before, but are you really serious, and would there be enough people to make a real go of it?"

"Yes."

"How many do you think would join us if we took such a step?"

"Difficult to say. I know 50 . . . perhaps . . . perhaps, oh, 200 maybe."

"That would be risky."

"Yes, it would, but it is also an indication of the impact you have had on my people."

"I am just a person."

"No, Anod, you are not just a person. You have accomplished things others could only dream about. You have a strength that defies the imagination."

Nick walked across the meadow carrying a crying Zoltentok at his shoulder. "I am sorry to interrupt, but I have tried everything. I think he is hungry."

Anod glanced at the position of the θ27 star – slightly more than three hours had passed. She would not have guessed they had been outside talking for that long. She took her son in her arms and gave him what he wanted.

"Again, my apologies."

"No need," she answered. "I did not realize we had been out here that long."

"It must be a productive discussion."

"I think so."

"As well."

"Then, I shall leave you to it," Nick said then returned to the cave.

"Nick," she said to stop him. He turned to face her from about four meters away. "Are you really prepared to leave this beautiful place?"

He walked back toward them. "Yes, I suppose I am."

"Why?"

"Because I know the three of you are leaving," he answered

without hesitation. "I wish to stay with the only family I have."

"It will not be easy."

"I know."

"And, you would leave this magnificent planet."

"What price glory," he chuckled.

"We have been discussing the possibilities," Bradley said.

"As I surmised. And, what have you decided?"

"Nothing, really. However, I think this concept of combining the best of Beta and the best of the Society has some actual merit."

"Now, that is a risk," Nick said.

"Yes, it is."

"Technology can amplify our skills. Bradley estimates that around 200 Betans might join us. That is not a large number to settle a new planet. Technology can help us and protect us from certain elements. The technology of the Society can mend wounds or broken bones many times faster than the natural biological processes."

Nick smiled. "As we have seen with you alone."

"Yes, well, it works. That technology has saved my life many times."

"Indeed."

"So, what do you want to do?" asked Bradley of Anod.

Anod glanced down at her son, then back to Bradley and Nick. "If we are agreed, I think we should assume Colonel Zontramani will be successful, and we should meet with the 50 known supporters and lay out a plan."

"Precisely," Bradley added.

"Then, let us make it so," added Nick.

Over the next several days, arrangements were made with each of the known supporters Bradley had identified. They wanted to meet in Providence, but the process of rebuilding after the destruction inflicted by the Yorax was still too far from completion. In the end, they agreed to meet at a small public house in the community of Delphi, which had not been touched by the Yorax.

Nick, Bradley, Anod and Zoltentok arrived several hours early. The proprietor of the Wayfarer's Inn, Tung Wan Foo, was one of the supporters. The community occupied a spot in a large, fertile valley in the foothills of a mountain range. Nick estimated that 30 families lived in the valley, mostly in dwellings around Delphi. Only ten families actually lived in the village. There was one other eating establishment in the town, but Tung's Wayfarer's Inn was the only complete boarding facility in the valley.

Anod recognized the configuration of the Inn immediately as they entered. A large room with numerous pillars made the entire ground floor. A combination refreshment bar, servicing area and registration desk occupied the full left wall of the room. Five simple tables with chairs filled the right side of the room. Memorabilia covered the walls.

Mister Tung was a small man with a round friendly face. He recognized his guests as they entered his public house and came out from behind the bar.

"It is an honor to have you at my humble establishment, Mister Prime Minister," he said as he extended his hand to Bradley.

"Thank you for being the host for this meeting, and I hope you realize that I resigned as prime minister."

"Oh, yes, yes, but I still think of you as our prime minister."

"Well, thank you for that." Bradley turned, motioning toward his father. "This is Nick SanGiocomo, my father." They shook hands, and then he turned toward the mother of his son. "This is Anod and our son Zoltentok."

"Ahhhh, so, this is the famous woman who saved our planet."

"Not really," said Anod.

"Yes, it is," Nick answered.

Anod stood about 12 centimeters taller than Tung. She took his proffered hand.

"Oh, you are a very strong woman," he said looking at their clasped hands. "It is truly an honor to have such important people here. I shall always remember this day."

Tung showed them the rest of his inn. Several complete rooms made up the second floor. Behind the inn was an open picnic area with ten bench type tables among the trees and occupied the area between the back of the building and gurgling stream that ran through the center of the valley. They all recognized the site as a near perfect place for their initial meeting.

Others arrived over the next hour. Betans who knew and supported Anod when her presence was a threat to them and the safety of Beta came to Delphi. Otis Greenstreet was the first to arrive. The chocolate-skinned security man was nearly Anod's size as well as her first lover – her original sin – and now her devoted friend. He embraced Anod, kissed Zoltentok on the forehead and shook hands with Bradley and Nick. Mysasha Nagoyama, the midwife who assisted Anod in the birth of her son and taught her to understand and appreciate her motherhood, was next. Even Guyasaga, the wet nurse who tended to Zoltentok while Anod defended Beta against the Yorax, came to join them. Anton Trikinov, Otis' partner and comrade, and the man who helped Otis move the critical fuel pods to the secret hangar at Astral, added his expertise to the growing band. The entire Gibritzu family, led by Dahar and Naomi, who harbored Anod at a pivotal time during the defense of Beta, decided they wanted to be a part of the new endeavor.

Anod felt considerable relief when the scientists and engineers who helped her repair the damaged Yorax interceptor she used to defend Beta walked through the Wayfarer's Inn and into the growing crowd in the picnic area. There was Natasha Norashova, George Robbins, Tim Bond, Maria Verde, Gerald Oscarson, and even the older members James Brown and Armand Bellier. Both Brown and Bellier told the group they could not join them, after all they were much older than the others, but they wanted to lend their support. Anod glowed with the physical demonstration of those Betans who supported her and wanted to continue to support her.

Others, Anod did not know, trickled in and introduced themselves. Some heard the stories of Anod's exploits and just wanted to meet her. Most had either seen or heard about what happened during the Yorax incursion, had been impressed by Anod's commitment and selflessness, and just instinctively knew they had to be a part of the next step. In all, 77 Betans were present at the Wayfarer's Inn in Delphi, of which 12 indicated their curiosity but not commitment to the group.

"May I have your attention," Bradley shouted. He was not entirely successful. He stood on one of the benches in the center of the area, and shouted again. "May I have your attention, please." He waited for the last of the discussions to die off, and all faces and eyes to be on him. "As most of you know, we are gathered here, thanks to the generosity of Mister Tung of Delphi, to discuss and debate the possible migration to a new planet."

"Is there a new planet?"

"Not yet. The Society Starship *Endeavour* has agreed to search several possible systems for an appropriate planet."

"Why leave? Why not stay here?"

Bradley cleared his throat. "We are proposing to form a new

society that combines the character of Betan culture and the advantages of technology used by the Society – a hybrid of sorts."

"Why?"

"Well," he paused to look at Anod as if he wanted her to answer the question. Anod knew it would only work if Bradley could answer satisfactorily. "There are several reasons I shall submit to this debate. One, we have recently experienced an episode that graphically demonstrated passive resistance or passive defense does not work in every instance. We need certain technology to ensure our survival in a sometimes-cruel universe. Two, Anod has been banished from her society because she became more like us. She needs our support and friendship. Three, by taking this step, I think we can grow more, become a greater contributor to the diversity of the universe around us."

No one spoke. No one moved. The group seemed frozen in place and inanimate. Then, as Anod looked around the group, she noticed a few beginning their own scans to determine the mood – first Otis then Mysasha. They were thinking about what Bradley had said.

Armand Bellier, the 81-year-old mechanical and structural engineer repeated the original question, "So, why leave?"

"I think the answer lies in our culture. We have, for several centuries now, rejected technology in favor of our agrarian ethos and the fundamentals of human interaction. I have talked with several of you," he said waving his hand across the crowd, "and, many of you share my belief that infusing higher-order technology into our society would compromise those who want to retain the traditional values."

"Perhaps," answered Bellier.

"Where do we get this technology?" asked Natasha Norashova, the 30-year-old chemist.

"From the Society."

"At what price?"

"The price brings me to probably the fourth reason," said Bradley. "The Society has agreed to search for a suitable planet for us, and we believe they will give us the requisite technology if we join the Confederation of Planets with them."

Again, the crowd was frozen in contemplation. Anton Trikinov was the first to move. He stared at Anod. She tried not to return to his gaze, but it gave her an odd shiver, nonetheless.

"Does that mean we must accept their laws, their morals, their rules?" asked Naomi Gibritzu.

"No. A confederation is a loose collective of states that share many common stately objectives. We would retain our laws, our morals, our values, share defense, and trade practices and procedures."

"Would it exclude trade with others outside the Confederation?"

"No."

"We need to think carefully over this," stated George Robbins.

Discussion continued in smaller groups throughout the afternoon. Anod moved from group to group trying to stay out of the discussion, but occasionally answered a direct question. She felt the mood was positive. There were no negatives other than normal caution, concern and some apprehension. As evening approached, they agreed to meet again in a week in Delphi. The high speed, levitation, rail line passed directly through the valley. There were only two directions to leave. Slightly more than half the group went the same direction as the SanGiocomos. The discussion continued even as participants left the cars at their stops. Eventually, only the SanGiocomos remained. It had been a long but fruitful day. They let the words rest.

Every day messages came in via the rockphone – the ingenious, subterranean, seismic, communications system. Some of them were too complex to interpret in the simple language necessary for the functioning of the rockphone. In singles, small groups or families, they came to SanGiocomo to continue the discussion and debate. Most of the people who attended the Delphi meeting seemed to be in favor of the move if the details could be worked out with the Society and among themselves, and a comprehensive plan was drawn up, ratified and implemented.

As Bradley predicted, others began to join the immigration band. As the news spread, the reaction was not all positive. Some saw this move as a serious threat to and fragmentation of the Betan society.

The intellectual struggle among the visitors and within the SanGiocomo family continued unabated as the days rolled on. There were very few who remained neutral. People were either strongly supportive or dead set against it. For the most part, Anod watched, listened and absorbed the debate. She tried to place herself in the position of each person regardless of the side they fell into on this dialogue.

On a particularly cool, overcast, misty day, Anod took advantage of the quiet time as Zoltentok napped, and Nick and Bradley were preoccupied with other things. She went outside to walk through the damp forest. The leaves did not sing, and the ground did not crackle beneath her feet. She stopped several times on her short excursion to absorb the fine points of the vegetation or terrain around her, but mostly to think.

The dimensions and broadness of the Betan personality spectrum impressed her. She learned from others. She learned what she admired and what she did not like. The more she absorbed, the more she began to understand the feelings and developing emotions within her. As with everything she had done in her life, Anod tried to sort things into beneficial and detrimental buckets.

Anod had an epiphany regarding what her thoughts meant. She wanted to share her revelation with Bradley and Nick. She moved smartly through the forest. Upon her return, she found Bradley standing at the cave entrance.

"Did you have a good walk?"

"Yes. How is Zoltentok?"

"He is fine. My father is keeping him occupied."

"Is he hungry?"

"Not yet. He seems to be happy playing with my father, who is probably more happy playing with ZJ."

"I think I am beginning to understand what it means to be human."

"Well, now, isn't that a big step."

Anod ignored the lighthearted sarcasm. "Life is like a circle, a continuum, with the slightest, thinnest gap, or maybe connection, necessary to complete the circle. On one side of the gap is love, and on the other side is hate. The examples among the populace have become more graphic since the confrontation with the Yorax and this debate about the future. There are also similar relationships between pleasure and pain, female and male, happy and sad. They are at either end of the spectrum – complete opposites – and yet, they are almost the same. The spectrum, is often represented as a straight line, but it is a circle, and the boundary between either extreme of the spectrum is often difficult to perceive."

"Just as you described men and women in the Society, complete opposites, and yet virtually identical," Bradley added.

"You are correct, but my life in the Society did not feel like I was on one side of the connection in the continuum. Now, I can look back and say, I was on the opposite side of the circle from the connection. All our emotions were neutralized. The Society purposefully made everyone equal, the same in fact . . . other than physically."

Nick joined them carrying a passive Zoltentok. "Maybe we should think about our relationship with the Society as a continuum," he suggested.

"It might solve the misgivings of some of our people." The possessive reference reflected the growing stretch between the fundamentalist Betans and those who wanted a new direction.

The three of them considered Nick's suggestion. Could the union of technology and emotion really work to everyone's advantage? It was a question worthy of the debate, but one that could only be answered with the clarity of hindsight. All innovative, or even sometimes evolutionary, changes possessed a certain amount of risk, a potential for failure.

Bradley eventually offered his response. "A more beneficial relationship with the Society can be reached, I should think." The myriad of unknowns attached to the topic produced a modicum of pensiveness among them.

"Yes," was Anod's simple answer.

As the time for the second meeting approached, the level of interest among the people clearly defined the seriousness of the topic at hand. This time they knew others less inclined to the immigration plan would be in attendance. Bradley thought the crowd might be twice or maybe even three times the size of the first meeting. They agreed it would not be fair to Mister Tung and the tiny community of Delphi to have so many people descend on the village. The government square in the capital of Providence, still strewn with the rubble of destruction and construction, was the best place for such a large group.

The citizens of Providence, knowing this important meeting was to take place in the government square, cleared most of the debris away or pushed it to the sides. The space was large enough for 200 to 300 people. Nick, Bradley, Anod and Zoltentok arrived early as they had for the last meeting. As the people gathered in the square, Anod could tell the mood and tone was different from the meeting in Delphi.

Anod did not want to be in front of this group as a symbol of something bad that happened to them. She leaned toward Bradley's ear. "I am going take Zoltentok to the back of the square." He nodded his head without the slightest hesitation. He understood her concern.

Zoltentok straddled her left hip supported by her left arm. People she did not know smiled and slightly bowed their heads toward her in recognition of her child and the future. Those who recognized her greeted her cordially as they would any friend. Anod wanted to blend into the crowd.

She overheard words of encouragement, along with harsh, critical words, and arguments between friends, neighbors and citizens. This question represented a challenge to their way of life. Anod finally found a spot, a flat stone perched halfway up a pile of rubble that would be a reasonable bench enabling her to see over the crowd and stay back away from the others.

Bradley raised his arms above his head. The crowd quieted quickly. "Citizens," he shouted then waited for that last of the mumblings to dissipate. "Thank you for coming."

"Why are you trying to tear us apart?"

"We trusted you."

"Yeah, why are you doing this?"

They did not wait for any statement of explanation. There was anger among some of the people.

"Let's discuss this . . . ."

"Yes, let's do. We want to know."

"We thought you were our leader . . . you cared about us," a woman shouted.

"I do. Now, please. Let's have some order," Bradley said raising his hands again. This time silence was not so quick in coming. He shook his hands and pleaded for attention. It took several minutes for a sufficient reduction in the clamor to allow further dialogue. "This does not have to be a bad thing," he said causing another roar from the crowd. "Let me speak," he shouted.

Anod could see the strain in his face and body from her perch. Several people turned to look at her, but it was Anton's determined eyes that caught her attention, again. She moved Zoltentok to a seated position on her lap and concentrated her physical attention on him, although her senses were focused on the crowd. Anod measured every person – their body language, their position, their words, although she could not see their faces or eyes. She did not want to be surprised. Her lack of experience with large, assembled groups of people that were somewhat unruly and potentially hostile did not help her sense of unease.

"Please let me speak," Bradley shouted again. "You can each have your turn, but at least let me present the question."

That seemed to be the magic word. The crowd nearly instantly went silent.

"Thank you. Now, I know this is an emotional topic, but let me present the question," he repeated for effect. "We have been through a very trying time for our community. As in most events in life, these times bring about evolutionary change. It is a natural course of life. Such is this time. For several reasons, some of us believe it is time for us to grow, to expand, to branch out from the strong roots we have created. This juncture will only be bad if we make it bad. I submit to you this should be viewed as a very positive move."

"So, what is the question?" shouted a man from the faceless crowd.

"The question is, how shall we branch out our society?"

"Why isn't the question, whether?"

Bradley hesitated. Not a good sign from Anod's perspective. "While we have not discussed this collectively, as free citizens any of us have the right to define our future, our destiny. Some of us believe it is time for us to add an additional facet to the gemstone of progress. We want to retain the humanness of our culture, but also infuse technology to allow us to grow and expand."

"We have rejected technology because it takes away our humanness. Why do you think this will be different?"

"It will be different because we will make it so."

"Our ancestors, in their wisdom, decided it was not possible. Are you saying you know more than the ancestors?"

"No, I am not saying that. What I am saying is, we have seen more; we have experienced more; and, we can see more clearly than they could in those tumultuous times."

"You want to tear us apart," someone repeated.

"No, I do not! I want us to grow. As I said, we can make this positive or negative. It is our choice. I propose that we make this positive."

"How?"

Bradley explained the situation and the tentative agreement with the Society. He told them what was happening, and what the objectives were for the present search process. The questions changed from challenging and confrontational to curious. The mood settled down to a deliberative circumspection as the Betans examined many aspects of the proposed new society, and Bradley added his views of how the relationship between Beta and the new society could be maintained. As the tide changed, others, who were supporters but had been silent, began to add their embellishments to the discussion. The fundamentalists still outnumbered the revisionists by about two to one, but the tone of cooperation and support carried through the preponderance of the dialogue.

"So, what exactly do you propose?" someone finally called the question.

Bradley held up his right hand as if he were going to take a pledge. "Assuming the planetary search by the Society starships is successful, I propose that those who wish to migrate to the new planet and help build the new community sign on to this plan. As part of this plan, the new group will forge an agreement, an alliance, with the Society as part of the Confederation of Planets. I also propose that Beta join the Confederation, or we should create an alliance between brothers and sisters."

"Why would we want to join the Confederation?

"Our ancestors were banished from Earth because they wanted to retain their freedom of choice."

"Why would we want to go backward?"

"We are an equal with Earth. We would join the Confederation as an equal, not as a subject. The Articles of Confederation clearly state that no culture has the right to impose upon another. The Confederation is designed for a symbiotic relationship of primarily defense and trade. We can join as equals."

Bradley's statement quieted the crowd for a few moments.

"Are we to trust them? After all, they expelled our ancestors several centuries ago."

A rumble washed through the group. Bradley held up his hand, again. "It is the Society's starships that finally routed the Yorax. It is Society's starships that are currently searching the galaxy for other, suitable, inhabitable planets. What more assurance do you need?"

"Much."

"Yeah."

"Perhaps, then we must define conditions. Likewise, there is no obligation, implicit or otherwise, regarding Beta's membership in the Confederation. So, the central question is, given satisfactory conditions, who wants to join the new group, then we can begin to decide terms and conditions for both Beta and the new colony."

Zoltentok began fidgeting and would not accept more bouncing on Anod's knees. She rose and began to walk behind the crowd, placing her son on her shoulder and rocking him softly. His irritation grew. Anod quickly decided to give him the one thing virtually assured of satisfying him. It worked. She cradled him to her chest as she continued to pace slowly behind the crowd. An occasional head turned to see who was moving behind them.

An older woman did a double take as Anod approached then took several steps toward her. "Dear God, woman," she said in a low but harsh voice. "Have you no modesty? Cover up when you are feeding your child."

Anod could only stare back at her. She had no towel or blanket or other material with which to cover Zoltentok's head and her exposed chest. She looked around for something to use, found nothing and decided to leave the square. She found a destroyed shop and a damaged chair. As she settled in to allow Zoltentok to finish, the same old woman found her.

"Why aren't you covering yourself?" the woman pressed.

Anod smiled, wondering why the woman could not see the obvious. "I do not have a towel, madam," she answered as she tried to adjust her shirt for some coverage without much success.

"Where is your modesty?" she said, standing squarely in front of Anod with her fists on her hips. "Why weren't you prepared?"

"Madam, I do not mean to offend, but I was told this was the proper way to feed an infant."

"Not with your chest flopping in the breeze for everyone to see, it isn't," she responded with mounting anger.

Anod began to feel strains of self-consciousness. She wanted to cover her exposed breast then decided she was not wrong. In defiance, Anod pulled the other side of her shirt back exposing her unoccupied breast and smiled directly into the woman's eyes.

"Well!" she grunted and stamped her right foot raising a small cloud of dust. "I never," she added as she turned and stomped away.

Anod allowed Zoltentok to finish his meal, tended to his needs, then returned to the meeting. She considered leaving her chest completely exposed to antagonize the old woman then decided there was no purpose in such provocation. As she moved back to her perch, she saw the old woman attract the attention of several of her friends and point toward Anod. A few shook their heads in the old woman's disapproval. A younger man, who happened to be listening to the exchange, looked at Anod, nodded his head, and then said something to the sub-group that changed their expressions instantly from outrage to fear. Anod turned her head toward Bradley and tried to ignore the episode.

The meeting was concluding with an amicable tone as they decided upon subsequent meeting times and places as well as committee assignments for further plan development. As they terminated, Bradley descended from the makeshift platform into the crowd. Many people surrounded him and Nick. The crowd began to dissipate. Friends passed by to pay their respects to Anod. Everyone smiled. She did not see the old woman, again.

Eventually, they boarded the rail car for the journey back to SanGiocomo. Anod waited for the dialogue to open then told Bradley and Nick about her confrontation with the old woman. Bradley apologized for not remembering to bring a towel and other supplies, but neither man seemed upset.

In the end, Anod did not feel good about her exchange with the woman in Providence. Against Bradley's protests, she left them at SanGiocomo and climbed through the mountains to High Cave – the place that had become her sanctuary on Beta. She asked for Bradley and Nick to remain at SanGiocomo and tend to the process of negotiating and refining the migration plan. Colonel Zontramani or one of his colleagues could return at any time, and they needed to be as prepared as they could be for a serious and significant move into the future.

Anod and Zoltentok remained at High Cave with no visitors other than animals, birds and insects. Although she was certain Zoltentok did not understand her, Anod talked to him and showed him various detailed features of the forest, from the geology to the flora and fauna. She found a truly satisfying inner peace and contentment alone with her infant son. The attachment between mother and son, more and more, occupied the dominant place in her mind. Occasionally, Anod felt the urge for flight, but the urge quickly passed when she heard his gurgling or cry. The daily, mounting animation of her infant commanded her attention, interest and consciousness. The growing life in her arms fascinated Anod. She reveled in telling Zoltentok about her experiences in the area of the small mountain cave from her very first hiding from the Yorax search, to his birth with Mysasha and Nick helping her as the Yorax began their campaign of destruction to flush her out of hiding. She knew she would retell the stories many times as Zoltentok became more aware and curious. She wanted him to know her history.

The days passed uncounted, with weather changes to add variation, until one day Bradley joined them. She accepted and gave the various forms of intimate affection to Bradley and was happy to see him. She did not ask what brought him to High Cave. She allowed him time to play with Zoltentok and enjoy the peace of the mountain retreat.

Several hours passed before he opened the topic. "We have concluded the agreement."

"Excellent."

"I hope so. We have just under 400 citizens in the new group."

"Now, there is a surprise."

"Yes. It surprised us all when we asked for commitments. It also raised a few problems, too. The number is a little under one percent of the total population of Beta. Many see that as a serious risk. But, we negotiated an agreement. The population finally took a version of my original recommendation. We will have a close alliance between Beta and the new colony, and both have agreed to join the Confederation. It was the protection of the Society that won the day."

"Very will done, Bradley. So, we are ready?"

"Nearly so. There are still arrangements to be made and will probably continue until the embarkation day comes."

"I suspect so."

"Have you enjoyed your time at High Cave?"

"Yes, indeed. While I have always found this place attractive, it is Zoltentok that has been the best for me."

"It is wonderful watching new life, isn't it?"

"Like nothing else I have ever experienced. It has made me wonder why the Society would not want people to share this reward. There is much I do not understand."

Bradley laughed. "I imagine there is much all of us do not understand . . . part of the wonderment of life."

Bradley spent two days with them as a kind of vacation to celebrate the conclusion of the negotiations. They continued to discuss various facets of the plan interspersed among their mutual enjoyment of their son. It was a good time for all of them. They descended the mountains to rejoin Nick and await the return of the Society.

Chapter 3

"Survey complete," announced the science officer, Major Astridag, as the last of their probe and scan efforts concluded on the second of five possible planetary systems to be examined, surveyed, charted and classified.

"Classification?" asked Colonel Zontramani as he continued to stare at the image of the planet on the large display screen before them.

"By the strict guidelines, I agree with Mostron. This is a marginal Class D planet. Carbon Dioxide levels approach the non-scrubbable limits of our current technology. There are adaptive, low-order, lifeforms present. In short, this is not exactly a great place to live for species *Homo sapiens*."

Zontramani felt a certain amount of frustration. The long-range evaluations had indicated possible Class E planets, and so far neither of the newly explored worlds qualified as Class E. He wanted to find some success for those Betans who wanted to find a new planet. However, a forced fit would serve no useful purpose. What they were learning did have positive value. Their model that defined conditions for possible Class E planets was being further refined with each example.

"What is next?"

"Our search plan calls for the fourth planet in the Murtauri star system."

"Very well. Set course for the Murtauri system. Warp nine."

The helmsman repeated the Captain's command and executed the order.

Zontramani watched the starship change heading toward a distant spot of light indistinguishable from most other stars in the panorama. The ship's counter-gravity field that constantly adjusted to maintain a ship vertical acceleration vector of 9.8 m/s² – standard Earth gravity – negated the acceleration forces. Even when the visible electromagnetic field smeared in the distortion of the jump to hyperlight speeds, there were no physical sensations associated with the incredible acceleration and velocity. The counter-gravity technology had been one of the key, fundamental, break-through, leaps in science and engineering that enabled inter-stellar travel. While Colonel Zontramani and the other humans aboard SS *Endeavour* had lived their entire lives with the technology, he never took it for granted nor did he forget history as he reminded himself of what space travel was like without counter-gravity field generators and plasma drives.

Most of the bridge crew departed to carry out other duties. Astridag joined Zontramani and sat in the first officer's chair on the left side of the captain. Other than the captain and science officer, only the helmsman and her second remained. Both senior officers sat lost in thought as if they were mesmerized by the distorted visual image in front of them.

Zontramani was the first to move. He turned his head toward his science officer. "Did you refine the classification model with the result from the last search?"

"Yes."

"Does Murtauri Four look different?"

Astridag rose from the first officer's chair and walked to the science station. She input various commands and eventually attained the result she wanted. "Yes, it does look different. Based on the refinements of the last two searches, Murtauri Four has moved up the Class E scale somewhat. Rich in oxygen. A bit of the low side for carbon dioxide. It appears to be above a J and below an L in terms of lifeforms. Of the three remaining candidates, Murtauri Four looks the best."

"At least it is a living planet, but not sufficiently living that we have to negotiate a mutual habitation treaty."

"Correct."

"Since we are too far away for any detailed evaluation, based on what you do know about Murtauri Four, would you want to live there?"

"Actually, Captain, I rather like it here, aboard *Endeavour*."

"Indeed, but if you had to find a piece of rock to live on, would this one look inviting?" he asked nodding his head toward the only point of light not moving on the screen.

"So far, based on our grossly insufficient data, I suppose it would." Astridag allowed a long pause for any further questions, and then she asked hers. "You have some empathy for the former lieutenant, Anod?"

"Yes, I think I do. She found herself in what we might otherwise call *in extremis* conditions. She responded the best way she knew how, given the situation, and now she no longer enjoys the status of our class nor the benefits of the Society."

"Yes, well, she did make choices."

"Would any of us have responded differently?"

"I have asked myself that question since the details of her

encounter were developed. Perhaps not, but I think I would have made different choices."

"Ah, isn't that what makes us human?"

They returned their attention to the visual display as Astridag rejoined her captain. "Do you think they will take the stipulations of our support for their migration?"

"Yes. I sensed a yearning in her and their former prime minister – her consort."

"We are pressing farther into the galaxy proper. If they do migrate and join the Confederation, we may have an advantageous base for inter-galactic exploration."

"What do you mean?"

"As I looked at the geometry, Murtauri is sufficiently down the home arm and on the fringe of the galaxy to partially see behind the galactic centroid. If the orbital mechanics are verified once we get there, we might find stars and galaxies never seen by humans before."

"That would make this journey worth it."

"Absolutely."

The peculiar alert whisper, like a distant birdcall, told them of an incoming communication. Zontramani simply commanded, "On screen."

A small box on the left side of the large display appeared with the reef of stars logo of Central Command, and then the clear image of Admiral Agginnoor replaced the logo. "Greetings," she said.

"Greetings to you, Admiral."

"Is everything as it should be?"

"Yes, of course. We are enroute to Murtauri, and we have completed nearly half our present search mission."

"Excellent. Have you found anything promising?"

"No. Both previous planetary systems were predominately gaseous, Class A planets. The best in either system was a singular but marginal, Class D planet in each system."

"Interesting."

"We have used the new knowledge to refine our models, and we think the fourth planet of the Murtauri system may qualify as a Class E. Major Astridag indicates that Murtauri Four may give us a better view behind the galactic centroid as well."

"Now wouldn't that be tantalizing?"

"We shall see."

Someone off screen handed her a single piece of paper. "Excuse me," she said as she read the message. When she was finished, she looked up and left as if to someone standing beside her but not visible, nodded her head, and then returned to Zontramani. "My apologies. Things are happening rather smartly at the moment, which is really why I called. It appears the Yorax want to conclude a peace treaty with the Confederation."

"Or, perhaps set a trap."

"Perhaps, but neither the Council of Elders nor Central Command believe that is their purpose. All the recent activity indicates our encounter with Yorax forces at Beta convinced them peace was better than war."

"That is quite a change for the Yorax."

"Yes, nonetheless, we believe this request to be genuine, and as you may have surmised, *Endeavour* is the closest starship to the proposed meeting place."

"Which is?"

"A research station run by a Norgekkian sponsored team in the Riiza system called Riiza-Strogon," said Agginnoor. Astridag went to the science station in preparation for the inevitable questions. "The Norgekkians are apparently studying one or more planets in the system for their commercial development."

"Some minerals and rocks there, but not much else."

"You know the Norgekkians?"

"Yes, I do. If there is even a hint of profit, they will not let go."

Agginnoor smiled for a brief moment then returned to her serious gaze. "The burden of negotiation falls upon you, Colonel Zontramani. Your objective is to conclude a substantive peace with the Yorax. If you can bring them to accept the precepts and join the Confederation, the Council wishes you to make the attempt. Furthermore, you should attempt extradition of the traitor Zitger. The latter two sub-objectives are remote at best, but we should be on record as requesting them. It is not known whether Zitger will be in the negotiating party. If he is, which is likely if for no other reason than to be an irritant to us, you are directed to treat him with the respect due a Yorax leader."

"How does that mix with the request for extradition?"

"You will have to use your judgment. The prime objective is peace. Nothing must obstruct that goal."

"And, Riiza-Strogon is presumed neutral?"

"Yes, however, as in all situations like this, you must make your own determination. Avoid confrontation. Remember, the objective is peace."

Zontramani recognized the dichotomy of his instructions. He was also experienced enough to know that life was rarely bipolar; it was usually a vast array of colors, tones, tints, textures and shades. "Understood," he responded.

"Good luck. Godspeed and following winds."

"Thank you, Admiral. We will let you know when negotiations are concluded."

She raised her hand, and then the communications link was broken.

Zontramani turned to see Astridag standing at the science panel. She looked up from the panel. "We are 23 days from Riiza at warp nine."

"Set course for Riiza. Warp nine."

"You have the coordinates," added Astridag.

"Course for Riiza at warp nine, aye," answered the helmsman.

The point of light that had been their destination moved smoothly off the screen to the left. Within a few minutes, a new destination star, more bluish in color and smaller, moved to the center of the display and stopped.

"Send a hyperspace message to the Yorax giving them our arrival time, and ask them for their estimated arrival time at Riiza-Strogon."

"Aye, sir."

Once Zontramani was satisfied with the state of things, he relinquished the bridge to Major Astridag. The starship would quickly complete settling into the routine of transit. The senior officers began the process of preparing for the pending negotiations with the Yorax.

The days passed as if there were no days as was most often the case for the warriors in service to the Society. Numerous conferences were held as each of the officers shared their research and opinions regarding the Yorax and their present mission. None of them thought the mission would be simple or easy. They rarely received simple missions, and when they thought they did, they even more rarely turned out that way.

They discussed primary and secondary approaches, as well as contingencies for every potential obstacle or hazard they might encounter before, during or after the meeting with the Yorax. The desire to capture Zitger and bring him to justice was also unanimously strong although they all knew, as warriors, they were bound by their mission directive.

Once the planning was complete, they allowed themselves a good period of rest and relaxation, each in their own way.

They returned to the plan and reviewed their research when they were two days away from their destination. Each member of the crew tightened their actions and attention.

"Captain," Major Astridag announced, "the scans of Riiza-Strogon, both open and covert, have been completed." Colonel Zontramani turned to see his science officer. "The open scan was acknowledged, so they know we have evaluated the station. The covert scan found nothing serious. There is an armory, and as best we can determine, it is secure and not active. This is about as close to a neutral conference site as we can get in this neck of the galaxy. There are no signs of the Yorax, yet."

"How many life forms?"

Astridag chuckled more to herself than for anyone else's benefit. "Well, Captain, that depends on how you define lifeforms."

"In our usual manner, major."

"Twenty-five entities in seven species. This station appears to be what they say it is, a research station for this planet and star system. Not exactly what we might call an inhabitable place, but for them, it is marginal enough to command their interest."

"Do we have an arrival time for the Yorax?"

"The last message, five days ago, is the best we have," answered Colonel Astrok, the *Endeavour*'s first officer.

"Very well, so we have a day or so to wait. Let's take up synchronous maneuvering position to keep the station in view so we can respond promptly to any threat. Raise the shields to Alert One. I don't want the Yorax to find us napping."

"Shields to Alert One, aye," answered the helmsman.

Colonel Zontramani sat in the command chair and waited for his powerful and agile starship to settle into a synchronous orbit of the fourth planet in the Riiza star system, 1,000 kilometers farther out from the research station. "Hail the station," he commanded.

The response took several minutes to achieve. A fine specimen of the Norgekkian merchant species finally appeared on the large visual display before them. The characteristic attributes of the large biped with distantly human male features and a distinctive shiny brown skin that made you wonder whether it is real or artificial – biological or android – although all the scans reported biological. What they could not see was the equally characteristic and noticeably mechanical, jerky gait, as if the Norgekkian was slightly off balance.

"You must be the Society representative," the Norgekkian stated.

"Yes. Colonel Zontramani, Captain of the Society Starship *Endeavour*."

The Norgekkian read a piece of paper. "Yes, as it states in the notice. I am Kegortron, chief of this research station. Will you be joining us?"

"No, unless you see a reason. We shall stay aboard our ship until the Yorax arrive."

"As you wish," he paused as if he was waiting for some further instruction. "Do you need any special equipment, arrangements or conditions?"

"No. A simple, quiet, conference room will be sufficient for us."

"Excellent. We have plenty of room. We look forward to concluding these negotiations."

"As do we."

Kegortron consulted his paper again. "Our latest information states the Yorax contingent is due to arrive in two days."

"Thank you for the update, Chief Kegortron. We shall be here if you need us."

"Then, thank you, Colonel Zontramani," he said as the screen insert disappeared.

Zontramani checked the status of the communications link to ensure the connection was broken and no further re-initialization was underway then checked their position relative to the research station and the other celestial objects in proximity. "Maintain the bridge watch and Alert One condition," he commanded.

"Aye."

He turned to his first officer. "Something bothers me about this – a sixth sense, gut feeling kind of thing."

"What about it?"

"Do you sense something?"

"Yes," answered Colonel Astrok without hesitation. "I sense an ambush."

"What would they hope to gain? Do they think we are the only starship in this sector? Do they think if they did overcome us, they would be able to deal with the weight of the Fleet?"

"Who knows what they think? We could go to Alert Five, however that is most likely to be viewed as provocative. I would if I was on the other side."

"Indeed. We gave them a rather sound thrashing at Theta Two Seven Beta. I imagine they are still smarting from that exchange. However, we shall stay at Alert One to give us some protection and avoid the confrontation stance."

An unspoken tension persisted among the senior officers. The captain, as was often the case, rejected the rejuvenation of sleep in his isopod simply because he could not afford the extra minutes for recovery. Even when he did try to sleep in the old way, it was a sporadic and fitful slumber – not a restful sleep.

The crew reviewed their preparations as they waited. They were as prepared for any conceivable action as they could be in this situation. The fine line between the diplomatic mission and the normal, uneasy, paranoia of the warrior with the potential for battle looming so close to the negotiating table added to the tension.

The intervening days disappeared. The senior officers of *Endeavour* were on the bridge when sensors first picked up the approach of the Yorax battlecruiser. They took all appropriate passive precautions as they monitored the arrival of the much larger, gnarly, Yorax warship. No offensive attributes could be detected in the Yorax ship other than a minimal shield similar to the *Endeavour*'s Alert One status. They watched to see if any other Yorax vessels might appear. Everything seemed as it should be for such an encounter.

The rather ugly battlecruiser settled into a synchronous position on the other side of the research station, so that the neutral site was directly between the two warships. They detected communications between the Yorax and Riiza-Strogon, a normal activity. Zontramani was content to wait for the proper time.

The hailing whistle announced the beginning of the negotiations. Kegortron appeared on the screen. "Good day to you, Colonel Zontramani," he said. The Society starship captain simply nodded his head, wanting to take a more conservative, reserved stance. "As you know, the Yorax delegation has arrived. As per the accepted protocol, I propose we complete the introductions and presentation of credentials via this communications link. Once accepted, we should meet in the general conference room aboard this station. Is that agreeable?"

"Yes."

"Then, with your permission, I shall initiate a three way link, now."

Zontramani nodded his head and waited. His stomach took a hard, nauseating twist when the interior of the Yorax battlecruiser joined the image from Riiza-Strogon. There, before them, with a devious, smirk on his sharp, chiseled, youthful face was the traitor Zitger in the contoured, reptilian armor plates of a Yorax general. Several Yorax warriors stood behind him. The image was an oddity. Zitger's head appeared to be on a large, out-of-proportion, Yorax body. The repulsive reptilian heads of the Yorax around him amplified his nausea. Beside his white skin, his black, wavy hair stuck out among the browns and greens of the Yorax.

Zontramani reminded himself repeatedly and continuously not to let Zitger's appearance on behalf of the Yorax affect his thinking. He tried to neutralize the images in his head. From his peripheral vision, he noticed Astrok and Astridag turn away from the main screen, pretending interest in one control panel or another.

Zitger was the first to speak. "So, it is the famous and successful Zontramani who shall negotiate for the Society."

The *Endeavour*'s captain slowly nodded his head as he fought the urge to demonstrate his revulsion over facing a traitor.

Kegortron took control. "May I begin the introductions? Representing the Confederation of Planets and carrying the full diplomatic credentials of the Society, I present Colonel Zontramani, Captain of the Society Starship *Endeavour*," he said motioning toward the screen although it had no real meaning. "Representing the Yorax Empire and carrying the full credentials of the Yorax Empire, I present General Negolian, Commander of the Yorax Battlecruiser *Strockgen*. And, for the record, I am Kegortron, Chief of the Norgekkian Research Station Riiza-Strogon and host facilitator of these negotiations." He waited for some response and received none. Zitger's smirk turned to a cold stare. "General Negolian, do you accept the credentials of Colonel Zontramani?"

"Yes."

"Colonel Zontramani . . ."

"Yes," he interrupted.

"Very well, with the introductions complete, would both of you be so kind to join me. I have sent the proper coordinates for the meeting room. I must remind you, according to the accepted rules of protocol, you are entitled to only one companion, and there must be no weapons, scanners or other support devices. Agreed?" Both leaders nodded their agreement without words. "Very well. We shall meet aboard Riiza-Strogon in ten minutes." Both images disappeared.

"To think he was once one of us," said Astridag.

"That traitor turns my stomach," Astrok added.

"Mine as well, but that must not affect us."

"A difficult task."

"Indeed, but the task nonetheless. And, so it begins."

"Did you notice he has apparently taken a Yorax name?" Astrok said.

"General Negolian . . . how presumptuous," replied Astridag. "I wonder what he has done to warrant this recognition after betraying his people and killing so many innocent citizens."

"Indeed," added Zontramani with a tone of impatience. "Colonel Astrok has the bridge and command. Major Astridag shall be with me. It is time to conclude the peace."

After the appropriate acknowledgments, the captain led the ship's science officer to the transport room. The environmental conditions were confirmed one last time, and then both officers were converted and transferred to Riiza-Strogon.

The conference room on the orbiting station was austere and functional. A long, gray, metal table with straight, gray metal chairs occupied the center and majority of the room. A large viewing screen along with a simple control panel covered one wall. Various charts, graphs, schematics and other diagrams covered the other walls. Astridag stood behind and one step to the left of Zontramani.

Although their scans indicated seven differentiated species aboard the station, the only locals were three Norgekkians, one smaller female and two similarly sized males. The apparent leader stepped toward them and extended his right hand. "I am Kegortron," he said.

Zontramani reached inside and clasped his elbow so that they connected forearm to forearm in the Norgekkian style of greeting. "I am Colonel Zontramani," the captain responded in a traditional greeting although both men recognized the other from the previous communications.

"Welcome to Riiza-Strogon, Colonel. Would you care for a beverage?"

"No, thank you, but I would like to introduce my science officer, Major Astridag," he said motioning toward her.

"Ah, yes, the Society custom of introducing seconds," Kegortron answered holding up his right hand in the universal greeting gesture. Astridag reciprocated. "Then, I should introduce my seconds. I have Rorsotron, the second chief of the station," he said motioning toward the Norgekkian male, "and, Dorrentra, our chief scientist." General greetings were exchanged. "I might suggest you take the other side of the table since I gave both parties those coordinates," he added glancing to an unspecified spot under the Confederation delegates.

Zontramani and Astridag moved to the other side of the room to wait. Astridag took advantage of the time to examine the wall charts.

"This is a survey station," said Kegortron, anticipating a question.

"What are you looking for?" asked Astridag.

"Oh, this is just a mapping exercise," he answered.

Astridag continued to closely examine the charts. She could see more than was being discussed. "For a system with only three Class B planets – solid mass, inert core, no atmosphere or water – this must be a very unrewarding exercise, as you call it."

Kegortron's expression turned cold. "Are you here to interrogate us?"

Astridag waved her hand as she turned around to face their host. "No, no, by all means, no. I am just a science officer." Zontramani wanted to add that she was the best science officer in the galaxy, but did not think the opinion would add to the conversation. "My task aboard *Endeavour* is to be curious, inquisitive and learn."

A slight smile returned. "As you say, then. You must be very good at your job." He paused for a response but none came. "We are simply looking for trace minerals that we can mine and sell. It is our nature, after all."

Astridag nodded her head and returned to her position beside her commander. Silence filled the room. No one moved as they continued to wait. Several minutes passed before two figures began to reassemble from the energy they had been converted to for the transport. Within seconds, the two Yorax delegates stood before them with their hands held away from their sides and palms forward. Zontramani and Astridag reciprocated to show they held no weapons.

The connected, contoured, plates of body armor, characteristic of a Yorax warrior's uniform, made up the majority of the visual presence on the opposite side of the room. The only uniquely distinguishable aspect of the two entities was their heads. As he appeared in the communications image, Zitger was the lead person. The reptilian second behind him offered no indication of rank or purpose.

Introductions were completed without physical contact between the belligerents before they sat at the table. The Confederation and Yorax delegates sat on opposite sides with Zontramani and Zitger, or General

Negolian, as he apparently desired to be called, directly across from each other, and their seconds sitting to the left of each leader diagonally across the table. The Norgekkian leader sat in the middle of the adjacent side with his seconds on either side of him.

"Shall we begin?" Both leaders nodded. "Very well. As I understand the situation, both parties have been engaged in warfare and now wish to conclude peace." Again, both leaders nodded without taking their eyes off each other. "Then, let us start with the respective conditions for peace," Kegortron said, then motioned toward Zitger to initiate the statement.

"The mighty Yorax Empire insists upon an apology from the Society for the wanton destruction of peaceful Yorax citizens, and a clear, binding line of demarcation and buffer zone to allow peaceful commerce without interference with the sector defined by the Yorax Empire."

"Is that all?"

"Well, actually, I must add that we must have assurance from the Confederation they will not violate the buffer, nor interfere in Yorax enterprise, and we must establish a process for arbitration to remedy any violations, unintentional or otherwise."

"Anything else?"

Zitger shook his head.

Kegortron turned to Colonel Zontramani. "And, the conditions of the Confederation of Planets?"

"Our conditions are simple," Zontramani responded looking directly at Zitger with an icy stare devoid of emotion. "We want peace. We want a peaceful existence for all living things and respect for life." He let his words float for few moments then looked to Kegortron and smiled.

"Is that all?"

"For now."

"Yes, well, then, it appears to have the makings of a peace treaty."

"Is the Confederation prepared to concede the territorial demands of the Yorax?" asked Zitger.

"The Yorax have made no territorial demands other than conceptual."

Zitger reached into a pocket beneath his left breastplate and extracted a clear, encased, memory chip. "Do you have a holographic projector?"

"Yes," Kegortron answered motioning with his head for the

Norgekkian science officer to retrieve the chip and set up the display.

They waited for the setup of the three dimensional projector with the coordinate data from the Yorax chip. Zontramani and Zitger stared at each other, neither one blinking or moving, each sizing the other against some undefined standard of their respective experience.

The image of the home galaxy appeared in the middle of the table with green and orange markings in one of spiral arms emanating from the dense center. Colonel Zontramani recognized the green circle as the Sun, the parent star of the Society, and the orange circle marked the position of Jnnsork, known on the Society star charts as Bellatrix, the solo star of the Yorax planetary system. The small orange and green boxes presumably identified the Yorax recommendation for defining respective sectors. The green box was farther out the spiral arm, while the orange box was toward the center of the galactic mass.

"Please amplify the volumes in question," Zontramani requested.

The two volumes of space now occupied the tabletop. Zontramani recognized that the Murtauri system was in the orange box. Since it was their best hope of finding a new Class E planet, he had to find the correct negotiating position. He needed time.

"A fair division," commented Zitger.

"Perhaps, but we will need time to compare with our charts."

"Are you suggesting we adjourn for the day?" asked Kegortron.

"Yes, I am."

"I am afraid I must insist we stay here to conclude this agreement. I have a mission that has been delayed."

"You shall do what you must do," answered Zontramani. "However, I am not agreeing to anything that I have not adequately studied."

"That does seem appropriate."

"Then, I shall ask that my protest be entered into the record of this proceeding."

"As you have requested . . . so noted," Kegortron said. He waited for a head nod from Zitger then added, "We are adjourned until six on the universal time measure."

The original chip was returned to Zitger, and a copy was handed to Major Astridag. The Yorax were the first to depart. Zontramani and Astridag departed immediately after them.

Zontramani gathered his senior officers in the command conference room. The ever-present Mostron remained an invisible participant.

Without words, Major Astridag loaded the copy of the Yorax memory chip then amplified the relevant portion of the galaxy. She began the briefing. "This is the proposal from the Yorax. As you can surmise, the green is the proposed sector of the Confederation of Planets, and the orange would belong to the Yorax Empire."

"They do not want much, do they?" said Captain Zalemon, the *Endeavour*'s security officer.

"There are several key elements, not least of which is that the Murtauri system is in the Yorax sector. In fact, the remaining three systems to be charted are on the other side of the boundary."

"To state the obvious," began Zalemon, "they are blocking the trade routes out of the home area."

"We have to cross the void to expand or explore," Astridag added, pointing to that portion of the image between adjacent arms of the spiral galaxy.

"What do you want to do?" asked Astrok.

Zontramani considered the options. "I would like to find the means to move the line to place Murtauri in the Confederation sector."

"We must examine the benefits to each party," said Astridag. "Perhaps, we can argue an adjustment based on some parameter like inhabitable worlds, or mineral deposits, or something."

"That will take time," Astrok stated.

"Yes, but it may be our only way," Zontramani said. "Mostron, do you have the regions defined on the subject memory chip."

"Yes."

"Please search your records to determine the number of documented as well as probable and possible inhabitable worlds."

"To include what planet classes?" asked the mechanical voice of the ship's central computer.

Again, contemplation.

"May I suggest," interjected Astridag. She waited for a nod from her captain. "We should make the search broad. It will take longer, but it may tell us more. We need to know the stars with planets from Class B through L, and as a secondary objective, those star systems with any planets A through L, in each sector. Also, we should know basic facts like, respective volumes in each sector, the number and class of stars in each sector."

"Agreed."

"I might also suggest, Captain, that we think about what happens from this position," Astridag nodded toward the holographic image above the table. "History says we will want to expand our knowledge of the universe. Our present mission, other than these negotiations, is to explore new worlds. There are not many star systems remaining outboard on this arm of the galaxy, while the Yorax have the implicit ability to expand across the entire galaxy. It will take several years to cross to the adjacent arm, and chances are, the Yorax will claim the rest of the galaxy."

"Good point."

"Then, we need the data."

"How long will it take you to complete this search, Mostron?"

"Approximately three point seven hours."

"Then, execute the request."

"As you command," Mostron stated.

"We have ten hours until we reconvene on Riiza-Strogon. As soon as Mostron has completed his search, we shall rejoin here to assess the results and map our negotiating position."

They left the conference room to return to their other duties or activities of their choosing. They would eat and sleep in preparation for the next phase.

Mostron finished his search and was ready for the meeting, but several leaders were still in their isopods. Zontramani, who more often than not, avoided the sanctuary and refreshment of recovery in his isopod, reviewed the collected information with Mostron as they waited for the others to return. The process took another two hours. The group rejoined with less than three hours until the opening of the negotiations.

They reviewed Mostron's search data. It gave them some leverage. They wanted to focus on the future without making expansion an issue. The Yorax would not appreciate the deluge of statistics and numbers. The wild card was Zitger. He knew too much about the Society, the Confederation and would probably anticipate the negotiating tactics. After several mock debates, with Zalemon acting as Zitger, the direction and alternatives were established.

Zontramani and Astridag returned to Riiza-Strogon . . . this time as the last delegation to arrive. As Kegortron requested, Zontramani stated the results of their search. As the numbers, descriptions and statistics rolled along, he could tell the Yorax second had already lost interest, and Zitger fought his own impatience. The strategy was working. Their hosts asked several questions during the presentation, more out of curiosity than as factors in the negotiations.

"So, what are you suggesting?" interjected Zitger as his patience reached a limit.

Zontramani stared at his opponent as if he did not understand the question. "Well, I suppose I am suggesting that we adjust the sector boundaries slightly."

"Do you have a proposal?"

"Yes, we do," he answered motioning for Astridag to provide the modified data.

"This is the original proposal," she said as she manipulated the controls of the display system. "Although Colonel Zontramani has not completed our presentation of the data, we are suggesting the borders be adjusted as follows." The parallel orange and green lines moved farther down the spiral arm of the galaxy.

The expected debate bloomed as numbers and statistics balanced against unspecified territorial objectives. In the end, after several retirements for consultations, the two sides agreed upon a clear definition of borders, the meaning of policy between the two groups and a process for remediation of any infractions or transgressions.

"Are there any remaining issues to be discussed?" asked Kegortron.

"No," answered Zitger.

"Well, yes, I am afraid so," Zontramani said looking directly at Zitger through the image of stars.

"And, what may that be?" asked Kegortron.

"There is a traitor among the Yorax who has committed multiple murders and other violations of universal law." Zontramani paused. Zitger did not twitch or show any reaction. "We want the traitor returned to the Confederation and specifically the Society for trial and punishment."

A long silence filled the room as all the participants remained frozen. Zontramani was perfectly content to let the moment ferment.

"What is the answer of the Yorax Empire?" Kegortron finally asked.

Zitger slowly turned his head toward the facilitator and smiled slightly just before his eyes shifted. "We have no extradition provisions in the treaty."

"Perhaps, we should add them," said Kegortron.

"No," responded Zitger. "The Yorax Empire has no desire for any contact with the Confederation. Therefore, no extradition process is warranted."

"But . . ."

"No, buts!" exclaimed Zitger.

Stung by the sharpness of Zitger's reply, Kegortron stared back with incredulity. He turned to Zontramani with the question in his eyes. He opened his mouth several times as if he wanted to speak, but no words came. His expression picked up an element of desperation as he recognized the undercurrent.

Zontramani held up his right hand as a director might signal a halt to whatever action was before him. "The Confederation wishes to place on record the demand for extradition of the traitor and the eternal desire to seek justice."

"Since you have made this request for the permanent record," said Kegortron, "would it not be appropriate for the Confederation to specify the identity of the alleged traitor that is the subject of this request?"

Zitger did not flinch or even move his eyes as he stared at Zontramani.

The *Endeavour*'s captain nodded his head, smiled slightly, and then turned to Kegortron. "For the record, the accused traitor is Captain Zitger, now apparently known as General Negolian of the Yorax Empire."

Kegortron's razor thin mouth fell open slightly as he scanned quickly back and forth between the two leaders who remained locked in some invisible grappling hold. "This cannot be true."

Without moving his eyes, Zontramani responded. "I can assure you it is precisely true."

"This is most unusual. I don't . . . I cannot imagine . . . what are we to do?"

The two belligerents continued to hold each other as the Norgekkian leader could only observe the two hoping for an opening. This impasse remained unchanged for several minutes until Zitger turned his head toward Kegortron without taking his eyes off Zontramani. At the last moment, he shifted his gaze.

"As I stated earlier, the Yorax and the Confederation have no extradition provisions. Does the accomplished starship captain wish to negate this treaty over this issue?"

"No," Zontramani answered without allowing the Norgekkian his procedural step. "We simply wish the record to state our demand."

Kegortron flashed between them for several seconds then raised his hands as if to concede the point. "Do the Yorax accept this demand?"

Zitger moved his up-turned, open hand from Zontramani to Kegortron to signify his acceptance of the protest, not that it would change anything.

"The Yorax have accepted the statement. Any other remaining issues?" Both leaders shook their heads in the negative. "With both parties consenting, we shall now sign the treaty and conclude these proceedings."

An electronic document device was placed before each party. The principal and second signed, and the signatures were witnessed by the Norgekkian representatives.

Zitger and his second did not waste time in their departure. As a smirk grew across Zitger's face and with a flippant salute, the two disappeared.

Zontramani thanked Kegortron for his efforts. The revelation of Zitger's betrayal explained the events for the Norgekkian. Colonel Zontramani provided a brief synopsis of Zitger's traitorous acts from the ambush of his colleagues of Team Three, Saranon Detachment to the brutal bombardment of Beta. Kegortron wished them good fortune in seeking Zitger's punishment. However, they all knew the desire would not likely lead to a result. With the last gestures of gratitude, Zontramani and Astridag departed.

Once back aboard *Endeavour*, the captain checked on the status of everything. His first officer reported that the Yorax Battlecruiser *Strockgen* departed immediately upon the conclusion of the meeting. The direction was consistent with a return to the Yorax sector by the shortest route. Colonel Zontramani reported the results of the treaty meeting to the crew, and then reported to Admiral Agginnoor. She was pleased with the treaty, would present the document to the Council, but was disappointed they could not apprehend Zitger and bring him to justice. As the Council considered the treaty, the *Endeavour* was ordered to resume her search mission.

"Set your course for the Murtauri system. Warp nine," commanded Zontramani.

The powerful starship changed direction then jumped to hyperlight speed. The crew quickly settled into a routine. As they continued their search, Colonel Zontramani sent a status report to Beta. He was not sure they had the technology to receive the high-speed communications of modern space travelers, so he also sent the same message via ancient radio medium. Communications with Beta had never been good. During the battle with the Yorax, several unilateral messages had been received from

Anod calling for help. He could not recall any bilateral communications. At least he made the effort to keep them informed.

The transit to Murtauri was uneventful. The survey of the Murtauri system took ten days to complete. The leaders of *Endeavour* gathered to consider the results.

Astridag began the report. "Murtauri is a young, stable, solo star of about 1.2 Sun diameter. Of the 11 planets and 27 moons, there is only one Class E object – the fourth planet. So, of the 11 planets, we have two Class A's, seven Class B's, a Class I, and the Class E, I mentioned."

"A Class I?" asked Astrok.

"Yes. The fifth planet would otherwise be a Class E object, but there are no detectable life forms."

"Now, that would make only the second Class I planet in the entire registry," added Zontramani.

"Correct. A planet with an adequate atmosphere and water with no detectable lifeforms is even more rare than the Class E planets in the surveyed universe to date."

"What about the moons?"

"There are 27 moons orbiting the various planets, with 22 of them orbiting the two Class A, gaseous planets. All are Class B objects except for one, which is a Class C, having no atmosphere but some detectable, subterranean water."

"Where is the Class C moon?"

"Orbiting the fifth planet – the Class I object."

"This is an interesting system," Zontramani said. "What about the fourth planet, you said?"

"It is a marginal Class E. All parameters are within nominal limits except carbon dioxide, which is about 7% above the high side value. The only consequence would be time to adjust to the higher carbon dioxide levels, very much like acclimatization."

"What are the lifeforms on Murtauri Four?"

"There are no high order lifeforms, but a substantial spread from bacterium to mammalian, low to middle level lifeforms. There are many new lifeforms that must be evaluated. Statistics would say there could be organisms that might be antagonistic to unsupported humans."

"A true Class E?"

"Yes, except for the atmospheric carbon dioxide levels," answered Astridag.

"Then, this would appear to be a good candidate for colonization

. . . with proper medical support."

"Yes, except for the proximity of the Yorax frontier."

"If we believe the treaty, that should not matter."

The search of the remaining star systems along the Yorax frontier yielded several new discoveries, but nothing that would support human life. With their search complete, Colonel Zontramani had Mostron complete the data transfer as well as learn about the results from other starships. Murtauri Four looked like the best site. The *Endeavour* began the return journey to θ27β.

Chapter 4

Time continued to roll on as the Betans waited for news of the search. The effort to find a new home was in someone else's hands, and they had no feedback regarding the prognosis. Anod guessed that Zontramani might try to communicate their progress, but the ancient Betan radio system was not helpful. She knew the starship would probably return before they received a radio message. Even the aperiodic and widely interspersed visits by the merchant traders including Alexatron could not add to their knowledge of progress other than one message intercepted announcing the peace treaty with the Yorax.

The size of the immigration group fluctuated as the weeks passed into months without any sign from the Society. The progress of the *Endeavour* and her sister ships was beyond the awareness of the inhabitants of Beta. Although there was no communication between the Society and Beta during the protracted period of the search, an intuitive link was active between Zontramani and Anod.

Neither of them could explain the feelings they had, nor could they communicate on a conscious level. The best that could be done was a belief in what they thought was happening. Anod simply knew the search was progressing well and probably with some success. Colonel Zontramani possessed a certain empathy for the condition of the separated Kartog Guards warrior. The intuitive link gave each of them an additional strength with which to persevere.

Although Anod periodically maintained her linkage with space, it was the continuous connection to her son that dominated her life. She talked to him, instructed him on everything she saw, did or thought, although she knew and recognized that the infant could not yet absorb her teachings. Zoltentok was beginning to make intelligible sounds when Guyasaga came to teach her the next important passage of life. The only disappointment, a very personal and unspoken disappointment, was Zoltentok's weaning. Both Guyasaga and Mysasha had discussed the duration of suckling and the process of weaning as part of her continuing education on motherhood. Having the two experienced mothers close at hand helped Anod learn the skills she needed every day. In the end, Zoltentok had decided the issue on his own. His mother missed the physical connection, like the discarded umbilical of his gestation and birth, much more than the growing boy. Anod's frustration came when she compared her learning rate with that of her son. It was difficult to stay ahead of him.

Anod vowed to keep the bond with her son strong despite the severance of their physical inter-dependence. The small acts of affection came naturally to her – a further demonstration of those repressed and subdued forces long dormant in the mind of the warrior.

Zoltentok's learning process accelerated sharply as his walking and talking became more stable and recognizable. Everyone marveled at the speed he learned life skills. This process was not without bumps and cuts, but the boy healed quickly, like his mother.

"No one told me being a mother was so hard," she mused to Nick.

He laughed hard. "You never asked," he bellowed.

"There is a body of facts I should have known before Zoltentok was created."

Nick's expression softened quickly. "Yes, my dear. There are many things you should have learned when you were much younger, but your life has been different."

It was Anod's turn to chuckle. "You might say that. It seems like one day I was a warrior, and the next day I was a mother."

"A difficult transition for the best of us. You have done well, Anod. Better than anyone expected or could have dreamed. The blossoming of your abilities as a mother brings refreshment to my soul. There were no mothers in the generations before you – no examples or roll models – and yet, those instincts remained strong and powerful despite their dormancy."

"I have certainly learned a great deal more than I could have imagined."

"Yes, and you shall learn much more about what it means to be human."

Anod considered his words. She had not taken the time to project herself into those situations, but she knew those lessons would come from her son. There was much more to learn about the marvel of *Homo sapiens*.

Nick helped Anod make the SanGiocomo cave dwelling safe for the voracious curiosity of her toddler. Once the task was fully accomplished, Anod began to relax a little. The process of keeping up with young Zoltentok proved far more fatiguing than any other activity she could remember including the days of survival training or the intense games of rumbleball. She learned, as the safety of the rooms grew, to let

Zoltentok have his lead. Occasionally, he would throw a tantrum over the physical denial of his access to one area or another, but it gave his mother some piece of mind.

Anod felt the need for more advise and counsel, and it was also time for another dose of peers for Zoltentok. Mother and son made the four-hour journey to Guyasaga's home. Zoltentok's former wet nurse – while Anod was in space fighting the Yorax – had just given birth to her sixth child, a third son, four months earlier. Her six children ranged from the newborn to a young female of 13 years. People gravitated to this family. Guyasaga held the distinguished reputation of being the Betan expert on motherhood and the rearing of children. She had held dozens of Betan children to her breasts almost continuously since the birth of her first child. Citizens, both male and female, talked about her in very reverent terms. On occasion, Anod needed the reinforcement, and Guyasaga was always ready with a smile and open arms.

Zoltentok jumped from his mother's arms into the crowd of children around them. His light complexion became a blur among the sea of darker skin. Anod smiled as the squeals of joy erupted from the mass of small people running around the shrubs, trees and grass.

"How have you been, my child?" asked Guyasaga when the first moment of quasi-peace came to them.

"Tired. Very tired."

Guyasaga laughed hard and spoke between heaves, "A mother's world, my child."

"I would have never guessed this was such hard work."

"It is not the work, child. It is the attention." She turned serious for a moment. "You cannot ever relax . . . no rest. Your only moments of peace are when they are asleep, and then you must use that time for other chores."

"I do not think I have ever been so tired. How do you manage with so many children?"

"After a certain point, the older ones begin to help with the smaller children, and it does make life a little easier."

"Then, I should have more children?" asked Anod.

Guyasaga smiled a wise and knowing smile. "Perhaps." She paused to look deeply into Anod's eyes as if she were searching for some valuable object. "Only you can decide that, Miss Anod. However, I have known you for most of the time you have been with us, and certainly since your Zoltentok was born these nearly two years ago. I have watched you, as a woman, as a mother and as a warrior." She nodded her head as if to agree with herself. Anod sat patiently and continued to listen. "I know you are a devoted mother. I know you want to be the best mother you possibly can be, and maybe you should have more children, but you are a warrior, Anod. I have never seen a woman like you, nor has anyone I know ever heard of a woman like you. You are more powerful than any woman and most men, if not all men, on this planet. You have a gift."

"But, I have never known the meaning of pleasure until I came here. The pleasure of a union with a male. The unworldly pleasure of my son. It is very confusing."

Guyasaga rubbed the chocolate skin of her soft cheek, turned and walked toward a group of chairs arranged in the shade of a large tree. She sat down. The laughter of the children and occasionally the heavy breathing of one or more the children could be clearly heard among the shrubbery. Anod joined her host.

Guyasaga began, "It is always difficult when we must make life choices. I have always known I was destined to be a mother of children, many children. It is the only world I have known since as far back as I can remember, and I have never considered nor dreamed of anything else. You, on the other hand, have really only known the life of a warrior. Motherhood was foisted upon you by the happenstance of your presence on this planet. It was not of your choosing."

"So?"

She held up her right hand. "If you were to ask my opinion, Anod, your destiny lies in that which you are best at doing."

"Am I not a good mother?"

"Yes, you are – a very devoted mother – but you have not been trained all your life to be a mother, as I have. You have been trained to be a warrior. While my Samuel and I are peaceful people, we respect the strength and leadership you have brought to our planet, which is why we have chosen to take the risk and join the immigrant group."

"Then, are you saying I should not be a mother?"

"No, Anod. Listen. You are a woman, free to do as she wishes. Perhaps you can find balance between the two roles. All I am trying to say is, people look to you. It is a heavy burden, I know, but it is just as vital to all of us as your commitment to Zoltentok is to him and you."

Anod turned her eyes toward the small voices beyond the bushes. There was an appreciation of the natural state all around her. While her eyes saw the natural world and her ears listened to frivolity and pleasure in the children's voices, her mind considered Guyasaga's words. There was the dilemma for her.

"I am having some trouble with this weaning process, as you call it."

"Why? Is Zoltentok not giving up the breast?"

"No. It is not him. He is doing fine with regular food . . . well . . . mashed up a little. It is me that is having the trouble."

Guyasaga smiled broadly, showing all her white teeth, and waved her head back and forth several times. "Dear woman, now, I suppose you are truly one of us. Most mothers miss that contact with their children."

"Yes, but it was pleasurable for me," Anod stated. Guyasaga cleared her throat but did not answer. "Is it pleasurable for you?"

Guyasaga cleared her throat again. "Well, child, I suppose that is a very personal question."

"Then, I have asked too much. I must apologize."

"No need. To answer your question, it is one of those few true pleasures in life that we keep to ourselves. We certainly do not tell the men, or they would be seeking equal time. And, we definitely do not want that."

The words floated for a moment. "I see," said Anod. "So, it is pleasurable for you as well."

"Yes."

"And, it is hard to wean, as you say."

"Yes, it is. I think it is much harder on the mother than it ever could be for the child, but it is a normal and important passage milestone."

"Is the pleasure why you suckle other children?"

"Now you are getting very personal."

Anod looked away and lowered her head. "I am sorry. Sometimes my curiosity sees no boundaries."

"Well, child, you are new to this, so I will make an exception, but I certainly do not want you talking to others about this." She waited for agreement and attention. "The answer is, yes. Yes, there is a physical pleasure I feel throughout my whole body, but more importantly, it is the glorious ecstasy of watching that oh-so-small person, cradled in your arms and drawing nourishment from you. The pure, unadulterated contentment and peace of that child at your breast is the opiate that keeps me sedated. I know you have felt the same."

"Yes, I do. Well, at least, I know I was not experiencing some clinical, psychotic episode."

Guyasaga laughed so hard, several of the children poked their heads through the vegetation to make sure everything was all right or to see what was so funny. Their curiosity satisfied, they disappeared, again. Anod waited for Guyasaga's laughter to subside.

"I am not sure I see the humor, Guyasaga."

"Perhaps you don't," she answered as she tried to regain control. "Just remember what I said, Anod. Your destiny is to lead our new colony, not to be a wet nurse like me."

"Maybe."

"No, maybes. You know I am right. We need you to lead us to the future. There are several of us who can take care of Zoltentok and your other children should you have more. There is only one you."

"I never wanted to be your leader."

"As you say, but nonetheless, you are."

"I am not sure I want to be your leader, to take that responsibility. I rather like the rewards of being a mother."

"Anod, listen to me. I will help you be a mother, but the risks we face in this migration plan require your expertise."

"I was not here when your ancestors came to Beta."

"No, and neither was I. However, our folklore tells us, many died in the first years of the immigration to Beta. I do not want that to happen to us. We have decided to incorporate some of your advanced technology to minimize the risks, and you are the only one among us who knows this technology."

Anod could only nod her head in agreement as she looked away to the vegetation, again. She looked around at the shadows to determine the time. It was getting late. She and Zoltentok would have to make their way from the waystation to the cave through the forest and up the hill in the dark, as it was. The later they waited, the longer it would be.

Zoltentok threw a fit when Anod tried to remove him from the group. Guyasaga offered several times to take care of Zoltentok for a few days, but Anod needed Zoltentok more than he needed her. He remained upset for only a short time once they began the rail journey back home. He was completely asleep and deadweight as she carried him up the hill through the dark forest to SanGiocomo Cave.

Anod changed his clothes, wiped him down with a warm, damp cloth, and then dressed him for bed. The boy never opened an eye. Nick and Bradley asked about her day, but she said very little other than the visit was quite enjoyable. Her thoughts ground away on Guyasaga's words.

Anod knew she was correct, but the truth somehow did not sit well with her.

It took Anod several days to reach a point where she was ready to talk to anyone. Bradley was off somewhere continuing to negotiate support for the immigration plan. Nick was working in his laboratory when Zoltentok finally decided to take a nap.

"Nick," she said and waited for his attention.

He finished his precision task then looked up. "Yes, Anod."

"Do you think I am a good mother?"

"Oh my, is this the source of your mood? Are you having some kind of crisis of conscience?"

"Guyasaga believes I should concentrate on leading our people as opposed to having more children."

"Well, Guyasaga is entitled to her opinion. Did she tell you not to have children, or that you are not a good mother?"

"No."

"Well, I would agree with her in a sense. Many of our people look to you as a leader including Bradley and me. But, that does not have any bearing on your ability as a mother. Anyone can see you love Zoltentok very much and care for him as well as any mother on this planet."

"I have considered her words. I want to have another child."

"Then, you should do what you want. You are a good mother, Anod, and if you want to have another child, you should." Nick allowed a pause to occupy a few moments. "Have you reconsidered our custom of marriage?"

Anod smiled. "I still see no reason."

Bradley returned to his bench work. Anod wanted to ask him more about the relationship between community leadership and motherhood, but she had received the opinion she wanted. She was ready for another child.

Anod decided to announce her decision at a family evening meal they chose to eat outside in the calm, moderate air. She waited until they finished the meal. Zoltentok walked from one object to another trying to tell his observers about his findings.

"I want another child," Anod blurted out.

"Really?" asked Bradley.

"Yes. Zoltentok does not need as much personal care any more. I miss that connection with him."

"It changes, Anod," added Bradley, as if she had not considered the obvious.

"I know, but I want those feelings."

"I think it is great that you want more children. I can help there."

Nick was the first to notice the change in the situation on Beta. The elder SanGiocomo was standing in the middle of the clearing watching the setting of the θ27 star – their life source – when he saw the distinctive shape of the Society starship passing above in the darkening sky.

Pointing to the moving shape, Nick asked, "Isn't that a starship?"

The confirmation was not long in coming. "Yes, it is."

"Is it the *Endeavour*?" asked Nick.

"I'm sure we will find out soon enough," answered Bradley.

Young Zoltentok was old enough to comprehend what was happening and something about what the adults were talking about. His many flights with his mother in the interceptor had given him a strong, indelible impression of flight and space travel. Nick and Bradley waited patiently as Anod explained what the object was. The battery of questions from the lad was predictable and amusing. Anod answered each of every one in simple concise terms that Zoltentok could understand.

"Fly," said Zoltentok looking between his mother and the orbiting starship, motioning for them to fly up to see the starship.

"Maybe later," Anod responded with characteristic patience. "We are waiting for one or more of her crew to visit us. We need to stay here until we know who it is, and why they are here." Without any additional information, Anod instinctively knew why the starship was orbiting above them although she did not want to offer her thoughts to the others.

In the waning light of the descending star, the eerie scintillation and changing colors, from blue to broadband, indicated the arrival of two humans through the energy-matter conversion transporter. After a few additional seconds, the complete bodies of Zontramani and Astridag were standing in front of them.

"Welcome back," Bradley said with enthusiasm. "Welcome to Beta."

"Thank you, Prime Minister SanGiocomo," responded Colonel Zontramani. "It is good to see you, again."

Bradley chose not to correct his guest on his diminished governmental status. "Would you like to join us for a drink?" asked Bradley.

"Actually, we would like to invite you to dine with us aboard *Endeavour*. We have completed our planned search, and we have some data we are eager to provide to you."

"Go?" asked Zoltentok in an excited voice of youthful anticipation.

Anod looked first to Zontramani who smiled and nodded his head in the affirmative, and then to Bradley who shrugged his shoulder to indicate his neutrality.

"We have already eaten," responded Anod.

Colonel Zontramani nodded his head then said, "Quite all right. I am sure Major Astridag and the others will not mind missing a meal for the moment."

"We can certainly wait," Bradley added.

"It is not necessary. I am eager to show you the information we have collected."

"I don't know if it's a good idea to be decomposed and recombined," Nick stated with noticeable concern.

"The process is quite safe. There are several layers of safeguards. The system will not initiate if there is even a remote chance something might go wrong," said Major Astridag in an attempt to soothe Nick's apprehension.

"We have both done it," Bradley added motioning toward Anod. "Please join us, Nick."

After a few moments of further consideration, Nick reluctantly agreed. "Well, I have lived a long life already, and it has to end sometime." The elder man's acquiescence and funereal comment brought a sympathetic laugh from the assembled group.

"Shall we go, then?" asked Zontramani.

The four residents and two Starfleet officers gathered together under the direction of Astridag and were transported to the *Endeavour*. Upon arrival, Colonel Astrok greeted them. Nick was inwardly impressed with the array of instruments in the austere, no nonsense, operational, transporter room. Young Zoltentok was ecstatic and quite animated in his enjoyment of the new experience. With Anod's approval, Zontramani haled Captain Zalemon and upon arrival asked him to take their young guest on a tour of the ship. The others proceeded to the command conference room for a briefing on the results of the exploration.

"We believe we have some prospects for you," began Colonel Zontramani. "I'd like Major Astridag to brief you on the findings to date."

On cue, the science officer stood and moved to the far end of the oval table from Colonel Zontramani. "*Endeavour*, with the assistance of four additional starships, conducted a comprehensive search." Reaching down to a small control panel near the edge of table, Astridag touched two positions. A large hologram appeared behind her. "As you should recognize, this is an image of our galaxy." To the Betans, the image was a conglomeration of little points of light arranged in a large, spiral, galactic formation hovering over the table and passing over their heads. To the *Endeavour*'s crew, it was an illustrated map of the home galaxy – the Milky Way. It was slowly rotating in an erect position such that most of the audience was looking at the characteristic pinwheel disk from beneath the image. "Viewing it from above," she continued. The large circular image about two and a half meters in diameter reoriented on her voice command so the rotation axis was now pointing across their heads. The pinwheel projection stopped spinning.

"Here is Earth." A small, but oversized, bright, blue sphere appeared in the field of white pinpoints. "And, here are the previously known class E planets." Six green spheres materialized. They were scattered across the same spiral arm in a thirty-degree sector at the top of the image and around the blue sphere.

"Before she jumps into our findings," interjected Zontramani, "I must say, we have explored parts of the galaxy previously outside of our sphere of examination. We have made many discoveries all to the benefit of the citizens of the Confederation and the Society. This search would not have happened at this time if we had not received your request. So, on behalf of the Confederation, thank you."

Bradley answered, "We are most grateful."

"Continue, major."

"We examined numerous star systems and potential planetary star systems," which appeared as red spheres, "and discovered several possible inhabitable systems during the search." The small sector of the galaxy was enlarged and an array of colored spheres was now depicted within the sector image.

Astridag continued the briefing, which lasted nearly two hours, using various holographic images. Each of the red spheres were systematically examined using a one meter, full visual color, recreation of the respective planet that expanded rapidly from its place in the galactic image to a place centered in front of the galaxy. Each object was used as a talking point.

Nick's progressively puzzled expression led to raising his right hand like a school child. "Excuse me."

"Yes, sir," answered Major Astridag.

"You have used this term, class, in categorizing your findings. I thought I could figure it out, but unfortunately, I am not able to ascertain your classification system, thus I am not able to understand your findings."

"My apologies."

"We use the Confederation standards for classification of any object below an infant star, in other words, any object that has not reached critical mass for ignition of its internal nuclear fires, or is not a substantial net emitter."

"I understood that."

"So, for those sub-star objects we use broad classes. I will try to summarize these briefly. A Class A planet is a gaseous or excessive atmosphere object. Classes B through D are generally defined as rock objects with insufficient or inadequate atmospheric parameters and the differentiation determined by the quantity or toxicity of the atmospheric gases. Class E is most like Earth. Beta is a Class E planet. Classes F through H segment objects for the lack of water or the materials to produce water. The remaining categories, Classes I through L, define the presence of other lifeforms with Class L recognizing the existence of higher order lifeforms that would prohibit any visitation without a treaty or other form of reassurance regarding interaction."

"So, we are looking for a Class E planet?" asked Nick.

"Yes, although most other objects are inhabitable with various support mechanisms."

"We are not interested in constructed environments."

"My father speaks for all of us," interjected Bradley. "Those of us in the migration group are willing to accept some technology as Anod has helped us see the benefits, but we want to live a simple life without the worries of maintenance, leakage, or other factors of deterioration."

"Understood. With that constraint, you could also inhabit Class I and J objects."

"And, those are?"

"They have acceptable atmospheres and water conditions with no detectable lifeforms as in a Class I planet, or only low-order lifeforms – a Class J object."

"If there is no life, how can it support us?" asked Bradley.

"That is where we must be careful," Zontramani said. "There could be many reasons for no life, for example, all the ingredients are present, but no initiator has been introduced like a high energy discharge. The end point is, for any object other than a Class E, other more detailed criteria must be used to evaluate the usefulness of any particular object for any reason, actually."

"I need to learn much more about these classifications," Nick said, "but this is sufficient for me to absorb the information you are providing."

The remainder of the discussion focused on the attributes and detractors of the candidate planets. The process of discovery was left to the Betans as the Society presented the collected information. Many possibilities were discussed. One was a solo satellite – more arid, possessed moderate terrain, limited life forms and the atmosphere had higher oxygen content. The parent star was actually a relatively young binary set. The other planet was the fourth of fifteen orbiting a mature singular star near mid-life. The planet possessed a stable, uniform and symmetric orbit, and was endowed with ample vegetation, high atmospheric moisture and abundant life forms. The detractor for the second planet was the higher than desired CO_2 content which produced an elevated ambient temperature.

"None of the candidates are gems like Beta," observed Nick.

Astridag thought about the comment. "If you mean, they are not nominal Class E objects, you are correct, although a remote appraisal even with our sophisticated sensors is most likely inadequate."

Nick waved his hand, not wanting to respond to the rather sterile response of the *Endeavour*'s science officer.

"You now possess all the summary data we have accumulated," Colonel Zontramani added with finality. "You are welcome to examine the details of our search results as you wish."

The mood of the assembled group was decidedly more subdued than was earlier the case. The survey found a couple of reasonable candidate planets although neither was an idyllic place. The three visitors each considered the information provided in their own way and were arriving at essentially the same conclusion. Either site could be made comfortable with some adaptation of methods, processes and customs. In most other categories and by the majority of parameters, both planets were within the acceptable range of values, and they were inhabitable.

Bradley spoke for the visiting contingent. "Thank you, Colonel Zontramani, for the extensive effort you and the others of the Society have expended. We are grateful for your assistance. We must consider collectively the information you have provided and decide on the direction we desire to head."

"How much time will that process take?"

"It is difficult to say," responded Bradley.

"Have you considered the method of transport, if you decide to migrate to one of the candidates?"

"No. This journey demands deliberate steps of small stride to ensure acceptance of the objective."

"Very wise," added Zontramani.

"We will have to reach a decision, soon, however."

"With your permission, we will remain here for some rest and relaxation for the crew, then we will have to be on our way."

"As always, we have no problem with your visitation," Bradley said almost without thinking. His thoughts were actually on other topics.

The breakaway Betans were preoccupied with the consideration of less than optimum planetary choices. The Starfleet officer empathized with the unspoken concern.

Anod noticed her young son watching the Starfleet officers, their mannerisms, their movements and their speech. Zoltentok was clearly enthralled with the new characters within his immediate realm of understanding.

The visit ended earlier than expected much to Zoltentok's disappointment. The boy was not particularly bashful about his feelings as most young children through the ages often displayed. The departure was friendly, respectful and temporary.

Back at SanGiocomo Cave, it was dark and nearly the middle of the night. Inside, they fidgeted with things, doing various mundane household chores, until Zoltentok fell asleep.

"What do we do now?" asked Nick.

They both look to Anod. She chose not to respond.

"Well?" asked Bradley of Anod.

"This is up to you."

"Wait a minute," Bradley said. "Are you with us or not?"

"Yes. I am just trying to say I have already formed my opinion. I know what I want to do. What we must determine is, what does the rest of the group want to do?"

"As you say, then," said Nick. "It would be helpful if we knew what you thought about this situation. After all, you are the only one among us who has lived out there," he added with the glance to the sky above.

Anod searched the eyes of both men. "There are really only two choices, well perhaps others. First, we can remain here. There may be several possible options with that, however, I think any deviation from the culture and mores of Beta would be corrosive and potentially injurious. The best choice beyond Beta is Murtauri Four. The other planets are just too far off the baseline values. They are all possibles with substantially greater support. The levels of carbon dioxide are within adaptable values."

"How long?" asked Bradley.

"She is correct. It would probably take several months, maybe a year at most, based on our knowledge of human physiology."

"So, you really think Murtauri Four is the best choice?"

"Yes, I do."

"Do you think we can convince the others?" Bradley asked.

"You are the best judge of that. However, my opinion is, yes. It is unfair and unreasonable to impose further upon Beta. The information provided by Colonel Zontramani indicated that Murtauri Four, in some ways, would be better than Beta, and of course, in some ways, worse. In all, with the benefits of the technology I think we can obtain from the Society, we can make a very good life on Murtauri Four. There are many assets on Murtauri Four that we can use for trade. There appears to be many more possibilities or alternatives."

"You are saying, we must present an image of what will be or what might be," Nick said.

"Yes."

Both men stared at Anod as if she had spoken some unintelligible language. She wondered what they were thinking, and then let her puzzlement show on her face.

"It is late. We must go to bed," offered Nick.

"Yes. Tomorrow, we need to establish our plan or at least the next few steps to gain the acceptance of the group."

They all nodded their heads and retired.

Zoltentok did not let them sleep long. Anod rose to retrieve her son while the two men slept. She gathered up the requisite things including some fresh porridge for her son then went outside. The early morning light meant she had only managed a couple of hours sleep, and she felt it. Anod tended to Zoltentok's needs first. Once satisfied, the lad bounced from his mother's lap to begin a further exploration of the meadow and treeline in front of the cave. The warmth on her face coupled with her general fatigue pulled her toward slumber. The rich aromatic mixtures of the fertile soil and scents of the forest compounded the sense of relaxation, of release, for Anod. She fought the urge, knowing her son was not self-sufficient regarding what not to do. One scare too many forced her to get on her feet. She chased Zoltentok around the meadow listening to his squeals of delight.

To keep her mind busy, Anod found a particular plant or bird to use as a point of instruction. She could only hold his attention for so long on any one specific item, but it did serve her purpose. Anod stayed awake, shepherding her son, until Nick then Bradley joined her at the talking stumps.

"How long have you been up?" asked Bradley.

"About four hours."

"Then, you did not get much sleep," Nick observed.

"No, and I am feeling it."

"We can take over, if you want to get some sleep," said Nick.

"Thank you. I think I will."

"First, before you go inside," Bradley said, "I think we need to talk to a key group of our strongest supporters to prepare the decision process."

"Yes."

"As soon as possible."

"Yes."

"I will try for this afternoon after you awaken from your nap."

"As you say," Anod answered, then turned to go to the cave.

"Wait, Anod. Do you have any thoughts, any suggestions on who?"

"No, Bradley. I still believe it is the will of the Betans that should decide."

"Questions of the technology will come up."

"I will be prepared to handle those questions, but the group must decide what is best for all concerned. That is not something that is up to me."

"Very well. We shall be waiting for you. Now, go rest."

Anod nodded her head toward Zoltentok who was now seven meters away near the edge of the clearing. Both men looked toward the boy. Nick rose to move closer to him. When they looked back, Anod was half way to the entrance.

She slept four hours. A small group had gathered among the talking stumps. Several children of various sizes bounced among the adults. Anod recognized most of the attendees, although there were a few she had not met, yet. Greetings were exchanged as Anod joined the group.

"The discussion began without you," Bradley said.

"Good."

"Yes, well, there are probably more questions than answers at this stage."

"That is good, I should think."

"While I have tried to describe things like terrain, vegetation and other lifeforms on Murtauri Four, there are many things we do not know." Anod nodded her head in agreement, not knowing what exactly he wanted. "Yes, the general consensus is there are too many unknowns."

"As there probably will always be," Anod responded.

"You have said that technology can reduce the risk."

"Yes."

"What technology?" asked Otis Greenstreet.

Anod looked into her former lover's eyes. "There are many elements that will help."

"Like what."

"The Society uses respirators that can alter the inhaled gas mixture within certain limits. The atmosphere on Murtauri Four is within those limits. Those respirators can help us adjust to the higher carbon dioxide levels. I think we should have isopods, cleansing stations and the central computer to monitor our health."

"Isopods?" asked Guyasaga.

"It is a device that enables you to gain the most efficient recuperative period, sleep as you call it, and allows the central computer to constantly evaluate the health condition of your body," and make appropriate repairs, Anod thought, although chose not to add too much information that might overwhelm her Betan friends.

"The pod constantly scans . . . ," she hesitated, ". . . well, actually, it would be easier to explain with a functional isopod. Can we wait for that?"

Guyasaga and several others nodded their heads.

"With a properly configured central computer system, environmental conditions can be continuously monitored and reported, such that changes in the atmosphere, the biological profile and any other basic condition can be detected for us. The system also serves, to a certain degree, as an early warning system if there is a problem. It takes a while for the computer to learn everything it needs to know, but it would be adequately configured once it has experienced one full seasonal cycle of the planet. Actually, it does not need a full cycle, but it is better and more useful if it does. So, we will have some exposure."

"Then we will not have protection?" asked another.

"Well, I suppose so. Yes."

"Very risky."

Anod wanted to ignore the concern for the moment. "We will also need converters and an array of satellite reflectors to use converters for transport."

"Converter?"

"Yes. The device changes matter to energy for transmission short distances, then reassembles the matter at the new destination."

"You are not talking about doing this to human beings."

Bradley jumped in to avoid the risk of losing the audience in some scientific exchange. "My whole family has used these converters including little Zoltentok. These are successful devices commonly used by travelers."

"Then, you are talking about human beings."

"Yes," answered Bradley, "but there is no risk."

"There are many safeguards including a messenger signal that verifies the transfer prior to anything, object or otherwise, being transported," interjected Anod.

"What else?"

Anod looked first to Nick then Bradley, who both nodded back to her. "Although I find your ancient growing processes charming and attractive, I would suggest we have replicators that can assemble atomic material using genetic prints into virtually any substance we need."

"Food?"

"Yes, or virtually any other material, biological or otherwise, as well."

"These replicators assemble substances?"

"Yes."

"Where do they get the atomic material as you say?

"The systems extract what matter it can from the environment, disassembles then reassembles the basic matter into the desired form."

"Can we see these technologies? Can we use them?"

"I am sure we can make arrangements with Colonel Zontramani and *Endeavour*."

"But, these devices will not eliminate the risk, will they?" Guyasaga asked.

"No," answered Anod. "They will not."

"This is a very serious step," Bradley said for the group. "We must decide carefully, and we must develop a consensus among all the immigrant group."

"If you consider the risk too great," Anod added, "I believe we could send a reconnaissance team to Murtauri Four to explore portions of the planet before we make a final decision to move. Or, we might be able to convince the Society to place a detail monitor probe on the planet for us."

"Do you think that necessary?"

"I do not. I am satisfied with the information we have from the *Endeavour*'s search and the advantage we gain from the technology, assuming we can obtain the technology from the Society. I am prepared to move, now."

"Pardon us, Miss Anod, but some of the rest of us are not quite so confident."

"That is your decision to make."

"I would suggest," interjected Bradley, "that we divide up the entire group and each of us take a portion. We must know what the others think. This is a decision that belongs to the body of the whole as well as a very personal decision for each of us."

They agreed. The process of division was completed quickly as well as the timetable for accomplishment. An additional question was added regarding the mechanism to make the final decision. Five days were set aside to contact each of the known immigration group.

The SanGiocomos waited for the returns. Their neutrality in this process had been requested and agreed.

The debate among the separatists took much less time than either Bradley or Anod thought it would. The only extra effort involved several visits to *Endeavour* for those who wanted to gain some comfort with the technology. They had underestimated the conviction to move. Those among them, who wanted the new beginning, wanted the move, wanted the adventure. The preference was virtually unanimous for the tropical planet, Murtauri Four. Those who desired one of the other planets easily agreed to the change. Even the skeptics among them overcame their fears.

So, the decision was made.

Bradley James SanGiocomo, on behalf of 387 men, women and children, informed Colonel Zontramani of their collective decision and sought Society assistance for the colonization of Murtauri Four. The discussions regarding the acquisition of necessary technology items took several additional days. Anod added her request for a team of androids to join them. Specifically, she asked if her life-long android, Gorp, who perished in Zitger's ambush of the patrol from the Saranon Outpost, could be recreated and programmed. Her personal request proved to be the most difficult. In the end, *Endeavour*'s captain was prepared for the requests and quickly consented once the details had been established. The *quid pro quo* surrounding the migration plan was the Murtauri Four colony would be required to join the Confederation of Planets and participate in the joint governance and protection process. The last vestiges of uncertainty vanished. Their course was set.

Chapter 5

"There is still a considerable amount of apprehension regarding the technology," Bradley said.

Anod closed her eyes and leaned back, supporting her torso with locked arms on the back of the massive rock. The heavy dampness of the fog nearly obscured the entrance to SanGiocomo Cave. She could hear the faint squeals of her son inside the cave playing with Nick. Anod savored the variety of ambient, atmospheric conditions on Beta, something she did not experience in the habitats of Saranon Outpost nor during her years of service to the Society.

"Anod," Bradley nudged, wondering if she had not heard his statement.

"Yes, yes, I know."

"How do we help them become comfortable?"

"There is only one way I know of, and that is to use it."

"Can we get Colonel Zontramani to bring these devices here for a demonstration?"

Anod chuckled softly then opened her eyes to connect with her partner. "Some of them, such as the respirators, can be transported down here, but most of them cannot, since they are linked to the central computer for many reasons."

"So, we must go to *Endeavour*."

"Yes. That is the only way I can think of at the moment, unless we build a mini-station on Beta, which would not be advisable."

"Agreed."

The two leaders stared at each other as they contemplated the possibilities. A large mass demonstration would not likely be successful. Anod tried to place herself in the mind of a Betan skeptic who has lived for several generations without any of this technology, never felt the need for supporting devices, and is only now being confronted with the potential.

"Here is a suggestion," she began. "Let us identify those among us who are the closest to accepting the new devices. We can have the others divided into planning groups, working on various aspects of the detailed migration plan, while we do small demonstrations hopefully to convert a segment of our population. Then, perhaps, they can help the others go through demonstrations for small groups, so we have Betans working with other Betans, rather than me or the crew of *Endeavour* trying to convince them."

"Excellent idea."

"You have been the closest to some of these devices. We should go do our own demonstration. I know you and Nick are not quite comfortable with these things."

"You are, of course, correct. When you say, we, you mean the four of us?"

"Yes. Zoltentok must learn about these things. We can also use the time to make the appropriate arrangements with *Endeavour*."

"Then, so be it."

Anod and Bradley joined Nick and Zoltentok. They talked over lunch. Nick was not particularly enthusiastic about the plan, at first, but as they talked, he warmed to the opportunity. The conventional radio call to *Endeavour* brought a quick response and invitation.

The solid antratite rock walls of SanGiocomo Cave prevented any signal penetration. The transportation process would have to wait until the *Endeavour* could detect them.

Since the *Endeavour*'s sensors could not 'see' inside the cave of solid antratite, the signal for the converter to bring them to the starship would be when the four of them appeared, outside, where the sensors could detect them. They walked outside the cave. The process did not take long. Within seconds, they were aboard the Society Starship *Endeavour* once again.

Major Astridag greeted them. "Good to see you, again."

"Likewise," responded Nick for the small group.

"As I understand this visit, you want a demonstration of the equipment you have requested for the colonization of Murtauri Four."

"Yes," Bradley answered.

"Since Anod is just as familiar with these devices as any of us, I can leave you to perform your own demonstration." Anod nodded her head, although the others were not quite so sure. "I have taken the liberty to arrange one of the guest quarters with the various items you requested."

"Excellent," Anod said. Bradley shrugged his shoulders as if to concede, and Nick reluctantly nodded his head.

"If you would follow me, I shall take you to the guest room, and leave you to your own discovery."

They walked through several corridors, and passed various crew and working spaces. The guest room was actually a suite including living and sleeping chambers. Anod recognized the space and accouterments of the flag guest quarters, the best space on any starship, better than the captain's quarters. The captain and the crew obviously wanted this process to go well.

"Here you are," Astridag said swinging her arm for them to enter. "Anod, I believe you are familiar with all this equipment."

"Yes."

"Then, I shall leave you to it."

"Thank you."

Astridag turned to leave. "Oh," she said turning to Anod. "Are you familiar with *Intrepid*-class starships?"

"No."

"Then, call me when you are ready to leave. I shall retrieve you. I know Colonel Zontramani would like to talk with you regarding the desired arrangements for the subsequent demonstrations."

"Very well."

Astridag left. The sliding, automatic door closed behind her, and they were alone.

The three males stood staring at Anod. Zoltentok was the first to break as he fluttered from one place to another. They started several times only to be interrupted by Zoltentok's voracious curiosity. Anod suggested they ask one of the crew to watch him, while they worked with the equipment. Nick's patience won out. They enjoyed the view of Beta and the universe beyond the observation window until Zoltentok ran out of energy and fell asleep on one of the soft chairs.

Anod wasted no more time. "This is the respirator I mentioned earlier," she said holding a flexible, cage-like object. She placed it over her head. The various soft bars moved to her skull. "As you can see, it automatically adjusts to your head shape. This bar goes across your upper lip, and these two probes go in each nostril. The respirator continuously senses the inhaled and exhaled gases and adjusts primarily the oxygen level to achieve the correct blood gas levels. The units can be quickly outfitted with small head mounted reservoirs or a large, multi-gas back pack for the more extreme atmospheres that require a special supplemental mouthpiece or a nose and mouth mask."

Bradley and Nick both tried on the respirator several times. Nick laughed each time the device adjusted to his head. They examined the various attachments. Bradley donned the backpack to feel its weight and center of mass.

"There are three other support devices," she continued. "This helmet is used when there is one or more elements present that could prove harmful. The light suit is generally used when there are hazardous agents that can penetrate by other means beyond inhalation. And, the full or heavy suit is, of course, designed to support human life in the void of open space with all its associated radiation and lack of appreciable pressure."

"Do we need all of these?" asked Bradley.

"Probably not, but it would be a good idea to have some with us, just in case something happens."

"Of course," Nick said. "Better safe than sorry." They all chuckled.

Anod walked to the far wall separating the living and sleeping chambers. She touched several buttons, and said, "Korric juice." In seconds, the clear container of clear, green liquid materialized in the small chamber. When the process completed, the clear door lifted. Anod reached in, took the glass, and drank several swallows. She smiled as she held out the cylinder of juice.

With pronounced hesitation and reluctance, Bradley slowly reached for the container. He held it in front of him to examine it very carefully. He smelled the contents then touched the tip of his tongue to the liquid. Anod smiled patiently as the Betan leader tested the juice. Satisfied, he took first a small sip, then waited to feel any adverse response. Feeling none, he took several more swallows. "I am dumbstruck," he said holding the container out to Nick. "That is the best Korric juice I have ever tasted. And, it came from that machine?"

Anod continued to smile and nodded her head. She moved to one of the other tables. "These are, of course, weapons. I guess I shall handle these."

"Do we really need them?" asked Nick. "Weapons just attract others with bigger weapons."

"The universe is not all friendly."

"We will need to discuss that later," injected Bradley.

"As you say, then. The last devices I think we need to demonstrate are the cleansing station and isopod." Anod led the two men into the sleep chamber. She moved to a floor to ceiling, clear, cylinder and turned to face Bradley and Nick. She placed her hand on a small, black box with several colored buttons beside a tall section of the cylinder that appeared to be a door. "This is a cleansing station. It has many purposes, however the primary use is to clean and evaluate our bodies. We use the cleansing station, as a matter of routine, before we retire to the isopod. These two devices really work best together," she said pointing to both the cleansing station and isopod.

"How does it work?" asked Nick.

She pointed to the top of the cylinder. "Do you see that thick ring at the top?" She paused but did not look to confirm their attention. "That is the action ring. Once you are inside and the door closes, the ring descends. A complex array of electromagnetic and sub-aural acoustic energy is used to completely scan your body while other features remove any contaminants detected. The information is evaluated against a baseline plus most recent profiles for identification, health examination, minor repair and profiling."

"My gosh," Nick said. "It does all that?"

"Yes. If the computer detects any abnormality, such as a wound or alien virus or bacterium, it will repair some of the damage like minor cuts. So, depending on your state of health when you enter the chamber, the process could take anywhere from ten seconds to several minutes to complete. The information gathered by the cleansing station is used by the central computer to program the isopod for extensive repair work." Anod thought about telling him about the disease, wound and damage repair capability and the DNA refurbishment function but knew it would be too much for them to absorb.

"Fascinating."

Anod began to remove her clothes.

"That is not necessary," Nick said.

Anod did not hesitate. "Yes, it is. Clothing will inhibit some significant features of the device."

Curiosity overcame his prudishness. Nick looked behind him, into the living chamber, as if to see if anyone else was with them. Both men had slowly adapted to Anod's lack of inhibition. They had seen her naked more times than they could count, and this was just family.

Anod pushed two buttons, opening the door. Once inside, she turned to face the men, then pushed another interior button. The door closed. Anod kept her eyes open looking at both men and stood with her legs shoulder width apart and her arms straight and away from her body with her palms facing forward. She smiled. A blue-green light filled the darkened room. Airflow lifted her hair straight up. The ten-centimeter tall ring descended inside the cylinder. As the unit reached the top of her head, a narrow, blue-green, horizontal band with a brighter, thin, grid pattern illuminated the contours of her body. As the band descended, various small beams of red, yellow, green and blue danced over her body. Small sparkles leapt from her ascending into the ceiling. The process continued until the band of light reached the floor, then the band changed to red and ascended more rapidly up her body to the ceiling. The door opened.

"Now, the system recognized me by my genetic print and everything in my body must be within normal limits," she said as she stepped out of the chamber. "The computer said nothing. If either of you entered the chamber, since it would be your first time, the computer would ask you several questions, and the process would take longer since there is no profile for you in the system." They nodded their heads. Anod walked to the horizontal unit, a long, shallow, ellipsoid device on a short pedestal. The bottom half was a bluish-silver and the top was clear. "This is an isopod. This is where you sleep."

"Inside?" asked Nick.

"Yes." Again, she pushed several buttons, this time on the isopod, and the top opened length-wise. "Computer, do not initiate sleep cycle and enable full, visual and audio transfer."

"As you command," answered the voice of the unseen, omni-present computer.

Both men looked around as if to see the person who just spoke. Anod waited patiently. They turned back and smiled.

Anod sat on the edge of the bed then lay down. Once she lay still, the top closed over her. Within seconds, her body rose several centimeters inside the device. She turned her head toward them. "This is all normal. You can move," she said as she shifted her position several times. Her height above the bottom adjusted continuously so that her body never touched the isopod. "Normally, at this point, the system would trigger numerous key elements to induce a deep sleep, but since I have instructed the system not to place me in suspension, I remain awake. The system continuously monitors your physiological functions and can perform a multitude of tasks to ensure that when you awake, you are fully rested. The system also has the ability to darken the interior making it devoid of light as well as unilaterally or bilaterally eliminate any audio transfer. I like the bilateral audio block and remain transparent." Both men stared. "Any questions?"

"This is like the machines they used after the battle, when I first saw you again on the ship."

"Yes, precisely, although this model is primarily for recuperation. The medical pods have far greater capability." Anod waited for other questions that did not come. "Anything else?"

"No," Bradley said.

"Me neither."

Anod nodded her head. "Open," she commanded. Anod was lowered to the bed and the top rotated away as it had done before. She dressed quickly. "The isopod provides the most efficient recuperation possible. What takes us six to eight hours in your conventional bed, can be done in four hours with an isopod, and you feel much more rested."

"What does it feel like?" asked Nick.

"Try it."

"No," he said holding up his hand. "I will in time, but not now."

"Do you have to be naked?" asked Bradley.

"No, but as I said earlier with the cleansing station, the devices will not work as well with any obstructions present. For example, it would not work at all if I wore a suit of antratite because the sensors would not detect key physiological indicators." She looked to Nick. "It feels like you do not have a body any more. You feel no weight, no touch, and no sensation of presence. Of course, you can see yourself or touch your body to confirm that you are indeed present, but when you lay like I did, you can feel nothing, no up or down, no pressure points anywhere. It does take a few times to adapt to the lack of sensation, but you will find the isopod to be an exceptional sleep."

"So, you think we need these?" Bradley asked.

"Would you not want this capability?"

"I suppose that was a rhetorical question."

"You do not have to take your clothes off. You can try it as you are."

"Maybe I will," said Nick bravely.

Both men, in turn, lay inside without entering into the sleep cycle. Each of them began to giggle as they activated the various functions on the isopod. The levitation state fascinated them the most. They each came to the realization clothing did provide touch sensation, and they convinced themselves of the benefits of no clothing in the isopod.

"Now, I understand why you like these things," Bradley said.

"It is not that I like or dislike these devices. They simply improve my capabilities and performance."

"Yes, yes," added Nick. "Now, we must help the others appreciate this technology."

"The best thing we can do is keep Anod out of this and conduct demonstrations with small groups as we have just done. They will convince themselves."

"Right you are. Are you in agreement, Anod?"

"Yes."

"Then, we must talk to the captain and make the appropriate arrangements."

"Computer, Major Astridag, please."

Without any words of acknowledgment, the science officer's voice came to them. "Astridag, here."

"Major, we are complete here. We would like to discuss the possibility of further demonstrations for our people."

There was a slight hesitation. "Yes, of course. Colonel Zontramani and I shall join you."

A short set of light chimes announced the arrival of the captain and science officer. Anod acknowledged and gave the command to allow entry.

"So, what do you think of our little gadgetry?" asked Colonel Zontramani, looking at Nick and Bradley.

"Most impressive," answered Nick.

"None of us fully appreciated Anod's descriptions, but we do now."

"Excellent. Are there any questions?"

"None about the technology, but we would like to talk about the migration plan, and specifically the acquisition of this technology for our people when we move to Murtauri Four."

"You have decided upon Murtauri Four?"

"Yes. However, Anod has convinced us," Bradley said glancing at Nick, "of the necessity for this equipment. We also need to convince the others."

Zontramani motioned toward several chairs. "Would you care to sit down?" They each found a chair with Bradley retrieving one from the sleep chamber. "Since our last discussion, I have had several conferences with various leaders at Central Command. They have endorsed our plan as we sketched it out. The Society will provide transport and the desired equipment," he said waving his out-stretched hand across the various items, "as required, in exchange for the membership of Murtauri Four and its inhabitants in the Confederation of Planets."

"Agreed."

"Then, you want to do more demonstrations?"

"I know it would be an imposition, but yes, it would be most helpful."

Colonel Zontramani looked to his science officer, who nodded her head in agreement. "Very well. We shall make this room available to you at your will and provide transport services from the surface and back."

At the conclusion of the meeting, Bradley lifted the still sleeping Zoltentok onto his left shoulder. The Betans paid their respects and offered their gratitude for the generosity of Colonel Zontramani and his crew.

Several collective meetings were held over the next few days to warm the other Betans to the capabilities of the new technology. The reluctant acceptance of their participation in the demonstrations aboard SS *Endeavour* brought the group to an important juncture.

The requisite demonstrations took several weeks to complete in a reasonable, orderly and methodical fashion. The intentions and objectives of the demonstrations were fully met. Most of the colonists were impressed but not convinced. There were still skeptics among them who maintained their aversion to the new capabilities. Surprisingly, to Anod, the most prevalent apprehension had nothing to do with the technology they were about to embrace, but the propriety of sleeping, virtually unconscious and completely naked. The ability to make the cover translucent or opaque made the need more acceptable to those.

Once the final details of the plan had been solidified within the team and accepted by the Society, Bradley and the others began a campaign to present their intentions and the plan to the Betans who chose to remain behind. They had time to accept the idea. Although there was no particular enthusiasm for losing such good people from their midst, they understood the drive to define a new culture, a new society. Many even referred to Anod and her accomplishments as a temptation for them to join, but in the end, the comfort and security of their lives on Beta became the deciding factors.

Despite the enormous distances between Beta and Murtauri Four, the two groups completed an alliance agreement to preserve the connection between them.

The preparations for the move took several more months to

complete. The *Endeavour* had departed on several missions then returned at the prescribed time. Arrangements and agreements were made with the Society for the transfer of some technology, the construction of fundamental facilities and the transportation of the people, their belongings, equipment and other life forms that would not destabilize the planetary ecosystem of Murtauri Four. As the departure date neared, Anod and Bradley were also presented with an additional gift. Anod was pregnant with their second child. The child would be born about three months after their arrival on Murtauri Four.

The day came for embarkation. Emotions ran deep and strong. Tears flowed as words of farewell and *bon voyage* marked the departure of the colonists. SS *Endeavour* would escort three conventional transports. When the actual day came, only 362 Betans actually ascended to the transports – 82 females, 85 males and a nearly even gender split of children of various ages. There were 78 family units.

As the boarding process continued, Anod, Bradley, Nick and Zoltentok waited aboard the starship. Colonel Zontramani joined them in the guest quarters.

"I know this is a difficult time for all of you," he said waiting for expressions of consent. "This is also a time of hope. There is a bright future ahead."

"Indeed," answered Bradley, not feeling particularly talkative.

"I think this might be an appropriate moment to say," he found Anod's eyes, "I can only imagine how difficult this has been on you. After some amount of negotiation with Central Command and the Council of Elders, we would like to soften the pain of your separation, somewhat."

"How so?"

"Lornog, enter," he commanded.

The automatic sliding doors parted allowing an android to enter the room. The android looked and moved like a human. His skin tone was pale, bleaching his short, light blond hair. His build and facial features made it very difficult to determine the identity, but Anod knew the vast majority of androids were produced with a near neutral, but slightly male gender identity bias.

"Anod, this is Lornog. He has assimilated all we know about you, as well as received that last record from your former android, Gorp."

Anod stared at Zontramani then shifted her gaze to Lornog. She nodded to the android.

"Please to meet you, Anod," said Lornog.

"You can never replace Gorp," she said softly.

"It is not my intention to replace him. I have been assigned to you, as your assistant to make this transition better."

Anod extended her hand to the android, who took her hand in a traditional greeting of friendship. "So, you know all about me?"

"Not exactly. I only know about you until your departure from Saranon, and then the record of your evaluation once you had been repatriated aboard *Endeavour*. I might add, I truly and eagerly look forward to getting to know you better."

Anod introduced the others present and explained to them about Gorp, her android since her genesis, who perished in the ambush by Zitger, as well as the purpose of an android, as a personal assistant and companion, and a loyal servant of the Society. The Betans struggled with the reality that androids performed all the manual labor within the Society. Questions returned regarding the evolution of culture on Earth.

With the boarding process nearly complete, the final arrangements for their departure to Murtauri Four were concluded. They busied themselves with the departure and settled into a routine of transit.

The journey involved a menagerie of spacecraft and four months of travel. Everyone remained in good spirits despite the uncharacteristic confinement for the colonists. Most of them had never ventured off Beta. There were second, third and fourth generation Betans. Even Nick, as the eldest among the pioneers, could not remember space travel. Anod was much more comfortable with being back in space despite the uncertainty of the future. She devoted a good portion of her free time, beyond Zoltentok, Bradley and Nick, to Lornog.

"This has been a most fascinating experience," said the android.

"For me as well."

"I must say it is an honor to serve you, Anod."

"It is nice to have someone who really understands me. My family understands me as a person, as a mother, as a woman, but none of them understand the profession that was my life for 46 years."

"I, of course, am not familiar with this term, family, but I am learning from you. Most fascinating concept."

"Yes, indeed. A family is like a small, close, intimate team, each bound to the other by commitment or genetic material, and working for the collective benefit."

"Does that not describe the Society?"

"Yes, I suppose it does, although these feelings, these sensations, the intimacy of the union between us, is very hard to describe for someone who has no concept."

"I shall learn," said Lornog proudly.

"I am sure you will. By the way, I have been meaning to ask you, what are your capabilities?"

The android hesitated from a moment. "To answer the question in some convenient manner, I shall use you as a standard. I have monitored you through Mostron's daily scan of your body. To succinctly summarize, I have a 22.4 percent greater audio range, just about equally distributed on either end of the acoustic spectrum. I have 31.7 percent greater visual range, plus I can sense ionizing radiation at alpha, beta and up to gamma levels. I, of course, do not need an atmosphere or sustenance. I believe you are quite familiar with my strength; it is essentially similar to Gorp's strength. I am conversant in over 1,000 languages and dialects. More importantly, I know you better than you know yourself."

"I would say that is rather impressive."

"Modesty aside, you are correct."

Anod stared at Lornog for a very long time. "Can you feel?"

"My sense of touch is quite refined."

"No, I mean, do you have emotions?"

"Emotions . . . in the sense of mental images that elicit some other internalized response, often manifest as some other externally evident reaction?"

"You could put it that way."

"Given that definition, the answer would be, no."

Anod smiled at Lornog as if he could appreciate the subtleties of the topic. She was glad she had found that part of being human.

"Do you?" he asked.

"Yes."

"Why?"

Anod ignored his question. "As you know, then, I was breed from inception to focus on facts without any qualifying or amplifying response. I am still learning from the Betans about the other dimensions of being human. As a Kartog Guards warrior, I was not much different from you except I was totally biological rather than cybernetic." She smiled at him again. "Emotions give me relief to life . . . the ups and the downs . . . the elation and disappointment. It adds color to life."

"Color?"

"Yes, color. I am not talking about the wavelength of reflected light from an object, but rather the dimension, a depth of field if you will, to everything. To you and me before my arrival on Beta, a flower was simply a biological manifestation of organic reproductive processes for a particular genus of plant. After Beta, the bloom can stimulate a sense of wonderment, relaxation, excitement or contentment by the sheer beauty of the shape, texture, smell or subtle variations in its coloration."

"I think I understand."

"Until you have emotions, you cannot understand. Agreed, you know my words, but you do not know the feelings."

"Interesting."

"Indeed, but carried to the extreme, the birth of my child, Zoltentok, and the growing life within my womb, bring the greatest emotions of all. There are no words to describe the pure, unadulterated elation and joy you feel when you hold your newborn child in your arms and to your breast for the very first time."

"I shall try to learn from you. I am not familiar with ancient reproductive and birthing processes. I have acquired as much information as I can, regarding those processes especially since they were fundamental in your dismissal from service. I must learn as much as I can in order to assist you."

Anod laughed hard. "Yes, you will," she grunted out.

Time became a precious commodity. Anod, Bradley and Nick used the transit to continue preparations for their debarkation including the training of their people on the new equipment and procedures they would soon use on Murtauri Four. Discussion groups were established on each ship to collectively deal with the concerns, apprehensions, issues and worries of their citizens. They wanted to keep everyone busy with some activity or another.

Anod used some of the time to fly. The Yorax interceptor she had used to defend Beta was hangared on the largest of the transports. Zoltentok often went with her, as he had done on Beta. Even Lornog joined them, although he was relegated to a small storage compartment behind the cockpit. He had rigged an interface connection for him to communicate with Anod, and some rudimentary controls and displays for him to use.

Lornog, despite his lack of emotion, had good social skills. Bradley and Nick took to him in short order. Lornog had become part of their family.

As they approached the Murtauri star system and their future home, the immigrants picked up strains of excitement and anxious anticipation. The preparations had been completed weeks before their arrival. There initial actions had been rehearsed many times along with the variations possible when they would execute the real thing.

Upon arrival, a detailed survey of the planet was conducted from orbit. Final adaptations to the plans were developed from the preliminary, inhabitation outline generated from the acquired data provided by the crew of *Endeavour*. The Society continued to provide assistance to the settlers for the construction of temporary lodging, transportation and communications systems. The transfer of technology was comprehensive including replicators, a powerful central computer system – a clone of Mostron they affectionately named Morgan – isopods and a wide range of other equipment along with all the other baggage they brought with them.

Bradley, Anod, Nick, Otis and others provided initial governance through individual leadership with a formal charter to be developed and implemented at a later date. One principle habitat was constructed in the temperate zone of the upper mid-latitudes near the confluence of two large rivers before they emptied into a vast sea.

The first months of life on Murtauri Four were arduous and difficult more from the unknown than from the task of construction. The assistance of the Society made the transition more efficient and effective with the additional tools available to them. The array of orbital reflectors for the converter-transporter system was positioned by the Society.

A governing council was created and empowered for the task of refining the rules of their community. The need for rules was actually quite low since there was a general unanimity of opinion for the population. Most of the former Betans embraced the new technology with excitement and enthusiasm, and made the necessary adjustments in their life styles to take full advantage of the benefits. A liberalization of mores accompanied the expansion of the group allowing for a blossoming of thoughts, ideas and feelings. There was excitement associated with the span and pace of change.

Adaptation to their new environment was rapid and relatively painless. Each and every one of the pioneers exhibited the spirit, dedication and focus of generations of their genetic ancestors. On several occasions, the lack of community introspection over their migration decision was discussed as if it were a strange bird passing through their field of view.

There had been no doubts about the move.

"We must carry out the exploration of our planet as well as the other planets of this star system," Anod announced one evening at a community meeting.

"Why?" asked an anonymous voice.

"We must understand the environment in which we live as thoroughly as we are able, to prevent irreparable abuse. We must also explore the objects of space around us. Exploration is stimulation for the human mind – our consciousness. Just as we must exercise our muscles to avoid atrophy, we must exercise our minds through exploration, science and growth."

"Don't we have enough to do just establishing ourselves on M4?"

"Yes," answered Anod, "but exploration will help us live better."

Anod's words were new to the former Betans. The majority had quickly assimilated the technology of the Society, but projection of that technology, of their intellect, was still a new concept.

"What would you propose?"

"First, I think we should catalog the resources of our planet. Others in the galaxy have benefited from development of natural resources. Second, I would suggest we should slowly expand our inhabitation and maintain a close network of communication not only internally like we had on Beta, but externally with other peoples around us. Third, I would recommend we utilize the spacecraft we have to perform the same exploration of the other planets in the Murtauri star system."

"I endorse Anod's recommendation," offered Bradley.

"Of course you would, she is your wife." The anonymous comment generated a volley of laughter among the settlers.

Bradley allowed the jocularity and related barbs to continue for a short time then raised his hands. "As you say, I would not deny. It is appropriate that we decide on the referendum offered by Anod." Bradley paused to allow any rebuttal. There were no objections. "Will all those in favor of Anod's suggestion please signify their approval by saying, aye." A resounding chorus conveyed their approval. "Those opposed, say nay." Although not as prevalent, there were a substantial number who did not agree. "Considering the number of objections despite the affirmative vote, it would appear we should debate this issue further. Will any of those objecting, please offer their arguments."

With the invitation, the dissenters articulated their concerns. The discussions took more than four hours building in tempo and vigor as the voices were heard. The central theme of the protests was the speed with which the pioneers, the former Betans, were casting off the principles that had helped them survive through the years. It was a fear of the philosophical unknown that was the greatest obstacle. What if actions were set in motion that might become impossible to turn around? This was a common question among explorers, searchers and pioneers. The answers did not come easily.

In the end, they all agreed, although many chose the conservative path. Anod taught a half dozen of her compatriots the techniques of operating the interceptor and two other small shuttle spacecraft provided by the Society. There were mineable minerals on several of the other planets, but life support would be required for the humans. The information was catalogued for the future. They also created other communities around the planet as each family or group found the place they wanted. The SanGiocomos found their own site 320 kilometers up the coast then moved up a medium river where it left a mountain range onto the coastal plain. Among a thick stand of conifer trees, they cut out a space for a simple house built of the felled trees and rocks from the river shore.

It was during this process, before the new house was completed, that the SS *Endeavour* and the Society transport vessels departed. The colonists and the majority of the Society crews met one last time on the surface to celebrate the new world. The communication system had been set up, established and tested. All the colonists had found their homesteads across the planet, although most, like the SanGiocomos, had not yet completed their new dwellings. They were at least reasonably settled and stable. Although no commitment was made for a return visit, Colonel Zontramani indicated that various ships of the Confederation, the Society and friends or trading partners would visit from time to time.

The celebration lasted for the better part of a day as all the colonists gathered at the original landing spot to rejoice their new beginning and to thank the crews that had helped them make the move safely. With much fanfare, the *Endeavour* and her entourage departed on other missions. The Murtaurians savored the moment then returned to the tasks at hand. For the SanGiocomos, it was completing their new home among the trees.

The largest room of their family house was the main room that occupied the entire front half of the structure, where they ate, talked, and played. The back half of the house was divided into three rooms, one larger than the other two. After considerable discussion, they decided to put the new equipment – isopods, cleansing station, replicator, communications console and weapons, secured in a small closet – in the larger room. Nick wanted conventional beds, like they had on Beta, just in case he wanted an old style sleep or they had guests. They had six pods. Since space was limited, they figured out how to stack the isopods, two high. By the time the house was finished, Lornog made the communication link to the central computer and tested all the equipment. Despite the perfection and efficiency of the Society's cleansing station, they all agreed they needed a conventional, water shower like they had on Beta, which Anod had become so accustomed to during her stay.

The day came, several months after they arrived at their new homestead, the entire family stood in front of their house and marveled at their accomplishment. They held hands with Zoltentok between Anod and Bradley. Anod's seriously distended abdomen forecast a new member soon to join them.

"I would say we did a respectable job of this," Nick said.

"Yes, we did," added Bradley.

"Shall we call this place SanGiocomo as we did on Beta?" asked Anod.

"No," Nick answered. "This is not the place we used to live. This is a new place." He hesitated, staring through the house to some distant place. "Let me suggest . . . we will soon have new life among us," he said gently patting Anod's belly, "and, I feel a sense of continuity here. Would you mind if we named this beautiful place for my wife – Bradley's mother?"

"Megan?" asked Bradley.

"Yes. Well, actually, I was thinking of Meganville."

"An exquisite name," answered Anod. "If there are no objections?" she asked, looking to the three males. Nick and Bradley shook their heads, and Zoltentok just stared back at his mother with innocent eyes. "Then, hearing no objections, I christen this place, Meganville."

They all clapped as if some important award had been bestowed upon someone.

The final days of Anod's pregnancy brought a shift in priorities for the family. For this birth, Mysasha Nagoyama joined them for the preparations. Guyasaga also arrived as news of the impending birth spread. Friends stopped by to visit, see their new home, and celebrate the approaching birthday. The wait lasted only another two days.

A daughter was born to Anod and Bradley. They named her, Sara Jean SanGiocomo. She was the first native Murtaurian. A celebration of life accompanied their announcement and the future it foretold.

The community on Murtauri Four continued to thrive as they expanded their inhabitation of the planet. The communications and transportation systems enabled global activities with little difficulty. The other families were prolific, as well, in many ways. Offspring were brought to life on a regular basis and each birth was celebrated. Surprisingly to Bradley and Nick, the people shed many of their inhibitions, restrictions and constraints as their society pushed forward through the blending of human emotions and the power of technology.

Most of the people shared a common feeling they often vocalized at small as well as large gatherings. Growth was all around them and a synergistic energy fueled the changes. Everyone was intoxicated with the challenge and accomplishment of the growth, the changes that were occurring in all of them. There was a new freedom. There seemed to be no limitations to what could be done, or what they wanted to do. One of the common threads among them was a mutual respect that pervaded all their actions, activities and plans. The respect bred trust, and their trust enabled a collective performance of unparalleled strength.

Discoveries added to the excitement of those early days on Murtauri Four. New minerals, compounds and materials were found or created. Anod maintained her flight skills with the interceptor that had become a symbol of their rebirth as most forgot the origin of the craft.

Every member of their society from little children who were barely old enough to understand to the oldest among them knew what had happened at $\theta27\beta$. Anod was highly regarded by men and women alike for her exploits, capabilities and the potential she represented. Passing down of her martial arts knowledge was becoming part of the culture, also. The techniques and knowledge brought a greater awareness of the power of the mind and the strength of the body. Even Anod was becoming a stronger blend of the old and the new. Motherhood never ceased to provide Anod with new lessons, new experiences and a new appreciation of life that was not fully comprehended in her previous life.

The years passed and the community of Murtauri Four evolved. The process of education in all its forms was a pre-eminent priority among the population. The nurturing of their young in combination with the constant stimulation of their elders was seen as essential as breath and sustenance. Visitors to their haven were, more often than not, impressed by the mood of the people, the accomplishments of the community and the prospects for the future. Many visitors decided to remain and absorb the monumental changes they were living.

Their success also attracted the more pernicious of elements among all creatures. The Murtaurians, as they began to refer to themselves, had also learned to deal with unwanted intrusions with strength and compassion. The relationship with the Society remained strong although a need for the breadth of power their starships represented had never been needed. Every starship stopover was an enjoyable event.

The Murtaurians began the long journey to greatness among other peoples through respect for others, respect for their environment, respect for lesser planetary creatures and a reverence for life. The unique combination of creativity, imagination, energy, science and exploration brought new achievements and new pleasures to the Murtaurians.

For Anod, the content that would heal the wounds to her pride would come with the maturation of her children. Watching them absorb life, like perfect, limitless sponges enabled her to look back at her rejection from the Society as a positive step on a journey through life. The passing of knowledge to the next generation was a community objective as well as avocation. The cooperation among disparate and dissimilar minds was also an element of societal pride. It was out of the breadth of ideas, suggestions, recommendations and hints that an impenetrable bond among the Murtaurians was created. They used technology to expand and protect life around them.

Out of a crucible of conflict and the randomness of chance was born a fresh, expansive and engaging community of human descendants that would ultimately change life among the stars. History took a long time to realize the changes, but the participants knew something great was now growing on its own. They all instinctively knew it.

Chapter 6

"Are you sure?" asked Bradley as he stood in the doorway of their cabin having just returned from helping their closest neighbor several dozen kilometers away.

"I am not certain what I am sure of," answered Anod.

"Do you know what you want?"

"Yes."

"Then what?"

"I have come to recognize the Betan custom . . . many have told me the Betans retained from ancient Earth . . . of a union you call marriage. I know this is important. I have learned much from our friends. I also appreciate the conflict, the contradiction I have caused, and yet both you and Nick have not applied any pressure. Well, I think the time has come."

"Are you sure?" he asked again.

Anod looked deeply into his sparkling blue eyes. "Yes, I am sure. I know this is an important custom for Betans and thus for Murtaurians."

"Are you doing this for them, or for yourself . . . for us?"

She reached with both hands to grasp his head below the ears. "Bradley, have you ever known me to do anything because others want me to do it?"

Bradley chuckled softly as he looked away from her determined eyes. "No, of course not."

"Then, this occasion is no different. I want to be a part of this community. I am a Murtaurian, and I want to live like one."

With levity in his eyes, he said, "So, you are no longer a warrior of the Kartog Guards?"

"No," she answered sharply. "I am not. I am a mother of two beautiful children, and I hope many more. I want to be the wife of Bradley James SanGiocomo."

Their eyes remained joined. He smiled then nodded his head in acceptance. "Then, so it shall be."

"Good."

Bradley's expression turned serious. "Can I ask a sensitive question?"

"I have never known you to be bashful."

"Right you are. Then, I shall ask it. Are you to take my patronymic name?"

"You mean, SanGiocomo?"

"Yes," Bradley answered.

"I suppose if we are going to get married, custom also dictates that I take your family name."

"So, your name will become Anod SanGiocomo?"

Anod laughed. The sound of it seemed too foreign and perhaps even a little bizarre. "Yes. Perhaps I should change my name completely, like maybe Anne Marie SanGiocomo."

"There is no need for sarcasm. I was just trying to understand how much of our customs you were going to accept."

"Yes, well, I see no need to change the name I have lived with for fifty one years."

"Does that mean you will accept our family name?"

"Yes," Anod said, then smiled gently. "I thought about taking a middle name – of your mother – Megan."

"Are you serious, or are you being sarcastic, again." Anod kept a serious expression and nodded her head. "You do not have to do that, you know. Meganville is quite enough." She nodded again. "My father will probably cry when he hears of this."

"Why?"

"He loved my mother very much. When he hears her name invoked and especially associated with someone of your prominence, he will find it quite emotional."

"Then, perhaps I should not take her name."

"*Au contraire, mon ami.* He will probably be beside himself with joy. Just that gesture alone will bring you two even closer, as if you are not close enough, now." He paused as if in contemplation. "In fact, maybe that is not such a good idea. I don't think I will stand a chance if you two are any closer."

Anod smiled. "Then, so it shall be. Once we are married, I shall become Anod Megan SanGiocomo."

Bradley stepped the several meters between them, leaving the door open behind him. He embraced her. They kissed affectionately at first then quickly transitioned into the more passionate form. Anod felt his response and reached for him. Within a few minutes, they were naked and joined on the floor. The motions of their love absorbed them until Bradley suddenly froze at the point of their fullest contact. He scooped her up so that she straddled him.

He looked into her eyes. "Where are the kids?" he asked as though he just now realized they had two children.

"They are asleep."

Bradley moved his hips against her several times then stopped again. "Where is my father?"

Anod laughed, squeezing him with all her muscles. "You wait until we are in the throes of passion to wonder whether we are going to be discovered."

"I got carried away."

"I guess so. Anyway, he left this morning to visit some friends. He said he would return by supper time."

Bradley smiled as he returned to the movements of their union. "Then, we have the moment to finish what we have started."

"Yes, and while you are at it, why don't you give me another baby."

"Are you sure?"

This time she gripped him hard making it impossible for him to move. "Am I in the habit of being unsure?"

"No," he answered.

Anod relaxed on him. He lowered her to the floor. They moved together as lovers seeking their own pleasure as well as the pleasure of each other. As with all the other times, Anod was thankful for her growth as a human.

The sounds of their love woke Zoltentok before they finished. Anod noticed her oldest son watching them from his bedroom doorway. She smiled and winked at him. The boy smiled back as he watched with object fascination.

Bradley must have sensed her distraction then noticed Zoltentok himself. He froze again. "Damn," he muffled his exclamation.

"Don't stop. You must finish."

"No. I can't with him watching."

Anod looked into Bradley's eyes. "Why? Isn't this what men and women are supposed to do?"

"Yes, but not with other people watching and especially our children."

"Do you breath with others watching?"

"Yes, but . . ."

"Do you eat with others watching?"

"Yes, but . . ."

"No, Bradley. You have told me this is natural – what two people in love do. Our children should see what their parents do when they are in love."

"I can't."

"Yes you can. I need you," she said as she moved her hips against him.

Bradley glanced at Zoltentok who smiled at them, and then Bradley closed his eyes and returned to the rhythm of their union until the convulsions of his climax shook his body in repressed silence. As his spasms of pleasure subsided, he lifted her to him, again. They kissed then both looked to their son. They extended their closest arms to him. The boy ran to bury himself in the embrace of his parents. They kissed him repeatedly on each cheek.

"What were you doing?" Bradley asked.

Zoltentok looked to each of his parents. "You woke me."

"What did you think about what you saw?"

"You and Mommy were together like the animals."

They both laughed. "Yes, I suppose we were, ZJ. Mommy and Daddy love each other and enjoy being together like this. It is also how we make babies like Sara Jean."

A broad smile lightened his expression. He captured his mother's eyes. "Are you going to have another baby?"

"We hope so, Zoltentok. We hope so. But, it takes several weeks before we will know for sure."

"I like little Sara. I want another baby like her."

"That is good. Perhaps we shall be lucky," said Anod. Sara's little cry for attention announced the end of her nap. "Why don't you go check on your sister? I shall be there shortly," she added.

As the young boy gleefully skipped out of the bedroom, Anod and Bradley separated and dressed. Satisfied, they kissed.

"I love you," whispered Bradley.

Anod smiled and kissed him again. "I love you." She lightly grasped both of his cheeks. "Thank you."

Bradley knew precisely what she was thinking and returned her smile. He kissed her again then turned to leave the cabin. His chores beckoned. Anod went to Sara.

The planning process as well as the announcements to the

community took the better part of a month to accomplish. Provisions for adequate food and drink for their guests and for the supervision of the children took several days to complete. A dozen brightly colored tents had been erected among the trees, complete with cots and other accoutrements for the guests who wished to stay.

The families gathered at Meganville on the appointed day. A nervous energy passed among them as the group busied itself with the final minute adjustments to this and that. The occasion took on a greater significance because of the two people who were about to publicly recognize their partnership. It was also the definitive statement that Anod had become one of them. She was fully joining the greater community. The celebration was as much for Anod's conversion as it was for her marriage with Bradley.

Dusk was coming when Mysasha Nagoyama found Anod at a quiet moment. "Congratulations, Anod," she said. "We are proud of you."

"Thank you, Mysasha. I am sure I do not fully appreciate the significance of marriage, but I understood enough to know it is important to Bradley and the community."

"It is. We tend to think of it as a commitment to each other as well as to the community. While the marriage event does not define a family, it does establish a public demonstration of your commitment to each other."

"Then, I am glad we did it."

Mysasha looked around the crowd, not so much to find someone but to buy some time for her thoughts. "How are you doing?"

"Fine."

"And, the kids?"

"Zoltentok is growing and talking."

"He is . . . let me think . . . five years old, now?"

"Yes. Sara is six months old and also doing quite well."

"Are you still nursing her?"

"Yes. I have not tried to give her any solid foods, yet. She seems to be doing quite well on my milk."

"From the looks of her, I would say you are precisely correct."

"Thank you," responded Anod.

"Once you begin to wean Sara, are you going to get out among the community more, and assume your role as one of our leaders?"

Anod chuckled as she turned to face Mysasha. "Did Bradley and Nick put you up to that question?"

"No. I have not talked to them about this," she answered with appropriate seriousness. "You are a natural leader."

"Perhaps. They have been pushing me as well."

"The community needs you."

"My children need me. In fact, I think I would like to be pregnant, again."

"So soon?"

Anod began to walk slowly toward the edge of the clearing. Mysasha stayed with her. "Not for me."

"You like motherhood. It agrees with you."

"Yes, Mysasha, it does. This may not seem like much to you, but I feel like a three-dimensional person . . . I feel alive . . . because of those children," she said pointing to the cluster of young ones, "because of every aspect of life those children represent. I was happy as a warrior with the Kartog Guards in service of the Society, but I did not know pleasure or contentment or elation. I am thankful for the experience."

"It is good, isn't it?"

"Yes. For someone who lived forty plus years without the depth of pleasure, it is truly fulfilling. From the physical and emotional pleasure of making love, to carrying a child in my uterus and feeling her move within me as her life develops, to even the pain of bringing her from my body to the great world around us. There is no greater pleasure. But, you have always known those pleasures?"

"I suppose you are right. And maybe, I have taken those pleasures too much for granted."

"I have not." Anod stopped among the trees and raised her head like an animal drawing scent. "Just the smell of the forest upon the breeze brings its own pleasure."

"Indeed, Anod, indeed." Mysasha allowed the moment to float quietly between them. "So, you want to have many children?"

"Yes . . . as many as I am able. I do not want to be a leader within the community. I just want to be a mother. I enjoy it more than you can imagine. It is that third dimension I mentioned earlier. This," Anod said rubbing her lower abdomen and cupping her left breast, "is what I want to do."

"Then, that is what you should do, but I would like to say just a few things about what you mean to this community, of which you are a part." Anod looked to Mysasha to indicate her fullest attention. "The reason many of these people decided to leave the only community they have ever known was simply . . . you. While they were perfectly comfortable with what they had, you represent the future to most of them. Your strength, your skills, your understanding of the technology impressed people and enabled them to embrace things they have shunned for generations. It is you who has made this happen," Mysasha said as she waved her arms and spun around as if Anod had created everything.

"I never wanted that responsibility."

"No, I'm sure you didn't, but you have it nonetheless." Mysasha waited for Anod's nod of acknowledgment. "Now, let's return to the celebration of your marriage." Anod smiled and turned to follow Mysasha.

The party lasted into the evening as laughter, light and the words of friendship filled the forest. Some folks left after paying their respects to Bradley and Anod. Many remained to spend the night at Meganville rather than press the journey home after a long day of rejoicing.

Lornog found Anod. "Bradley suggested I put the children to bed as it is passed their bedtime. I tried to give Sara some of your stored milk, but she would not take it, and Zoltentok says he cannot go to sleep as long as Sara is crying."

Anod smiled for his expression recognition algorithms. "I know what she needs, Lornog. Sometimes she just wants the reassurance of her mother's warmth."

"Which I cannot give her."

"No offense meant."

"I understand."

Lornog followed Anod into the children's bedroom. Sara was crying in her crib and Zoltentok was sitting straight up in his conventional bed. Bradley and Anod had agreed to start the children out in conventional beds, and then let them transition to the isopods when they were older.

"Mother," Zoltentok said in protest.

Anod motioned for her son to lie back down as she quieted Sara. Anod lifted the baby out of her crib, found the ancient rocking chair passed down through generations of the SanGiocomo family and cradled Sara in her arms. The infant girl's crying subsided to a mere whimper when, even with closed eyes, she found the nipple of Anod's left breast. Anod began to hum a non-descript tune. Feeling the little girl draw nourishment from her body brought the usual surge of the unique bond between mother and child. Within just a few minutes, both brother and sister were sound asleep. Anod returned little Sara to her crib.

As Anod partially closed the door behind her, Lornog asked, "How do you do that? I have watched you and tried to imitate you, and yet the infant seems to know I am not you."

Anod chuckled. "To put it simply, Lornog, you are a machine. I am not."

"Is that really what it is?"

"I do not know, actually. I was raised by my first android, Gorp. I did not have a mother. I can only guess as to what is significant to Sara beyond what I was taught by the others. It is probably the warmth of my flesh, the smell of my skin or the sound of my voice. I do not know, but there is definitely something between us that is unique, just as there was between Zoltentok and me when he was her age."

"I can see."

"It is also why I do not regret the loss of the excitement of the Kartog Guards."

"Being a mother must be very rewarding."

"Yes, it is."

Nick entered the cabin before Anod and Lornog could rejoin the celebrants. "Anod, dear, I think you need to help your husband."

"What trouble is he in now?"

"He is trying to instruct a few of our more doubtful citizens on the proper use of the cleansing station and isopod."

"Perhaps I can help," Lornog offered.

"I am sure you could, but I think this may take Anod's touch."

"Then, perhaps I can learn from Anod," Lornog added, as was his nature when there was a task for which someone felt him not well suited.

Anod nodded her head, and led the human elder and ageless android to the clot of humans gathered around the moderate size bonfire. The crowd had thinned substantially just in the short time Anod had been inside. She stood back a few meters, remaining in the shadows, to listen to the conversation. Mysasha was on the periphery. Nick rejoined the group. Bradley was in the middle with his back toward Anod. She could see Otis Greenstreet and several of the scientists that helped her rejuvenate the Yorax interceptor on Beta – Natasha Norashova, the chemist, George Robbins, the specialist in microcircuitry, and Maria Verde, the so-called computer doctor. The doubters in the discussion appeared to be Tung Wan Foo and Naomi Gibritzu, wife of Dahar. The argument seemed to center around the covert physiological interrogation by Morgan, the central computer, when they used the cleansing station and isopod.

"Here is Anod," said Otis. "She will tell us."

The group turned toward her. She moved closer. "What is the question?" she asked.

The entire group hesitated. Naomi was the first to speak. "The idea that some machine is probing my body while I sleep is really creepy . . . unnatural . . . just plain not right."

"What bothers you about it, Naomi?"

"If that machine can probe my body, then it can do other things, other things that are not so good."

"Perhaps. However, Morgan is programmed to do no harm. I have lived virtually my entire life within this arrangement."

"But, why does it need to do that?"

"First, the objective is to preserve your health, to find abnormalities and treat them before they become serious or life threatening. Many of those anomalies are best spotted when there are routine, consistent, periodic and frequent physiological observations, in essence, comparing one day to the next. Second, Morgan needs some elements of information to constantly adapt the suspension field for optimal performance of your sleep cycle."

"What is so wrong with conventional sleeping?" asked Mister Tung.

"Nothing, actually. The isopod is just more efficient. Plus, my experience is testament to the effectiveness of Morgan's medical monitoring and preventative measures. I can also tell you the cleansing station is the most thorough examination of your body I know of, and the isopod is at least twice as effective with the renewal of sleep and the maintenance process as any other method. It takes half the time and is precisely consistent. There is even a dream mode with the isopod that will allow or prohibit dreams."

"But, still . . . ," said Tung as he shrugged his shoulder and held out his hands.

"Look," Anod responded looking at each of the group, "we all agreed that no one would be forced to use the technology the Society has given us. I have learned to appreciate the simplicity of the Betan culture. I do not think we should cast off those traits. As in all our debates, we agreed this would be a personal choice. If you want my opinion," she paused but no one spoke, "this technology enables me to enjoy being human to the greatest extent possible, in my mind. In the end, it is the personal choice of each and every one of us," Anod said pointing to each person. "It is your choice, no one else's."

"We understand what you say and what you have told us before, Anod," Naomi continued, "but, some of us are torn. On the one hand, we believe you. We want to gain the advantages of using the technology. However, it scares me. Just the concept that some machine is looking inside my body while I sleep frightens me."

"Perhaps, you could show her," Bradley interjected. "Maybe go to their place and help her with the technology."

"Yes, if you wish," she said to Naomi.

"No, that is not necessary." Naomi hesitated. "Well, maybe sometime, but I know you have your own family to worry about as well."

"This," said Anod as she looked to each of the crowd, "is really an issue of understanding and more importantly trust. I can see there are some aspects of these items that could appear threatening if you believed they could do harm. If you use the equipment, then you must build trust in Morgan, in the isopod, in the cleansing station."

"How do we do that?" asked Tung.

"I would suggest by using it just a little everyday until you gain confidence with it."

"I don't know."

"Again, there is no requirement. It is available if you want to use it."

"I suppose."

"It is getting late," said Nick, "and after all, this is my son's and daughter's wedding night."

There was general laughter. They paid their respects to the newlyweds and said goodnight as the various guests went to their tents. Bradley doused the fire, and spread the remaining wood to ensure all the embers were out and the fire could not restart during the night. Lights were extinguished.

Inside their cabin, Nick said, "Goodnight." He closed the door to his small room.

Lornog busied himself with little chores as Bradley and Anod retired to their room. Sometime during the night, Lornog would position himself outside their door. He might stand or sit, fully alert, until morning. Bradley had grown quite comfortable with their 'guard' outside the door.

"Let's not use the isopods tonight," Bradley said.

Anod smiled. She knew what that meant – an excellent conclusion to a wonderful day. As the first steps of their passion were taken, for some reason, Anod remembered the first night they actually spent together in the little hut at the end of one of the escape tunnels as they fled from the Yorax in Providence, the capital of their former planet, Beta. His fumbling aversion had been almost comical. Bradley had become much more comfortable with her naked form as well as his own. She wondered if it was their relationship that helped him overcome his prudishness. Whatever it was, she was thankful. Soon, the passions of a man and a woman occupied them – body, mind and soul.

The early months of their presence on Murtauri Four had been difficult. If it had not been for the support of the Society Starship *Endeavour* and the other ships of the convoy, it would have been much worse. As the months passed and they learned more about their new planet – M4 as they began to refer to it – the colonists found a more bountiful planet than they realized. The nearly perfectly erect rotation axis relative to the planet's orbit allowed a constant growing environment. Seeds and seedlings brought from Beta thrived.

The small fusion generators immersed in the plentiful water of the streams, seas and oceans provided virtually limitless power in various forms. For the SanGiocomos, their generator sat at the bottom of deep pool at the base of a modest waterfall downstream a few hundred meters from their cabin. Their vegetable and fruit garden occupied not quite a hectare of a clearing in the forest several hundred meters upstream.

The Murtaurians quickly began the process of trade among themselves. Barter naturally filled in the gaps for the various families. As word spread throughout the sector of the galaxy, visitors began to arrive. A very few were rogues looking for trouble or get-rich-quick schemes. The preponderance of the visitors to M4 were traders looking for new items to add to their selection. They also found a natural haven for those visits. A group of four families located on an open plain on the coast of the planet's largest body of water. It was the first location to be named as a community and by unanimous consent – New Providence. It became the hub for trade between the citizens of Murtauri Four and their neighbors in the Confederation sector of the galaxy. As the utility of New Providence grew, other families chose to move to New Providence – some keeping their original homesteads, others choosing to abandon them.

One day, a visitor to Meganville landed a shuttlecraft at the prepared landing area where Anod's modified Yorax interceptor was hangared. A single entity walked up to the cabin. Lornog alerted the humans to the approach. The visitor broke into view as the SanGiocomo clan walked out onto the small porch.

The adults recognized the large figure of Alexatron, the Norgekkian galactic trader who rescued Anod after the Zitger's traitorous ambush. The large biped with shiny brown skin and the flowing light brown, woolen appearing, robes did not uniquely identify him. His noticeably mechanical gait and his jerky, maybe even slightly off balance motions, as he moved across the open space marked him clearly as Norgekkian. He held up his right hand, palm forward, in the universal peaceful greeting sign.

"We are honored to welcome you, Alexatron," Nick said in a loud, friendly, commanding voice.

"The honor is mine," answered the Norgekkian.

Nick, Bradley, and then Anod touched both hands in front of them, the traditional Norgekkian friendship gesture. Lornog was introduced as well as Anod and Bradley's two children.

"To what do we owe the pleasure?" asked Bradley as the cordiality waned.

"I finally made it to your little sliver of paradise. I landed at your trading center . . . what is it called . . . New Providence, is it?" All of them nodded their heads in acknowledgment. "They indicated to me where your home was located. I knew I just had to make the journey to say hello to my favorite family and especially my favorite warrior," Alexatron said as he nodded toward Anod.

"I am a mother now."

"The warrior is never far removed, of that I am certain, but it is good that you are raising the next generation from such perfect stock."

"Thank you," answered Anod.

"Won't you come inside for some refreshment," Bradley offered motioning toward the interior.

"Yes, of course."

Alexatron looked around the interior of the cabin then followed the lead of his human hosts. The process of him sitting in small chairs built for humans smaller than him took considerably longer as he shuffled, leaned, shifted and worked his way into a chair. Lornog served the requested drinks. Zoltentok sat quietly on his father's knee. Sara dozed, cradled in her mother's arms.

"Are you finding materials you can trade?" asked Nick.

Alexatron took a good long swallow of his Norgekkian ale. "Nothing in particular, at present, but there are some interesting prospects."

"Such as?" Nick asked with genuine interest.

"I have several woven materials that have promise. I will want to see a greater selection before I ascertain their worthiness in some markets, but as I said, they do look promising."

"Anything else?"

"I understand there might be some marketable mineral deposits. Some of your citizens will have to play that out." Alexatron looked to each of his hosts. "To be honest, I do not see much else at this early stage."

"As you say," answered Nick. "We have only been on this planet for a few years."

"We are quite happy here," added Anod.

Alexatron looked at her with a strange expression, as if she had spoken some language he did not understand. "Happy, you say. Aren't you the human female who I rescued from oblivion, and who did not have emotions?"

"Yes, but all that has changed."

A crude, forced smile bloomed on his face. "I should say, so." His smile disappeared. "I hope you do not loose those skills that enabled you to survive in adversity."

"There should be no need," answered Anod. "We are a peaceful people, and as you have indicated, we have nothing anyone else would want. There should be no reason for us to have to defend ourselves. We just want to live peacefully," she repeated.

"Doesn't everyone," said Alexatron. He stared at Anod making her wonder what was on the Norgekkian trader's mind. "There have been rumors the Yorax are not content with the current treaty. There are also stories that the human general . . . ."

"Zitger."

"Yes, except he goes by the Yorax name of Negolian . . . General Negolian, I understand. Anyway, your old antagonist is not content to leave you alone in peace."

"Do you know this to be true?" asked Bradley.

"No. I do not. They are only loose rumors intoxicated space pilots throw around to impress others."

"Then, it is quite possible these stories are not true," Nick stated.

"Yes, but it is better to be prepared."

"Are they going to hurt you, Mommy?" asked Zoltentok.

"I don't think so, ZJ," Bradley answered for Anod.

She nodded her agreement, although she was not as convinced. It was something she needed to worry about and be prepared for if the threat ever materialized. Anod pushed those thoughts from her mind.

"How long can you stay with us?" asked Anod, wanting to think of something else.

"Actually, not long. I have business to conduct."

"We certainly appreciate the visit from a friend," added Nick.

"Is there anything I can do for you?"

"Listen as you travel and tell us when you can, anything that might be of interest to us," Bradley said.

"That is a given."

"We will continue to look for those opportunities we can add for trade," Nick said.

"Good. I am always looking for business."

They said good-bye to the Norgekkian trader. Anod waited outside until she saw the chopped up cubic shape of Alexatron's shuttlecraft rise straight up beyond the treetops. She waved as though he might be watching her. Anod knew she owed her very life to his initiative and courage. She sensed those events would not be the last time she would be thankful for Alexatron's friendship.

The SanGiocomos returned to the routine of chores that never seemed to be complete. It was not until supper was finished and the children were asleep that the conversation returned to the serious topic raised by Alexatron.

"What did you think of his news?" asked Nick, knowing all of them knew what he was referring to.

Anod ignored the question.

Bradley recognized Anod's sensitivity. "It is just a rumor. Why would the Yorax tempt fate with the Society?"

"Anod," whispered Nick.

"You think they would risk peace for one person?"

Sebastian Nicholas SanGiocomo glanced at his daughter-in-law. Anod lowered her head and stared at the empty table. She knew Nick was probably correct, although she did not want him to be right. The children brought a whole new dimension of happiness to Anod, beyond the companionship she found with Bradley and Nick. She did not want him to be correct.

Anod looked up to see all eyes on her then looked back down at the table. "Nick is probably right. Zitger, or whatever he is calling himself these days, is probably obsessed with eliminating me. After all, I am the only witness to his treachery."

"But, you have testified to the Society. They do not need you to do more," Bradley protested.

"Personal testimony in a criminal trial, where interrogation is possible, is far more compelling to a jury. If Zitger is ever captured and placed on trial for his crimes, the Society will want me to testify in person against him."

"But, he would risk war with the Society."

"Yes, he would," she said finally looking up from the table. "He is not likely to rest until he completes his mission."

"Can't we ask the Society to intervene?"

"Sure, we could ask . . . however, I doubt there is much they would want to do. If they took preemptive action, it would virtually guarantee a war with the Yorax. They would be acting against a possibility, not a certainty."

"There must be something that can be done," Bradley said.

"Like what?" asked Nick.

"At a minimum, I suppose we should notify the Society. Perhaps, there is some diplomatic action they can take to reinforce their comment to us."

"That would not hurt," added Anod. "However, I cannot live my life worrying about what might happen. There are some precautions I should take to avoid any temptation by Zitger or the Yorax."

"Such as?" asked Bradley.

"We brought some antratite from Beta. I should craft some protective materials to hide my existence on this planet."

"You can't accomplish that a hundred percent of the time," Nick stated.

"You are correct, but I can reduce my exposure substantially."

"How?"

"Well, while I am in the isopod, Morgan controls access, and he can block any scanning. I thought I would craft some antratite armor to substantially reduce my scannable mass. We could also use some of it in sheets to cover the interior walls of the cabin."

"And, you are proposing that you wear this armor all the time, forever, just because there is a rumor bouncing about the galaxy?" Bradley asked sarcastically.

"Actually, no, I was just thinking out loud. You asked what could be done."

"Then, what is practical?"

"I don't know, but some precautions are probably warranted."

"You seem to attract attention, Anod," Nick observed.

"Yes. I suppose I do. One thing is certain. I will be of no use to anyone if I do not keep my body and mind rested. So, if you will excuse me, I am going to rest."

"I will come with you," said Bradley as he stood to join you.

"I need the isopod tonight," Anod responded to avoid any confusion.

The next day, Anod asked Bradley to watch Zoltentok while she went on a day excursion. She needed the thinking time.

Anod loaded Sara into a chest pack so that the infant girl faced forward, and could watch where her mother was going and what she was doing with her hands. She also carried a backpack with some supplies for a day's journey with her daughter. Anod went into the mountains, partly for the exertion of the climb and partly to think without other interference of any kind. The mountains were always beautiful to her. While she also enjoyed the oceans and the vegetation of the plains, the mountains added dimension she found particularly pleasing, soothing and stimulating. By midday, Anod reached the top of a relatively small hill with a bare crest that gave her a full, panoramic view of the high mountains with their jagged peaks on one side and expansive coastal plain with the blue of the ocean's water in the distance on the other side.

Anod found an appropriate rock and disassembled her various packs. The breeze evaporated her accumulated perspiration giving her a chill on her chest and back. Sara recognized that she was no longer confined to the chest pack, and she was hungry. Anod cradled Sara in her right arm and began to feed her. With her left arm, she fumbled with the backpack to retrieve the container of water. She took a long drink then found several biscuits to eat before taking another long drink. Sara drained one breast and wanted more. Anod shifted her to the left side.

"What should we do?" Anod asked her speechless daughter.

Sara looked up to her mother's eyes without missing a beat. Her eyes did not seem to see, but she remained spellbound nonetheless. Anod took a deep breath and looked around the complete horizon.

"This must not be spoiled, little Sara. I cannot let Zitger ruin this for any of us."

Sara continued, although her eyelids were getting heavier.

"Maybe I should go."

Anod looked down at her daughter. Sara's draws from the breast were becoming less strong and less frequent. Her eyes closed. A few more draws then she held the nipple firmly for several seconds.

"But, I cannot leave you, nor can I leave with you. As long as Zitger is out there, he will be a threat no matter where I am."

The little girl finally relaxed. The gentle rhythms of her slumber brought contentment to Anod.

"And, as long as he is a threat to me," she said then looked down at her sleeping child, "he is a threat to you . . . and that . . . simply, will not do."

Anod formed a little recessed bed of some rocks and her packs. She lay Sara in the recess and covered her daughter with her shirt to keep the direct light from her. Anod stood and walked around the hilltop. The star's warmth overpowered the cooling of the breeze.

"This is too perfect," she said to herself. "Zitger cannot be allowed to spoil this beautiful planet."

For the better part of an hour, Anod paced among the rocks, sat for a couple of minutes and paced some more. She considered her options. There was only one. She must continue to live her life without fear as she had done for fifty plus years. As she had suggested to Bradley and Nick, she would use some of the antratite they brought from Beta to reduce her exposure however much she could, but she would stand her ground. If the threat materialized in some form, then she would deal with it in the best manner she could. Anod enjoyed the comfort of knowing that Zoltentok and Sara would be well taken care of by Nick and Bradley. After all, Nick raised Bradley alone for many of her husband's youthful years. What they could not handle, Lornog would be able to supplant.

Sara whimpered underneath Anod's shirt. Anod used her body to shield Sara from the light before she uncovered her. She tended to Sara's needs before returning everything, as it had been when they arrived.

They reached home just prior to sunset. A trail of smoke rose from the chimney. The clan including Lornog was inside. Nick crouched in front of the fire at the hearth, stirring the contents of a black kettle and poking the roasting body of a large bird.

"I guess no replicator food tonight," Anod said as she announced their arrival.

"Welcome home," Bradley answered as he moved toward Anod, kissing his wife first before he kissed his daughter on the forehead.

"I thought we would have a proper Betan supper," Nick said without looking up.

"Where did you go?" asked Zoltentok.

"Sara and I took a long walk to the top of Mommy's mountain."

"I wanted to go."

"Perhaps, next time, Zoltentok. Mommy needed some time alone."

"Why?"

"To think."

"But, you weren't alone."

Anod chuckled. "Well, now, you are correct. Sara was with Mommy, but she slept part of the time."

"Did you get everything worked out?" asked Bradley.

"Nothing new, actually. I think my suggestion last night is still the only option."

"What? Stay here and use the antratite?"

"Yes."

"That's good," answered Bradley. "I thought you might go back to that crazy notion of yours on Beta."

"Leaving?"

"Yes."

"That is not an option, I know. I cannot leave you, and I know I cannot leave the children. This is where I belong, with my family."

"Yes," Bradley said. "We will stand together if we need to defend our home."

"Which reminds me," she paused to eat a bite of bread. "While I was on the mountain thinking, I wondered about Anton Trikinov. When was the last time we saw him?"

"Several months ago."

"What is he doing?"

"I don't know. Why?"

"I had the oddest feeling."

"In what way?"

"Like he is not one of us."

Bradley stared at Anod. "He is just a solitary man."

"Perhaps."

Several days passed before Anod made the journey to New Providence to assess the small cache of antratite slabs they brought with them from Beta. There were sufficient pieces to accomplish most of what

Anod thought appropriate.

The SanGiocomo clan decided to discuss Alexatron's information along with the proposed actions with the community. A series of meetings were held as well as more personal family-to-family meetings. The response of the community was unanimous. They all supported Anod's proposal.

Several of the men who specialized in making clothes and special cloth along with a couple of the women helped Anod fashion a set of garments with a variety of sealed pockets that contained thin sheets of antratite. The finished, black garments covered the majority of her torso, arms and legs. They also formed a set of hats, although one would more properly be called a helmet, with many small chips of antratite sewn into the contours.

The Murtaurians also managed to shave numerous large sheets of antratite from the blocks that remained. These sheets would cover the ceiling of the SanGiocomo cabin.

When all the items were complete, they were transported to Meganville. Anod chose to wear one of her armor suits. When they arrived, she called out to Nick and Lornog announcing their arrival. Nick carried Sara in one arm and held Zoltentok's small hand with his other hand. Zoltentok immediately burst out crying at the sight of the large, black form several meters from the porch.

"It is Mommy, Zoltentok," she said trying to stifle a laugh.

"Look, ZJ, it is Mommy," said Nick.

Anod held out her arms, which made him cry harder. She quickly took off her helmet to show her face and head as she stopped to avoid getting any closer until he understood. Anod kept talking to him until his cries muffled and then stopped. She knelt down on one knee and continued to hold her arms out to her son. Nick gently pushed the reluctant boy toward his mother. After several seconds of coaxing, Zoltentok eventually covered the distance.

"See, it is just Mommy inside this ugly suit."

"It scares me."

"I know, but Mommy needs this suit for protection."

"From what?"

"From the Yorax."

"Are they coming here?"

"We hope not, but we want to be prepared, just in case."

"Take off that suit, Mommy. I don't like it."

Anod did as her son requested, leaving only a thin undergarment to cover her torso. The coolness of the air felt good. However, the enthusiastic embrace of her son felt far better. The tests they had done on the suits proved they worked. Now, they had only to install the antratite sheets on the ceiling of the cabin.

The last of the project was completed within the week. Even Zoltentok began to accept Anod's black suits. She tried to wear them regularly as much to help Zoltentok as for her real purpose. The suits were not particularly comfortable except when the weather turned cold. Anod soon developed a routine. She wore the antratite suit when she journeyed away from the homestead, or when she was outside for long periods of time. Anod knew the benefit of the suit's protection could only be realized with consistent and rigorous use. She accepted her condition and so did her family and community.

Chapter 7

"They have called a community meeting," announced Bradley when he returned from New Providence.

"What for?" asked Anod.

"Some are concerned we are becoming too dependent upon the replicators."

"What exactly is behind all that rubbish?"

Bradley took a drink of water then poured some in a glass before he sat at the kitchen table. "Apparently, we are now finding some of the seeds and seedlings do not enjoy the Murtaurian soil and weather. They have begun to fail."

"But, they were thriving a few months ago."

"Yes, well, something is happening we do not understand."

Anod placed herself in the position of a native Betan, who had only known natural grown foods. She remembered Naomi Gibritzu's articulated fears about technology. "Perhaps we can use Lornog and Morgan to help us sort out the problems with the growing processes."

"Good idea. If they are successful, in addition to helping the crops, it will show the doubters the technology can help them solve problems.

"Excellent point, Nick."

"When have they called the meeting?"

"Tomorrow noon."

"That is rather short notice, isn't it?"

"Yes, but it is also a measure of the importance."

"This is not something that just happened. What set them off?" asked Anod.

"Actually, I think it was you."

"How so?"

"Your little speech to Naomi Gibritzu and Tung Wan Foo on our wedding day made them think. They talked to others who had not participated in the little chat of yours, and they began to compare notes. As they looked at the larger view, they realized something was wrong. They collected some information from the various families and saw the trend."

"If their information is correct," said Nick, "there is reason for concern. Genetic diversity is important to any ecosystem."

"As you will recall, this was and still is a stable system," Anod offered.

"Indeed. Then, perhaps the solution lies in adapting our tastes to the local offerings."

"That is one choice, but I would submit, unless there is some detrimental effect, that introduction of other genetic strings is not a bad thing, and, if done correctly, can enhance the diversity of this ecosystem."

"We shall not solve the problem tonight," said Bradley, "so, let's eat the delightfully smelling supper and get a good night's sleep."

As was usually the case in the SanGiocomo household, they took their time, enjoyed the meal and laughed about anything with which they could find humor. They loved to laugh. This was one of those nights Anod and Bradley decided the conventional bed was more to their liking. They took full advantage of the closeness and warmth.

The meeting was scheduled to take place at zenith time in New Providence. The SanGiocomo family arrived early. All the families gathered or at least representatives of all the families since some of the adults remained at home with their children. Several volunteers tended those children that came with their parents. All the chairs, benches and other objects to sit on were brought to the grove of tall, leafy trees in the center of the growing community. Not everyone would be able to sit on something. Those without chairs would sit on the ground or stand on the periphery. A two-meter high pile of rocks among the trees was the marker for their community meetings, but they built a small wooden platform in front of the rock pile for the speakers.

Tung Wan Foo stood before the assembled community and raised his hand for attention. He waited until there was quiet, except for the chatter of children in the distance. "Since I collected most of the data, I suppose I should frame the question before us." He opened a small folder with bound pages. Anod still found such antiquated methods of information retrieval very inefficient and otherwise wasteful, but she did not want to voice her opinion. "We brought sufficient quantities of 47 crop seed types – 64 percent were passed along by our ancestors, while the remainder were native to Beta or others imported by trade partners. Of those two groups, 64 percent of the ancestral seeds have failed to germinate and 53 percent of the Betan native seeds have failed as well.

Worse, 82 percent of the seedlings have died."

"Do you have any idea why?" someone asked.

"No. As I understand this, each of us has tried everything within our knowledge as well as various new ideas. Nothing has worked."

"Of those that have grown," said Dahar Gibritzu, "is there any consistent reason for one seed type to be successful and another to fail?"

"None that we can find," Wan responded.

"Maybe this is a sign we should not be here," Guyasaga said.

"Perhaps," answered Wan.

Bradley must have sensed the turn in the argument. "This is a bountiful planet. There are no deserts and even the polar regions have substantial plant life."

"There are fish," said Anton Trikinov, the tall security compatriot of Otis Greenstreet. Everyone turned to look at Anton as though he had mentioned some unspeakable observation. No one spoke. "Well, there are," he added as if no one had heard him.

"There were not many fish on Beta," someone added.

"We need to adapt to our new home planet," Bradley said.

"Yes," interjected Dahar. "However, we do not know what the native foods will do to us. We must be very careful. After all, there are not that many of us that we can afford to lose anyone."

Bradley leaned toward Anod to whisper in her ear. "Don't you think it is time for you to say something?"

"What do you want me to say? I don't think they want to hear from me."

"Yes, they do, Anod. Now, stop being so reserved. You have something to offer. Contribute." Bradley waited for her to act. She shook her head that she was not ready. "Excuse me," he shouted, interrupting numerous smaller conversations. "If I may have your attention."

"Bradley," protested Anod as she squeezed his elbow.

"Anod has something to add to this discussion," he said loudly and with force. He motioned to her. Everyone turned to face Anod and waited for her to speak.

"Contrary to Bradley's encouragement, I do not see this as a topic to which I can contribute."

"Nonsense, Anod," shouted someone.

"You know more about these situations than any of us," stated Otis Greenstreet, who usually did not participate in public discussions.

"Actually, I am afraid I don't. I am a warrior, or I was a warrior. I am a mother now who only wishes to care for her children and her family."

"As Otis says," said Natasha Norashova, the chemist, "you have explored more worlds than any of us. You have seen more than any of us. You know more of this universe than any of us."

Bradley nudged her as if to say, now is the time to speak. She nodded her head.

"First," she started and paused to scan the faces of the crowd, "I am keenly aware that some, perhaps even many, of you are not entirely comfortable with the technology of the Society. So, I shall save that option to the last." She heard several muffled affirmative acknowledgments and saw the nodding of many heads. "There are three primary actions I see for this situation. One, we simply adapt to the resources available on this planet. I do agree with Bradley, this is a bountiful planet. There is a process I was taught that probably began millennia or more ago on Earth that has served humans quite well, and still does to the best of my knowledge. It is a method of finding edible materials in an abnormal situation, which I suppose this qualifies." Lighter laughter rippled through the group. "Simply stated, you use your senses."

"How's that?" asked Dahar Gibritzu with an air of impatience.

"First, you look at the fruit, vegetable or whatnot. If it looks good, not ugly, then it passes. Second, if it feels good to the touch, in other words, it does not have spines, thorns or cause a tingling sensation or other reaction when you touch it, then it passes the touch test. If it smells good . . . does not have a foul or offensive odor . . . then, it passes. Lastly, you must experiment using your taste."

"Isn't that dangerous?" asked Naomi Gibritzu.

"Not if you are careful."

"How so?"

"You cut open or crush whatever it is you are checking and repeat the previous steps. Tradition says if it has a clear juice, oil or liquid content that smells good, then it can pass. However, if it has a milky or non-clear liquid, then it should not pass. Lastly, you touch your tongue to the liquid and wait. It is best if you have someone watch you, but you are looking for any adverse reaction like dizziness, nausea, blurring of vision, and so on. If there is any observed reaction whatsoever, then it does not pass. If there is no reaction either sensed by the tester or observed by a friend, then the material can be considered edible by humans."

"I know of plants that have milky juice, like the Sorachika fruit, that are perfectly good, even delicacies," said Tung Wan Foo.

"The process does eliminate good foods, but more importantly, it generally prevents ingestion of bad materials," Anod answered.

"Isn't that too narrow?" asked Natasha.

"As a starting point, yes, I suppose it is, but it has worked for many centuries, in many different worlds. You can always go back to do other tests on those materials you think might be all right, for example, those that pass all the tests except one, like the Sorachika fruit."

"That makes sense," Dahar said.

"What are the other options?" asked Naomi.

"I would like to hear more about these taste tests," Natasha interjected.

"We can come back to the adaptation option," responded Anod. "The second option is to prepare a growing environment similar to what we had on Beta."

"We tried that," Tung stated. "Or, at least some of us have, I know."

"Have you tried hydroponics?" Anod asked.

"Yes," answered several people. "Some work." "Some don't." The flurry of comments floated among the group.

"Well, then, perhaps that isn't an option. The third option I thought of was to let Lornog work with Morgan . . . ."

"They are machines," protested Naomi Gibritzu.

"I am an android, madam," Lornog said as he took a few steps toward the group. "I have many human attributes without the emotional confusion."

"Kind of like Anod was," interjected Otis.

The group laughed. Several patted Anod on the shoulders.

"Between Lornog and Morgan," said Anod, "they possess far more knowledge than any of us. Lornog can gather information for Morgan, who in turn, can search his memory and if needed link up with the other systems like him to see if they can find us a solution."

"Will it really work?" asked Tung.

"There is only one way to find out, and what will it hurt to try," Anod answered.

"So," Dahar said forcefully as he stood to join Wan on the platform in front of the rock pile. Everyone listened. "As I understand this, we are going to use Anod's methods of finding native foods." Various forms of affirmation rippled through the group. "And, while we are doing that, Anod's machines will attempt to analyze our horticultural predicament to find a solution." Again, there were signs of affirmation.

Lornog leaned toward Anod's ear. "I think I should say something about the genetic pool."

"Say it, Lornog. You have every right to speak as the rest of us."

"Are you sure?" he whispered.

"Yes," she answered, touching the thick cloth that covered his cold skin and giving him a slight push toward the front.

As Lornog moved through the few folks between him and the pile, he raised his hand like a schoolboy. "May I say something?"

"What does a machine have to say?" said Dahar.

Lornog ignored the gibe. He waited until the group quieted, and he had their attention. "There are some scientific elements to be aware of on this issue." No one interrupted him. "While this was or appeared to be a stable ecosystem when we arrived, we have introduced numerous new species into this system, not least of which are the human primate mammals," he said swinging his right arms across the crowd.

"And, your point is?" Dahar asked.

"We must be concerned about the gene pool. Attempting to keep one genetic string pure, in essence, isolates that genetic material, which in turn makes it more vulnerable to distress and injury. This could be part of the problem here." He paused to allow reaction. No one was eager to interrupt him. Lornog held their attention. "While we have not analyzed the specific details of our various crop failures, it is entirely possible the genetic strings were too fragile in this environment. There could be and most likely is a myriad of reasons why that might be the case. The logical action would be for us to cross-breed various imported materials with robust native materials."

"How do we do that?" asked Dahar.

"There are numerous techniques that could be employed here, but first we must ascertain the cause of the failures we have experienced." Lornog waited for other questions. The group sat or stood virtually spellbound, probably lost in their own thoughts. "The narrower or more focused the gene pool is for one species or another, generally, the more at risk that species is when it comes to survival and propagation."

"Then, that must hold for us as well," said Mysasha Nagoyama, aloud but more to herself.

"Yes, in principle," responded Lornog innocently. "The human adults on this planet appear to have sufficient diversity for healthy propagation. However, the numbers are not great. While statistically above threshold margins, there is not an enormous foundation or margin."

"Which means?" asked Otis.

"The genetic strength of humans is, in general, not fundamentally different from any other biological entity. We must be mindful of the genetic health of all living elements."

"Back to seeds," said Dahar. "What do we need to do now?"

"The best thing to do is exactly what Anod suggested," Lornog answered. "Allow Morgan and me to analyze several of the successes and failures to see if we can derive a set of cause factors as well as potential solutions. That process could take days, weeks or several months. During that time, a judicious investigation of native materials would be prudent."

"Sounds fair," Dahar said.

"It is reasonable," added Tung. "Since I called the meeting and our business appears to be concluded, I shall call for any other business." He scanned the crowd. No one responded. "Hearing none, I move to adjourn."

The gathering broke up. Numerous small social groupings formed and dispersed. Gradually, they moved to retrieve their children, those with children, while others began the journey to return home.

Anod left her family and sought Anton Trikinov. "How are you?" she asked.

His eyes stared back with an odd combination of resentment and apprehension. Anod motioned with her eyes and hands . . . well?

"I am fine. How are you?"

Anod's stone cold expression made him look down at his feet. She watched him for several seconds. He appeared evasive. In the end, she chose to ignore the response.

"Where have you been?" she asked.

"I have been alone," Anton responded without looking at her.

"Doing what?"

"Trying to get my farm going like everyone else."

"Why do you live alone so far from anyone else?

Now, his shot back to hers. "Why are asking me all these questions?

Anod kept her expressionless eyes focus on him like surgical instruments. "I sense something is wrong."

"There is nothing wrong. I like living alone. I like being by myself."

"Are you one of us?"

"Damn, Anod. Of course I am one of us. I am fine. No problems," he snarled then turned and walked away.

Anod watched him disappear among the buildings. She returned to her family without conveying her apprehension regarding Anton's actions. The others glanced at her. She gave them no reason for concern. They returned to discussions although Anod was not listening.

Lornog made his way back to the SanGiocomo's position. "Well, I think that went just as you wanted," he said to Anod.

"More or less . . ."

"More of what or less of what?"

"It is a figure of speech, Lornog, meaning within a reasonable band of outcomes."

"I see. Then, we accomplished what you wanted, more or less."

"Yes, I would say we did."

"What next?" asked Nick.

Anod motioned toward a large table with integral benches on either side situated near the trunk and shade of a very large leafy tree. Once everyone was positioned around the table, Anod said, "Beyond collecting the children and returning home, we need to lay out a plan for you. Morgan will give you a data acquisition sequence, I am sure."

"The sooner you get started the better, Lornog," added Bradley.

"This could take many days or weeks to collect sufficient information for conclusions to be reached and recommendations formed," Lornog stated.

"Yes, it might," added Anod.

"Then," Lornog said looking to Anod, "I shall not be home to help you."

"It is just one of those sacrifices we all must make for the common good." Anod stood and looked around at the few remaining people. "Let's gather up the children and head back to Meganville," she added.

The process took an hour. The children and supper kept them busy for the additional time until the little ones tired and went to bed. With the family routine complete, they congregated around the object that represented the focus of the Society's technology on Murtauri Four – the console. In addition to the replicator that they used on occasion, the console contained the principal interface with Morgan – the center computer – who was actually located in an underground building near New Providence. Bradley, Nick and Lornog stood behind Anod as she sat at the console to work whatever controls might be required.

"Morgan, request please," said Anod.

"Good evening to you, Anod. I see you have your family behind you there as well as your faithful partner, Lornog."

"Good evening, Morgan. We need your assistance."

"How may I be of service?"

"It seems we may have a problem with some of the seeds and seedlings we brought from Beta."

"A goodly portion have failed," interjected Nick.

"Have you determined the reason?" asked Morgan.

Anod thought the question odd, coming from such a powerful computer. "No. We cannot find it. We need you and Lornog to help us determine the cause and hopefully correct the problem."

"Some of the failed seeds," said Nick, "our ancestors brought through our many moves from Earth. They have never failed to germinate before now. Our citizens are worried."

"This is important, Morgan," Anod added. "We would like you to work out a plan, give Lornog your collection requirement and help us figure out what is happening, so we can correct it."

"Very well," Morgan responded. "Let me think for a moment."

"Think?" asked Bradley almost to himself.

Anod turned to face her husband. "It is not a word he usually uses since humans tend to take the word in a very egocentric manner. In many ways, his memory-processor combination has a far superior cognitive capability especially when it comes to logical reasoning. I think humans still have the lead on the illogical."

"I just never heard that term used before with a computer. When I consider the thinking process, I see original thought, creative thought and deductive thought beyond the obvious regurgitation of facts."

"And, Morgan has original thoughts as you will see the more you work with him. He is capable of all those aspects of thought."

"Perhaps."

Anod turned back to the console panel. Various symbols were presented on the screen as an animation of Morgan's thought processes in very simplified form since humans could not assimilate information fast enough to keep up with his thinking. In an instant, the display stopped.

"I have a starting point for this task," announced Morgan.

"Yes."

"First, I need to review as much of the observation information as possible to include at a minimum the geographic location by inertial reference, time, type and quantity of material, preparation and maturation efforts. If practicable, it would be helpful to have composition analysis of the soil and water used for irrigation if other than atmospheric precipitation. It might also be helpful to know the experience of the humans for each location."

"That is a lot of information," said Nick.

"Yes, it is. I can help," said Morgan, "with those sites where I have an agreement for access, but that is only about half by my count."

"That could take several weeks to accomplish," Lornog said.

"Here is a suggestion," Anod interjected. "Morgan, define a standard set of observation questions in some simple form that is useable by all the citizens. We will send a notice to everyone about what we are going to do. Those that will contact Morgan directly, can give him the information he seeks without the need for Lornog or any of us being involved. For those that do not have an agreement, we will tell them Lornog will visit them to collect the requisite information. Does that sound reasonable?" Anod asked more in rhetorical tone.

"Yes," said Nick and Bradley simultaneously.

"With this observation information," offered Morgan, "I may be able to find some answers, although statistically it is not likely. Under the assumption there is no logical conclusion, I shall specify a series of controlled experiments to first replicate the natural results, then alter the outcomes to arrive at a recommendation."

"It is possible, Morgan," Nick began, "that this planet is not as compatible as we initially thought."

"It is certainly possible. However, the original search and preparatory analysis does not justify such a conclusion."

"But, it is still possible?"

"Yes, Nick. A conclusion of incompatibility for any one of a myriad of reasons cannot be eliminated at this stage."

"Then, the sooner we know that the better," said Bradley.

"While there may be some underlying element of doom here, I would like to remind everyone that we are doing quite well. The births exceed the deaths. People are not ill. Many things do grow, and the planet has ample vegetation and animal life. Plus, the replicators can produce virtually anything we want," Anod added.

"That is not how these people want to live," Nick responded.

Anod let the comment float for the moment. She really did not want to enter a discussion about the rewards of the simple, agrarian life they had known on Beta. Anod just wanted her simplified life. They seemed to be able to grow healthy children, and she definitely wanted more. Anod could not see a limit to the number of children she wanted. The distractions of all these other problems produced a frustration she worked hard to contain. Anod recognized she was still learning to acknowledge her long suppressed emotions without letting them interfere with her decision-making.

After what seemed like a long time, Anod rose from the console seat. "I am tired. It has been a long day. I shall leave you to the debate."

"Did I say something wrong?" asked Nick.

"No," she answered as she walked to the bedroom.

Anod started to shut the door, only to find Bradley right behind her. She did not acknowledge his presence as she disrobed. Anod moved in one fluid motion into the cleansing station and closed her eyes as the process began. The warmth of the air flowing over her entire body along with the tingling, almost flirtatious, fingers of energy from the scanner and the residual of her invigorated muscles and skin offered the satisfaction she needed. Once the process was complete, she remained in place with her eyes shut until the last of the sensations passed. She opened the door to the station and walked directly to her isopod.

"You are angry about something," said Bradley, having waited patiently for the course of events to change.

"No, I am not," Anod answered as she opened the pod and lay on the bed. "I am just tired."

"So, you are sleeping alone tonight."

"Yes. I need the rejuvenation."

"Without even a kiss goodnight."

Anod turned her head toward Bradley, closed her eyes and pursed her lips. She waited patiently for her husband to come to her. She felt his presence just before she felt his lips upon hers. Before she turned her head back, Anod felt his hand touch her breast. She ignored the embrace as she touched the proper control spot and the cover began to close.

Bradley removed his arm to avoid interference with the operation of her isopod. Anod glanced at his concerned face before she looked back to find the desired position on the control panel.

She felt her body rise into free space with no contacts, no pressure, and no sense of weight on any minute portion of her anatomy. The last vestiges of any element of awareness drained her body of every tension, thought or reality like life itself being drawn from her. The darkness, quiet and solitude of her rejuvenation cycle claimed the last dismembered thoughts of her mind.

The rush of warm, life giving, fluid flowed like smooth, slippery oil through every fiber of her body as her brain returned to full function. The soft light of the awakening isopod added to her sense of warmth and well being. Anod enjoyed the moment as she often did for several minutes. As her contentment plateaued, she opened her eyes and looked from her pod. The room was dark except for the soft greenish-blue light from her pod.

Bradley was asleep in their bed. He chose conventional sleep, which meant he would probably be asleep for another two to four hours if he had gone to bed shortly after she had entered her sleep cycle. She checked the clock on the wall of their room. Her guess was probably correct. The enlightenment of dawn was still several hours away. Anod smiled as a simple physical manifestation of the urge she felt.

Touching the correct place on the panel lowered her gently to the soft, warm bed of the isopod and opened the cover. The cool air of the room gave her a spasm of shivers as her body adapted. The night was her time. She intended to enjoy it.

Anod opened the door from their bedroom to the main room. Lornog was standing as he always was to the right of the door. He turned his head to greet her as he always did. Anod held a single finger to her lips signaling him to be quiet. Lornog started to move, only to stop when Anod held up her full hand. She wanted the solitude of her own enjoyment to be protected.

Anod paused to look at the antratite suit hanging of the wall by the front door. She decided against it. She wanted nothing between her and nature.

The colder night air outside their cabin gave her another chill, but she quickly adapted. There was something almost celebratory about being outside in the natural world with nothing between her body and the breeze, the scents, the touch of the night air. The light from the array of stars above the treetops gave her ample illumination for her sensitive eyes.

Anod filled her lungs as fully as she possibly could several times. The surge of release coursed through her entire body. This was what it meant to be alive. She walked slowly and deliberately through the woods. The feel of leaves and needles as she avoided the branches and rocks added an odd exhilaration to her movement . . . like it was the only connection with the real world for her . . . that, if she became detached from those soft pricks on the soles of her feet, she might float away.

The gurgling of water passing over rocks in the stream added a natural music to the scents and feel of the forest. Anod walked in the narrow strip of sand along the edge of the stream, stopping to pick up a shiny rock or examine a uniquely weathered and worn piece of wood from some tree who knows how far upstream. These physical features of a natural environment still fascinated her. Until she found herself on Beta and was given the opportunity to explore the Betan world, she had never known the feel of a wet, worn smooth, rock resting in the palm of her hand. While she had felt air move over her bare skin and even had some scent artificially added for an appealing effect, there had been nothing in her entire life that could compare to the exquisite combination of sensory stimulation she found so seductive on Beta and Murtauri Four.

Anod stopped to slowly scan the entire darkened scene around her. The mountains rising beyond the treetops on either side of the stream provided the perfect backdrop to the panorama of stars spread so elegantly across the sky in every direction, from horizon to horizon. "This is just magnificent," she said aloud as if to make her thoughts more real.

The broad pool at the base of a waterfall composed of large rocks called to her. She stepped into the water up to her ankles. The cool temperature was not as cold as she expected. The night air brought her skin temperature closer to that of the stream. Anod waded into the pond, immersed herself to her neck, and took several rapid breaths as her body made the final adjustments to the cool water. She took a couple of gentle strokes to the center of the calm water then turned over on her back. Her head was semi-immersed. She could hear the gurgling of the water from the rocks downstream from her and the crashing sounds of the water plunging into the pond from the falls above her. The canopy of stars appeared even more vivid.

Anod's thoughts returned to Beta. Floating on her back in a cold pool of water looking up at the brightness, patterns and variations of the stars reminded her of those days when she hid from the Yorax at High Cave in the mountains beyond SanGiocomo Cave. She also remembered making her way to High Cave as she sought a safe place to give birth to her first child. The same sense of safety that enabled her to relax in adversity on Beta brought the peace she sought. Anod felt a distinct embrace of contentment. Between the joy of her children, the love of her husband and his father, the occasional flight, and the solitude of the moment, she needed nothing else.

Anod moved slowly around the pond, remaining on her back and looking up at the stars. She eventually found her way under one outcropping to feel the water cascading onto her face and chest. Little tiny pinpricks of water hitting her chest took her mind to the cleansing station and provided a similar invigoration. Anod felt very much alive and attuned to the world around her.

She watched the stars move across the sky until she began to see the first shades of the approaching dawn. "Time to go home," she said aloud to hear the words. She waded out of the water and without any attempt to remove the residual water she walked back through the forest to the cabin.

Lornog acknowledged her return with a slight nod of his head as he continued to stand guard next to their bedroom door. "Did you have a nice swim?" he asked as Anod approached the bedroom door.

"Yes, indeed."

Anod entered the bedroom. Bradley was still sound asleep. She dried her short auburn hair and ran the towel over her body although it was already dry from the walk back to the house. She dressed quickly and quietly then left the bedroom closing the door behind her.

"So, what do we do now?" she asked Lornog.

"It is nearly dawn. The household shall be rising soon. While you were swimming, Sara awoke. I tended to her and gave her some juice, so she will probably sleep until the noise of our movement wakes her."

"Thank you, Lornog. I just needed to feel the freedom of nature," Anod said as she moved to the replicator.

"No need to explain to me. I believe I can understand, although I shall never experience such an urge."

"Darjeeling tea, please," she commanded. The replicator produced a cup of hot tea prepared in the English fashion with a hint of sweetener and milk to make it the rich brown color of a fine potter's clay. The curl of steam identified the correct temperature. She sipped slightly then sat at the kitchen table facing Lornog. "It is difficult to describe since it is not something I ever experienced either until I was stranded on Beta."

"All of this," he said waving his right arm in a broad arc across the room, "must be very important for you to sacrifice all you had know before."

"I would not quite say it that way."

"How would you say it?"

"The ambush by Zitger was not of my design or desire. I was fortunate he did not recognize my escape pod taking me away from my destroyed fighter. For whatever reason he missed it, I was lucky. Then, to be found, nearly dead, by Alexatron and deposited on Beta was probably even more lucky." She took another few sips of her tea. "In no small measure, this life was thrust upon me." She paused. Lornog decided to sit across the table from her. "Yes, if you must know. I learned, or rather began to learn, about life – real life."

"Weren't you human before?"

"Yes, but I was a biological machine before. It was good, and I derived a sense of satisfaction from our accomplishments." She stared at her tea. "But, there is so much more to being alive."

"I have tried to assimilate that information since I joined you, but I must say, I do not understand what you mean."

"I suppose if I had to describe it in one word, I would say, emotions."

"Emotions?"

"Yes. They are sensations, feelings, and urges. They are ups and downs – peaks and valleys. They are the constructions of pleasure. Emotions, or at least my recognition that I was even capable of emotions, added a third dimension to my existence – a depth to my life. Perhaps only finely crafted poetry, that draws upon those emotions, can describe the feelings."

"And, you felt these sensations on your swim tonight?"

"In a manner of speaking, yes. They were different sensations, though."

"This is very complex."

"Indeed. I am still learning to recognize these emotions, to find the ones that are the most rewarding to me, and trying to hold those sensations, to savor them."

Zoltentok entered the large room rubbing his eyes as he adjusted to the light. "I heard you talking, Mommy."

"Sorry, ZJ. We did not mean to wake you. Would you like some porridge to hold you until the rest of the family is ready for our morning meal?"

"Yes, please," he answered as he gave her a hug and kiss on the lips.

Lornog rose, commanded the replicator for Zoltentok, then placed the precisely and specifically prepared bowl of boiled, crushed grain in front of the boy, whose chin barely reached the lip of the bowl despite kneeling on the chair.

"Did you have a good night's sleep?"

"Yes."

"Excellent. So did I."

"Good," the boy answered as he took another spoonful of the cereal.

They listened to the sounds of the boy's eating for several minutes. Anod thought, there is even pleasure in this.

"I have never asked you this question, Anod, but do you think your sacrifice was worth the outcome?"

Anod smiled. The broad, abstract question was not characteristic of Lornog's precision. Perhaps, the ambiguities of human life were rubbing off on the android. All the assumptions necessary in such an open question tempted her curiosity.

"Interesting question." Anod place a finger to her lips as if she was signaling her children for quiet and looked up at the ceiling. "In a simple word, yes. While there are emotions I am learning that I do not like, there are others that truly make the change worth the sacrifice. There are no boundaries to the joy I feel when a child moves within me – kicks me from inside the womb. I could do anything, but this seems to be the most rewarding to me."

"I still do not understand. However, I can fully appreciate your impressions of the value these changes have for you."

"That should do, then." Anod looked out the window at the angle of light passing through the tree branches to the forest floor. The rest of the family would be up soon. "I feel like an old fashioned breakfast like Nick makes," she said as she stood.

Anod gave the commands and the replicator produced the ingredients she wanted. The urge to produce the meal pushed her to cook the food over the rekindled fire. She was well into the process when Nick joined them. The smell and crackle of the meat cooking on the griddle, hung over the fire at the correct height, woke him.

"Do you need help?" he asked.

"No, thank you."

The process continued and picked up pace until Sara's cry for attention came to her.

"Do you want me to take care of her?" Nick asked.

Anod thought for just a moment. "If you would be so kind, Nick, would you finish this. I would like to tend to her."

"Sure," he answered then took the utensils from her.

Anod satisfied Sara and returned with her daughter within a few minutes. Bradley joined the group shortly after her return. Anod allowed him to sit first then gave Sara to him to cradle in his arms before she relieved Nick. The preparation was nearly complete. Nick had already prepared the table for their hearty meal.

Breakfast moved at a leisurely pace with small talk about the weather, or the day's chores, and off and on about Anod's urge to cook breakfast this morning. Zoltentok was the first to leave the table driven by some project he was working on outside. Lornog began to play with Sara who was perfectly content with the stimulation.

"Do you feel better this morning?" asked Bradley.

Anod knew what he was referring to but chose to prod him a little. "I feel great."

"You did not appear very happy last night."

"Yes, well, sometimes I get frustrated and lose my patience over this illogical resistance to technology and what it can do to amplify our lives."

"So, that was it," interjected Nick.

"You have to understand," Bradley added before she could respond.

"I do not understand."

"Our ancestors were banished from Earth because they refused to submit to the rules of technology."

"What does that mean?"

"The leaders, as I understand our history, of Earth at the time of the split, created strict rules to control population growth, reduce crime and other such diminishments of our society, by using technology to do things they thought were the root sources of society's problems. Our ancestors believed it was the technology, the dehumanized aspect of technology that was the root cause. They chose banishment from Earth rather than submit to the conditions and constraints."

"Doesn't that seem a little silly?"

"Not to them it wasn't."

"The technology does not hinder mankind. It enhances mankind. The use of technology is in our control, not the other way around."

"That is not how our ancestors saw it," Bradley stated.

"So, because there were differences or issues a couple of centuries ago, we are going to deny the advantages of technology today?"

"No," answered Nick. "That is not it, Anod. All we were trying to say last night was, some of our people are having trouble accepting this technology you have brought to us from the Society."

"The technology, as you call it, may very well save our lives," Anod said as she searched deeply into their eyes, "and, there aren't very many of us, yet." She paused for a response but received none. "I have tried to be patient, to allow our citizens time to warm up to the benefits these devices offer us, but sometimes that patience wears thin."

"I know you know this, Anod, but I feel compelled to say it," Nick said. "You must give these people time to learn. Most of us have lived our entire lives, several generations, without any of these devices."

"I understand that," Anod responded as she rose from the table to clear the dishes and other implements of breakfast.

Bradley joined his wife. He embraced her from behind and placed his chin next to her ear. "I love you, Anod," he whispered.

"I love you."

"I don't like it when we sleep apart and especially when you are angry."

"I was not angry, Bradley."

"You know what I mean."

"I suppose I do."

"Anyway, I love all of you – the sharpness of your mind, the feel of your skin and the strength of your embrace."

Anod stopped what she was doing to press his arms against her body. "Me, too."

"Excuse me, Anod," said Lornog.

Bradley and Anod unwound. "Yes, Lornog."

"I think I should get started on the plan."

"Yes, I suppose you should."

Bradley and Nick finished the clean up as Anod finalized the plan with Lornog and Morgan. An itinerary was created for Lornog's visits. Messages were sent to each of the sites. Morgan issued instructions to those places where the Murtaurians accepted the technology and their interaction with Morgan. Positive replies began to arrive before Lornog completed his preparations.

Once Lornog was ready and confirmed the sequence with Morgan, he turned to Anod. "Are you sure you think this is a good idea?"

"In what sense?"

"I shall be away for perhaps a week or two."

"And, you worry that I might not be able to handle things without you."

"Not precisely, but I am alert continuously."

Anod looked at Lornog's crafted face and optical sensors that had no depth. She knew exactly what his carefully structured statement was intended to mean. She glanced toward Bradley and Nick to ensure they had not picked up on his meaning. Anod nodded her head in acknowledgment then said, "We will be fine."

"I shall endeavor to keep in touch via messages or through Morgan where appropriate, so that you know where I am in the plan. If there are some preliminary findings, I shall let you know immediately."

"Very well, Lornog. Good luck."

Lornog turned toward the males. "I shall say good-bye to you, now – Nick and Bradley. As I shall be absent for some time, please take good care of Anod and her children."

"We shall do our best, Lornog," answered Bradley. "May you find success."

"Thank you."

Lornog departed the cabin. Anod, Bradley and Nick watched from the doorway or the window as Lornog searched for Zoltentok, found him, mussed his hair, and then waved farewell to all of them and disappeared into the woods.

The plan called for Lornog to use various conveyances on his journey. His first stop was a homestead several hours walk from Meganville. Lornog chose to walk the distance for some reason.

Chapter 8

"Have you heard from Lornog?" asked Anod as she entered the front door.

"No, not yet today," Nick responded.

Anod removed Sara from the chest pack where she usually rode when Anod walked somewhere. Once the child was safely in her grandfather's arms, Anod disassembled the front and backpacks she wore. She decided a few days earlier to visit several of the sites where Lornog had already visited in order to calibrate his reports in her terms.

"How did it go?" asked Bradley as he stirred a kettle of thick, hearty soup slowly cooking over the small fire.

"As I suspected, Lornog has been very methodical in his data collection. While it was not clear from his early reports, he has been doing far more than we originally planned. He has even collected samples from several notable sites."

"Do you see his reports any differently than you did yesterday?"

"No."

"So," said Nick, "as we discussed last night, he has probably not seen any trend in potential cause factors."

"Correct. He is reserving any conjecture for the conclusion of the first phase. Lornog, like most other personal androids, is programmed and trained to use scientific processes in any examination. He wants to collect all the data he can in this segment before he and Morgan evaluate what they have."

"Based on his progress to date, when will he be complete with the data collection and be able to offer some opinions?" Bradley asked.

"I can estimate that, but let's see what Morgan says." Anod paused for an affirmative head nod from Bradley. "Morgan," she said to the central computer.

"Yes, Anod."

"Based on Lornog's progress and the sites yet to be visited, what is your estimate for completion?"

"The median duration of Lornog's task is eleven days, four hours and seventeen minutes with one sigma variation of one day, twelve hours."

Anod turned to Bradley and smiled. "There you go."

"How do you think everyone is handling this study we are doing?" asked Nick.

"Quite well, I should think. Of those I have talked to, the attitude seems to be unanimous optimism, which would tell me they think Lornog and Morgan will be successful in finding the cause of these failures and finding a remedy."

"That would be nice."

"Yes, it would," added Bradley.

Except for those families that worked with Lornog or collected information for Morgan each day, the routine of life returned to Murtauri Four. The same was true for the SanGiocomos. The days began to roll along with similar content.

Several hours each day were devoted to tending the large and growing garden that supported the SanGiocomo family. They had not experienced any seed failures. The garden contained most of the popular vegetables and fruits from Beta. Many of the plants actually thrived in their garden, while the same plants had failed in other places on the planet. It was the fact that specific plants did thrive at a few locations that convinced Nick the causal factor for those failures had to be something specific at the various failure sites. They performed their chores around the homestead, tended to the education of Zoltentok, now a part of their daily life, and enjoyed the growth in both their children. They also settled into exchanging information with Lornog, wherever he might be, during the evening hours after supper in Meganville. Zoltentok and Sara were asleep.

"Here comes the nightly report," Nick announced when he noticed the message light blinking.

Within seconds, Morgan announced, "Lornog is asking me to setup a holographic exchange."

"Morgan, go ahead and set it up. We will use it as well," she said without consulting Nick or Bradley.

"As you wish."

Anod moved a chair into the 1.5-meter box they marked on the floor next to the control console then swung the scanner poles into their proper positions around the cube of space. She also had to position the receiver poles around an adjacent 1.5-meter box and move several objections out of that space.

"Do either of you want to join me?"

"No. I will just watch," answered Nick.

Bradley shook his head to decline then motioned with his hand and arm toward the projection space as though a gentlemanly courtesy to let her be the advocate. This was the first time for them to actually use the holographic communicator function.

Lornog appeared in the receiver section while Anod was still checking on some unrelated things in the kitchen. The image was so nearly perfect except for just a hint of transparency. The colors, motions and features made Lornog's image appear as though he had been transported to the site, and in a manner of speaking, he had indeed been transported in image form.

"Oh, I see we are going to be seated," he said as only the chair appeared in his receiver.

"I will be right with you," said Anod. Morgan's communications circuits passed her voice to wherever Lornog was.

"I will get a chair." He stepped out of the image space and reappeared with a chair, and sat down. "Well, Anod. I can see you are not quite ready."

"I will be right there," she repeated.

"Anod, whatever it is you are doing can wait," protested Bradley.

"Yes, yes," she said as she stepped quickly to the send box, sat down and looked at her android sitting across from her. The holographic projector made Lornog appear even more human than his meticulous exterior construction. "What have you?"

"First, I hope everything is at it should be."

"Of course it is. Did you think we would founder without your assistance?"

Lornog actually smiled in a scarcely perceptible way. "No, it is just that I heard today from Igor Stokolvic that a trader visited his site just before I arrived, told him he encountered a Yorax battlecruiser on this side of the frontier."

"Interesting. Any other information?"

"According to Stokolvic, the trader was scanned by the Yorax, but there were no communications, so the trader could not determine intent."

"Anything else?"

"Yes. Stokolvic wanted you to know this information, and he wanted me to tell you he is worried. His family remembers the murderous rampage on Beta when the Yorax were looking for you."

"Understood. Morgan, please notify the Society of this report."

"As you command," he answered.

"Have you learned anything more from your mission?" she asked, wanting to change the subject.

"Yes, as a matter of fact, I have. We will need to analyze the data more closely, but there are several interesting elements. I have seen and collected samples that appear to be parasitic damage to several seed types and young plants."

"That would suggest a solution."

"Yes, but that is premature, as you know."

"Understood."

"I am just past halfway. I thought I might comment, there are some very beneficial ancillary consequences of this effort. First, we are creating a rather extensive survey of the planet and its population. Second, we have also created an exchange with a common baseline for addressing future questions of this nature."

"All to the good."

"I must also say, I am able to train people on the use of these tools. The training does slow me down, but I suspect it is time well spent. They are interested in learning."

"That is the best news, yet."

"I thought you would be pleased."

"Indeed."

"That is about all I have at the moment. We can certainly talk about the details, but I have given you the essence of what I know to date."

"Excellent."

"Can I try it?" asked Stokolvic from outside the projector volume.

Lornog turned his head to look at Igor although Anod could not see him. "Yes, certainly." Lornog stood and moved out of the projector. Igor Stokolvic sat down.

"Can you see me?" he asked.

"I see you perfectly, Igor, as well as you can see me."

"It looks like you are sitting right here in my living room. This is so real."

"This is one of the many tools we acquired from the Society," Anod said as though compelled to raise his awareness.

"Indeed."

"Yes, Igor. There is much we can do with this technology."

"I see. I see."

"Is there anything else we need to talk about?"

Lornog appeared behind Stokolvic. "I do not think so."

"Then, we shall hear from you tomorrow night."

"Yes, Anod . . . tomorrow."

Anod rose, waved to Lornog and Igor, then stepped out of the projector box and said, "Morgan, end transmission." Lornog disappeared. Anod promptly returned the accouterments of the holographic projector to its stowed position. "Would you like some tea?" she asked Bradley and Nick.

"Sure," they said in unison.

Anod prepared three cups of tea in the conventional manner, set one in front of each man, and joined them at the table. "What did you think?"

"I was impressed with that projector," said Bradley. "It was the same technology we saw on the *Endeavour* when we were searching for a new planet, correct?"

"Yes, precisely the same. It can do many things like magnify and reduce objects, just as we saw the entire galaxy on a table top, and we could see a DNA string down to the atomic level."

"Impressive."

"What did you think of the information from Lornog?" she persisted.

"The study information is encouraging," answered Nick, "but, the report about the Yorax is disturbing."

"I think you are going to have to wear that special suit, now," added Bradley.

"Regrettably, I must agree," Anod said and placed her face in her hands with her elbows resting on the table.

"What is wrong?" asked Bradley.

"Just thinking."

The two sipped their tea and looked at each other, but remained quiet to let Anod think things through to a conclusion. They waited several minutes. Bradley's patience was not up to the challenge.

"With Alexatron's information and now this, I suspect we must prepare for a visit," Bradley said.

"Yes," she responded in a muffled voice, not moving from her contemplative posture.

"What should we do?" her husband asked.

Anod lifted her head and looked into the eyes of both men. "I shall wear the suit outside until the situation is resolved. I think we need to request the assistance of the Society, just in case the Yorax have renewed their search for me. While we have no early warning system, we can ask Morgan to monitor those channels of information that might give us some warning. I should exercise the interceptor to ensure its readiness, should I need it."

"I have notified the Society's High Command," interjected Morgan in an unusual preemptive statement.

"Thank you, Morgan. Please let us know if there is any response by the Society."

"As you wish."

Anod stared off to some distant place. Her instincts told her the Yorax were coming for her, but there was not much she could do, and she was not going to live her life in fear. Her primary concern was not for her safety but for her family. She could defend herself, but she knew she could not defend the entire planet. She had been lucky on Beta. The Yorax would not make the same mistakes again. They were a formidable adversary, especially led by the driven, vengeful traitor, Zitger.

"What are you worried about?" asked Bradley, as if he did not know.

"I just want peace," she said.

"As we all do," Bradley responded. "Is there anything we can do?"

"I do not think I need to check the interceptor tonight. It will keep for tomorrow. I would feel better talking to . . . ."

"Incoming message from the Society's Central Command," announced Morgan. "The bipolar encryption algorithm has been activated."

Anod moved to the console in front of the view screen. "Ready, Morgan."

On the screen appeared the embellished star symbol of the Society, followed a few seconds later, by the image of Admiral Agginnoor.

"Greetings to you, Anod," she said.

"And, good day to you, Admiral."

"We received your transmission regarding the Yorax in your sector. Do you need assistance?"

"We have two reports from traders. We have no evidence of their intentions, but if the reports are correct, then it would seem logical they have violated the frontier to find me."

"We have no other information other than what you have provided. We agree. If true, they have violated the treaty. We shall assume the information is accurate. I shall order the diversion and dispatch of a starship to your sector to investigate."

"That should be sufficient."

"Unfortunately, the closest starship is several weeks away."

"We shall attempt to be as quiet and unobtrusive as possible," Anod responded.

"Please keep Central Command informed of any developments," said Agginnoor.

"We will."

"Excellent. Good luck," she said and disappeared with her image replaced by the Society's symbol for several seconds, then the normal collection of information Morgan normally displayed for them.

"Help is two weeks away," Bradley expelled.

"As we have always done, we shall do our best to cope with whatever comes our way," said Nick.

"That is all we can do. If the Yorax truly are intent upon finding me, they will most likely do whatever they feel they must do to accomplish their objective. If I am perceived as that great of a threat to them, then there is almost nothing that will stand in their way."

"They will even risk war with the Society?" asked Bradley.

"If it enables them to complete their mission or objectives, yes. I think that is exactly what it means."

"The admiral did not sound too alarmed," observed Nick.

"She was trained exactly the same way I was. She most likely is not capable of feeling fear or apprehension, and even if she was, it would be considered a weakness to show such emotions."

"Ah, yes, the famous Society unemotional world."

"It is considered a desirable attribute among the warrior class," explained Anod.

Both men fell into contemplation followed by Anod. Nick rose from the table, refreshed his tea and went outside. Bradley rinsed out his teacup and went into their bedroom to fidget with something. Anod followed Nick. She found him sitting on a stump in the clearing just beyond the porch. He was looking up at the stars. He did not even look at her.

"You should not be out here without that suit on," he said.

Anod looked up at the stars, as well. She quickly evaluated the array for movement, looking for an object exhibiting the angular motion of an orbiting spacecraft. She saw none. Anod knew she would not be able to detect a Yorax battlecruiser if it was masked, but then, they were not likely to feel the need for deception with such a peaceful planet. "They are not up there."

"How can you be so sure?"

"I am. They are not there."

Nick continued to scan the skies looking for something. Eventually, he looked at Anod, and then patted another stump signaling her to sit beside him. Only diffuse light came from the interior. It was another gloriously clear night.

"What are we really going to do if they come again?"

"The best we can, as you said earlier."

"I know what I said, Anod, but we do not have as many people as we did on Beta. We do not have many places to hide. We have no defenses."

"We have the interceptor and me."

Nick chuckled in an odd nervous, non-humorous way. "Not to lessen your skills as a warrior, Anod, but you have been a mother for several years now, not a warrior. And, somehow I do not think we are going to be so lucky this time around. I am a very selfish old man. I have become quite accustomed to having you around. You are a very good mother to the only two grandchildren I have. I do not want to lose you."

"Nick, I have become quite comfortable with this life. I will do whatever I have to do to preserve this peaceful, rewarding living."

"I know, but I still worry."

Anod looked up to the stars one more time. She could detect nothing abnormal among the stars above them. "It is sleep time. We are safe tonight."

Nick nodded his head and followed Anod into the house. They retired. Anod and Bradley chose the conventional bed.

Time passed. Anod wore her crafted suit of antratite without complaint. She completed her checkout of the interceptor – even flew a few test flights – and kept the machine in readiness. Without telling her family, Anod devoted extra time to vigilance. She tried hard to keep her caution hidden or transparent. Anod also used the early morning hours before dawn to perform her martial exercises. She felt the need for preparation, but she did not want to give her family any cause for worry.

Lornog completed his survey. They left Lornog and Morgan to their analysis that took two more days to complete. Others asked about progress, and each time, a request for patience was made.

"I am ready to report," announced Lornog after the family completed breakfast outside.

"Excellent," said Nick. "Let us devote the morning or the day to listening to Lornog's findings."

"Sounds good to me," Anod added.

"Should I begin, now?" asked Lornog.

"Yes," they said simultaneously.

"Very well. Do you want to discuss our report out here or inside?"

"Do we need to be inside?" asked Nick.

"No. I will connect with Morgan from here. He can pick up my communications stream, and I can speak for him." Nick nodded his head in agreement. "I visited every site of habitation on this planet. The survey has accounted for everyone, so in a form, this was a census as well. I collected a complete baseline listing of the relevant information like location, residents, materials involved, methods used, results and timing as best could be reconstructed in some cases, along with other data I found interesting. We can discuss the analytical methods Morgan and I used, but I do not think there are any issues with our methods."

"Agreed," Nick said as if, as a scientist, he needed to consent to dispensing with the methods portion of the presentation.

"Morgan wants me to tell you we learned many ancillary facts that will strengthen our community."

"Excellent," Anod responded, wanting to move back to the primary topic.

"There were three conclusions," Lornog continued. "One, the crop failures can be classified in two main groups – adaptation and methods. Namely, some of the seeds were not robust enough to adapt, or the timeliness or extent of modifications to the germination processes were inadequate. In most cases, Morgan and I believe these can be corrected. Second, the available data indicates your admonition at the last community meeting was correct, in that, we are not convinced that raising the imported seeds from Beta is the best for this environment. The assessment tells us the humans are better off adapting to this environment as opposed to trying to change this system to their liking. Third, although the Yorax have not found us, yet, it seems a virtual certainty they will find us."

"And, what do you think will be successful?" interjected Anod, feeling uncomfortable about the stress her presence was once again going to place on these people including her family.

"First, where appropriate, we must adjust our growing . . ."

"No, Lornog. Start with your last conclusion since that is apparently more of an immediate threat."

Anod held up her hand palm out to stop the conversation.

"We have done all we can do at this point other than arming ourselves with rudimentary implements of combat, and even then, we are not likely to be effective against the modern weapons of the Yorax, especially if they choose to carry out a bombardment as they did at the end on Beta."

"So, we should just await our fate?"

"If something was to happen soon, we must do our best with passive means of resistance until the *Reliant* arrives. Once our defensive posture is improved by the presence of the Society, we can discuss other options with the captain."

Bradley looked to Anod and caught her eyes. "We need to keep you hidden for a couple of more days."

"I do not like living my life in fear."

"But, Anod," said Nick, "Bradley is correct. Even if the Yorax do appear here, we will most likely be able to deceive them for some time if they are unable to detect your presence. To them, we would be just another band of humans near their frontier."

"It is you they are clearly seeking," Lornog said to Anod.

"I know."

"Then, we must issue instructions to all our people, they cannot acknowledge your presence," Bradley added. "We should also tell them the Society is coming to us and is a couple of days away."

"Is that what you wish Morgan to do?" asked Lornog.

They looked at each other and nodded in agreement. "Yes," answered Bradley.

"Very well. Morgan has begun the process. It will take him six hours to complete if we do not want to make this an emergency notification."

"We would have to wake people from their sleep cycle," Anod said.

"That would probably cause more alarm," Nick stated, "and there is no indication the Yorax arrival is imminent."

Anod considered the time and options. She looked to Bradley. "Perhaps, if you can take care of Sara, I should take the interceptor up. I have flown missions of several days before; I can certainly fly a patrol. It would remove me from the planet, and it would give at least some early warning capability we do not have, now."

"How much milk is stored for Sara?" asked Bradley.

Anod checked the cold box. "Twelve hundred milliliters."

"That should last us two days."

"You can always stretch it out a little by thinning it with water," added Nick.

Anod knew the topic was a sensitive one, but maybe this time was different. "You can always use the replicator. Morgan can reproduce my milk in what quantities you wish."

"Maybe you two have come to that acceptance, but I have not," Nick stated firmly. The old man had accepted many aspects of the new devices and resigned himself to eating the generated food from the replicator, but he was still too apprehensive about the consequences for a growing baby. He was against experimenting with his grandchildren.

Anod let it pass.

"What about you?" Bradley asked.

"What do you mean?"

"Your milk?"

Anod thought about the motherly task she had not considered in the small spacecraft. She also thought about Sara's age. The infant daughter was too young and had shown no signs of weaning her dependence on her mother. It was only two days, plus or minus at little. "I can express and discard it to keep things going."

"Are you sure?"

"Yes. I will need to take a pump. Plus, it will give me something to do during those boring hours on patrol."

"Of course," answered Bradley. He looked to his father then back to Anod. "As much as I do not want you to go, I suspect your suggestion is the best choice. In case the Yorax are able to slip by your patrol, you would not be here which would buy us some time. If you do detect them, some warning would help us."

"You must not attack, Anod," Nick added.

Anod smiled. It was nice to have a family that cared about her. "As you say. I am only one little interceptor."

"That did not stop you on Beta," Nick said.

Bradley and Anod laughed, and soon dragged Nick into their laughter. They all knew Anod's courage and singular resistance had saved many lives on Beta. They also knew that effort nearly claimed her life, again. The Betans and Murtaurians recognized, appreciated and honored Anod's heroism. Nick simply wanted his daughter-in-law safe.

Anod nodded her head. "I shall endeavor to be prudent despite the urge to engage those who torment us."

"We must let the Society do the engagement," Nick said. "They are properly equipped for such action."

Anod checked everything on the interceptor before starting the powerplant. She activated the masking function before she launched herself into space. It had been several months since she had flown last, so this was a great opportunity for her to refresh her handling skills. Once she was several hundred kilometers from Murtauri Four, Anod conducted a comprehensive, passive search of the universe around her and within the interceptor's sensor range. The process took two orbits of the planet and three and a half hours to complete. She found nothing extraordinary.

The conventional radio traffic she listened to coming from the planet meant their communications plan was working. A half dozen families located around the planet were secretly enlisted in the scheme. They made the antiquated radio messages seem like routine voice exchanges. Specific key words or phrases were embedded in the string of otherwise innocuous words to alert Anod to different conditions on the planet. They would not make any direct reference or address to Anod, or even acknowledge her existence. A set of agreed calls would be made to the Society starship to give her information about the status of the Yorax in the region. The plan called for her to either contact the starship from space or land to return to her place at Meganville as if nothing had happened.

Anod settled into a routine. The same alert support program she used during her defense of Beta was still quite adequate for this occasion. She remained in her moderate orbit hidden from all sensors and let her on-board systems monitor what was happening in their little corner of the galaxy. She ate, slept and did the other things she needed to do to keep herself comfortable and alert.

For entertainment, Anod would flip the spacecraft over on its back and marvel at the image of the planet as she orbited the sphere. Occasionally, she would use her optical sensor to examine a new geological feature she had not seen or noticed before. Every pass over Meganville when she was awake, Anod watched her home. Several times she lowered her orbital altitude so she could see members of her family outside their home.

Early on the second day, just after dawn at Meganville, she saw Bradley walk out of the house and hold Sara high over his head as if he knew Anod could see her from orbit. There was no way for Bradley to know her position, but the gesture brought tears to her eyes when she saw her daughter's face and peaceful state, and felt the hardness in her breasts and the developing wetness across her chest. She wanted to be down there. Anod continued to shed tears after Meganville passed from view. She had to keep them safe.

Late on the second day, her sensors detected a large craft dropping out of hyperlight speed. Anod maneuvered to watch that point of space. She also detected several broad scans that she recognized as precautionary active scans that would normally be performed if nothing presented itself on passive searches. This was the profile of a warship not wanting to be surprised by a potential adversary.

"People of Murtauri Four," came the radio hail, "this is the Society Starship *Reliant*."

The call was repeated four times before an answer came. "*Reliant*, welcome. This is Murtauri Four." Anod recognized the voice of Otis Greenstreet.

"We understand you have some trouble," said the female starship officer.

"In a manner of speaking," answered Otis. "It would be best if you could meet our leadership at my location in . . . perhaps . . . two hours."

"As you wish. We shall do a good search of the area and meet you at the location of your transmitter in two hours."

"Very well. I shall notify our leadership."

Anod did not hear any further radio calls from Otis. He was probably calling Bradley at Meganville using Morgan or their secure communications.

Anod took a long look at the graceful lines of the starship. She was tempted to make a close pass to examine a starship class she had not seen before. The several active scans from the *Reliant* convinced her not to press her luck by getting too close to the starship. Anod manipulated the controls of the interceptor to return to the hangar near Meganville.

She waited until she had the doors closed before she shutdown the systems and the powerplant. With the care of a professional, she secured the small spacecraft.

The twenty-minute walk through the forest and across the stream to the SanGiocomo house renewed her pleasure in the benevolence of nature around her and heightened her anticipated reunion with her children and family. When she saw the assembled logs of the cabin, she quickly searched the surroundings. Zoltentok was the first to see Anod.

"Mommy," the boy shouted and ran to her.

Anod buried her son in her arms and lifted him from the ground. "You are getting so big," she whispered to him. "I will not be able to lift you much longer," she fibbed to emphasize Zoltentok's growing status.

"I have been busy, Mommy."

"Doing what?"

"Building a fort."

"A fort? For what purpose?"

"For our protection," the boy said proudly.

Nick appeared, followed by Bradley carrying a sleeping Sara. They waited on the porch. Anod nodded her head toward them to acknowledge their presence then returned her attention to Zoltentok.

"Protection from what, ZJ?"

"The Yorax."

"Really?"

"Yes, Mommy. I am going to protect you. I will not let them hurt you."

"Thank you, Zoltentok," Anod said as she carried her son toward the porch. Before she reached the first step, Anod lowered him to the ground. She kissed Bradley, then Nick, and ever so gently stroked Sara's forehead. Anod slowly took Sara into her arms, kissed her daughter's forehead again, and then looked to her husband. "The Society has arrived."

"We just received word from Otis in New Providence," responded Bradley. "He indicated the first meeting will be in the square. We should head on down there."

"You go."

"Anod, they will want to talk to you."

"Perhaps, but you are our leader, and I want to be with my children."

"Anod," he protested. The instant washout of any warmth and the steely stare from her eyes told him the answer. "Very well." He looked to his father. "Are you going to come?"

"I would rather not. I want to stay here with Anod and the children."

Bradley looked back to Anod. "So, you really are going to make me go down there without you."

"Yes."

"Ah . . . ," he stopped when she lifted her free hand. "Damn, but sometimes you are difficult."

Anod simply smiled at him then returned her attention to Sara.

Bradley did not take long to gather a small satchel and departed for the meeting with the Society. Zoltentok returned to his activities. Anod wanted to examine her son's construction efforts but resolved to do it later. The ache in her chest tempted her to wake Sara, but again, she decided to wait. The thickening clouds suggested impending rain although she could not yet smell it. She found a chair on the porch. Nick pulled another chair close to her and sat as well.

"Anything happen down here over the last two days?" she asked Nick.

"Not really."

Anod looked around. "Where is Lornog?"

"He responded to the Gibritzu family. They asked for his help with some new crop plantings."

Anod smiled broadly. "So, they are warming to our android brother."

"It would appear so. We heard last night from him that Dahar had invited several other families for a horticulture meeting today. We expect Lornog back tonight or tomorrow."

"Excellent."

"We thought so," he paused. "How were things up there?" he asked.

"Boring."

"You found nothing?"

"No. Not a whisper."

"I suppose that is good," he said as he looked off into the forest.

"Yes and no. With all the little bits of information, I think it is fairly certain the Yorax are out there. The longer this takes to come to resolution, the longer we live with uncertainty."

Zoltentok's gleeful, bouncing exuberance attracted their attention. He had apparently found just the branch he needed for his fort. Without even a glance to the porch, he disappeared behind the corner of the house.

"He seems quite pleased with himself," she said.

"Yes, indeed. You need to see his fort. He is very proud of it. He feels he is protecting his mother."

Sara began to stir. As she woke up and her eyes focused, a smile grew on her delicate face. Sara's recognition generated a warm surge throughout Anod's body. Within minutes, the mother and daughter connected in shared nourishment of different forms.

The routine of life soon enveloped Anod. When Sara succumbed to her afternoon nap, Anod responded to Zoltentok's urgings. Her son's fort was an impressive, though not functional, structure combining rocks and wood into a fairly sturdy square building with a thin, peaked roof. It took Anod extra time to contort her long body into the small space and adjust herself to allow room for Zoltentok. The boy enthusiastically described the features of his fort and the process of defense he intended to employ. Anod listened intently and asked key, probing questions of the young warrior. The most striking revelation of their conversation was the level of understanding Zoltentok demonstrated of the ancient Chinese philosopher Sun Tzu's principles of war. She could only wonder how he acquired such knowledge at his young age? The warrior ethos was not something the SanGiocomo family discussed.

Anod had just sat on the porch after extricating herself from Zoltentok's fort, when two individuals materialized in the small clearing in front of her. She recognized Bradley before the process was complete. The other person was a female, slightly taller but more slight, than Bradley. She wore the uniform of a Society starship captain – probably the captain of the *Reliant*. Anod rose to greet her husband and their guest.

Before Bradley could begin the introductions, the woman saluted then extended her hand. "Anod, it is a pleasure to meet you. I am Colonel Arkinnagga, Captain of the *Reliant*."

Anod did not return the salute but did shake hands. Arkinnagga was slightly taller and of a similar build as Anod. Her dark brown hair was pulled back tightly against her head and wound in a roll at the back of her head. Her eyes were nearly as dark brown as her hair and matched perfectly with the creamy, light brown texture of her skin. She was a strong, handsome woman.

"A pleasure to meet you," Anod responded.

"I was disappointed you did not join us at New Providence, but Bradley explained and I understand. You have developed quite a reputation, and I must say, a respectable following."

"Thank you, although it is not deserved."

"That is not what I hear."

"A combination of events not of my choosing."

"Perhaps, but nonetheless impressive. Many of us feel a true sense of loss from your situation."

"I do not."

"I suppose that is good."

Nick returned with Sara. Anod completed the introductions of her family. Without a sliver of modesty, Anod tended to Sara's nourishment demands.

"I have never seen this before," stated Arkinnagga.

"It is the way humans feed their infants and one of the reasons I do not regret my banishment."

Arkinnagga showed minor signs of discomfort. She held Anod's eyes. "Bradley can explain what we discussed in New Providence, but in short, we shall remain here and ensure our presence is known to discourage any intrusion by the Yorax. The warrant for Zitger is still valid."

"Good."

"We must consider more permanent arrangements. We can not remain in orbit forever."

"We discussed several ideas," said Bradley.

Arkinnagga nodded her head. "I shall leave you to your debate. I would like to extend an invitation for your family to join my officers at mess for dinner, at your convenience."

"Thank you."

The starship captain waited as if she wanted a commitment. When none came, she said, "Please let me know."

"We shall," Anod responded.

Colonel Arkinnagga nodded her head, stepped away from the porch, waved to the SanGiocomo family, and then touched the wristband on her left arm. "One for transport."

Within seconds, the body of the *Reliant* captain was converted from matter to energy for the short journey back to her ship. Anod shifted her attention from the captain's departure to her daughter still nursing at her breast.

"It was a good meeting," Bradley stated.

"Good," she answered without diverting her attention.

"They plan to stay for several days at least. They will continue to search this sector. Colonel Arkinnagga indicated she would likely receive redirecting orders in a week or so."

"What did she say about subsequent defense?" asked Nick.

"First, their mission is to find Zitger and return him to justice. If that is accomplished, the threat should dissipate. Barring that, she suggested we deploy an array of electronic picket satellites." Anod nodded, not wanting to comment. "She said they could detect the approach of any visitor or intruder and could alert us as well as the Society. These satellites could also take some limited defensive action."

"Not against a Yorax battlecruiser or a determined adversary," Anod said.

"Perhaps not, but it would be more than we have now."

"Yes, it would."

"Where do we get these satellites?" Nick asked.

"The Society will deploy them as part of our alliance with them."

Nick looked to Anod. "What do you suggest we do?"

Anod wondered why he was asking her. They certainly had the ability to make decisions of this character. She looked back and forth between Nick and Bradley, expecting one of them to give her a clue as to what they were really after. "I would suggest we do what Colonel Arkinnagga recommends."

The two men looked at each other and back to her several times. Sara had fallen asleep. Anod shifted the baby's position to allow the return of her clothing to its proper place.

"Don't you have any other ideas?" asked Bradley.

"No."

Again, the two men shared their incredulity. Anod was no longer in the mood to talk. She rose to take Sara to her bed. With the task complete, she ordered up a cup of tea from the replicator then returned to the porch.

"You are sure this is the correct thing to do?" asked Nick.

"Yes."

"Anod, aren't you concerned about our defense?" Bradley asked.

"Yes, I am. I also know I cannot change the things I do not control. Arkinnagga appears to have a keen mind, and her recommendation is logical. I would rather worry about the things I can control, like raising my children and becoming a better mother."

"Anod, you are the only warrior among us. The entire community looks to you in such matters including us."

"I did not seek this role you suggest. You and the others can make this decision. You do not need me."

"But, Anod . . . ," Bradley said, then stopped when Anod raised her right hand.

"No, buts, Bradley. Now, I am quite tired, and I would like to get a good night's sleep."

"Are you going to use the isopod tonight?"

Anod searched Bradley's eyes. She could see the yearning. "No."

"Then, I shall be along shortly."

"As you wish." She rose, kissed and said good night to Nick, and then Bradley.

The next few days passed peacefully. There was no excitement. There was no news of any encroachment by the Yorax. The only conflict came in Anod's resistance to attending the dinner aboard *Reliant*. She did not want to leave her children, and it was not until Bradley relented to allow the children to go with them that Anod agreed to go.

The dinner had gone reasonably well. The children, each characteristic to their age, demonstrated the power of precociousness. The crew, unaccustomed to young children on a starship, seemed truly fascinated and intrigued by Zoltentok and Sara. Equally as interesting was the enigma that was Anod – an accomplished warrior . . . one of them . . . of burgeoning mythical proportion, and now a detached, doting mother. Through numerous confessions, the dichotomy was beyond their comprehension.

Anod chose to remain outside the decision process as the Murtaurian community accepted Colonel Arkinnagga's proposal. The proffered satellite system was deployed, tested and certified operational. The announcement of the starship's impending departure brought the community together for another collective meeting. Colonel Arkinnagga was invited to attend along with several of her officers.

The traditional introductions and explanation of purpose were completed. Arkinnagga became the primary speaker, at the request of the group.

"The satellite system is functional and should give you a reasonable warning time for any approach. Now, you must realize, the alerts will be for any craft approaching the planet, friendly or otherwise. You will need to learn the distinctions."

"Aren't there recognition codes, or something, to prevent nuisance alerts from friendly traders?" asked Otis.

"Yes, however we cannot give you the code sequence algorithms since you do not have a military force to protect them."

"We have Anod," Guysaga added, producing a rumble of laughter.

"Yes, you do, but she cannot be up there all by herself, no matter how good she may be."

Anod wanted to add her own rejection of the suggestion. She was appreciative of the faith some of the people had in her, but she also worried that faith could be carried too far. No one countered Arkinnagga's response. Anod let it pass.

Arkinnagga continued. "I will inform Central Command and the Council of Elders of the actions we have taken here and also suggest we try to keep a starship within a few days travel of Murtauri Four, but please understand, proximity is not likely, given all our other commitments."

"So, we could be on our own?" Dahar asked.

"We shall attempt to mitigate the situation, but the basic answer is, yes."

"Can we make peace with the Yorax?" asked someone.

Anod started to answer but gave way to Colonel Arkinnagga. "Technically, we are still at peace. After all, we have a treaty with the Yorax Empire. However, prolonged peace is highly unlikely given their history. The Yorax are a very vengeful creatures."

"Then, we shall do the best we can," interjected Nick.

Muffled conversation erupted among the group like the rumble of a distant thunderstorm. It was difficult to detect a drift to the mutterings.

"And," said Arkinnagga, pausing to quiet the crowd, "we shall do the best we can to protect you." The murmuring continued. Colonel Arkinnagga held up both hands high above her head. She waited for quiet. "The *Reliant* must depart soon. Are there any other questions for me or my officers?" She scanned the crowd. "As we leave you, on behalf of my crew and the Society, I would like to thank you for your hospitality and wish you the best of luck."

A chorus of thank-you's punctuated the meeting. Colonel Arkinnagga and the three other officers she brought with her stepped away from the group then disappeared.

"Who will make the decisions on the alerts, and what actions will be taken given an alert?" Dahar asked to finally refocus the meeting.

"We have a choice," said Bradley as he made his way to the front. "We can set up a duty cycle where we either define a cadre of watch officers, or we rotate the duty using the communications system."

Before anyone could answer, Otis said, "We can also let Morgan do the monitoring. He can make these kinds of decisions."

The debate ensued around turning over their collective security to a machine. Anod felt her frustration mounting once again. For her, the answer was quite clear and simple. She tried to listen then gave into the tug of her children. The debate continued for nearly an hour. It was not until other citizens began to pick up their children that Anod recognized either the conclusion or suspension of the defense debate. Nick and Bradley soon joined her.

"What was decided?" she asked.

"The group was not comfortable making the jump all the way to Morgan, so Otis, Anton and seven others agreed to attend the alert system and work with Morgan then report back to the community," Bradley answered.

"Anton?"

"Yes. Why?"

"He is so distant, to himself, almost like he is not one of us."

"He is fine, just a loner."

"I trust you will not have objections if I ask Morgan and Lornog to give me additional information."

"I don't see why."

"Excellent. Now, can we go home?"

"Yes, sure."

Chapter 9

The trial worked. The Murtaurians gained sufficient confidence in Morgan and the early warning system to let the central computer manage the alerts. Morgan performed well, as Anod had known he would.

Time passed. The focus of the people returned to the crops. The horticulture improvements progressed. Recoveries were accomplished in several areas. A half dozen seed types were declared unsuccessful. Those involved wanted to acquire some more of those types to make further attempts, but they would have to be imported and that would take time. Morgan and Lornog continued to refine their knowledge and adjust their advice to growers.

For a period of several months, not one single rumor or other piece of information even remotely suggested any Yorax activity on the Confederation side of the frontier. The sense of peace grew. Even Anod began to relax her dress code, venturing outside without her antratite suit on occasion.

Trade expanded as more of their neighbors became aware of their mercantile goods. The Murtaurians gradually expanded the selection and quantities of materials. This was a time of prosperity for Murtauri Four.

Even Anod's life changed. Sara decided the day had come to wean herself from her mother's milk. Anod marveled at the child's sense of direction as well as her determination. Zoltentok had stayed with her longer. The weaning process was more protracted for him, and he occasionally sought his mother's breast after he was eating solid food – usually when he was hurt. The loss of the intimate motherly stimulation brought a mounting yearning for another pregnancy, and the removal of one of her primary excuses for not traveling. Their recent attempts at conception had not been successful.

The majority of her time was spent with the children. Zoltentok was big enough to travel with his father and learn the lessons of leadership and diplomacy. Sara was beginning to show the first signs of personality and ravenous curiosity. Anod did not want to acknowledge the reality that the growth and progressing independence of her children was giving her more time. Emptiness began expanding within her. She wanted more children. As she watched her children grow and their reach stretch beyond her, Anod felt the nibbles of her yearning for flight resurface.

"Would you mind if I went flying?" she asked Nick.

Bradley had taken Zoltentok with him on a two-day journey to the other side of the planet. Sara was preoccupied with the examination of various shaped blocks around her.

"No, of course not. You deserve the time. I shall be perfectly fine with Sara."

Lornog stepped forward. "Would you like me to go with you?"

"No. Thank you, though. I would like you to stay here and help Nick with Sara."

"As you wish," Lornog responded then stepped back.

Anod gave Sara a kiss on the forehead that did not disturb the child's intense interest in the blocks. She also kissed Nick on the cheek before departing for the hangar.

The interceptor was in fine shape with plenty of fuel – days worth, actually, although she only needed hours. Without activating the masking system, Anod took off for some atmospheric maneuvering. She made several low passes over the site where Bradley and Zoltentok were working. On the second pass, they were outside the house. When they recognized Anod's craft, they waved feverishly. Anod performed several rolls as she pointed the nose toward space.

Once clear of the atmosphere, she pushed the throttle forward, accelerating through light speed transition out to three, four, five times the speed of light. Anod accelerated and decelerated as she visited each planetary object in the Murtauri system – six primary planets with thirty-one secondary satellites of natural origin. She committed herself to exploring other planets someday in the future – *mañana*. With those visits complete, Anod slowed the interceptor to a near stationary speed, switched off all the displays and lights in the cockpit, and then tilted her head back to absorb the stars. She carefully found the stars she needed to establish her location without the aid of the on-board systems.

Anod found the solo star the Society called, the home star, or simply the Sun. It was a mature, stable, yellow star of modest size. While she could not see the orbiting planets, she new the third body was the wellspring from which her genus had come. For all the beauty and good that was the Universe, or at least the only galaxy they knew, it was the ugliness of Zitger's betrayal that occupied her. Why had one of theirs betrayed his own people? What had pushed Zitger over the edge to treason? He had to know that his treachery was now documented with the Society, which meant he could never go back. Why would he continue to risk whatever life he had with the Yorax just to pursue her? Why couldn't he just leave her alone?

The irritating whistle of the communications alert brought her back to the craft she occupied. Anod switched on the various displays and usual lights. A conventional radio message had been received containing the name of her daughter. She activated the replay.

"Sara Jean, return home," the message said. Morgan repeated the transmission three more times – the prescribed number – indicating the situation was safe.

Anod turned the interceptor toward the lighted side of the dusk terminus. It would be nearly dark by the time she landed, secured the interceptor and returned to the house. Anod pushed the throttle forward then immediately pulled it back as she quickly approached Murtauri Four.

The entire family, including Lornog, waited for her on the porch. They were smiling, so it probably was not bad news. Zoltentok burst from his father's arms to run into Anod's embrace. She lifted him to straddle her left hip that supported a good portion of his weight. Anod knew she would not be able to do this for many more months.

"How is my boy?"

"Fine, Mommy. It is time for supper."

"Well, thank you, Zoltentok."

As she approached the porch, Bradley said, "We thought you might be having too much fun up there, and we wanted you home for supper."

"So Zoltentok told me," she answered as she lowered her son to the porch and kissed her dozing daughter's forehead. "I am glad you called. I was lost in the stars."

Bradley and Nick laughed, followed by Zoltentok. "As we figured," said Nick. He rose from his chair still cradling Sara and led them into the house.

Lornog held Sara while the family ate their supper. The meal conversation revolved around Zoltentok's observations about plants. He had obviously spent the day listening to his father discussing the various elements of the growing process. Nothing much happened beyond the routine.

The evening was spent in laughter and play once the dishes were cleaned, and Sara woke up to join them. The little girl was moving on her own although not quite ready to walk. She was very much aware of what was going on around her. Anod absorbed this life she was immersed in fully. These children were the ultimate celebration of life – the next generation – the continuation of the species. They deserved the devotion of their parents, and they received it in full measure.

Once the children were in bed and asleep, the conversation briefly returned to one topic.

"Did you detect anything while you were up there?" asked Bradley.

"No . . . not a whisper."

"Perhaps, those rumors were just idle speculation," Nick added.

"Perhaps."

"Is there anything more we can do?" Bradley continued.

"No, not that I am aware of. I think we should put this behind us. We certainly cannot live our lives in fear of something that might never come." Anod paused to let the others speak. The two men were caught in their own contemplation. "While I was in space, I thought about Zitger and his betrayal. I cannot see any purpose in his further pursuit of me. If the Yorax actually did cross the frontier, I surmise it may have been for other reasons. I really think I would have been easy enough to find."

"So, they were not after you?"

"I suspect not. I really do not think I am that hard to find."

"I hope you are right," Bradley responded. "We are harming no one. We are not a threat to anyone including the Yorax. They can leave us in peace."

"Indeed."

"What purpose would it service to compound his crimes?"

Anod looked at Nick then Bradley. She even glanced to Lornog who stood in an inanimate state beside their bedroom door. "My thoughts precisely, but I suspect normal and reasonable logic is not at work here. There is still no reason, no rationale, for his original crime. While I could probably understand his quest for my head on Beta, before the Society intervened, I cannot understand any further transgressions."

Nick rose from the table and walked outside into the cool night air. Bradley just stared for many long moments. Anod realized she had other responsibilities, a duty of sorts. She needed to train others to fly. She needed to train her children in her skills. Until her children were old enough to master those skills, she knew she had to train others who accepted the new devices of their community, like Otis, Anton and others.

"Bradley," she said and waited until he returned to her. "There is something more we can and should do."

"Like what?"

"I think I should train others to fly, to prepare them to defend us, in case something should happen to me."

"First, nothing is going to happen to you. Second, who did you have in mind?"

"I was thinking Otis and perhaps Anton since you vouch for him."

Bradley chuckled. "You think they can fly?"

"They are the closest we have to security forces. They already have some of the skills. I will have to teach them the other skills they will need, and they are both without family."

"And, you think you can teach them what has taken decades for you to learn."

"Yes. They are intelligent, capable and absorbent."

"You really think that would help?"

"It is called risk mitigation." She stared at him expecting something. "Now, I must confess . . . I do not want to be the sole protector. Otis and Anton are much younger. They are more enthusiastic for the challenge and the adventure."

"That is quite a switch."

"My turn to ask, what do you mean?"

"When I met you on Beta and during the confrontation with the Yorax, you were the ultimate warrior. You accomplished feats of magnificent martial skill. I have never known such courage."

"Thank you."

"So, what changed?"

"Those two children sleeping in the other room. I found a special fulfillment. I cannot return to service in the Society, and I am not sure I really want to return. Those children represent the most fascinating achievements in my life."

"Well, maybe you could use some help. When do you want to start?"

"Tomorrow."

"You were never one to waste time," Bradley said with a quiet voice, nearly a whisper. "Could you wait a day?"

"Sure. Why?"

"ZJ wants to go with me tomorrow, but I need him to stay here."

"You do not need to ask me twice."

"Good."

Nick returned, did not speak other than to say goodnight, and then went to his small room. Bradley finished those tasks that needed to be finished before bed, then grasped Anod's hand and led her to the bedroom. Tonight they shared each other.

Anod kept the process low key. She did not talk about her added duty, and she asked Otis and Anton to refrain from discussing their activities with anyone. Neither one of the men was married, nor had any family to be worried, so they made natural choices. It was not that Anod wanted to keep anything from the citizens, it was just prudence. The more people who knew what was happening, the more likelihood the Yorax might find out if they were looking.

She trained them on the basic principles of space flight and the operation of the interceptor's gravity neutralization feature. Anod enlisted Lornog's assistance in the initial flight tasks since he did not require life support, and there was insufficient room for two adults in the cockpit. While Lornog did an acceptable job, some of the fine points were being missed. She needed a craft with at least two seats.

Anod tried to convince several traders to allow her to borrow their craft, but none would oblige her request. A call went out to the Society. Anod struggled with her decision to ask for more help, but she saw no other choices. Murtauri Four did not have a manufacturing capability. They had to acquire spacecraft by one of only a few means. They could trade for a vehicle, but they were still an immature merchant culture. There was only one path she had confidence in that would result in the correct machine. Her primary reluctance came from all they had asked the Society for already. The leadership of the Society offered to garrison a detachment of warriors, similar to her last duty station on Saranon. The thought of having some of her old comrades from the Kartog Guards or one of the other of the Society's elite units on Murtauri Four had a certain attraction, but she was a voice of only one.

Her sense of security and survival overcame her reticence. Within a month, the Society delivered an old Korbon fighter, the predecessor to the Guards' fighter she flew on Saranon, and a standard Society shuttlecraft that most starships carried. The blocky, inelegant, shuttlecraft had one distinct advantage – two pilot stations. It also had a cargo capacity that could be used to carry ten people and some equipment, or two metric tons of mass within a twenty cubic meter rectangular cargo bay behind the pilots' compartment. The Korbon fighter was actually crude in comparison. The anti-gravity, field generator was rudimentary at best and consumed an enormous amount of power. As a result, the engineers built it with old, conventional, lifting wings and thermal protective materials to withstand atmospheric reentry in the event the vehicle ran out of fuel. Masking technology had not been perfected when the fighter was built. There were very few defensive systems. The primary advantage of the fighter, other than it was another flying machine, was the dual cannon armament firing anti-matter projectiles the warriors called slugs. At least the Korbon fighter had hyperlight capability, which was some consolation for the antiquity of the vehicle.

Once the Murtaurians constructed hangars for the additional craft in widely dispersed locations and Anod completed her checkout of the machines, she began her flight-training program with Otis and Anton. Once they settled down in basic control manipulation and she was satisfied the two students could perform fundamental tasks, she decided it was time for a change when they finished their tenth flight.

With the shuttlecraft secured in its hangar near Anton's modest cottage one third of the way around the planet, Anod motioned for both men to sit under a large shade tree. "I think both of you have learned the basics."

"I am not so sure," interjected Anton.

"Neither one of us is comfortable, yet, with this act of flying," Otis added.

"Nonetheless, you both can control the craft."

"So, what did you have in mind?" asked Otis.

"To be blunt, I need to spend more time with my family. I am going to ask Lornog to teach you the rest of the skills. I will monitor your progress and check on you, now and then."

"He's an android," said Anton.

"Yes, he is. However, he has a brain, in some ways more sophisticated than ours, and he knows everything I know and more. My previous android, Gorp, taught me how to fly, and Lornog is more advanced than Gorp. Just listen to what he tells you. Do what he says. Do not think of him as an android or a machine, think of him as my friend, and a very capable friend, I might add."

"Are you sure this is a good idea?"

"Yes, Anton, I am."

"I don't know."

"I did not want to do this," Anod continued. "I agreed to do this training as a means to increase our protection against the Yorax or other potential aggressors."

"What are we going to do with only a Yorax interceptor, a Korbon fighter and an unarmed shuttlecraft?"

"What did I do with only a Yorax interceptor on Beta, Otis?"

He remembered and nodded his head. "All right, so a determined warrior can overcome a superior adversary, but we are not you."

"You are both more than you think you are. You simply must believe."

"Perhaps," answered Otis in a muffled tone.

"No perhaps," Anod responded sharply. "Just believe."

The next day, Anod gave Lornog his instructions and set out the remainder of the training course for the two fledgling pilots. On the first flight with the two students and Lornog in the shuttlecraft, Anod joined them, flying a loose wing position, in the Korbon fighter. They talked on simple, low power radio, so she could hear the conversations and occasionally contribute when she thought it important.

As she guessed, both of the former Betan security officers learned quickly. They progressed rapidly through the tactics and weapons segments. Since neither Anton nor Otis had seen what an anti-matter projectile did, Anod felt it important to give them the experience. On two separate occasions, they all went away from the Murtauri system, found a wandering asteroid and conducted a mock engagement. While one pilot fired from the Korbon fighter, Anod observed from the Yorax interceptor and Lornog and the other pilot watched from the shuttle. The slug traveled at sub-light speeds, but the high-order flash was dazzling and made the desired impression. Despite its age, the projectile was not a weapon to be used indiscriminately.

The conclusion of their training and the associated pronouncement of their qualification came at a community meeting in New Providence. Anod reported the result of their work. The questions and concerns were minor. They also agreed to a set of action plans if they were threatened. Otis would operate the Korbon fighter; Anton the shuttlecraft; and, Anod would continue with the Yorax interceptor. Anod did not discuss their contingency plans should any one of them be compromised. Only Anton, Bradley and Otis knew. Anod finally felt some relief. There were other warriors on the planet beyond her, and they were capable of defending their people, at least for a little while.

As time passed, the Murtaurians gained confidence in their early warning system. Only a handful thought in terms of defense.

Life slowly became easier. Trade continued to grow and even some of the crops began to flourish with the adjustments recommended by Morgan. Several additional visits from Society starships as well as other friendly warships added a degree of shared commitment. The only dark cloud in this otherwise gorgeous scene was the now reoccurring rumors of Yorax incursions into Confederation space.

To Anod, the visits by various Confederation warships meant there was some veracity to the rumors. It was not something any of them discussed. Anod tried to keep her sense of unease to herself. She tried to make everything appear as though she did not devote one scintilla of thought to the Yorax. Only Lornog and Morgan knew of her concerns.

Anod hid her apprehension behind other activities. She even began to hide her black, antratite, protective suit under flowing robes with high, bunched, collars or hoods. Some people even began calling her the high priestess . . . in jest.

"Anod," said Lornog, "Bradley is calling you to New Providence."
"What for?"
"He indicated Alexatron arrived with a proposal for a special trade alliance with Beta. He has asked several citizens to attend for discussions with Alexatron and his colleagues."
"Very well." Anod knocked on Nick's bedroom door.
"Come in," came the subdued answer.
Nick lay in his bed underneath a blanket. He had not been feeling well for several days.
"How are you doing?"
"Better, I suppose, but still not too good."
"Bradley has called me to New Providence for some trade agreement brokered by Alexatron. Do you feel up to coming along?"
"No, not really."
"I shall leave Lornog here with you."
"Leave the children as well. You don't need the extra burden of tending to them."
Anod considered Nick's suggestion. On one hand, she knew they would be well taken care of, as always, but on the other, she wanted them with her. "You need to rest. I will take them with me."
"Are you sure, Anod? Between Lornog and me, we can tend to the children quite well."
"I have no doubt, but you can also get more rest, which you

desperately need, if they were not here."

"Please, Anod."

She considered his plea, but she knew what was best. "No, Nick. I want you to rest."

"Very well," he responded as he pulled the sheet and blanket up to his eyes.

"Good. Now rest."

Anod closed the door as she left the room. She also instructed Lornog to take care of Nick and keep him in bed until he felt better. They should be home for supper.

Gathering up both the children, Anod headed off to New Providence. In the interest of time, she used the interceptor with the kids stacked on her lap to move quickly. She found Bradley, Dahar, Otis and several other Murtaurians along with Alexatron and one of his colleagues who was never introduced, in a modest building that had become a public meeting place for refreshment, sustenance, conversation and exchange.

"Good-day to you, Alexatron," Anod said as she joined the group.

"And a most good-day to you, Anod. These are your children?"

"Yes. This is Zoltentok," she said placing her hand on the boy's head, "and, this is Sara," she added holding the little girl against her chest facing forward.

"Most beautiful children, Anod . . . for humans anyway."

They laughed. "Thank you," she answered as she sat at the table with them.

"We have been waiting for you," interjected Bradley. "Alexatron has brought us a trade agreement amendment from Beta. His group of Scorbions would be the traders to facilitate the transportation."

"Excellent. We have been waiting for this." Anod spoke to Alexatron. "When we left Beta, we had an alliance in principle but never took the agreement to the practical stage because of the transportation obstacle."

"Our thoughts precisely," Dahar said.

Zoltentok lost interest in the adult conversation and decided to wander around the pub. Sara continued to sit quietly on Anod's lap, scanning the group with curiosity and occasionally holding out an arm as if she was pointing at someone or something.

"You did not need me here to consent to this agreement," she said to Bradley.

"Not the trade portion. However, there is more to the agreement."

"They want your protection," Alexatron stated.

"My protection? What do the Betans think I can do, and what am I supposed to protect them against?"

Alexatron looked quickly at each of the other participants as if he expected them to answer her question. When none of them did so, he answered. "They do not want to join the Confederation as M4 has done, and you are the only one they have confidence in for their defense."

Anod took her turn looking into the eyes of each person, now looking at her. "Did I miss something? Protection against what? The Betans are a peaceful people, just as we are."

Alexatron stared at Anod intently as though he was trying to telepathically communicate with her. "The Yorax have been there twice since you left."

"That is insane. Beta is much deeper into Confederation space as defined by the Treaty of Riiza-Strogon. Why have they gone there twice? What did the Society do to enforce the frontier? Was anyone injured?"

"Anod, they know you are here."

"Then, why haven't they come here to get me?"

"That we do not know," Alexatron responded solemnly. "I happened to be on Beta during their last visit."

"So, they cooperated with the Yorax."

"Yes. They are afraid, Anod."

The group continued to keep their eyes on her. What did her husband and these other men expect of her? What did they think she could do for the Betans? She seriously doubted she would be able to defend Murtauri Four against a concerted Yorax assault. There was no way she could protect Beta, even if she moved back and remained stationed there.

"I just want to live my life in peace," she protested.

"We know," Bradley responded.

"We are trying to help," added Otis.

"Can we agree to the arrangement?" Dahar asked.

"What does that mean . . . can we agree? Does this agreement commit me to jump in my single seat interceptor and make the journey at warp nine back to Beta in two weeks to defend that place against a Yorax attack that will probably be over by the time I get there? Is that what you are asking me to agree to?"

"No."

"Perhaps, the Society . . ."

"They do not want the Society alone or as part of the Confederation." She looked sternly at Alexatron. "You said they wanted me. Now, I will tell you what I think of this agreement." She paused as if to allow a response of some kind, but she expected none. "I think this is a trap – an ambush, plain and simple. They are trying to use the Betans as bait to lure me into a response. Am I the only one who sees this?" Only Alexatron shook his big head. The Murtaurians just stared. "If this is the condition of a trade agreement with Beta, then I say, no. I want enhanced trade with Beta. I would encourage some exchange process to ensure we maintain the cultural ties of our people. However, the price is too steep. There is nothing I can do. I am no longer a warrior," she nearly growled. "I am just a mother, and why doesn't anyone understand that," she added softly as she wrapped her arms around her daughter sitting quietly in front of her.

"Mommy, are you all right?" asked Zoltentok.

Anod looked down at her son, who must have sensed her agitation and tugged on her sleeve. "Yes, son. Mommy is fine." Zoltentok felt the need to stand next to his mother and hold onto her arm. Anod scanned the group. "This is my life, now," she stated, glancing in the direction of her two children.

"Are you saying you want me to reject this trade agreement?" asked Alexatron.

"If the price entails a commitment that I must defend Beta? Yes, that is what I am saying."

"Isn't there some compromise?" Dahar asked.

"Yes. We want the trade agreement, but there is nothing I can do. I have trained two, capable warriors to defend this planet. The Betans can learn to defend themselves."

"Perhaps, you can train them," Alexatron said.

Anod stared hard for several seconds at each of the Murtauri men. "Do any of you think that is an option?"

"Maybe they have changed as we did."

Anod chuckled. "Do you really think so, Dahar?"

"I don't know, but probably not."

Again, she chuckled. "Yes, probably not."

"Could you visit them to find out?"

Her eyes bored deeply into Dahar's head. "Do you even suspect a trap? Do you have even the slightest twinge of doubt about where the Yorax are, and why they have visited Beta, our former planet . . . twice?

And, more significantly, knowing that I am here, why haven't they even come within sensor range of M4? Have you asked yourself these questions?" Anod regretted the harsh tone of her voice. Dahar Gibritzu shook his head. "If you think a visit will help anything, send Otis. He has the skills to defend himself if he is jumped, and he is capable of this assessment. The Yorax, who are most certainly going to be watching the route between Murtauri and Beta, will most likely not suspect him."

"I can do that," responded Otis with some enthusiasm. Otis quickly looked to each person hoping for some support.

Bradley kept his eyes on Anod for several seconds, and then glanced at Otis, shook his head and turned his eyes to Alexatron. "I know Otis could do this task, but I am not sure it is the correct choice. I might add, before my wife scolds me, that I agree with her. Sending Anod or committing to this trade agreement as currently defined would not be wise." He turned his eyes to Anod. "Do you think you can ask the Society for a unilateral agreement without sponsorship to include Beta under our umbrella defense covenant?"

"We continue to ask the Society to give . . . give . . . give. When will we give back to the Society and the Confederation of which we are also a part?"

"You are right, Anod. Then, I would propose Anod's suggestion is probably the correct one at this stage." He looked to Alexatron. "Are you going back to Beta?"

"I can, I suppose. I do have other plans."

"Then, I think we should send Otis, as our emissary, in the Korbon fighter, back to Beta to: one, ascertain the interests, adaptability and flexibility of the Betans; and two, negotiate a compromise agreement he can bring back to us," Bradley said as he looked to Otis, whose excitement and enthusiasm was barely contained. "You must make no agreement, implied or otherwise, with the Betans. The message to the Betans should be clear. We want a trade agreement between our two planets and peoples, however, the stipulation of Anod's protection is unreasonable and beyond her ability to deliver." Otis nodded his head in agreement. "Good." Anod nodded her head in agreement. Bradley returned to Alexatron. "There you have it. We shall dispatch Otis to Beta, so as not to interfere with your trading plans. We shall endeavor to keep you informed of our negotiations with Beta, and especially any agreement with them."

"Thank you."

They all stood. Anod clutched her children. The men shook hands with Alexatron who displayed his reluctant acquiescence to the traditional human contact. Alexatron waited for some dispersal and found Anod for a private word.

"Anod, I have the utmost respect for your skills. I must tell you, I think your instincts are correct. I felt compelled to deliver the message from Beta, but I also happen to agree with you. I think this was a not so elaborate trap orchestrated by the Yorax through the unwitting Betans. I am certain they wanted to catch you alone in space between the two star systems. You have done the wise thing."

"Thank you, Alexatron. I shall strive to keep my foot from the snare."

"You have my support, as always."

"Thank you, again."

They stood outside as Alexatron waved good-bye, boarded his craft and departed. Dahar Gibritzu left shortly thereafter. Otis waited with anticipation.

Bradley placed his hand on Otis Greenstreet's shoulder. "I would suggest you prepare for this journey and embark as soon as you are ready."

"I will."

Anod handed the now sleeping Sara to Bradley. She stepped toward Otis, embraced him tightly, and then kissed him on the lips. Anod placed her head next to his and whispered to him. "You must be careful. Take no chances. I do not want anything to happen to you. If you need help, call. I shall come to you immediately. You must return safely."

"I shall be careful," he answered then placed his massive hands on either side of her face and kissed her again. Otis shook hands with Bradley's free left hand then turned from them.

Bradley kissed Anod as well. "Let me take the children. Why don't you take the interceptor for a little sprint into space? We have time before supper."

"Your father is still not feeling well. I really should get home."

"You know how long it will take me and the children to reach home. You take that time for a little flight. Lornog is more than capable of helping father."

Anod considered his suggestion. He was, of course, correct. Some dashes about the near space would help relieve some of the tension she felt. Her mind also felt the need for her own scan of space using the interceptor's sensors. She nodded her head in agreement, kissed both children, and then kissed Bradley again. Anod watched her family leave before she mounted her interceptor and flew off into space.

Chapter 10

The diffuse light from the window dimly illuminated their bedroom. They woke up together with their warm flesh touching in many places. They embraced without words. The muffled sounds of both children along with the instigating levity of Nick and the attention of Lornog told them the situation outside their bedroom door was under control.

"Well, Otis is on his way," Bradley finally said.

"Yes, he is."

"Do you think he will be successful?"

Anod pushed her apprehension about Otis' mission aside. "I think so."

Their touching became more purposeful.

"What do you want to do today?" Bradley asked as her hand went to specific places and his hand idly passed over the smooth skin covering her firm muscles.

"I thought we would try again to make a baby."

"Now?"

"Yes. It is that time of my cycle."

"But, it is time to get up," Bradley protested weakly.

"The children are in good hands." Her hand made her determination quite clear. "We have no commitments this morning."

Bradley smiled and focused himself on the task at hand. As was usually the case, he saw to her pleasure first and continued to caress her until she returned to him. They joined. He moved slowly, with extra care to allow her another rise. She began to move with him, to enhance his efforts. She was rewarded with another climax before Bradley attained his own pinnacle and left his essence deep within her. She kept him to her until their passion subsided and their hearts returned to normal.

"That should do it," she whispered.

"I am glad to be of service."

"And, a great service man you are."

They tickled each other and played to heighten their warmth. They enjoyed their moment of peace and companionship even more in the light of their infrequent occurrence. They tended to savor those moments they found scattered among the events of life.

ANOD'S REDEMPTION 175

"I suppose we should join our family," Anod said softly into Bradley's chest.

"I suppose."

They played as they dressed then joined the others in the main room. The usual excitement greeted them. The others had already eaten breakfast, and it was nearly time for lunch. Anod and Bradley scrounged up a few scrapes to tide them over.

"Anod, Mysasha Nagoyama sent a message this morning. She has asked for your assistance."

"What does she need?"

"She wants you to help her with some technology procedures."

Anod stared at Nick trying to determine if he was teasing her or not. "She lives on the other side of the mountains," she said as if neither of the men knew where she lived. "It will be more than a day's journey unless I take the interceptor or have Anton pick me up with the shuttlecraft. Can't Lornog help her?"

"She does not want to talk to anyone else. She trusts only you."

"She delivered both our children," Bradley added, taking his turn to remind Anod of what she already knew.

Now Anod stared at Bradley. She did not want to leave home. Anod also recognized her loyalty to Mysasha. The midwife had done more than deliver her two children. She was a good friend.

"When does she want me at her place?"

"Her message said as soon as it is convenient," answered Nick.

"Why don't you take the interceptor?" Bradley suggested.

Anod considered the option. "I think it would be better to save the fuel rather than have to refuel soon. I will call Anton."

Before she could turn her head toward the console and speak to Morgan, he spoke to her. "Anton reported ready and available. He could be here in thirty minutes."

Anod sneered at the console as though her dissatisfaction with his efficiency would be noticed. "I want to play with the children, Morgan. Please ask Anton to be at the interceptor hangar in an hour and notify Mysasha I will join her," she paused to calculate the flight time to the Nagoyama residence, "in ninety minutes."

"As you wish," answered Morgan.

"It will be evening time there," Bradley added.

"Yes, I know. If she has no objection, I can probably answer their questions and teach them the necessary procedures within a few hours . .

. before their sleep time. Then, I can return home by supper time."

"That sounds reasonable," said Bradley.

Anod rose from the table. Before she could reach the door, Morgan responded. "Anton indicates he will be at the interceptor hangar at the appointed time, and Mysasha agrees to your arrival. She wants to pass her sincerest appreciation for your accommodation of her request."

"Thank you, Morgan."

Anod found Lornog with the children playing around Zoltentok's little fort. She sat down next to the fort and was promptly hit by Zoltentok's charging body. She embraced him as she fell back into a layer of leaves. She kissed and tickled him until he began to push back to escape her grasp. Anod stopped her movement then grasp his head, holding it just above hers. "I love you, little boy," she whispered as her eyes watered, and she kissed him again.

"I love you, Mommy," he said, then placed his head on her chest and hugged her.

Anod sat up and helped her son to his feet. "Now, you defend the fort while I give your sister some loving."

"As you command, Mommy," Zoltentok said as he spun away and leapt to the fort.

Anod held her arms out to Lornog. He delivered the fidgeting girl to her mother's arms. Anod swallowed her into her embrace. Anod watched her eyes move as she kissed the tiny girl. When Sara began to fuss a little, Anod lifted her to an erect position. Sara could stand without support and spouted her gurgling pride with each accomplishment. Anod held her hands and pulled her gently forward. Sara responded by placing one foot forward and then another in an effort to balance herself.

"She will walk any day, now," Anod announced.

"I think you are correct."

"The odd thing, Lornog, is I cannot remember ever feeling such reward as I do watching these children grow and learn about the world around them."

"I can only trust your words."

"Let there be no doubt, there is nothing better in all the Universe."

"As you say, then."

"I must go to the Nagoyama residence, soon. I wanted to play with the children before I left."

"So, you are going to satisfy Mysasha's request?"

"Yes."

"I suggested it would be more appropriate for me to respond, but Mysasha said, no. She wants only you."

"I can understand. It is a good sign actually. She and her family are recognizing the benefits, and are ready to use these devices," she said waving her arm toward the house.

"Would you like me to go with you?"

Anod tried to think of the balance between his assistance to her and to the family. "No, thank you. I think it would be better if you were here since I am not taking the children."

"Where are you going?" Zoltentok asked from the top of his fort.

"I am going to Mysasha's house."

"Can I go?"

"Not this time, Zoltentok. It will be nighttime there, and Mysasha's children will be asleep. Mommy wants to make the trip as quickly as possible."

Zoltentok nodded his like head. "OK, Mommy. I shall take care of things here until you return."

"Thank you, my big little man."

Zoltentok smiled and returned to his tasks. The Murtauri star was nearly at its zenith on its daily passing across the sky. The wind was beginning to increase. The trees began to sing and dance in the breeze. Anod rose to her feet and handed Sara to Lornog.

"There may be a storm coming."

"You are correct. Morgan estimates the rain should reach us in another hour or so."

"I had better be going. Take care of everyone," she said without knowing why.

"As you command," Lornog responded.

Anod went inside. As had become her habit on journeys away from home, she donned her antratite, protective suit and a flowing, light brown, robe to hide the menacing appearance of the suit. She kissed Nick and Bradley, and then kissed both children again before entering the forest. As she crossed the stream, she saw the shuttle landing beyond the trees. Anod made her way through the remaining patch of trees to find Anton Trikinov walking around the shuttlecraft in front of the interceptor's hangar.

"Thank you for the special mission, Anton."

Trikinov continued his scrutiny of the machine. "No problem, Anod . . . gives me an excuse to fly."

"Anything to be of assistance," she bubbled. "Now, can we get on with this?"

"Sure."

They loaded up and locked the hatch behind them. Anod thoroughly enjoyed sitting beside Anton and watching her student perform. He actually had a natural flow to his actions. Without the slightest doubt or hesitation, Anton found the perfect landing spot next to the Nagoyama house. By the time they exited the vehicle, Mysasha and her husband, Hyoshi, were waiting for them outside their front door.

"Good evening to you, Mysasha . . . Hyoshi," Anod said loudly across the five-meter distance between them.

They waited until she walked closer. "And, a very good evening to you, Anod," responded Hyoshi. "I see you decided to come in your limousine," he said nodding toward the shuttlecraft. "How are you this evening Anton?"

"Just fine, Mister Nagoyama. Anod gave me an excuse to fly the machine."

"So, you have become accustomed to these machines?"

"For the most part, yes."

"Please come in," Hyoshi said motioning toward the open door.

"How are you, Mysasha?" Anod asked softly, as Anton followed Hyoshi.

"Fine, thank you."

They kissed each cheek, and then Anod followed Mysasha into the house. The door was closed behind them. Hyoshi motioned for them to sit at their dining table as Mysasha served tea. They talked about the weather, the improvement in the crops, but it was the discussion of children that thinned Anod's patience.

"I understand you want to use some of the new devices," she said.

Mysasha nodded her head. Hyoshi stared at her for several seconds as though she had rudely interrupted an important topic. He then looked toward his wife.

Mysasha spoke for them. "We have heard from Guyasaga and a few others that you can sleep fewer hours and actually be more rested."

"Yes, that is true."

"I worry about what the machine is doing to me while I sleep," Hyoshi said.

"The best testament I have available is myself. I have used isopods virtually my entire life. If anything, they have extended and improved my life . . . not hindered it."

"And, a fine example you are," interjected Anton.

Anod did not respond to Trikinov's comment. "The isopod, along with Morgan, examines your entire body and can even do minor repairs, like small cuts, contusions, or muscle injuries." It actually did much more, but she did not want to go too far too soon.

"Is that why you must be without clothing?" asked Mysasha.

Anod nodded her head. "Yes. While the isopod will work in its most fundamental mode, clothing disrupts the energy fields it uses to probe, evaluate and repair your body."

"But, naked? Anyone could see you in there."

"As I said, you do not have to be naked. You can also program your pod to make the cover opaque, if you so choose."

"We cannot sleep together," Hyoshi observed.

"No."

"If both of us are in our isopods, how do we tend to the children when they wake up?" asked Mysasha.

"Well, there are perhaps several options. In our case, Lornog is awake continuously, and he is quite capable to tending to the children."

"But, you cannot have them at breast."

"No. However, that is no different than if you are on a journey without them."

"Of course."

"You can also alternate using the pods. You can place the children in their own isopods. The only limitation is, I would not recommend you both use isopods without the children also using them or having an android help you. A rapid awakening will not harm you, but it will cause an inordinate amount of fatigue."

"We want to try them," said Mysasha. "We have heard that they extend your workday. They could help Hyoshi and the older boys work more ground for all of us."

"All true."

Mysasha looked to Hyoshi for several seconds then back to Anod. "Would you be so kind to show me exactly how to use this isopod?"

"Yes, by all means."

Mysasha lowered her head.

Anton understood. "I shall wait for you in the shuttlecraft," he said then left.

Hyoshi was the first to stand. Anod and Mysasha followed him into their sleeping room. They had a low, conventional bed as Anod and Bradley did. Their two isopods occupied opposite sidewalls. The room was filled with a subtle, fruit blossom fragrance.

Mysasha began to shuffle her feet slightly as she kept her head lowered to avoid making any eye contact. "It is embarrassing," she whispered.

"Would you feel better if I demonstrated the isopod?" Anod asked as she began to pull her robe off.

Mysasha noticed the black plates of Anod's antratite suit and remembered why. "No. You should not. It is just that I have never been naked in front of another person other than my husband."

Hyoshi stood in the middle of the room with his arms folded across his chest. He was obviously not going to participate as anything other than an observer. Anod had never been close to Hyoshi, and this was another illustration of why. Mysasha began to remove her clothing. Anod stopped her.

"You do not need to disrobe, Mysasha. I can show you everything you need to know about the operation of the isopod."

"Thank you, Anod, but I want to do everything correctly. I shall swallow my pride and reluctance. You have always set this example for me."

Mysasha was visibly uncomfortable, but she endured. Hyoshi did not budge a muscle. Anod moved as though nothing had changed which was her way.

They started with the cleansing station. Mysasha had never used it. Anod tried to describe every action before it occurred and every sensation she would feel, so that the devices did not surprise her. By the time her cleaning cycle was complete, Mysasha was far more relaxed, animated and less inhibited. Both women ignored Hyoshi. Anod stepped through each command as she taught Mysasha to program the isopod to do everything it was supposed to do except induce Mysasha's deep sleep. She stepped through each action one more time, again describing exactly what would happen and what she would feel. Mysasha showed some uneasiness when the isopod cover descended, but she began to giggle like a little girl when her body rose effortlessly within the chamber.

"This is absolutely fascinating," said Mysasha.

"You should feel no pressure, no weight, no connection with the physical world."

"That is exactly what I feel. This is amazing."

"Normally, at this point, the isopod would begin your sleep cycle," Anod explained. Mysasha turned her head to make eye contact with Anod. "As the process begins, you would feel a sensation of everything draining from you, and yet feel a warm flush as your consciousness is removed."

"Will it feel like I am dying?"

Anod chuckled. "I have never died, so I do not know what it feels like." They both laughed. "However, I imagine, logically, that the sensations are probably similar except for the warmth."

"Then, how will I feel when I come out of the cycle?"

"First, while you are in the cycle, you have no sensations whatsoever. All your sensory nervous activity will be suspended."

"Will I dream?"

"Normally, no. Your brain functions are suspended as the device maintains those involuntary impulses required to sustain and refresh you. There is a mode that will induce dreams. It is not as restful, but it does serve a function in creative thought. Few people use that mode. I do not believe I have ever used it. I suppose I should try it sometime."

"I don't think I will use it either until you can tell me what is involved."

Anod nodded her head. "Anyway, when you come out of the sleep cycle, the process is simply reversed. Your awareness returns and the sensations of life refill your body."

"I am curious."

"Once you have tried it a few times, you will gain confidence, and I am certain you will appreciate the advantages."

Mysasha extricated herself from the isopod, hugged Anod, and then dressed. "What if something happens to the isopod, or Morgan, or the power supply while you are in the sleep cycle?"

"Good question. There are many fail-safe modes. The worst that will happen is a rapid awakening."

"Then, fatigue."

"Yes."

"So, it is safe."

"Yes."

"How do we tell the system to monitor what is going on outside and to wake us if something is wrong?"

"Simply tell Morgan what you want. He will repeat back your instructions to make sure they are what you want. If you would like, I can ask Lornog to begin constructing an android for you."

"No, not yet. I think we shall alternate using the isopod, at first, so one of us can deal with the children if they wake up during the night."

"As you say, then," Anod said.

"Do you want to try it, Hyoshi?"

He looked stern and disinterested. "No. Later."

Mysasha spoke to her husband. "I think you will like this. This will help you feel better, and as Anod says, it will help you recover faster from the rigors of your field labor."

"Then, I shall be happy."

Mysasha led them into the main room. "We have even begun to use the replicator, although we are not relying on it."

"Good," answered Anod. "The more you use these devices and gain confidence in them, the more you will see their benefits. I believe they enhance the quality of our lives, not detract from them."

"I am beginning to see your point," Mysasha responded.

"Good. Is there anything more I can do for you this evening?"

"I don't think so. Thank you, Anod, for taking time to come see us and help us. Hyoshi and I will use the isopods, and tell you of our experience. Perhaps in a few days or weeks, you can come back or one of us will come to you so we can share more."

"Perfect, for me."

They said their good-byes, and Anod joined Anton in the shuttlecraft. They departed as they had arrived. Once enroute back to Meganville, Anod turned to Anton. "Lornog could have done that," she said.

"Sure, but Lornog would not have made the connection with them that you did. They have confidence in you. They are not so sure of Lornog with such intimate tasks."

"I suppose, but he is a very helpful person."

"But, he is not a person, is he?"

"No, technically, he is not, but I think of him as a person."

"Maybe the rest of us will as well, one day."

"No problems?"

"None for me. I assume your demonstration and training session went well."

"Yes, it did, Anton. Thank you. It was good to see them, although I have not gotten through to Hyoshi Nagoyama, yet."

Anton laughed. "I don't think anyone has other than Mysasha."

Anod watched him fly for several minutes, glanced outside at the terrain passing beneath them, and then back to Anton.

"Is something bothering you?" he asked.

"Why have you been so distant?"

Anton stared at her without expression, "you are very direct."

"Yes I am," she answered then just watched him waiting for an answer.

He focused his eyes on some point ahead of the craft. "You have talked to me about this before in New Providence."

"Yes I have."

"As I told you, I just like living alone."

"That is not what I ask?"

Anton glanced at Anod then back outside. "Do you suspect me of something?"

"That is not my place. There has been all this discussion about the Yorax, and I look for activities or action that are out of place or do not seem normal."

"So, I am not normal."

"You tell me."

"I am not sure what I have done to upset you, but believe me I have done nothing wrong nor have I done anything to deserve your suspicions."

Anod's eyes surgically dissected her subject, watched every twitch and blink. She did not detect even the slightest sign of deceit. Was her suspicion misplaced? Was she overreacting to some related stimulus? She decided to back off. "I guess my worries have clouded my judgment. I am sorry if I have offended you."

Anton glanced at her then nodded his head in agreement. "We're here," he said then made the proper control inputs.

They approached the mountains that marked the location of Meganville and her family. Anton maneuvered the craft for landing. Anod looked out the forward canopy transparency at the mountain peaks darkening in the descending dusk. Instead of making a buttonhook turn for landing, Anton decided to land straight ahead over the top of the interceptor hangar. Anton gently landed the craft.

"Thank you for transporting me, Anton. Why don't you stay? Supper should be just about ready. You are most welcome to eat with us."

"Thank you, Anod, for the invitation, but I think I need to get home and take advantage of the isopod myself."

Anod laughed. "I think I understand. Thank you, again." She

saw Anton nod his head in agreement, turned to open the rear docking hatch and stepped out into the cool evening air. The partially open hangar door caught her attention. She jumped to the door. The scorched and broken remains of the interceptor covered the floor. Her heart leapt into her throat and pounded hard. "Oh God," she bellowed. "The kids."

Anod sprang back to the shuttlecraft. "Get out of here, now," she shouted. "Do not come back until I call you."

"What . . . ?"

"I said, now!" she commanded in a strong but cold, harsh voice short of a shout.

Anod disappeared in a flash. As fast as her long legs would move, she ran hard like a panther weaving through the trees, around rocks, and jumped the stream in two long bounds using one small rock. Her instincts grabbed her. Anod froze and crouched near a large tree. She struggled to control her heaving chest and silence her breathing. She methodically searched the entire area.

Nothing moved. The house was dark – not a sliver of light – not even a wisp of smoke from the chimney. The door was open, beckoning to her. Anod checked the ground in front of the house. The distinctive triangular tracks of Yorax troopers mottled the dirt.

Anod burst from her position, sprinting toward the door. Her sensitive eyes picked up the bloody tracks on the porch. Anod spun around several times in a semi-crouched, defensive position. She scanned everything in sight. If the Yorax were out there, they would have rushed her by now.

She smoothly stepped inside and immediately slid away from the open door that would silhouette her. "Nooooo!" she screamed in a near howling groan as her eyes absorbed the scene.

Blood covered everything. She stepped toward the first bare leg she saw and immediately slipped in the blood, falling hard on her back. She deftly returned to her feet and ignored the pain in her wrist and back. It was Bradley's leg. Anod tried to ignore the wounds and injuries. Bradley was dead. His body was cold. The surrounding blood was thick and still slippery. She found Nick in the same state.

"Oh, God, please not the children," she said aloud. They were not in the main room.

Anod checked the children's bedroom. Nothing! She checked Nick's room. Nothing! She pushed open her sleep room door only to be greeted with spatters of blood everywhere, but no bodies.

"Where are the children?" she whispered to herself. "Where is Lornog?"

Anod thought of Morgan. The interface console was smashed into unrecognizable bits. Anod considered turning on a light but decided against it. She returned to Bradley. He was completely naked, and his head and genitals were missing. Sharp, crisp gashes covered his entire body. The leg she had seen first was the only part of his body that was not wounded. His other leg and one arm had compound fractures, the bones protruding from his flesh. The gaping wound at his groin nearly thrust her stomach out her mouth. Everywhere there was blood and signs of blunt force trauma as well as sharp, knife-like wounds. Bradley had suffered a very slow, agonizing death. The blood around numerous stab wounds was dark and dried. There was very little blood around his neck. He had been decapitated after he died. Anod knew his head would be somewhere close-by, probably with a message of some sort.

She went to Nick. The old man's death had only been slightly more merciful. He was naked as well with multiple wounds and signs of blunt force trauma, but at least he had not been broken up and dismembered. Nick's resistance had been less and thus received less sadistic attention from the Yorax.

Something touched her shoulder. Anod spun in a blur and thrust the heal of her right hand into the chest of the dark body. The heavy thud marked the fall. Anod leapt over the body to apply a *coup de grâce*, if necessary. It was only then she saw his face – Anton Trikinov. He was struggling for air. Terror filled his eyes, as he lay virtually helpless from her disabling blow.

Anod knelt beside him, leaned forward, placed her mouth over his and blew into his chest. His convulsions subsided as his breathing returned to normal. Anton took two deep breaths as if he was recovering from a near drowning. The shock and fear drained from his eyes. He coughed several times as he tried to gain control of his body.

"Anton, I told you to leave," she protested.

He tried to speak. It took him a couple of attempts before he could say, "I heard your scream."

Anod tried to smile to ease his concern. "Anton, listen to me. The Yorax have been here. Bradley and Nick are dead. I have not found my children or Lornog, but I suspect they may be dead as well."

"I want to help you."

"No, Anton. You cannot help me. They will surely come back

here. Maybe tomorrow morning . . . maybe in a few days, but they will come back. If you are anywhere near me, you will be killed."

"But, Anod, you need help . . . ."

"No. There is nothing you can do here. The best help you can give me is, stay alive. You tell our people the Yorax are here, but do not tell them what you have seen here or what you know about me. You must stay out of sight, and you must leave as quickly as possible. The longer the shuttlecraft remains here, the more they will suspect you know my whereabouts. Anton, you must leave, now."

"But, Anod . . . ," he said and stopped as she pulled him to his feet. He wobbled somewhat as his cardiovascular system struggled to return to normal.

"I appreciate your concern, but I need you alive, in case I need you and the shuttlecraft in the future. Now, Anton, listen to me carefully." She paused for him to nod his head. "You will probably be stopped by the Yorax. They know you were here. You must convince yourself you have not seen this. You must convince them you were on a routine training flight, decided to stop here, found no one at the hangar, and then you departed. Try to erase any memory of what you have seen or of me. You can tell no one . . . no one, Anton . . . do you understand?" Again, she waited for his agreement. "If you get back to your place, hangar the shuttle and do not leave. I will come to you, when I need you."

"I understand. I will do as you command."

"Good."

"I shall be ready to fight when you call."

Anod placed her left hand on his shoulder. "I know you will, Anton. But, you must do as I have said, now."

"I will."

"Remember, once you get back home, tell the others the Yorax are here. Try not to resist and do not send a message to the Society. Any action on your part like that will be seen as an act of aggression, and they will respond harshly. They must feel they have me cornered. They will tighten the snare until they have me. No matter what happens, do what I have told you . . . until you know for certain I am dead."

"You shall not die."

"No, Anton," she sneered. "I intend to finish this."

"I will be ready."

"Good. Now, go, and do not deviate. Go straight home and stay there. Run!"

Anton nodded his head and left.

Anod turned back to scan the ugly scene laid out before her. The mounting darkness had not exceeded the capability of her sensitive eyes. "Oh, Bradley," she began to cry, "what have they done to us?"

Anod touched his cold corpse then moved to the back door. She hesitated. Her mind blasted an image of what she suspected she would find on the other side. "Please let the worst be that the children were captured and held hostage. Please, please, do not let me find them here," she whispered as if to some friend who would do the searching.

She opened the door. A violent burst of nausea expelled from her as she fell to her knees, when she saw Bradley's head on a post two meters directly out the back door. She vomited several times. His eyes had frozen wide open. They had stuffed his genitals into his mouth, and a spike protruded from the top of his head. Anod fought to control her body. When she finally gathered the strength to stand, she noticed a piece of paper had been impaled at the top of the spike. Anod removed the paper as tears began to stream from her eyes. "Oh, Bradley, my sweet Bradley, what have they done to you?"

Written in blood as though from an ancient fountain pen was the message:

Your companions are dead.
You are dead.
Come to me.
Z

"Oh Bradley," she cried as she tried to close his eyes without success.

Anod folded the paper and placed it in a pocket. She scanned the area. The leaves had been stirred. Large scrapes were evident in the dirt. There had been a mighty struggle. She saw a foot. As she approached, more parts of what once had been Lornog began to appear. As she rounded the corner of the house, she saw the casing of Lornog's severed left arm with the wires, cables and other devices. She brushed the leaves away. The android's hand still clutched a small human hand.

The strength in her legs vanished. "Oh, no . . . no, no no," she said as her voice faded to a whisper. Anod cried . . . cried so hard as she tried to stifle her scream she induced a bone numbing vomiting episode.

Her stomach heaved without result as she buried her face in the dirt beneath her. She cried until there was nothing left inside her.

In the dark of simple starlight, Anod found the courage to move the leaves covering the limp body. "Oh my little boy. I am so sorry," she wailed. Zoltentok had mercifully died instantly from a single blast to the center of his chest. Anod gently caressed his cold cheek. "Oh Zoltentok. Why did they do this to you?"

A slight movement attracted Anod's attention to a pile of branches and leaves. She crawled to the pile. She reached for the closest branch then froze. With all the loss she had suffered this day, could she stand any more? Sara was the only member of her family not accounted for in this massacre. Anod wanted this to be a mound of dirt, or some small creature rummaging around under the leaves. Her instincts told her she was not to realize any luck this day.

Slowly, Anod pulled the branches away. It was Sara. In a blur, she threw the remaining branches and leaves aside. The gash across her throat told the story. Sara blinked her eyes. She was still alive. Anod gently lifted Sara's cool body into her arms and close to her chest. The little girl's mouth moved as if she was trying to say some words or cry out, but only the hiss of expelled air from the gash could be heard. Anod could feel Sara trying to move her arms without success. Anod cradled her and touched her. Sara's shirt and clothes were red from her blood. Sara continued to blink her eyes and move her mouth as Anod's mind raced through any possible means to save her little girl's life. The last threads of life flowed from her body. Anod knew there was nothing she could do other than hold her close.

Sara peacefully closed her eyes. In another few minutes, her tiny chest stopped moving. Anod held her daughter's lifeless body until dawn began to lighten the sky.

A cold rage replaced the grief and sense of total loss. Everything she lived for had been destroyed. She was no longer in the service of the Society as a lieutenant in the elite Kartog Guards. The family she had learned to love and especially the two children she had given birth to and suckled beyond infancy were gone. Even the android the Society had assigned to her had been eliminated. All of this loss at the hand of one savage madman – Zitger – former captain in the Kartog Guards, and now self professed General Negolian of the Yorax.

A cold purpose replaced her grief. With detached determination, Anod moved all the bodies including Lornog's parts into the house. For some strange unexplainable reason she did not understand, Anod moved Nick's body nearest the kitchen with his feet facing the front door. She adjusted Bradley's position beside his father and placed his head at the top of his torso. Next, she arranged Zoltentok and Sara. Lastly, just to the right of Sara, she placed all the parts she could find that once defined Lornog. It took her nearly an hour to find Lornog's head. Fortunately for her, it had only been severed. Oddly, Zitger either failed to recall the construction techniques of Society androids, or perhaps, did not feel he needed to worry about such things.

Anod found a blue, canvas bag the family had often used to carry picnic items and placed Lornog's inanimate head in it and tied it tight. If she ever did link up with the Society, they could connect the head and recover the entire memory of the android. They would be able to reconstruct Lornog's observations up to his termination including the visual scenes around him. For Anod, it was a precaution, not something she needed or intended to use for her purpose.

The former Kartog Guards warrior checked every space of the house as well as the entire area within ten meters of the house to ensure she had everything. She collected a few clothes including her spare antratite suit, several variations of dark clothing and other items she might need for her mission. With her backpack and the blue canvas bag at a safe distance outside, Anod doused everything inside the house with a flammable fuel and dispensed a stream out of the house. Without a moment's hesitation, Anod ignited the stream. The house exploded in fire. She stood in front of the house in the searing heat until she was convinced the entire house was involved and unrecoverable. She grabbed a branch and obliterated the Yorax tracks in the dirt. Only she and Anton would know what happened for the time being.

Anod pulled the antratite helmet over her head, moved quickly into the forest, evaluated the avenues of approach, and found a proper position with cover and concealment. She sat there patiently for the visitors she knew would come to investigate the fire.

The house had collapsed but was still burning when the first Murtaurians arrived. Tung Wan Foo led the first contingent of six from New Providence. They ran around the remains several times and recognized the futility of any effort. Others began to arrive. Several feebly threw dirt into the fire. One even threw a bucket of water, all to no avail. They looked into the forest around them. It was not until four Yorax troopers appeared that she felt the urge to move.

Anod watched intently, keeping track of each trooper. The Murtaurians retreated to the edge of the forest to avoid any confrontation with the Yorax. Two of the troopers found long sticks to probe the smoldering remnants. One of the probers turned and spoke in their irritating, screeching, string of sounds like a very angry dolphin. The other prober went to him. They were in the area of what was once the main room of her house. The other two troopers began pushing the Murtaurians away. Tung Wan Foo was a little too slow to move and resisted more than he should have, and nearly got killed.

She waited patiently like some big cat waiting for the correct moment to ensure success. Once the two security troopers were confident the Murtaurians had left the area, they returned to assist their comrades poking through the smoldering ash of the SanGiocomo house.

The screeching sounds conveyed agitation. All four began looking around. They probably figured out the human remains of two adults and two children, plus the mechanical remains of an android, arranged in a line and not in the positions they were left after the massacre, meant someone else had done the work. They also probably recognized that whomever arranged the bodies and set the fire had not been detected by their sensors. The facts as they collected them, added up to danger. With their light rifles at the ready, the Yorax troopers began an expanding search out from the ash pile.

Anod adjusted her position as she carefully watched the movements of the Yorax troopers. Her mind continuously calculated her options. She had no urge to run. If she died here, then she intended to die with honor and courage.

One trooper passed within several meters of her. Anod considered the distance and chose to remain frozen in the dark shadows. Their method of search would bring the next trooper nearly upon her. That would be the one.

The process took a couple of minutes. As the next Yorax trooper approached in all his large clumsiness, Anod quickly checked the positions of the other three. One had line of sight. The other two were fleeting and perhaps ten to twenty meters away. She waited for the approaching trooper's scan to turn his head away from her. She took the moment to refine her position. Anod could hear his footfalls in the leaves.

The hapless Yorax trooper stepped first one pace, then another, past her. Anod sprang toward his head and upper torso. She hit him at the same time her powerful arms grasped the egg shaped head and twisted it sharply. The trooper fell to the ground like a sack of flour without a whisper. The thud of his fall alerted the others.

Anod snapped up her victim's rifle. With cold precision, she fired, hitting the second trooper squarely in the chest. He fell dead. The third trooper managed to find a tree for cover before she could fire her second shot. She aimed toward the fourth. Nothing. Shifting back to the third, she waited. Anod knew time would be on their side. She had to end this quickly. She found a rock and threw it several meters from her into a small group of larger rocks. The bouncing clatter proved too much to resist. The third trooper exposed a shoulder. She fired. The pain sent him to his knees, and unfortunately for him, exposed his head. Anod fired again with surgical precision.

A flash attracted her attention. The fourth Yorax was running, not trying to defend himself. Anod sprang like a graceful cat, sprinting as hard as she could. She gained on the now fearful trooper. He continued to make no attempt to defend himself. His only focus was escape.

Anod caught him before he could reach the stream. At the proper moment, she jumped onto his back forcing him to stumble and fall not quite to the water's edge. She struck him once in the middle of his back. He screeched in pain and flipped in a futile attempt to fend off his attacker. Anod sharply hit his throat stopping all sound other than his thrashing in the leaves. Anod then hit him as hard and swiftly as she could in the middle of his chest. He doubled in mortal pain. She waited until his writhing gave her the target she sought. In a blur, Anod hit him between his scared, bile green eyes. All movement stopped other than the heaving of her chest. Anod kept her striking arm cocked until she was absolutely certain there was no life in the Yorax trooper.

Although she had no means to tell whether they had been able to send a warning, Anod had no choice but to assume they had had time to send out the alert. Without regard to her safety and with the intent to send a clear message of her own, she dragged each of the dead Yorax troopers back toward the ash pile, arranged them in a neat little row, and quickly covered the tracks and death spots.

With her task complete, Anod took one last look at the scene. She bowed toward the ash pile, retrieved her baggage, and then moved smoothly into the forest and toward the mountains. She was careful to leave no trace of her passage. She stopped every hundred meters or so to listen intently. On her fifth assessment stop, she heard the screams of more Yorax. The dead troopers had sent the alert. If Zitger attended the death site, he would certainly know it had been Anod's work. Nonetheless, she needed sometime to think things through carefully, to plan her next moves, and to ready herself for the battle that would most assuredly come to this planet. Her salvation would come. The memory of her family rested solely in her survival. Her margin of error had nearly vanished.

Chapter 11

Anod spent several days in the seclusion of a remote cove toward the headwaters of a large mountain lake. She tried to focus on honing her martial skills even more. Memories of all she lost kept creeping back into her consciousness. She fought with her memories. She cried for her loss in all its selfishness. She cried for her children and their innocence. Her thoughts became her immediate adversary. Memories were distractions for her, now. Thoughts of her family would never bring them back, plus they would not help her on her final mission.

She tried to sleep during the day in a cool recessed scoop in the rocks near the lake's edge. At night, Anod watched the heavens and refined her skills. The Yorax battlecruiser orbited the planet in a moderately inclined orbit and apparently made no attempt to mask its presence. Why hadn't she received any warning? Why had their early warning system failed to alert them? What had happened? They must have figured out how to compromise Morgan. How could they disregard the Society? She began to imagine the Yorax occupying the Society in one or more other areas along the frontier. That could be the only explanation for their disregard of defensive measures.

On the fourth day since the massacre, Anod began an ascent of the highest mountain in the region. Early on the sixth day, she reached the summit. The weather was near perfect. She could see several hundred kilometers in every direction including both sides of the mountain range.

Black and gray columns of smoke marked spots of Yorax destruction. No smoke appeared in or around New Providence. To Anod, that observation meant the Yorax trap for her was probably there. She tried to pinpoint the sites of the smoke. Who had been hit? How many more deaths would there be?

"It is time for the hunted to become the hunter," she growled with stone cold termination aloud as if to some unseen friend then started down the mountain.

The descent took half the time of the ascent. Anod took another few days to complete her preparations. She found a straight, hardwood staff, sharpened one end and rounded the other end.

Eight days after the tragedy, Anod gave herself the luxury of a languishing bath in the cold mountain water. She dried, dressed, and checked her antratite suit before she gathered up her belongings, and headed out of the mountains. Her first stop would be Guyasaga's house.

As she had become accustomed, Anod moved at night when her senses offered the greatest advantage. She cautiously walked out of the mountains. She avoided all living creatures. Once she arrived, she watched Guyasaga's house and surrounding area for a day and a night. Activities appeared to be perfectly normal.

Early in the morning on the following day, Anod waited for Guyasaga to venture away from the house alone. The woman who had been a wet nurse to Zoltentok while Anod defended Beta went to the river 200 meters from their house. Anod moved like a predator, keeping sufficient distance to remain undetected, but close enough to observe everything around Guyasaga. The sturdy, black woman took a bath in the river. Anod waited until she was finished and dressed. Anod purposely rustled some bushes. The sound startled Guyasaga, but recognition came quickly.

"My God, woman, where have you been?"

"I suppose you know what happened?"

"Yes, dear," she said as tears came to her eyes. "I am so sorry. What they did was savage, cruel and deserves to be severely punished."

Anod cracked a slight grin although there was not a scintilla of humor. "They shall indeed be punished. I am going to end this."

"Oh, Anod. I am so sorry for you," she repeated. "We have been worried sick about you. No one knew whether you were alive, or dead as well." She paused. "Then, we figured you were alive and somewhere since the Yorax were burning and killing, and clearly still searching for you."

"Yes, they are, but it is my turn."

"Good for you."

"I shall not compromise you or your family, Guyasaga. I am afraid I must ask you to tell no one of my existence or our meeting. I came to you because your homestead appeared, as yet, untouched by the Yorax, and I need some intelligence."

"What do you want to know?"

"Have they established a headquarters or base of operations on the planet?"

"Yes, outside New Providence. I have seen it. They brought several rectangular buildings, put them together, and put fences and guards around it."

"Good."

"Good?"

"Yes. That is where they will take me and interrogate me before they intend to kill me."

"Anod!" Guyasaga said in shock.

"Do not worry. They shall not succeed."

"What are you going to do?"

"I am going to hunt them down and thin them out a little before I go to the complex."

"Why?"

"They must know I am hunting them."

"But, won't that intensify their revenge upon our people?"

"Perhaps, Guyasaga. I will do my best to protect our people, but in war, there are causalities, including innocent people in the wrong place at the wrong time."

Guyasaga stared at Anod for several seconds. "What if they come here?"

"Do not defy them too much. You will need to judge what you must do to appear resistive, but eventually helpful to their purpose. That way, they will not likely harm you, your family or your home."

"Many have already been killed and their houses burned."

"I know. I have seen the smoke from the mountains."

"They have killed many, Anod," she repeated.

"I shall try my best to protect you, but I cannot move as fast as they can. That is why you must not resist them too much."

Guyasaga nodded her head. She clearly was not happy with the situation. Her sense of protection for her family was in direct conflict with her sympathy for and loyalty to Anod.

"Do you know anything about their patrols or their search patterns?"

A scream from the direction of the house ended their conversation and sent Guyasaga running. Anod first searched everything around her. She moved as quickly as she could without making any sounds. She heard more screams. They were not screams of pain or loss, but fright. By the time Anod reached a concealed observation spot, Guyasaga stood defiantly with her arms behind her and four of her younger children huddling behind her. Samuel, her husband, stood with his head down and the other two older children beside him. There were two troopers, their deactivated land scooters several meters away. In their squeaky version of the Society's language, they interrogated the family. They were indeed looking for her. She smiled. This was too easy, she told herself.

Anod evaluated the ground between her and her prey. It was mostly bare dirt or covered with short grass. There did not appear to be any branches or other objects that might make an alerting noise.

The troopers had intelligence that Guyasaga was a friend of Anod. They hit her several times. Guyasaga tried to protect her children rather than herself. The Yorax started several times to drag her away, only to be met each time by the passive resistance of her family. This was not going to turn out well if Anod did not act.

Anod shifted her position, waited for the moment the Yorax had their backs to her, and there were the fewest possible eyes to see her. She sprang from her position. Anod covered the intervening four meters in a flash, before either Yorax could react to the startled expression of Guyasaga's oldest child.

She jumped high, straddling the closest trooper's head and snapping her legs together. As the first trooper fell forward from the impact, Anod lunged, striking the second trooper directly on the end of his snout, driving bone fragments into the creature's brain. Still stunned, the first trooper barely moved when Anod struck the back of his head. The trooper went limp. In an instant, Anod grasped his head and snapped it to finish her work.

Guyasaga's family stood, wide-eyed and frozen in disbelief or shock at what they had just witnessed. The family remained motionless and silent as Anod checked her two latest victims to confirm their deaths. Anod grabbed the collar rings and dragged the two dead Yorax troopers away from the house.

"Good to see you, Samuel," she said calmly as she extended her hand to him.

Slowly, Samuel grasped her hand with an expression of disbelief still on his face. His mouth moved but there was no sound.

Anod greeted each of the children as though she had just arrived on a friendly visit. The façade of normalcy was not going to work.

"I am sorry you had to see that, but I did not like the way things were going."

The rest of the family remained frozen as Guyasaga spoke. "Thank you," she said meekly.

"I had no choice. Someone would have gotten hurt, and you

certainly would have been taken away for a more final interrogation."

"They will surely come for us, now," protested Samuel.

"Wow, that was impressive," said their oldest boy.

Anod ignored the youthful comment. "I will remove the bodies. We shall clean this area so no one will know these troopers died here."

"Maybe they already know?" Samuel added.

"Perhaps. But, it is too late to worry about that now. I shall dispose of these two, and then I will try to watch over your place in case they do come back."

"How?"

Anod turned to Guyasaga. "Where is the closest burned out place?"

The mother of six thought about the question. She looked at Samuel, who nodded his head back as if in the prescribed direction. "Probably Natasha Norashova's place."

The image of the young chemist who had helped her on Beta burned in her brain. She could only hope Natasha was alive and well, and just without a house. "Is she all right?"

"As far as we know. I have not seen her. I have not heard anything about her, one way or another. I just know they burnt her house," said Guyasaga.

"That should work."

"What if it doesn't?" Samuel asked.

"As I said, I shall do my best to protect you. There are not many other choices, unless you want to go into hiding, which would virtually confirm to the Yorax your involvement."

"No."

"Good. Now, I need a strong rope with a sturdy board of about one meter length."

"I think we can find that," responded Samuel as he went to a separate building.

As they waited, Guyasaga turned to Anod. "I cannot imagine how you must feel."

"What do you mean?"

"Having lost your entire family, Anod, I cannot even think about how you must feel."

Anod fought the sharp pain that jolted her thoughts. She pushed that pain away. "There is nothing I can do for them, now," she answered solemnly.

"Yes, but, Anod, the loss."

"I do not want to talk about it," snapped Anod as the struggle with her memory grew rapidly unbearable.

Samuel returned with the material Anod requested. She took the board and rope, went to the scooters, and activated both devices. They bobbed to a stable height of 30 centimeters. Anod lashed the two scooters together, nose to tail, tightly against the board. This was not the best configuration, but it would suffice if she was careful. This way she could remove the two scooters, the two bodies, and not need any assistance. After she checked the adequacy of the lash-up, she loaded the two Yorax troopers. Samuel helped her lift the two, heavy corpses onto the rear scooter and tied them down. Anod found an appropriate branch with leaves and obliterated any signs of the Yorax presence.

"Thank you," Anod said as he mounted the Yorax land scooter.

"Thank you," Samuel said.

"You saved our lives," added Guyasaga.

"Necessity. You have helped me enormously. I shall try to protect you."

"We will be grateful for whatever you can do for us," said Samuel.

They said their good-byes, and Anod squeezed the throttle to slowly move the two scooters away from the house. She checked several times over her shoulder to make sure everything was as it should be.

Anod constantly scanned the horizon all around her as she moved toward Natasha's house. Within a kilometer, she slowed her progress, stopping numerous times to listen. She maintained her caution until she was satisfied there was no one around the destroyed house. She examined the remains of the house and found nothing that indicated Natasha might have died there. The burnt and damaged remains of Natasha's husband were among the ashes.

Satisfied the area was clear, Anod set about unloading the two bodies and arranging them in such a way as to suggest some very brief but violent confrontation. If they examined the bodies carefully, the Yorax would probably be able to figure out the two troopers had not died at that spot. Anod was fairly certain they would not be able to figure out where they had actually died. She scuffed up the ground to be consistent, but removed all tracks that might implicate a human attacker. Anod mounted the lead scooter again, obliterated the last of her tracks, and then moved carefully out of the area. Once she was clear, she accelerated toward the mountains.

Anod found an appropriately secluded spot. She decoupled the two scooters, hid one among some rocks along with her spare antratite suit and other items she did not need at the moment, and then covered the spot with brush.

She needed some intelligence to determine her next move. A good start would be a control panel having access to Morgan. First, if the Yorax had not compromised Morgan, which was unlikely, she might be able to gain some valuable information. Second, again if Morgan was not compromised, he would be able to guide her in reactivating Lornog's head and memory to recover additional information regarding the final moments at Meganville and perhaps learn how much the Yorax knew of her. Anod waited for nightfall to chase the dusk terminus to Anton Trikinov's place. She was losing ground since the best speed of the scooter was not quite half the planet's rotation velocity. She arrived an hour before dawn.

Anod searched the area as she had become accustomed since the Yorax alert and especially since the massacre. The shuttle was in the barn they had built for it. Anton was asleep in his isopod, and he was alone. Anod moved back to where she hid the scooter, among some modest bushes and small trees, 80 meters from the house. She wanted to sleep, having driven through more than one night, but she fought her fatigue. Anton could keep watch over her once their morning exchange was complete.

Flashes of movement and the wafting smoke from the chimney marked Anton's return from sleep. Anod wanted to go to the door, but she stayed in her hiding place. The initial moment of exposure was always the most dangerous. Part of her wanted to avoid exposure until she was absolutely certain his situation was as it should be, and yet another part wanted to sleep under his protection. Initial meetings could change in an instant. Anton made his second journey outside before Anod moved closer. It was his fourth trip when Anod met him.

"Damn!" he exclaimed. "You scared the hell out of me."

"My apologies, Anton, but I needed to be sure you were alone."

"That I am." Then, he thought about her capabilities. "How long have you been here?"

"I arrived before dawn."

"How did you get here?" he asked as his head swiveled trying to find her conveyance.

"A Yorax scooter."

"I should have guessed. Word is, you have killed four, maybe ten, of those bastards."

"Not quite."

Anton smiled. "How many?"

"Have they been here?" she asked.

"No."

"Did they stop you?"

"Yes, that first day, but I told them what we had rehearsed, and the idiots believed it."

"Do not underestimate them, Anton. It could be your last mistake."

Trikinov took the admonition well. He knew he would continue to learn a great deal from her. This time was no different. "Yes, of course."

"Is Morgan still accessible?"

"Yes, but I cannot tell how he is doing. He appears to be normal, but the Yorax could be monitoring him. Their base is at New Providence."

"I will find out."

"How . . . ?" he said to her back as Anod headed toward the house.

She did not wait for an invitation. His house was furnished with the ultimate simplicity and was reasonably well kept. The control console looked normal. Anod approached the console from the side, covered Morgan's eye, then pulled up a chair and watched the three screens for several minutes. The activity was still normal.

Rather than talk to Morgan or otherwise identify herself, Anod touched two spots on the middle screen, then one on the right and three on the left. The meaning reached Morgan. A single word came back on the lower portion of the center screen – OCCUPIED. Morgan had been compromised but left running – most likely with specific monitors to detect possible communications with her.

"What . . . ?" he started to ask, then stopped when Anod held her right index finger to her lips.

Anod motioned for Anton to follow her outside. With Morgan compromised, the shuttle was most likely compromised in one of several ways, as well. She checked her antratite suit to make sure everything was in place before she stepped outside. Anod looked around, found a medium tree with some shade and space for two standing adults.

"Morgan has been compromised, and probably the shuttle as well," she said.

"Really. How do you know? Everything runs normal."

"I agreed on a random code with Morgan months ago that we could use if this should happen."

"But, it looks normal."

"That must be Zitger's doing. I imagine they gave Morgan the choice, stay alive and help our people or be destroyed."

"So any information we get from Morgan should be suspect."

"Yes."

"That is why you covered up his eye and did not speak. He did not have to recognize you, which could possibly be detected by the Yorax, if Morgan was indeed compromised."

"Precisely."

Anton looked around as if in search of something. Anod watched him with an element of suspicion. She knew it was possible Anton had been subjugated as well.

"What do we do now?" he asked.

"I need to know what the Yorax are doing. What has happened since that first day?"

"They have ordered everyone to remain at their homes. They have forbidden any travel or assembly. The Yorax have begun a systematic interrogation of our people."

"I have seen houses burned. I imagine some people have been killed or imprisoned."

"Other than your family," he added with solemnity. "Yes."

"How many?"

"Twenty to forty, the best any of us can tell."

"Have they issued demands?"

"Yes." Anton looked into her eyes. Anod shrugged her shoulders as if say, so what are they? "They want you delivered alive."

"Or, what?"

"All the males will die . . . one by one."

Anod looked coldly at Anton. "That will not happen."

"How will we be able to stop them? They have powerful weapons. There are many of them."

"First, we will not do it. If you are discovered helping me, you will be executed instantly, or at least after they feel they have retrieved as much information as they can get from you."

"It will not be that easy," Anton protested.

"Perhaps not, but I need you alive, not dead."

"That's good. Me, too."

Anod smiled briefly and slightly, as a small concession to the emotions she had known. "What do you know about Otis?"

"Morgan received the message. He arrived on Beta. We decided to tell him to remain there."

"Why?"

"Well, for obvious reasons. We did not want him to be just another captive here. Plus, there is probably more he can do for us there."

"Did you tell him that?"

"No."

"Did you ask for help from the Society?"

"No. The Yorax told us they would exterminate us all if we did."

Anod did not wait for his question. "The best thing you can do for me is to do exactly what the Yorax tell you to do, stay here, listen as best you can, and I shall try to come back here as often as I can to collect what you have learned."

"Are you going to take the shuttlecraft?"

"No. It is most likely monitored by the Yorax, if for no other reason than to see if you decide to break your restrictions."

"But, the scooter will take longer to travel."

"Yes, it will, but my only other choices are walk or ride an animal."

"I see your point."

"Now, I have one big favor to ask." Anton nodded his head. "I need to sleep."

"You can use my isopod."

"I cannot. Morgan will identify me by the biological scans."

"Oh, yes . . . sure. Then, I have a nice bed. The sheets are clean," he said and smiled.

"Good," she said as she walked toward the house. "I need you to go in, cover up Morgan's eye again, to let me pass into your bedroom, then uncover it so he can see. Whatever you do, do not use my name or refer to me in anyway, or the Yorax will be here in an instant."

"No problem," Anton answered, and then did as he was requested.

Anod passed through his main room and far enough into his bedroom to observe the console. She watched Anton remove the cover from Morgan's eye. He walked to the bedroom door and closed it. Anod lay down on the bed without removing her antratite suit. She wanted to feel the exhilarating stimulation of the cleansing station, but knew that was a luxury she could not afford at the moment. She was asleep in a few loose thoughts.

The house was dark when Anod woke up. She saw a faint, flickering light reflected off the trees beside the house. She opened the door a crack, enough to see the control console. Morgan's eye stared into the room, absorbing everything within line of sight. The flickering light was brighter in the main room. Anod considered walking quickly across the room but decided against it. The risk was not worth the convenience. She opened the bedroom window and climbed out.

Anton sat on a chair near a small wood fire, staring into the flames. She made no effort to disguise her movement. He noticed her soon enough without being startled.

"Did you have a good rest?"

"Yes," she answered. "Thank you for staying awake. You must be quite tired by now."

"I will get my sleep."

"I shall be leaving soon, before dawn. Did you have any visitors?"

"None . . . not a one."

"Good."

"Where are you going to go?"

"It is better that you do not know."

"Oh, yes. I understand."

"Thank you again, Anton. You have been a big help to me."

"Anytime. I will just be glad when this is over, and we can live in peace."

"I will be, too. I will not let it go on much longer. I must set the bait carefully for the trap to be effective."

Anton nodded his head with fatigue. "If there is anything I can do to help you, just let me know."

"I will, Anton, and thank you again," Anod said as she touched his shoulder. "Good-bye," she added and did not wait for a response. She walked into the dark, not in the direction of the scooter. Anod saw no benefit in letting Anton know where she hid the scooter. The more facts she kept to herself, the better.

From the concealment of a small hill, she watched Anton extinguish the fire by spreading the pieces of wood, and then covering them with dirt. Once he was satisfied the fire was out, he went inside. Without turning on a light, he probably went directly to bed.

Anod scanned the sky above her. She saw the distinct shape of the Yorax battlecruiser low on the horizon and going away from her. She retrieved her backpack then mounted the scooter. Moving slowly until she was well away from Anton's house, she checked the sky one more time carefully again before she accelerated to full speed trying to stay ahead of the dawn terminus as long as possible.

As she drove the scooter, Anod had very little time for thoughts other than scanning for orbiting vehicles, obstacle avoidance and basic navigation. She had to stop several times as a precaution to clear her path. When she could devote a few moments to other thoughts, Anod's mind turned to Guyasaga and Samuel, to Natasha Norashova, to Anton Trikinov and even Otis Greenstreet, and to the Nagoyamas. She felt a sense of relief that Zitger did not dominate her consciousness. The traitor was never very far from her thoughts, but during this trip, she enjoyed a small respite.

The journey took two days going the long way around the planet and having to make the precautionary stops she felt she needed to be safe. Using the same processes, she finally reached the house she sought. Gerald Oscarson, the middle aged, conversion systems specialist who had been part of the team helping Anod on Beta, would be her best hope for weapons of some type.

Satisfied he was alone, Anod went to his door the next morning and knocked. His startled expression and quick glances around the exterior told Anod a lot. He quickly gestured for her to enter.

"They are looking for you," he whispered.

Anod scanned the interior. None of the Society technology devices could be seen. "I know," she whispered back.

"They have killed many, mostly males from what I have been able to learn." Anod nodded her head in acknowledgment. "And, I understand you have killed a few of them." Again, she nodded her head. "What can I do to help you?"

"I need weapons."

Oscarson shook his head. "I don't have any projectile weapons. I have a few antique swords and spears that you are welcome to use, but I don't think they will be much help."

"What about explosives?"

"I don't have any made up for fear of discovery, but I do have the ingredients and can make some quickly enough."

"How long?"

"Several hours, I should think." Anod heard what sounded like a faint screech. The change of expression on her face affected Gerald. "What?"

Anod went cautiously to the curtained window. Through the edge of the curtain, she saw two Yorax troopers five meters away from the house and five meters apart. She leapt to the back of the house – two more. Anod instantly considered the situation. There must be at least six and more likely eight or ten troopers surrounding the house. She returned to Oscarson. He figured out the situation.

"Let me handle this," he said.

"Don't resist, Gerald. They will kill you at the slightest provocation." He nodded his head and started to go outside. "Wait," she said strongly but as softly as she could. Oscarson froze one step short of the door and looked over his left shoulder at her. "They have not said anything, yet. Perhaps they do not know we are in here," she added, although she recognized the deployment meant quite the opposite. Anod suspected Gerald might be more relaxed if he thought this might be an innocent visit.

As she guessed, Oscarson stood back and wiggled his head as if to relax the tension he felt. Anod quickly searched the room for weapons. Only ancient swords and knives festooned one wall. She reached for the 14th century, two-handed, English broadsword, probably passed down, like the other old weapons, from generation to generation over the intervening centuries. Anod grasped it tightly with her right hand and swung in several wide arcs like a distorted, horizontal, figure eight. The swoosh of the blade through the air changed Gerald's expression from calm to worried, as though he was missing some essential element of fact.

"Human," came the screeching command from one of the troopers, "present yourself."

Oscarson connected with Anod's eyes. She smiled slightly to assure him then nodded her head. Gerald opened the door only enough to show his head.

"Step outside," the trooper ordered.

The middle aged, energy conversion specialist did as he was told.

"There is another in there as well."

Anod scanned the room again and quickly checked the other three rooms of the small house. There was no escape or reasonable place to hide. How did they know she was in here? Had they adjusted their scanners to detect something unique to her? Anod checked her entire body. Her antratite suit was a little dirty, but all the pieces were in place including her hood. Maybe they did not know it was her? Had they been watching the house from a distance where Anod could not detect them? She shook her head as she eliminated that possibility. She had been very careful in her preliminary search. Perhaps this was just a routine search. Anod looked around one more time. Nothing had changed. She stepped to the door, and then joined Gerald Oscarson at his right side. She rested the broadsword point down like a staff.

"Pull your mask off."

Anod did as she was ordered.

"So, we finally meet the mythical Anod," said the trooper directly in front of her, and the one who was probably the commander of the detachment.

Neither of the humans moved. The apparent leader of the Yorax raised his left arm, touched a spot of his wrist communicator, and screeched an irritating phrase. Something came back in the Yorax language. It took a few moments for the other troopers to gather. Six. A better number than eight or ten, Anod told herself. She watched her adversaries very carefully. They obviously did not have orders to kill her on sight. That was a good sign. The thought of a peaceful surrender did float through her consciousness for just a moment. They would probably kill Oscarson, anyway, and maybe even her. The thoughts of what she would face at the hands of the Yorax told her resistance and death in battle was better. After all, she was not quite ready to spring her trap.

Two Yorax troopers moved slowly toward them. None of them seemed to have much concern for the sword in her hand.

Anod whispered, "Don't move until this starts, then duck back into the house."

"Is this wise?"

"There is no choice. If I am captured, I will die. This is a much better place to die. I just do not want you hurt in this battle."

"Can you do this?"

"I do not know, but we will never know if I do not try." The dull slap of loose, non-metallic, material announced the next phase of the confrontation as the Yorax readied their light rifles. "I suspect they will try to avoid killing me, but they will not hesitate to kill you. You must move quickly when this begins." Anod saw the nod of his head in her peripheral vision.

She stepped forward one pace to give herself better angles. The movement stopped the troopers for several seconds as they evaluated the situation. The others raised their rifles, pointing them more directly at the two humans.

"Do not move," commanded the leader.

"You know who I am," Anod said strongly.

"Yes, we do."

"You also know what I am," she added.

The hesitation gave her an edge. They were still respectful of her skills. It might be just enough, but would it be sufficient to save Gerald?

"I will shoot you both dead if you resist."

Anod smiled. She knew their orders were different. If they had been authorized to kill them, they would have done so straight away without the risk of confrontation. The trooper closest to her right side made a grievous mistake moving his rifle away from his scaly body and pointing it past her.

In a blur of violent motion, Anod swiped the sword coming down and severing the trooper's arms. Everyone was frozen for an instant except Anod. She dove for the now free rifle. With the precision of choreographed movements, Anod rolled as she grasped the rifle, aimed and fired into the left trooper's chest knocking him back several meters. The red streaks of light projectiles filled the space.

Anod rolled back toward the writhing, incomplete trooper firing past him hitting another trooper in the chest. Several shots hit the first trooper propelling him onto her. The weight did not deter her actions, just slowed her movement slightly. The others fired several more times. She felt the impacts through the dead trooper's limp body. She thrashed against the weight and fired several precise shots, killing two and hitting the rifle of the leader knocking it out of his hand. Anod arched her back and threw her head back aiming her rifle at the last trooper who held his arms up. There would be no prisoners. Anod fired at his mid-chest killing the trooper instantly. She scrambled to her feet.

"Don't!" she shouted.

The Yorax leader froze. Anod kept the light rifle pointed directly at his chest. He turned toward her and stood at attention.

"And, what are you going to do with me?" he screeched.

Anod kept the rifle on him as she moved back toward the house. She glanced back briefly to find her steps. Oscarson lay flat on his back. She moved her eyes rapidly between the Yorax leader and her fallen friend. He was dead – two shots to the chest. Anod turned back to the trooper.

"I am going to ask you a few questions."

"And, then you are going to kill me?"

"Perhaps."

"Then, why should I answer any questions?"

"Your answers might be sufficient for mercy."

"There is no mercy."

"Perhaps. How did you know I was here?"

The Yorax trooper shook his large head in refusal.

"What were your orders?"

"To capture you and return you to General Negolian."

"Why?"

A nauseating grin of vile greenish red and obscene odor came back to her. "You are all that stands between us and victory."

Anod thought his response quite odd. She was only one warrior. What actions could she possibly take to obstruct a Yorax military victory?

"How so?"

Again, the trooper shook his head. "General Negolian has big plans for you," he sneered.

"Plans, you say?"

"I shall tell you no more. You can kill me if you wish, but your fate will come at the hands of General Negolian."

"We shall see."

Anod threw the rifle away from her. She would give him the respect of a warrior. She held up her hands, palms up at elbow height, to signify that she was unarmed. Anod's intention was the most basic mortal combat. The trooper dove for a rifle several meters away. Anod reached down, grabbed the sword and hurled it at the scrambling trooper. As he turned to aim the rifle at her, the sword buried itself halfway into the middle of his upper chest. The startled Yorax dropped the rifle and looked down at the hilt of the sword wagging back and forth like some bizarre tail. He looked back at her. He tried to raise his right hand in a jerky, feeble gesture of a universal salute, but never made it as he fell over dead.

Anod quickly checked the six dead troopers, and then went to Gerald Oscarson. He was indeed dead as well. She lifted his limp body, carried him to his bed, and gently placed him there. She covered up his entire body and head with a sheet. She searched his house thoroughly including several smaller outbuildings. As he had told her, he had the ingredients but nothing immediate she could use.

There was nothing else she could do. She did not have time to gather or transport anything of significance. Reinforcements might well be on the way and could arrive at any moment. Anod took one last look, and then sprinted away toward the hiding spot for her scooter.

Chapter 12

Anod found a secluded place in some rolling hills with lush vegetation to hold up until dark. She had several hours to wait. Once she was satisfied there was no one following her or anyone to observe her, she tried to find some sleep. The warm, gentle breeze rustling the leaves in the trees dissipated the adrenaline that had pumped through her veins.

As she relaxed, she replayed the events at Gerald Oscarson's house. The loss of another innocent life corroded her patience. If she did not act soon, there would be no one left to share life with around her. Her troubled thoughts settled on how. How had those troopers appeared at Oscarson's so soon after her arrival? How did they know there were two people inside? How did they know the other person was her?

Anod took the moment of peace to examine her antratite suit. It looked complete and correct except for the dirt and the stench of dried Yorax blood. She needed to take the suit off to examine every stitch and seam, but she did not feel comfortable doing so until she could see what was in orbit. Even that look was becoming questionable. The Yorax quite obviously knew she was on the planet – the evidence was mounting. If they masked the battlecruiser or any other craft, she would not be able to see it, and the craft would be able to detect her without the antratite suit. It was a risk she had to take.

She needed her mind clear for her next move. Anod forced the thoughts from her head and let her mind drift into slumber. The penetration of the defenses surrounding the Yorax base camp at New Providence would take all of her skills and mental concentration. She told herself to sleep as long as she could, even if it was all night.

She was not so lucky. Anod woke instantly with the sound of a twig snapping. She moved slowly to a ready position and scanned the area around her. She could not see, hear or smell anything unusual. She listened intently. Another twig cracking and the shuffling of leaves focused her attention. After several minutes in the reduced illumination of the vegetation, she saw glimpses of the source – a large wild boar of some sort with large white curving tusks protruding from its lower jaw. Anod watched the animal for several minutes to make sure it was what it seemed.

Once Anod was satisfied with her safety, and she was able to survey and evaluate the sky for observers, she stripped off the antratite suit. She carefully checked every plate, every seam and every stitch in the suit. Everything was in place. Anod started to put her suit back on, but then considered a bath of sorts. She remembered a stream several hundred meters away. It was barely ankle deep, but the water splashed and rubbed over her body was genuinely refreshing. The suit could stand a cleaning as well. As she enjoyed the water, Anod soaked, rubbed and rinsed her suit several times. An object moving rapidly up from the horizon caught her attention. She did not have much time and could not afford herself the luxury of drying her suit.

Anod quickly scrambled into her black antratite outfit. The evaporation of the moisture cooled her body rapidly giving her a deep chill. In another few seconds, she recognized the object – a Yorax battlecruiser. She wondered whether Zitger remained in the relative safety of the large warship, or was he on the planet . . . probably at the base camp if she was to guess. Anod stepped quickly to her backpack and rummaged through it to find the special gloves and mask she needed. As the large craft approached an overhead position above her, Anod completed an assessment of her body coverage. The only exposed spots were her eyes and mouth. Even her nose and ears were covered. Anod moved through a set of extension and contraction exercises partly to flex her joints and muscles, but also to squeeze as much water out of her suit as possible to aid the drying process.

Anod retrieved the rest of her things including the Yorax light rifle and four energy packs she had taken with her from Oscarson's. The Yorax would know she was now armed. They should be able to see that it was only her that was armed since the other rifles were available but left behind. Anod donned her backpack, went to the scooter, secured the rifle and headed across country at a modest speed toward New Providence.

The approach process slowed substantially within five kilometers of the town. Anod made numerous stops to assess the situation. When she was close enough to the town, she found an adequate observation post. She could not see clearly, but several crosses had been erected along the periphery of the square with dead or dying men strapped, nailed or somehow attached to them. The ancient Roman method of punishment, execution and public intimidation undoubtedly had a similar effect on the Murtaurians.

There was no movement in the town. The usual lights had mostly been extinguished. Only the Yorax compound at the edge of town was brightly illuminated. The configuration of the complex was basically as Guyasaga had described.

Anod carefully surveyed the terrain around the city as well as the avenues of approach. Activity in the town remained non-existent, other than the rare twist of pain from one of those tied to a cross. Anod found the spot she was looking for. She hid the scooter among some rocks along with her backpack. She took the rifle and a spare energy pack with her.

The Yorax had done a good job situating and preparing the site for their base camp. The use of lights and fences made any approach very risky. They undoubtedly had sensors deployed as well to detect any form of energy – anything that moved, anything that generated heat, almost anything at all. Anod considered trying to find one of the Murtaurian children to vandalize a light or throw a stick at the fence, but it was late at night and the risk of injury too great.

Anod patiently observed the facility. There were four, fairly large, single level, rectangular buildings arranged in a quadrangle. Three successive fence lines with very loose, powdery dirt regions between them meant fence penetration with sufficient speed to beat a Yorax reaction would be nearly impossible. A fifth building was the only apparent entry into the camp and straddled all three, fence lines. Six large poles, perhaps ten meters high, with a silver, one-meter diameter, ball on top each pole formed a circle around the inner buildings. Those had to be part of the primary sensor array. The light poles were half as high and situated at each corner with half the light pointed outward and half inward.

An hour passed with no detectable activity of any kind. Anod rolled over on her back to watch the skies. Convinced nothing of consequence moved above her, she adjusted her position, checked her escape route, and then aimed the rifle at the light tower closest to her and adjacent to the entry building. Anod fired one shot at the post just above the fences. She hit her mark but did not wait to see the result.

Anod moved swiftly back away from her firing point then laterally to her secondary observation spot. By the time she could see the camp again, the upper half of the light tower had fallen across the inner two fences. Sparks continued to splash up and out from the contact points. A dozen Yorax troopers had passed through the entry building and fanned out moving quickly toward Anod's firing point. Another covering group exited the compound but stopped outside the fences. They kept moving their heads and eyes to detect any movement. The reaction group reached her firing position.

Several loud Yorax screeches without further search activity gave Anod the last of the information she would gather from this reconnaissance by fire. The two groups of troopers continued to look around as they returned to the compound. Once both groups were together, they stopped and arranged themselves facing outward as though they expected something to happen.

"Anod, I have been expecting you," came the clear, distinct voice of Zitger from the direction of the compound. "I know you are out there to hear this. The sooner you give yourself up to me, the sooner this misery for these weak people will end."

She did not feel the slightest urge to respond. She had what she needed. They could not detect her or track their scooters, but they could detect the discharge of her weapon. They also believed she was the only armed belligerent. Anod sighed a deep relaxing breath knowing her antratite suit still worked against the Yorax sensors. A slight smile accompanied her thought that Zitger was inside the compound.

"Your foolish and impossible act of resistance will only cause other innocent people to be killed."

Anod watched everything very closely. The squad of troopers did not move. They expected something to happen.

"This singular defiance is futile. Surely you recognize you have no way to win. We shall continue to close the net around you. The only question is how many of these feeble creatures die to serve your ridiculous sense of honor. How many, Anod?"

Anod aimed the rifle at the silver sensor ball closest to her. She held her fire until the desired moment she knew would be coming.

"Your foolishness will only be rewarded with death, a slow agonizing death for everyone including you." Zitger paused to check all his sensor information. "So be it, Anod."

The Yorax squad began to withdraw into the compound. Anod waited to see if anything was going to happen like a demonstration or something. When the last troopers entered the building, Anod refined her aim and fired. The silver ball exploded in a brilliant blossom of smoke, sparks and fire.

Anod knew what was coming, ducked down behind the small hill and ran along her escape route. The return fire took only seconds to come, obliterating the top of the hill upon which she had so recently lay. The light of a small fire flickered against the trees, rocks and other vegetation. Anod retrieved her backpack and did not waste time securing anything.

She moved the scooter out of the clump of rock and accelerated carefully along her covered egress route. As she moved away from New Providence onto an open plain, she accelerated to full speed. When she found a chance, Anod glanced over her shoulder. The lights on a half dozen scooters followed her one or two kilometers back.

At the appropriate point, she turned and headed into the mountains along her pre-planned escape route. Anod found her spot. Stopping sharply, she turned into a hook promontory, shutdown the scooter and nimbly jumped from rock to rock until she looked down on the path she had followed. In seconds, the Yorax pursuit group came down the makeshift road a little faster than would have been prudent in this terrain. They were not looking for her. They were simply following the path they thought she was on. Eight scooters passed. Anod had no intention of moving. The Yorax would most likely follow the road through the mountains until they realized they had lost her, and then at least some of them would probably return to New Providence by the same route.

As she waited, four more Yorax scooters came along – trailers undoubtedly hoping to catch her uncovering herself if the primary patrol missed her. They were easy targets. In this rocky terrain, she could probably kill all four with no escape, but she held her fire. The immediate threat passed. She would be spending the rest of the night at this point. Anod rolled over on her back to watch the heavens. She saw the Yorax battlecruiser pass over her position twice before she heard the first sounds of the returning patrol.

This time the troopers scanned the rocks and trees all around them. They looked in her direction several times, but her concealment was near perfect. She could easily see them, but they could not see her.

Anod counted twelve troopers as their scooters moved slowly through the pass with much more professional spacing as they retraced their route. They were not going to find her this night.

When Anod was satisfied the Yorax were gone, she climbed down from her perch, found a secure crack in the rocks, piled up all the leaves she could find to camouflage herself, and lay down to sleep as long as she could.

It was the late afternoon brightness and warmth of the Murtauri star that finally woke her. When she was sufficiently awake, she slowly returned to her observation spot. She watched for many minutes and saw nothing of consequence. With the clarity of a good rest, Anod reviewed last night's exchange. She acknowledged that she did not have a particularly high probability of success for penetration of the Yorax base camp, but she remained convinced it could be done. Any facility is penetrable with enough imagination and courage.

Anod waited patiently for darkness. Although all the Yorax from the evening's chase had been accounted for, her instincts told her to use another pass through the mountains. The precaution added two hours to her transit. With last night's foray and the acknowledgment of their expectation of her presence, the Yorax would surely step up their pressure on her people. She did not have much time.

It was midday before she cleared the Gibritzu homestead. Anod entered the clearing in the grove of trees where their house was located. One of the younger children was the first to see Anod. The girl ran inside. Anod quickly realized she still had her mask on and pulled it off. Naomi came out by herself. Little faces poked out from behind curtains. Naomi looked around quickly then motioned for Anod to come inside. She closed the door behind Anod then frantically motioned for the children to go to another room.

"What are you doing here?"

"I came to learn what I can about what the Yorax are doing, and what we are doing, if anything."

"We are trying to do nothing . . . to stay out of the way. They are after you, not the rest of us."

The harsh tone surprised Anod, but she did not twitch a muscle or blink an eye. The situation was deteriorating faster than she suspected. Anod turned to leave as she said, "I shall not trouble you."

As she reached for the door, Naomi said, "No . . . wait." Anod stopped and turned to look at Naomi's strained face. "We are just scared. There has been too much death, too much injury."

"What do you mean?" Anod asked not questioning the reality but really needing more detail.

"Some people think the Yorax are killing the men and . . ." Her voice tailed off.

"And, what?"

"And, we think they are raping the women."

Anod concealed her shock and considered the statement. "That is impossible. The Yorax do not procreate as humans do. They are incapable of such mating."

"The human among them is doing it. Several women have been released and reported being raped. They were repeatedly raped until their pregnancy was confirmed."

Zitger's cruelty was going to even more grotesque depths beyond the taking of innocent life. He was contaminating the living.

"Have the Yorax been here since my last visit?"

"No."

"Where is Dahar?"

"He is in the fields with our two older boys. Why?"

"Do you expect him back this evening?"

"Oh, no," Naomi cried. "What is happening?"

"Naomi, I do not think anything has happened to him. I just wanted to know if you expected him to return from the fields tonight."

Naomi Gibritzu nodded her head. One of the older girls peeked out from behind an interior door. Anod noticed the movement and looked directly at her, forcing her to close the door.

"I just want to ask him a few questions to find out what he knows about the Yorax activity."

"He may know more, but I doubt it."

"Good. Then, I shall leave."

"Where are you going?"

"It is better that you do not know, Naomi . . . in case the Yorax do decide to visit." The head nod acknowledged the condition. "Try not to give the Yorax anymore information than they already have." Again, a head nod confirmed her understanding. "I shall see you later," Anod added and left.

Finding a concealed observation point in this flat generally open terrain was not as easy as it was in the forest or mountains. One of the trees was her only choice. Anod found the best one, checked her antratite suit, pulled on her mask, checked her gloves and then climbed the desired tree. She found a perch about 3.5 meters above the ground and wedged herself into a V joint of three large branches. While her view was partially obstructed, it was adequate.

The children played outside. Naomi checked on them regularly and refereed a couple of disagreements. They did not know Anod was in the tree. Anod's position was sufficiently secure to allow her to doze. The gleeful chatter of the children served as a sound of normalcy much like birds and other animals in the forest. Anod refused to let the memories of hearing the same sounds from her children enter her consciousness. She reminded herself over and over that she had only one purpose in life now. She could not let anything interfere with that mission. There would be time to remember and grieve in the future, but not now.

The method of alert worked. It was dark when the strong male voice marked a major change.

Anod instantly became alert. She watched carefully. It was Dahar and the two oldest boys, but he seemed agitated. Even with her sensitive hearing, Anod could not quite make out the words. She waited in the tree absorbing everything she could, using all her senses and scanning the entire detectable area. When she was ready, Anod left her tree and moved away from the house into the open ground beyond the grove of trees. She scanned the flat horizon. Nothing. She searched the skies. The telltale shape was retreating. She would be safe from observation within a few minutes. Anod returned to the house. As she approached, she pulled off her mask. She knocked lightly on the door. She heard Naomi say, "That is probably Anod."

Dahar opened the door, recognized the caller and stepped outside closing the door behind him. "It is dangerous for us with you here," he said.

"I know."

"What do you want?"

"Information."

"Such as?"

"What do you know about the Yorax?"

"They are a very cruel people." Anod nodded her head in agreement, wanting Dahar to continue. "We heard that Gerald Oscarson was killed."

"I was there."

"Really."

"Yes. They had come for me. They killed him outright before I could dispatch the six troopers."

"Six?"

"Yes."

"Your exploits continue to mount, but your presence is killing us."

"I know, Dahar. I shall try to end this soon."

Dahar just stared at Anod.

"Naomi mentioned earlier today some suspicion the Yorax are killing the males and raping the females."

"I do not know if it is so clear, but that is what it appears. As you said, Gerald Oscarson was killed yesterday. Natasha Norashova's husband was killed early on, and Tung Wan Foo and most of the males in New Providence, as well. Several women and older female children have been taken to the Yorax compound outside New Providence."

"They are inside?"

"As far as we know."

"Have any of them come out?"

"No," answered Dahar. "Why?"

"Yes," interjected Naomi. "Maria Verde was released. I told Anod earlier."

"I knocked a few things down at the Yorax camp last night. I need to know what is inside, and how it is configured?"

"Are you going to attack it?"

"Probably. We are running out of options."

"The Yorax made it clear they were only after you, and any attempt to contact the Society would be seen as a direct act of war."

"They have already declared war on us. They have killed some of our people."

"Many!"

". . . Many of our people, and I have killed a few of theirs."

"Yes. So, what are you going to do?"

"Learn as much as I can, then I shall go for the heart of the Yorax to stop them."

"Have you had anything to eat?" asked Dahar, changing the subject as if he did not want to know more.

"A little here and a little there."

"Are you hungry?"

"Yes."

Dahar looked over his shoulder as if he might see something, and then back at her. "Let us get our children in bed, then Naomi can bring you some food. Would you mind waiting out here?"

"No, as long as you don't mind me wearing my mask."

"Mask?"

Anod pulled her mask over her head. "This whole suit keeps me from being detected by the Yorax sensors."

"Very menacing."

"It is not intended for fashion, only functional obscuration."

"I am sure it works."

"So far, but the Yorax appear to be making adjustments. I am not sure how much longer I shall have this protection."

"Then, you can wait?"

Anod nodded her head. Dahar responded in kind and went back inside. Anod found a large tree near the edge of the clearing to sit down and lean against the trunk. She waited perhaps an hour. Anod stood as Naomi came out, found her in the dark and came to her with a small tray.

"Here is some food for you," Naomi said as she handed the tray to Anod.

"Thank you," responded Anod as she took the tray, sat down and immediately consumed everything as fast as she could chew and swallow.

"You must be very hungry. Would you like some more?"

"No," answered Anod, although she knew she could probably eat more. "That should be sufficient. Thank you."

"You cannot stay here, Anod."

"I know. I shall leave you. Good luck."

"Good luck to you."

Anod turned and disappeared into the woods. From a safe vantage point, Anod waited for Naomi to disappear into the house. Once she was satisfied, Anod decided to return to her tree. It seemed like a safe place to hide and let things settle a little from her raid of last night.

Safely wedged in her tree, Anod quickly went to sleep. Anod remained exactly in the same position throughout the night. It was a female scream of horror that woke her.

Beyond the leaves and branches between them, the area around the Gibritzu house was filled with Yorax troopers. The assailants knew their purpose and mission precisely. They dragged the entire Gibritzu family out of the house. The children cried. Dahar and Naomi shouted against their assailants. The Yorax did not waste time.

Anod carefully and quietly extricated herself from the tree. As she positioned herself for further observation, Dahar and the two older male children lay next to each other by the front door. The burns on their chests meant they were dead.

Anod started to move then froze. The screams continued as they dragged Naomi and the oldest girl into a small shuttlecraft. It was too late for her to do anything other than probably get everyone else killed. Within seconds, three shuttlecraft departed the area.

The two small children, one male and the other female, cried hard as they wandered among the bodies. They touched Dahar several times trying to wake him. She watched and waited. The two children eventually sat down among the bodies of their family still wailing. Anod wanted to go to the children and comfort them, but sacrificing herself would not help anyone. The best thing she could do was go directly to the center of the Yorax. She just needed a little more time to give herself a chance at survival, although part of her did not much care as long as she eliminated the Yorax threat.

She watched the children until they began to wander aimlessly. Dirt and tears stained their faces. They seemed to be looking for guidance, for some sense of direction, for their parents. Anod waited as long as she could then descended from the tree. As she walked toward the house, Anod pulled her mask off to avoid scaring the children. When they saw Anod in her black suit, they began to scream, frozen in their tracks. Anod held out her arms in a feeble attempt to ease their fears. The pain in their faces, in their eyes, was unbearable. Tears ran down Anod's face. She hurt for the children.

"It is all right, children. I will take care of you."

They continued to cry. As she got closer, she could see their little bodies shaking uncontrollably. They covered their faces with their hands as Anod reached for them. Embracing both children, she held them firmly kissing both foreheads repeatedly. As her warmth passed to them, they buried their faces in her chest. Their cries diminished to sobbing then subsided altogether.

When they eventually lifted their heads from her chest, Anod told them, "I will get your mother and sister back." There was no benefit to confiding her doubts. She would do the best she could.

Anod decided to devote her attention to the living, and then tend to the dead. She loaded the children in front of her on the scooter and sped off to Mysasha's place. The Yorax had not visited them yet. Anod dropped off the Gibritzu children without much explanation. She did not stay long as each second was simply more exposure to Yorax detection and possible compromise of the Nagoyama family. Mysasha understood Anod's concerns and accepted her duty to assist. She would tell Hyoshi when he returned from his local trading journey.

As dusk came to the day, Anod returned to the Gibritzu homestead to bury Dahar and the boys. She considered burning the bodies in the house, but she hoped Naomi might return to her home.

With that grim task complete, Anod headed back to the mountains. She needed time to complete the organization of her thoughts. Anod made it back to her original mountain retreat. There were no signs of disturbance even by small animals or birds. She needed a day to rest and think.

What exactly could she do and how? She could not be everywhere at once. She could not defend everyone at their homes. With only her determination and skills, Anod knew she could probably deal with individual Yorax troopers or small patrols. She also knew she had been extremely lucky during the Oscarson encounter. She could not depend on that luck.

Anod's recuperation process took a day longer than she anticipated. She cleaned her suit and her body. She took the few moments she could to let her body enjoy the caress of the cool mountain air. The bruises, cuts and scrapes she had received since the Yorax invasion healed quickly without the stress of combat or further injury.

The path of her offensive against the Yorax clarified as the fog of combat dissipated from her mind and body. She had a good portion of the information she needed, but it was not sufficient for her to act. Time was not on her side, and she knew it. Three more steps would be needed. The first one was relative easy. She needed the perfect terrain for the critical step. The reconnaissance process took three nights and those parts of the days she could risk the visual exposure. The next two steps would be progressively more risky, but there were no other choices she could think of among all those she considered. The next phase would be decisive, one-way or another.

Chapter 13

As she suspected, the Yorax substantially changed their routine around their compound. Anod had to take much more care in observing the Yorax facility. They had not yet repaired the damage from her previous raid, despite their ability to completely repair the facility in the days since her last visit. Why hadn't they repaired it? They undoubtedly had some alternative sensor coverage for those blind spots. Perhaps they wanted her to think they were blind in that quadrant. Perhaps they did not think they were going to be on the planet much longer.

More significantly, they now actively patrolled the surrounding ground. The observations she needed to make took much longer than she planned since she had to move her observation points many times. Anod knew she did not have the freedom of movement the Yorax enjoyed for the moment. She was not yet ready for the confrontation that was soon to come. Their operations did not leave her with the impression of a short stay or any threat of interference from beyond the planetary system. Her thoughts drifted toward imagining what diversion the Yorax must have carried off to occupy the Society so thoroughly. Anod had faith the Society would eventually come back to check on them as they had done many previous times, but it was clear the Yorax on Murtauri Four did not feel the Society's return was imminent.

Anod watched and watched. Several times she thought she could see a routine that could be exploited, then they changed. While the Yorax had their limitations, they were still formidable, disciplined warriors, and despite Zitger's treachery, Anod held a healthy respect for his leadership and martial skills. A misstep on her part would certainly lead to her demise, probably by some slow, painful, brutal process. While there was an element of relief in such an event, there was no guarantee her elimination would bring any relief for her comrades. She was the only immediate obstacle between the Yorax and the possible extinction of the Murtaurians. She intended to persevere.

It was dusk on the third day of her vigil when something drastically changed. From the gateway building came a naked human female. The woman wobbled and wandered aimlessly outside the compound. Anod moved quickly repositioning herself much closer to the town than she had previously been. The woman staggered and fell several times before Anod could recognize her – Natasha Norashova.

The Yorax guards outside the compound continued on their activities ignoring her condition and presence. There were no Murtaurians in sight anywhere other than those crucified around the square. The sight of some of her friends in death tied to those crosses knocked Norashova over several times. Anod heard Natasha's screams of anguish and calls for help carry over the distance between them. Her heart pounded with an awful mixture of sympathy, compassion and anger. She wanted to help her friend, but there was nothing she could do for Natasha as long as she remained within the observation range of the Yorax facility.

Natasha slowly began to regain her senses as she worked her way from building to building in New Providence. There were no signs of life or assistance for Natasha.

Anod watched the Yorax closely with a different purpose in mind. They no longer appeared to be interested in anything in the town. Anod used the darkness and cover of terrain and vegetation to work her way toward the far end of town beyond the view of the Yorax.

Carefully, Anod moved through the streets from building to building. As she checked various structures, she confirmed the absence of any humans. Each building was empty and cold. Many were left open. She searched several buildings until she found a large cape-like coat. Grabbing the coat, Anod maneuvered until she could see Natasha. What she saw turned her stomach. Besides being without any protective clothing, she was covered with bruises, cuts, dirt and dried blood. She was in awful shape. Her light brown hair was matted solid in an ugly helmet of some bizarre, misshapen form.

Anod checked the line of sight from the Yorax to Natasha. She could not risk any encouragement to Natasha that might change her movements or actions and thus attract attention. With agonizing slowness, Natasha continued to stagger and wobble her way, almost bouncing off buildings like an unbalanced ball, until she rounded the corner of a key building.

Anod had to wait for the moment she needed. The risk of any sound, disturbance or purposeful action would undoubtedly attract Yorax attention. Natasha turned away from Anod and toward a door. Anod sprang toward her. Using the coat, Anod enveloped her friend with the coat, one strong arm around across her chest and the other covering her mouth. Even in her diminished state, the shock caused a muffled scream.

"It is Anod, Natasha. It is me, Anod. Please be quiet. Shhhhh," she whispered. Anod continued to try to soothe the wounded woman. As Natasha calmed down, Anod leaned to her left side to enable Natasha's terror-stricken eyes to see her face, only to be greeted with more muffled screams. "Damn!" exclaimed Anod. She lowered Natasha to the ground so she could use her legs to control the woman's body and release her left arm for just enough time to pull her mask off. "It is me, Natasha. Look at me," she commanded.

As Norashova began to recognize her, tears began to mix with the dirt and blood on her face. The terror transformed into a total collapse of any control and almost violent sobbing. Anod kept her wrapped in the coat and felt bad that she had to keep her mouth covered as well. "It is all right, now, Natasha. I have you. You are safe, now. I need you to be quiet," Anod continued to whisper to her.

The process of quieting Natasha took an extraordinary amount of time for a solo warrior well within enemy territory. Anod scanned every angle around them between her efforts of compassion. She was in a very poor, vulnerable position if a Yorax patrol happened to come across them.

"Natasha, I need you to be quiet, to control yourself, so we can leave here." Anod had to repeat herself twice before Natasha finally nodded her head in agreement. "I am going to release your mouth, but you must not make any sound." Anod waited for the confirmatory head nod, and then relaxed her right hand.

"Oh Anod," cried Natasha softly before Anod covered her mouth again.

"Natasha, we are still in danger. I will get us out of here, and we will have time to talk, but I must insist you not make a single sound. You must do exactly as I tell you. You must say nothing and make no sound." Natasha nodded. Anod released her mouth to test her. "Do you understand?" Natasha nodded as she placed a single finger in front of her mouth.

Satisfied with the situation, Anod helped Natasha to her feet then secured the coat around her. Anod signaled for her to follow. Grasping her hand, Anod guided Natasha into one of the open houses. They swiftly and silently found oversized clothes and boots for Natasha.

"Are you ready to travel?" Natasha nodded her head and gave Anod the slightest smile. "Good. Now, I want you to stay here," Anod stopped when she saw Natasha's comfort turn to terror. "It is all right,

Natasha. I need to clear our exit route. It will take me five or so minutes to ensure our egress route is safe." Anod paused for a response. "Do you understand?" She received a reluctant acknowledgment.

Anod put her hood back on, started for the door, and then turned to place a single finger to her lips. Natasha nodded in agreement, again. Anod smiled back at her in the most confident form she could.

The clearing process took the form of climbing onto the roof of a selected building and watching. Although the Yorax continued their random movements, they were all at the other end of town around their base camp. Anod moved in swift, finite spurts, evaluating the conditions around her until she was convinced their escape path was clear. She returned to Natasha who stood in the same position as if she had been petrified.

"The way out of town is safe. Here is what I need you to do. Watch me as I move and try to duplicate my positions and movements. Stay to my left side and half a pace behind me so as not to trip me. Stop when I stop, and watch what you step on. Try to move on your toes to minimize the sounds of your footfalls, and don't step on anything loose. Do you understand so far?" Anod paused for the acknowledgment she sought. "If we are spotted, I want you to run as fast you can to the forest and make your way into the mountains. Find one of our people to help you."

"What will you do?" she whispered so softly.

"I will stand and fight. I will occupy all of them so you can make good your escape."

Natasha nodded.

"Are you ready?"

She nodded again.

Anod held her finger to her mouth, again, then signaled for them to move. Natasha performed perfectly as they left New Providence. It took most of the remaining night to reach Anod's sanctuary in the mountains.

They ate some dried meat Anod had stored in the area then settled into a protected partial cave to sleep. Anod was the first to awaken. The length of Natasha's sleep was yet another measure of her ordeal as well as the security she felt. Anod watched over her and patrolled the area never out of sight. It was morning twilight when Natasha awoke.

At first, she was disoriented, not remembering where she was or how she got there. When her eyes met Anod's, a smile bloomed across her face and in her eyes.

"Thank you for saving me," Natasha said.

"My duty," Anod answered then bowed toward her.

"Where are we?"

"In the mountains, a day's journey from Meganville," Anod responded, choking out the name of the family settlement.

"I am sorry for your loss."

Anod waved her hand. "It is the past. We live now for the future."

"Are we safe here?"

"As safe as we can be. For some reason, the Yorax have not used all the resources available to them, and they have not shown a desire to spend much time in these rugged mountains."

"But, they could come?"

"Yes, I suppose they could, but as long as we are careful, they will have no reason to come here."

"What do you mean?"

"The reason you are in this recess and I am wearing this black suit and mask is to prevent the Yorax sensors from detecting us from their orbiting battlecruiser."

"How do I move?"

"I had two suits made. My spare suit will be a little big on you, but it should work just as well as long as you keep your skin covered and wear this mask," she said touching her covered cheek.

"Always?"

"As long as you can be seen from the sky."

Natasha looked at her dirty skin. "How do I clean myself?"

"The same as I do. We wait until dusk or dark when we can confirm the position of the Yorax battlecruiser orbiting the planet, then we have about 60 minutes to remove the suits and wash before the next pass."

"So, I must wait until evening time."

"Yes."

"I guess I can do that."

"Good." Anod joined Natasha in the recess, sat down beside her and pulled off her mask. "I need to ask you some questions, Natasha. Do you feel up to answering some questions?" Natasha nodded her head. "Some of them might be very painful to answer, but the more complete your answers, the better I will be able to stop the Yorax."

"I understand. For that reason alone, I shall overcome whatever nightmare I may recall."

"Excellent."

Natasha looked at Anod like a child waiting for some wisdom from a parent. Anod looked across the lake then back to Natasha.

"Let's start at the beginning. What happened at your home?"

Natasha stared at Anod. Tears welled up and descended across her dirty face.

"I am sorry," Anod whispered and put her arm around her friend's shoulders.

Natasha waved her hand. She choked back her tears and sniffled slightly. "They came to search our home. I had some compounds they considered dangerous."

"What were they?"

"Some materials I was helping Gerald Oscarson with." She smiled. "The odd thing as I look at it now, the Yorax were correct. Those compounds were dangerous. Anyway, I tried to stop them from destroying my laboratory. When I tried to intervene, they hit me hard," she said touching the discolored remnants of a severe bruise on her right cheek. "My husband jumped to my defense only to be shot dead. I cried for him and could not answer their questions, so they took me away."

"To New Providence?"

"Yes, to their camp."

"Were they asking questions about me or our defenses?"

"No."

Anod's concept of the Yorax intentions and purpose was shaken. If they were not after her, what were they doing here? Anod's expression and diversion communicated to Natasha.

"They mean to destroy us," she offered.

Anod stared at her. "Are you sure?"

"As sure as I can be."

"What did they say to you?"

"It was not so much what they said, because they said very little. It was what they did."

"What they did?" Anod repeated.

"Yes. Several of us met inside that horror chamber." Natasha's eyes turned glassy and stared vacantly into the distance. Anod waited for her to continue. "There were no men, only women. They raped us all . . . everyday . . . in front of all the others."

"Zitger?"

"He calls himself, General Negolian."

"What is he doing?" Anod asked softly of herself, not Natasha.

"He is trying to eliminate the males and plant his seed in all the women."

"Why?"

"To take over this planet for the Yorax.

"By impregnation?"

"Yes."

"What? That is crazy."

"They held me. He raped me everyday until they confirmed that I was pregnant."

"You are pregnant?"

Natasha turned toward Anod and captured her eyes. "Yes, Anod. I think their tests are most probably correct. I think I am pregnant with his child."

"I am sorry, Natasha. I am so sorry."

"I'm alive. I shall survive this."

"There are others in there?"

"Yes. All females past puberty."

Anod's mind went instantly to Naomi Gibritzu. "Who did you see in there?"

"They brought in Naomi and her daughter just before they released me. They released Maria before me. They have Baktar, Susan, and young girls, just children, some of whom I have never met, Tao and so many others."

"How many?"

"In the room I was in, twenty-seven."

"There are others?"

"There may be at least one more room."

"That could be a quarter of our entire, fertile, female population or more."

"Yes, and if we do not do something soon, he will have our whole population."

Anod could not avoid the implications of a new and more onerous dimension to the Yorax intrusion upon their peaceful life. If she went ahead with her current plan, the ugly element added more weight. She would most likely have to endure such treatment. She did not know yet whether she might be pregnant with Bradley's child, but the thought of being raped by Zitger in the process gave her stomach a nauseating twist.

Even if she was pregnant with Bradley's child, Zitger might try to destroy her child before she could extricate herself. Once inside that compound, events would be unpredictable. If she was successful, she would just have to accept the outcome. If she was unsuccessful, she would be dead. The news did not change her mind.

"I am in the final stages of my planning. I will end this," Anod said in a positive, strong voice.

"I hope so, but what can I do?"

"I took the two youngest Gibritzu children to Nagoyama. Mysasha could probably use your help with the children. Since they released you, the Yorax will not likely bother you again unless you do something to provoke them."

"I won't."

"Good."

"Isn't there something I can do to help you?"

"No, Natasha. If you did anything to help me and the Yorax suspected something, you would most likely be killed immediately. Our priority at this stage must be survival. We must do whatever we must do to survive for our children, for our future."

Norashova nodded her head. Dusk was upon them.

Anod searched the sky in a leisurely manner and found the object she needed. She pointed to the bright light moving across the twilight sky. "See that?" she asked pausing to make sure Natasha was looking. "That is the Yorax battlecruiser. As soon as it passes down to the far horizon," she added swinging her arm along the expected path, "we can bath safely. I am sure you will feel much better once we have cleaned your body."

The two women washed themselves and each other. They enjoyed the refreshment of the water. Natasha actually laughed several times while they talked about the past. Anod checked all Natasha's wounds once everything had been thoroughly cleaned. There was nothing serious she could see. Natasha would recover completely in several weeks – several days if they could use a cleansing chamber and isopod. It was dark, and Natasha began to chill when they finally decided to leave the water.

"While you are up here, you should wear the antratite suit to avoid detection," Anod said. Both women dressed. "You can move around freely as long as you are wearing the suit."

"Good."

"You should probably stay here for a few days before we head down to Nagoyama."

"What are you going to do?"

"I should stay here with you, but I need to make my final preparations for dealing with the Yorax."

"Like what?"

Anod knew there was no need for Natasha to know her assault plan. She would not be a factor in the plan and could only compromise it if she was captured again and interrogated. However, she did not want to place Natasha outside the effort to drive off the Yorax. "I recovered Lornog's head – my android. He had memory circuits that might tell me some vital information."

"And, you think you can reactivate him?"

"I don't know, but it is worth a try."

"Can I watch?"

"I don't think that will be a good idea. One, I will need to move quickly and at night, and your night vision is not adequate. Second, I know Mysasha will need your help more than I will. However, as I said earlier, you should stay up here for a few days while I take the last few steps to rid this planet of those vermin." Natasha nodded her head in agreement. "Now, we should eat and get a good night's rest. While we eat, can I ask you some more questions?"

"Sure."

Natasha and Anod ate a very lean meal while they talked about the stars, the clean fresh smell of the mountains, and the goodness of the planet and its people. Anod discreetly interjected questions about the configuration and layout of the Yorax base camp. By the time, they decided to give into their fatigue, Anod had a sufficiently detailed view of what she would face when she entered the complex. The pieces were coming together. She could make her move in another day or two.

Anod woke before dawn, checked their status, and then woke Natasha. She wanted to get part way to Anton's place. She would race the dawn until it became too light to travel safely. Anod knew it would be better for everyone if she kept to herself until this crisis was over, and she had already said too much. She also realized her plan would require some other changes. Natasha deserved an explanation.

"I need you to change into regular clothes. I need to take the spare suit with me," Anod said to Natasha.

"Where are you going?" Natasha asked in a groggy, confused state as she started to open her antratite suit.

Anod saw the boundary pass. "I must find the tools I need to complete my preparations. As you said earlier, we need to do something soon."

"Didn't you say I needed this suit to hide from the Yorax?" Natasha asked still not completely awake.

"Yes, I did. However, you are no longer a threat to the Yorax. In fact, I suspect they will want to keep you alive and well to birth his offspring. I need the spare suit for a more critical task. Plus, as long as you act like this is a convenient campsite in the mountains, I do not think the Yorax will bother you. After all, they are going to have their hands full quite soon." Natasha simply nodded. Anod waited for her to change clothes. She packed away the spare suit and checked the small bag she had strapped to the back of the scooter.

"Anod, you can't do whatever it is you are planning to do, alone."

"There is no choice. This is not an article of debate. I need you to stay here. There is enough food to live comfortably for two weeks or longer if you had to, and you have unlimited water."

"But, you will be alone," Natasha repeated.

"Yes."

Natasha stared at Anod with a very worried expression. She lowered her head and eyes. "What if you don't come back?"

"This will be over one way or another in two to three days. If I do not return for you by the fourth day, then make your way to Nagoyama. It is that way," she said pointing to a pass in the mountains on the far side of the lake. "As I said, Mysasha and her family can use your help, and you can take care of each other."

"We can't lose you."

"As I am sure you know, I can make no promise regarding the outcome, but I can assure you I have no intention of losing."

"But, Anod," Natasha protested.

She held up her hand. "We have gotten you this far. You are safe. Let me worry about the Yorax. Please do as I have asked. I need to know you are all right." Natasha nodded her head in agreement. "Good. Now, I must be off. Dawn is approaching."

Natasha returned her tearful eyes to Anod. "Good luck and be careful."

"Thank you." Anod wasted no further time. She gathered the items she needed, mounted the scooter and promptly departed.

Anod initially headed in a direction other than her real path of travel to avoid any compromise. Once she was beyond visual range of their mountain camp, she checked her chronometer. She had adequate time to get beyond the horizon before she would have to stop again. Anod also planned her routine to reach a secure place to avoid as much daytime travel as possible – fewer people who might be aware of her passing.

She reached Anton Trikinov's house in the early morning hours. Everything appeared to be as it was when she left the last time. Anod waited for Anton to rise normally.

Anton grinned when he saw her, gave her a big hug and a kiss on both cheeks. "I have been worried about you. The news is not good."

"I know. I just left Natasha Norashova. The Yorax appear to be killing the males and trying to impregnate all the females."

"So, it is true."

"Yes. I am afraid so."

"Then, they will come for me."

"Have they been here since my last visit?"

"No."

Anod felt the need to search his eyes. Anton appeared sincere. He also detected the reason for her pause. "I am telling you the truth, Anod."

"I know," she answered as she began to unload her baggage. Anton looked puzzled. "I am in the final stages of my preparations."

"For what?"

"To deal with the Yorax. I must stop them from this senseless abuse. I intend to avenge the loss of my family and rid our planet of this virulent menace."

"Just you?"

"Yes, Anton. Just me. A single determined adversary with the will to succeed can overcome innumerable odds."

"You are crazy!"

"Yes, probably, but more importantly, I am committed," she said sternly. "I have lost my entire family and many friends. I haven't much more to lose."

Trikinov stared at her. A slight grin grew on his face. "All right," he chuckled. "You are obviously here because you need my help."

"Yes, in a manner of speaking." Anton's grin disappeared. "Here is what I need you to do. Is Morgan still functional?"

"Yes."

"Excellent. When I have finished briefing you, we will go inside.

I need you to cover up Morgan's eye and ear. I will need to make some connections to use Morgan."

"They will detect you."

"Yes, I know. They will also respond quickly, so we will not have much time. While I am doing what I need to do, you must get into this suit. It was made for me. It will be a little loose on you, but it should work. I want you to take the shuttle to Horvak, park it in the large open meadow, and then I want you to go into the hills and hide. You must stay there, and you absolutely must keep this suit on to avoid detection."

"What will you do?"

"I will do what I must then leave before the Yorax arrive. They will try to catch me. They might try to find you, but that is not likely. They will destroy this place."

"So, you want me to disappear."

"Yes."

"When can I return?"

"Not until I come to find you."

"You are going after them, aren't you?"

"Yes."

"Then, what if something happens to you."

"Give me a week. Either the Yorax will be gone, or I will be dead. In the latter case, you will have to make your own decisions."

"I should help you fight the Yorax."

"No, Anton. We cannot defeat them by fighting."

"Then, what are you going to do?"

"It is better that you do not know."

"In case I get captured?"

"Yes."

"OK. I can do that."

"Good." Anod checked her chronometer again. "Our window of opportunity will open in another fifteen minutes. When it is time, remember, I need you to first cover Morgan's eye and block his ear." Anton nodded. "Then, you get into the suit and leave as quickly as you can. You should have sufficient time to fly from here to Horvak before the Yorax can detect your movement. They will, of course, know the shuttle has been moved, and they will suspect you since you will disappear and I will have been here just before your disappearance." Anton nodded again. "Timing will be critical."

At the appointed time, Anod held a finger to her lips then motioned with her head for Anton to proceed. He covered Morgan, gave her a thumbs-up signal, and then proceeded to undress. Anod laid everything out of the kitchen table. He picked up the suit as she made the necessary connections between the tendrils at the base of Lornog's head and Morgan's console.

Anton went for the door, stopped to salute Anod, and then left without waiting for her return salute. Anod waited for Trikinov to depart in the shuttle. She checked her chronometer again. She had only ten minutes to complete her task and make her escape.

Anod took a deep breath and uncovered the console. "Morgan," she said.

"Yes, Anod."

"I have connected Lornog's head to your console here. I want you to activate his memory and replay his final moments for me from the first indication of any intrusion related to the Yorax arrival at Meganville."

"As you command."

Within seconds, the world as seen by Lornog appeared on the right screen. Within a few seconds of activation, Morgan displayed on the center screen among all the other data, a word in upper case letters – MAXIMUM. The Yorax knew of the activation and were monitoring her work. She had only minutes.

Anod watched the screen and saw the troopers burst into her house. Bradley jumped to his feet and was shot instantly but appeared to be only stunned. 'Where is Anod,' they squealed their demand. 'She is not here,' answered Nick. 'Where is she,' they persisted. Nick said, 'We don't know,' and was shot next as he sat in his chair. Lornog jumped toward the children. Anod saw terror on Zoltentok's face, then Sara's startled cries from the commotion. Then, black.

Tears streamed down Anod's cheeks. Her chest heaved with the sobs of a grieving mother. The fear on her children's faces tore into her heart. They had died a violent death. They died at the hands of evil beings. She also realized they tortured Bradley for answers after Lornog and the children had died.

An uncounted number of seconds passed before she noticed the words, End of Recording, and the blinking words at the bottom of the screen – THEY ARE COMING.

Anod tore Lornog's head from the console, ran outside, jumped onto the scooter placing the android's head in her lap, and hit the throttle to maximum nearly ripping the scooter from her vice grip.

She raced toward the dusk terminus dodging obstacles as she traveled at maximum speed. Anod scanned the horizon continuously until she saw the flicker she expected. She executed a maximum deceleration causing Lornog's head to fly forward like a shot. As soon as the scooter stopped, Anod hit the kill button, shutting off all power and dropping the vehicle to the ground with an abrupt thud. She jumped off the scooter and ran for a small clump of bushes surrounding a pile of large rocks. She waited, her heart pounding in her chest. Then, she realized in her haste, she left the light rifle on the scooter. Anod watched from her cover.

A Yorax shuttle passed a kilometer away from her, and then, two more. She strained to see if there were others coming. She climbed onto the highest point of the rocks and searched the entire horizon. She could see nothing. She checked the chronometer. The battlecruiser would be just coming over the horizon. The large warship would most probably have been alerted. She wanted to move the scooter to cover, but the risk was too great. Anod would have to wait until she could confirm the state of things. There was nothing she could do other than wait.

An hour before dusk, Anod saw one of the Yorax shuttles traveling at a much slower speed but farther away from her. They were searching for her. Travel would be much more risky and dangerous, now. She felt the net closing on her. Anod recognized that she had to execute her plan tonight, or as soon as she could get into position.

To her great relief, Anod saw the bright spot that was the Yorax battlecruiser rising above the horizon. Not only had the warship not changed its orbital characteristics, but it had also not activated its masking system. Everything appeared to be routine. Anod had to assume they would be using every sensor available to them from now on. That meant she could not move as long as the battlecruiser was above the horizon.

Anod took every available second of travel time during the night. She also stopped to reconnoiter any potential region of exposure before transiting the area or circumnavigating any place of unnecessary risk. She could only make the foothills of the mountain range between her and New Providence at morning twilight. Anod found a place to wait for the day to pass. The scooter was running out of fuel in its energy pack. She would not have time to go to the other scooter nor could she refuel. She deactivated the scooter. Anod calculated the available time she had on the energy pack. There was probably enough to get her to New Providence if she went directly there and at a relatively slow speed. That was her plan anyway, so that part fit. Then, she realized the low fuel state on the scooter would actually enhance her setup for the next phase of the *finale*.

After her usual checks around her and above her, Anod went to sleep. She was actually surprised she could sleep considering the events just ahead of her. In a manner of speaking, it was good that she had such a close call with the Yorax, yesterday. The adrenaline let-down helped her sleep.

Chapter 14

Anod woke before dusk. She foraged for whatever food she could find in the area around her. She did not need much to give her a full feeling since she had been on thin rations for quite sometime. Anod listened to the birds and animal sounds. They were similar throughout the day. Things were normal according to the wildlife.

Anod removed her antratite suit and stashed the suit along with other items, and then dressed in the common loose clothing of Murtauri Four. She stretched each muscle very carefully to ensure she could achieve full performance. Her body was ready. These were probably going to be the hardest days of her life in almost every way possible. And yet, the image of her children in the images of Lornog's last seconds burned within her like molten lead. Anod breathed precisely to clear her body and prepare her mind. This was the night her plan would come together.

Anod waited for complete darkness, and then worked her way slowly through the mountains. As soon as she could see the lights of the Yorax camp at New Providence, Anod stopped to observe. They had still not repaired the light pole as far as she could see from the great distance. She moved cautiously taking every opportunity to observe the compound as she approached. It was nearly local midnight when she reached her desired spot.

It was as though nothing had happened over the previous few days. The same patrol, randomly executed, occupied many of the Yorax troopers. The light and sensor poles she had shot down had been removed, but they had indeed not been replaced.

"This is it," she said aloud to herself.

Anod took a deep breath, aimed for the post of the farthest adjacent light pole and fired. The lights went out in a burst. The pole crashed to the ground. This time the scrambled troopers seemed confused as they exited the gateway. Anod aimed again, this time at the nearest sensor ball. She fired, exploding the ball in a shower of sparks. This time, the troopers saw her shot and her firing position. They deployed to engage. Additional troopers flowed from the complex. Anod watched their progress then casually walked to her scooter.

Anod waited until the troopers were close enough to see her attempted escape. They fired several times into the bushes that had been her firing position. Small fires started. When she saw the top of the first trooper's head, Anod accelerated slowly – almost too slowly. They fired, barely missing her. She wanted her escape to look genuine. The Yorax pursuit was more aggressive than she anticipated causing her to accelerate to stay sufficiently ahead of her pursuers.

The scooter ran out of fuel before she reached the desired box canyon. Anod abandoned the scooter and intentionally left the light rifle with the scooter. She ran at a moderate pace into the canyon and waited at the rock face until she detected the first flashes of light from their search. She carefully moved up the rock face several meters. She watched trying to gauge her progress with those of the Yorax troopers. At just about the perfect spot, a light projectile burst against the rock next to her. She froze.

"Come down, now," the trooper screeched, "or we shall fire to kill."

Anod did not think the last part was true, but she wanted to act as though it was. When she was on the ground, Anod turned only to be blinded by a half dozen lights pointed directly at her.

"Hold your arms out," the trooper commanded.

This was the risky portion of her capture, but she had to take the chance. As she raised her arms, Anod charged the line of troopers. One fired hitting her left shoulder like a massive ball nearly spinning her around. Another shot hit her in the chest knocking her down. Her vision narrowed as the approaching blackout almost took her consciousness. Her body hurt, and she had trouble catching her breath. She smiled to herself. She had been correct. They used a high-stun setting for their rifles.

Anod could see the troopers moving toward her and the shaking of her extremities, but she could not move anything. The Yorax screeched simple commands. They tied her with straps – her elbows to her torso, her wrists to her hips, her knees and ankles. The straps had large loops they used like baggage handles to lift her into a small shuttlecraft. Four troopers went with her in the cargo compartment.

She recovered her motor function, as best she could tell, by the time they reached the New Providence compound. The vehicle drove through the gateway into a quadrangle area before they opened it to remove her. A few more screeched commands preceded them carrying her into a rather large room. There were no others in the room other than Anod and six Yorax troopers. Various apparatuses occupied the center of the room –

a table with restraints, a round bench of some sort, and odd wide U-shaped chair. They were devices of torture. A control console occupied the long, far wall opposite to where they placed her. The troopers stood her, although her balance was not particularly good in the body restraints. She fell several times only to be lifted to the standing position again.

Several of the troopers placed manacles attached to long chains on her wrists and ankles before they began removing the straps. A single, wide, flat key with deep cut teeth was used to lock each device. Anod noted with some inner satisfaction, the key hung by the small chain around the neck of one of the guards. They started first with her legs. As soon as her ankles and knees were free from the straps, they pulled the chains taut drawing her feet beyond shoulder width apart. She lost her balance several times but was held up by one or more of the troopers. They did the same thing with her arms. The chains pulled her hands high above her head and also beyond shoulder width. Anod was in an X position with all four chains tight. She had very little movement other than a little fore and aft swing with the chains.

Several more screeches came. Four of them stood back while the other two retrieved knives from a drawer under the table. Carefully, they cut all her clothing away from her body until she was completely exposed. When they were finished, they all stood back looking at her using their irritating language to exchange words and laugh at her in their odd, disgusting way. Several of them poked at her body in various places. Anod commanded her mind to prevent even the slightest twitch or reaction. They were undoubtedly probing to find her weak or sensitive spots. Convinced she was not going to react as they had hoped, they left the room.

Anod used the time alone to examine every aspect of the room. A small winch type device held each chain at the prescribed length. She tried each restraint with as much force as she could generate at such odd angles. There was no movement. An array of slide tracks covered the ceiling and floor that probably meant they would move her around the room without releasing the manacles. She tried to slide the winch blocks along the tracks in either direction, but they were apparently locked in place. There appeared to be small teeth inside each track that suggested the winch block had their own propulsion mechanism. They probably moved by command from the control panel across from her.

The door opened. Two troopers with their weapons at the ready entered first followed by Zitger and two more troopers. Zitger wore a reduced size black protective suit similar to the Yorax, but had a large gold star on top of each shoulder.

"Well, well, well, look what we have here," he said as he walked to a spot directly in front of her about 2.5 meters away, just far enough that if she was not restrained she would have to take at least two steps to attack him. The four guards arrayed themselves on either side of him.

Anod fought the anger she felt in her belly and the pounding in every blood vessel of her body. She did not want to give him even the slightest satisfaction of a reaction. Anod knew that her moment would come, sooner or later. She had to be patient and non-responsive.

"So, you finally made a mistake," he said placing his hands on his hips as he swaggered in place. "I have waited too long for this moment. It is unfortunate your untimely arrival is after my sleep cycle was supposed to begin. By the way, aren't you even going to say hello to your old friend?"

Anod stared at him with as much blankness in her eyes as she could achieve. She neither smiled nor sneered. She wanted no response.

"I guess, not. Well, no matter. Your response is not required. Just so you know what is in store for you, I shall give you a little menu. First, I am going to get a very good night's sleep. In fact, I shall leave orders not to wake me. I want to be as rested as I possibly can, for tomorrow, I intend to have some fun with you. Rest assured, the pain and humiliation you shall feel is for my pleasure. I want this pleasure to last a good long time before you die." Zitger grinned at her. "I hope you realize you will not survive this experience."

Anod considered nodding her head in agreement just to give him the impression she had lost all hope, but her instinct told her not to react.

"I need nothing from you, Lieutenant Anod, nothing at all. I know your will is strong which simply means I shall enjoy your suffering until death, all the more." He paused as though he expected an answer. She gave him nothing. "Good, then. I shall bid you a pleasant night." He chuckled. "I must apologize for our rather crude accommodations for a person of your stature, but this is the best we can do for you," he laughed hard. "Good night, then." Zitger led the troopers out of the room. The door was closed and a heavy set of locks inside the thick door secured the double door set.

Anod very carefully searched every object, surface, edge or seam in the entire room. She had to assume they had observation devices, but she could not find anything that even remotely resembled an observation capability.

With her search complete, Anod smiled broadly. It was the oddest sensation for her. The elaborate, strong restraints and their apparent ability to control them along with her aloneness in this room meant Zitger and the Yorax had a very healthy respect for her capabilities. After all, according to Natasha's report, none of the other Murtaurian women had been subjected to these restraints and isolation. She had hoped she would be able to talk to the other captives, but that clearly was not to be the case. The extent of her isolation and the security of her shackles became a simple obstacle between her and her objective. She needed more information about the use of all this equipment before the last few details of her plan would come to her. The most important intermediate objective for her was to endure whatever they intended to do to her and somehow engage Zitger in a dialogue. She had to learn some of the reasons why he had done what he did. She also wanted to learn as much as she could about what his plans were with the Yorax, for Murtauri Four, and for this sector of the galaxy. She reminded herself to be observant, but to remain as passive as possible until the moment came for her to strike. Anod wanted them to think they had total and absolute control over her. She wanted them to feel safe and since she was not expected to live, she hoped they would share some of that vital information with her. She told herself, the more she learned about them and their motives, the stronger she would become and the more likely her mission would succeed. This would be a test of wills although she wanted to keep that from them.

Anod knew she had to be ready for even the slight instant from which to take her decisive move. Just as Zitger wanted his rest for her torture, Anod knew she needed to rest as much as she possibly could.

Anod lowered her chin to her chest.

She awoke with a start several times when her slumber disturbed her balance. The third time convinced Anod she would not get much rest trying to maintain her position. The flexibility of her body and the slight swing of her chains allowed her to lean back against the restraints. She thought she could lock her knees to keep her body from slumping in relaxation. Her sleeping weight would put an undesirable amount of pressure on her arms, but that was better as long as she could sleep. The adverse position would not be good on her joints, but the angle was good enough to keep her head on her chest rather than falling back. She gave her position a try. It worked.

The locks moving woke her. She quickly looked around the room as she returned herself to a standing position. Absolutely nothing had changed while she slept. Again, two guards entered first with their weapons drawn – a very good sign. They thought it was at least possible she might be able to slip her restraints. Her passivity and endurance would help to reduce or eliminate that caution.

Zitger again followed then two more guards. This time two new Yorax joined them. These two wore smaller silver stars on their shoulders – lieutenants of some sort.

The traitor returned to the same position he left. "I trust you had as good a night's sleep as I had," he said with an odd lightness to his voice. "Oh, no matter. We are not going to be particularly good hosts anyway, so it does not concern us." He moved to within a hand's distance of her face. "Aren't you going to say good morning?" She did not respond, not even a twitch. "So, you will not be civil. Again, no matter." He stared into her eyes. "Do you have anything you want to say to me before we begin?" He paused for a response but received none. "Aren't there any questions you want to ask?"

He was searching for some opening into her mind. Anod would not give him that satisfaction, not yet at least.

Zitger turned and walked to the control console. As he passed one of the silver star Yorax, he said, "Let's get the initial tests done."

The four guards stepped back to the walls on either side of her. The two silver star Yorax moved a small column device with a blue, flat face directly in front of her. The object looked like a scanner. Zitger activated the column. A line of bright blue light descended from the top. Anod closed her eyes.

"Open your eyes, if you please," Zitger said in a pleasant, normal voice.

Anod did not comply.

"Do you want us to open them," one of the Yorax screeched.

"No. We don't really need that information since she will not survive."

The blue light continued its descent. Anod kept her eyes closed until she heard them moving the column away from her.

"Well, now," said Zitger, "isn't this interesting." The two assistants joined him at the console. "I have some news for you," he turned to look at her. Nothing. He looked back at one of the screens, then back to her. "Oh, never mind. This does not change anything. The process and the result will be the same."

Anod's mind did grind through the possibilities. They must have found something that was either not normal, or not what they wanted. When she got out of this situation, she wanted to get her own cleansing station body scan to see what they found.

"With the painless preliminaries out of the way, it is time to begin the real festivities," he announced.

Zitger walked to the table, opened a drawer and removed a long, slender, fine edged, knife, larger than a dagger but smaller than a sword. He held it in front of him as he approached Anod. She prepared her mind for the pain that was surely soon to come.

He stopped about one meter away and extended his arm until the point of the blade barely touched the base of her throat. "So there is no confusion here, I am going to carve you up a little before we get on to the real fun parts. I want you to have some pain to focus on, to soften you up a little. By all means, feel free to scream out."

He did not wait for an answer. Zitger pushed the blade into her skin. Anod closed her eyes and tried as hard as she could to ignore the sharp pain at her collarbone. She stiffened her body against the blade. He slowly dragged the blade down the middle of her chest to her navel. She felt her skin open as the blade descended across her chest. The searing pain caused her facial muscle to finally give way in a silent grimace. Anod could feel the blood streaming down her abdomen and legs. She could hear the splatters on the floor as her blood dripped from various parts of her lower body.

Zitger, without words or sounds of any kind, took the blade to the front of her thighs and then the inside of her upper arms. Dizziness began to cloud her mind. Without seeing the amount of blood she lost, Anod felt certain the dizziness was from her enormous struggle against the pain rather than blood loss. She knew Zitger was more interested in her pain and the slowness of her planned death rather than a relatively quick and silent death by blood loss. He was probably cutting her just enough to cause the level of pain he sought without producing too much blood loss. He apparently did not want to cut muscle or any vital organs.

"We shall give you a few moments to allow these wounds to coagulate before we proceed to the next step."

Anod pushed the pain from her mind, and with her effort, the dizziness faded. Her suppression was working. When she felt she had regained sufficient control, Anod opened her eyes to find Zitger standing two meters away with the blade still in hand at his side.

"Good, you have returned to us," he said and smiled. "I am impressed, Lieutenant Anod. Your warrior's control over the pain your mind feels is truly admirable. Perhaps I have underestimated your capability."

Anod did not react. She tried to ignore her body and concentrate on Zitger's face. She bore into his eyes. Her adversary recognized the effort. A sinister grin grew across his face. He must have seen the determination in her eyes.

"Excellent," he said waving his long knife toward her several times.

As if by some pre-briefed or rehearsed plan, the two guards opposite the doors laid their rifles against the wall and moved to either side of her without touching her or the chains. Zitger and the two silver star assistants went to the console. All four winch blocks began to move. Anod was forced to shuffle and stumble. They moved her to the side of the round top bench. The two closest guards went to the opposite side of the bench. Anod could smell their foul odor like some stale decay kept bottled up for weeks.

The upper blocks moved forward bending her over the bench. She felt the bench lower itself slightly. To her surprise her arm chains slackened. Anod recognized the moment instantly. Within seconds, she was able to place her hands on the bench, and there was sufficient slack in the chains that she could easily sweep her arms and wrap the chains around the necks of the two guards. She could probably move quickly enough to snap their necks, but at the very least choke them to death if the others did not come to their rescue. Other than placing her hands on the bench for some welcome relief, Anod chose not to move. Her only concession was a quick examination of her wounds. A good portion of the front of her body was covered in her own blood drying into a caked mess.

The two guards cautiously grabbed the chains, probably not fully realizing how close they were to death, and pulled the looped chains down to hook a link of chain onto a small block that immediately began to move away from her. She was drawn snugly against the round top bench. The guards checked all four chains. She looked up to see Zitger wave to his entourage. The door locks were reengaged. They were alone for the first time.

Oddly, Zitger sat down in front of her so she did not have to strain her neck so much to see him. "It is just us, now. You do not have to put on any display of strength for me. I have given you that opportunity for my

Yorax brethren." He paused for a response, but again, got none. "Well, then, we shall proceed," he said as he stood and moved behind her.

Anod could not hear him or see him. For several minutes, she could have thought she was alone. She felt his hand on her left hip.

"You know, Anod, to be honest and candid, I have waited for this moment since before we left Saranon all those years ago. So, in my way, I was excited in a manly way when I learned you had survived the ambush."

Anod knew what was coming. She worked to relax her body and accept it. There was not much at the moment she could do anyway, so she saw her task as minimizing any collateral damage or injury.

His other hand grasped her right hip. She felt him press into her. Anod commanded her muscles to relax and let him enter. Zitger slowly pushed himself into her until they were fully joined.

"I have imagined this feeling. It is so much better than I thought. You are most accommodating, quite unlike the others." He began to slowly stroke into her, and then stopped as he moved his hands over her back and hips. "It appears you have learned this pleasure as well since your banishment from the Society." He stroked some more. "Isn't this fun?" he asked, not really expecting an answer.

Anod kept her mind in neutral although flashes of Bradley and Otis came to her, but she forced them out. She had to keep as independent and passive as she possibly could. If she allowed her memory of the pleasure she felt with Bradley to mix with this violation, she feared she might lose that contact with Bradley. This was no different than the cuts he inflicted upon her earlier.

His hands moved over more of her body, including her legs when he paused again at full insertion. "My, my, but you have a firm body. You are so unlike all these other women on this planet, even the young ones."

The image of his abuse of young Murtaurian women, not quite fully mature, wrenched her stomach. The first urges of her retaliation flooded into her consciousness. She must have subconsciously twitched against him.

"So, you don't like my valiant efforts to impregnate your young females."

Anod castigated herself silently for the momentary weakness. Her lack of control would probably lead to the pain and suffering of others. Surprisingly, she felt tears well up in her eyes. Fortunately for her and the others, Zitger was busy with his own activity and could not see her further reaction. Anod repeated in her mind, over and over, she could not react in any manner to any of Zitger's efforts.

His stroking became more purposeful. "We have other things to do, so I ought to get this first introduction finished." His conclusion came promptly. Only the slightest, erratic convulsions marked his completion. He stood up and did not touch her other than by their connection. "I want to tell you, I am really going to enjoy our time together. It does bring me some feathers of regret that you will not live to pleasure me for a very long time. But, alas, I have worlds to conquer for my people." At the appropriate moment, he withdrew from her. The sounds probably meant he was tending to himself.

Without a word, Zitger went to the doors and pushed two buttons to open the locks. Another good sign, Anod told herself. He did not feel a need to conceal the unlocking procedure from her. He obviously considered her escape impossible, thus there was no need to conceal the exit procedure. One of the guards opened the primary door without a weapon drawn. Once again, another good sign.

Once Zitger went down the hallway to the left, the four guards reentered the room, two with their rifles at the ready. They worked the controls to return her to the original position along the right wall. When they were satisfied she was secure, they departed leaving her alone, again.

Anod used the time to more thoroughly evaluate her wounds as well as the amount of blood on the floor beneath her. All of her wounds had sealed. Dried blood had already flaked off her body in places. Anod tested her restraints. The Yorax had done their job well.

Another visual room search revealed nothing of use to Anod. Her mind began digesting what she had learned so far. Natasha's information was confirmed, at least as far as Anod could tell. There was a carelessness about the Yorax actions earlier in her captivity. She was convinced her continued passivity would encourage further complacency on the part of the Yorax, especially as they perceived her weakening state and impending death. She had to be careful not to play the part too strongly too soon, or they might become suspicious. Likewise, she could not allow her strength to be depleted too far before she made her move.

The struggle for Anod, as with most warriors in similar situations, centered upon balance. She knew the longer she waited to act the more injury would be done to those in captivity, and yet, if she acted too soon, she might not achieve the advantage she needed to be successful. Anod remembered Natasha's description of the torture chamber where she had been held and repeatedly violated in front of and along with the other

Murtauri women. Her friends were still in that room and probably one other chamber.

The conditions she wanted should disarm whatever caution the Yorax might have remaining after a few days of her torture. Ideally, Zitger would be out of the room when she freed herself, and then she would convince him to a personal duel. In her diminished state, she would have to hope for some degree of complacency on his part or one minor mistake. While she did not want to die, Anod knew success depended upon her singular concentration on Zitger. If she lost her life after dispatching Zitger, it would be an acceptable and honorable price for a warrior.

Comfortable with her thinking, Anod decided to take whatever time she could to rest. She returned to her sleeping position.

There was no way for her to know how long she had been asleep, but once again she was awakened by the clacking sound of the door locks being moved. This time, the guards did not precede Zitger. Only the two older daughters of Naomi Gibritzu followed him into the room. Their heads rested on their chests, and their shoulders slumped into barely recognizable clumps.

"I brought two fine young examples of Murtaurian womanhood," Zitger announced.

Anod knew what was coming. She prepared her mind to ignore the graphic abuse of two innocent young women she was about to witness. Her momentary lapse in control caused this grotesque demonstration.

Anod suffered her pain and especially the pain of Cetia and Moma. Cetia was the beautiful 15-year-old young woman with an effervescent, enthusiastic individuality that amplified her boundless curiosity. Two years younger, Moma followed her sister like an avid fan. Both young women represented their mother, their family, in the best possible way. It was their outgoing personalities that made the transformation of their youthful excitement into the dejected, submissive, withdrawn shells he had rendered them – so gut wrenching. Neither of the girls looked at Anod or anything else. They just stood there with no apparent hope left in them. Zitger had taken their exuberance. Anod watched them. They did not move.

At least they were dressed. They both wore knee length, country dresses, unfortunately soiled by their ordeal. Cetia's was light blue with small printed flowers, and Moma's was deep yellow with little red dots. There were no signs of physical injury. The mental and emotional injury appeared to be so deep. Anod wanted to help them, to reach out to them, to protect them from the traitor. She could do nothing but witness. She thought about closing her eyes to avoid the disgusting display, but that simple action alone would undoubtedly be sufficient to encourage Zitger. Anod made her mind blank.

Zitger turned them to face Anod. The long knife he used to cut Anod was now used under each girl's chin to lift her head. Moma kept her eyes closed. Cetia saw Anod. Shock registered in her beaten eyes. The young woman probably could only see Anod's abused and exposed state. She could not see the strength Anod drew from her perceived weakness and vulnerability. Zitger did not miss Cetia's reaction.

"I have some delightful specimens for you," Zitger said to Anod.

The urge to plead for mercy for the two Gibritzu girls welled up instantly within her. She swallowed hard to control it.

"These two came here a few days ago with their mother, and they were the most resistive to their duty." He walked toward Anod. He kept her eyes. "This," he said glancing over his shoulder and waving the long knife toward the girls, "is what you have done to this planet, what you have brought to this planet."

Anod again swallowed hard and could only hope Zitger did not notice the slight response. He kept coming toward her. When he was beside her on the left, Zitger turned back to the girls.

"Look at your protector, girls," he said. Cetia was looking with horror in her eyes. Moma could only look down at her feet. "I said look at her," he commanded gruffly. Moma slowly raised her eyes to Anod, but stared blankly without the slightest noticeable reaction. "This was your protector – the great Anod. Look at her, now." The abhorrence in Cetia's eyes began to wash away as the sight went far beyond her saturation point. Zitger reached for and squeezed one of Anod's breasts very hard. The move caught Anod by surprise causing her to bite her lip. Fortunately, Zitger was not looking at her, and beyond the fresh rusty blood at her lips, Anod did not react. "You girls should feel good – honored, even." Zitger stepped back slightly and cut Anod across her breast and another down her side. Her blood flowed again. Moma just continued to stare blankly, but Cetia gasped and turned away. "Do not take your eyes off of her!" he shouted harshly. Cetia looked back but was clearly shaken by Zitger's action. "As long as you girls do your duty, you will not suffer the same fate. Your powerful Anod will not last much longer." He cut her again, this time across her stomach. "You girls should feel thankful that all you must do is carry my seed." Zitger cut horizontally across both thighs, went to her right side to cut her some more, and then walked backward away from Anod as if he was admiring his work. "In fact," he added turning toward the girls, "I think I am ready to give you your next dose."

To Anod's horror, Cetia went directly to the bench and leaned across it like a trained animal. She was facing away from Anod. Zitger went to her and turned toward Anod. Using the blade of the knife, he lifted her dress to reveal her naked posterior. Zitger smiled and wagged his head from side to side as though he was some successful hunter hovering over his prized kill. Anod strained to keep her eyes focused coldly on Zitger.

The beast turned to his prey. Anod glanced to Moma who was looking at her feet again. Zitger accentuated the sounds of his effort to make sure both Moma and Anod knew of his achievement. Moma showed no sign of recognition. Perhaps, her near catatonic state was actually a blessing, Anod told herself. When he was done, Zitger jerked Cetia's arm standing her up and brusquely waved for her to join her sister. Moma, almost by some unseen force, shuffled toward the bench.

"Oh, no, my little one," he said to her. "I want to see your face and you to see mine." He pointed toward the U-shaped chair. Anod watched Moma. She seemed to flutter along some invisible guide wire. The chair was obviously a device she had seen before as she positioned herself as she had been taught. Zitger looked at her then shook his head. He retrieved the knife. "I am not yet ready for you," she said to Moma then turned to Anod. "I need some inspiration."

Zitger crossed the distance. Without the slightest indication, he swung the long knife at her, striking the side of her chest with the flat of the blade. Bolts of electric pain shot to every corner of her body causing Anod to shake with tremors for a few seconds. He hit her again, this time across her stomach, and then on the bone of both hips.

"Why have you caused all this pain," he shouted at Anod as he continued to flail at her. "Why didn't you die when you were supposed to?" The rhetorical question gave Anod more strength to endure. Her pain gave Anod an inner contentment that she made the correct decision to avoid reaction.

Zitger cut her several more times although not as deep as previous occasions. His last attempt did not draw blood. As he used the point of the blade to poke into sensitive areas of her body, Anod noticed Cetia's expression change. Fear and abhorrence was replaced with anger, and she stepped toward Zitger. Anod caught her eyes and shook her head.

Cetia froze, but Zitger noticed the movement and turned to see Cetia's expression and position.

"Ah ha," he shouted with glee. "The fire of resistance." He walked quickly to her waving the knife menacingly. "You want to save your Anod, do you?"

Thankfully, Cetia did not respond other than to withdraw into her passive shell. Zitger flicked his knife blade at her. He flared the lower portion of her dress and stabbed it with the point. A muffled squeal came from Cetia as she tried to hold still. Even with the foolish little attempt to help Anod, he had not cut her or physically injured her. With both Gibritzu girls and Natasha Norashova, Anod confirmed the picture. Zitger did intend to kill her, but only wanted to impregnate the other women.

Satisfied that Cetia was under his control again, Zitger turned to face Anod. "Just what I needed to prepare me for my duty," he said with a broad smile on his face. He went to Moma. He tried to ready himself for the assault on Moma. The young girl just sat there, spread-eagled, waiting for the onslaught. Zitger was not as ready as he thought. After several attempts, he gave up. "Damn it to hell," he growled as he left Moma and stomped around the far side of the room. "I need some rest. Back to your cage," he said to the girls.

Cetia moved to the door and waited for it to open. Moma needed the encouragement of Zitger's blade, but eventually wobbled to the door joining her sister. Zitger walked directly to face Anod, placing the point of the blade on Anod's sternum between her breasts.

"I shall get a good night's rest and return to you in the morning."

Zitger did not wait for a response, probably convinced that if he had not been able to produce a response so far, he was not likely to get one now. He tossed the knife at the table causing it to clank and bounce across the floor.

Anod noticed with pleasure that Zitger was again careless in not trying to hide the exit opening procedures. It was identically the same as the earlier time. As soon as the door opened, Zitger pushed the two girls out and promptly followed them. The door locks shut.

Anod took a deep breath, released it slowly, and leaned back against her chains. She allowed her head to go back as she groaned softly with her accumulated pain. She could only hope she would be left alone for several hours. She needed as much rest as she could gather. Anod flexed all the muscles she could in her precarious position. Zitger's abuse was taking a toll. She knew she did not have many more hours of this torture before she might be too weak to act. As she allowed her mind to slip toward whatever sleep she could find she considered various options. The time to act had come.

Chapter 15

Anod's fatigue and depletion mounted to the point that it took her longer to regain alertness. The door locks had already unlatched and the door opened before she could open her eyes. Zitger entered the room. "Good morning," he said in a cheery voice.

Two unarmed guards followed him in before the door closed. The guards began moving her as they had done the last time. Zitger just stood aside and watched.

"I thought I would start the day off right by giving you a little pleasure." Anod knew there would be no pleasure for her. "I must confess I am wasting my precious seed on you since you will not live to deliver my child, but somehow, I feel compelled to tend to you when I am at my freshest. However, I must tell you I am tiring of this. I really would rather see your face, but I do not trust you. Anyway, today will probably be your last day. You are not much fun. I have found I enjoy the struggle, and many of your women give me what I want. So, you don't have many chances left. I want you to beg for mercy or resist me, and perhaps I will spare you."

Anod knew there was no way Zitger would allow her to live given his choices. He had to realize that as long as she was alive she was a threat.

The troopers completed their work and departed. Zitger did not waste time beginning his task.

He slapped her buttocks several times very hard. "Resist me damn you. Fight like I know you can."

Anod forced her body to do just the opposite. She would not give him more than he was already going to take. Zitger thrust his fist hard into the small of her back directly at her right kidney. The pain nearly blacked her out. She allowed herself to slump in total relaxation as her control continued to seep from her. Anod saw the end – one way or another.

"Come now, my lovely Anod, doesn't this feel so good?" he gushed as he purposefully sought his own pleasure.

Anod considered the moment for the change to the next phase of her plan. Her gut told her, no.

"Yes, indeed. This does feel good." He did not skip a beat. "I know you enjoy this." He took a deep breath. "After all, you have had two children through this process. I only want to give you another to enjoy." His motion began to quicken. "Tell me . . . you enjoy . . . this . . . just as . . . much . . . as I . . . do," he grunted as he exploded into her.

Zitger remained still and quiet. She could hear his heavy breathing. As he recovered, he withdrew from her and left the room without a word.

The previous two guards returned to undo her. One of the troopers had the key around his neck. Anod quickly calculated her position. Her mind began to transform into her preparations for action. Then, she stopped, forcing her thoughts to hold. She needed to talk to him before she made her move. There were some questions she needed to have answers to before the conclusion was reached.

As she had done each previous period of solitude, Anod tried to doze off. The next thing she was aware of was the door opening – Zitger again.

"I have decided I do not want to play with you any more," he said as he sat on the table in front of her. "I could keep you alive while I impregnate every female on this planet, but I have accomplished enough here. I have other things to do." He opened a drawer below him and pulled out a shorter knife. "I should let you have this to watch you perform *hara-kiri* as the ancient *samurai* did." He paused to watch her. Anod held her reaction. "But, then again, you would probably try to use it on me and my troopers." Zitger stood and moved slowly toward her. "I should give you the respect you deserve and disembowel you myself. Letting you die too quickly would be too easy for you."

"Why?" Anod asked for the first time since her capture.

Her word stopped him. "Well, now. You can speak."

"Why?" she repeated.

"I suppose I can allow you some last words before you die. So, why what?"

"Why did you kill my children? Why did you kill my family?"

"The answer is actually quite simple . . . I had to."

"What!"

"Yes. I must eradicate you. Your spawn continues the line – your line. They had to die. Your android and those males resisted and got in the way."

"You are a despicable beast."

"My, my, haven't you become emotional."

Anod knew he was correct in his last statement, and that was not good. She focused on his eyes, concentrated on him and tried to free her mind. Insulting him or displaying her anger over her loss would not bring her family back nor would it help her situation. Zitger had been trained just as she had, to avoid emotions or any other thoughts that might cloud his judgment.

"Why did you betray Zarrod and me at Saranon?"

"Does it really matter?"

"Yes. Yes, it does."

"Why? You are going to die, soon."

"My curiosity. What would it cost you to answer my questions?"

"Fair enough. I was bored."

"Bored!" she protested.

"Yes. Life was too sterile, too routine. The Yorax are an interesting people. They have made me a rich and fulfilled man."

"Then, why have you pursued me?"

"You are the only witness. Somehow you slipped my detection after the ambush, and someone saved you from certain death. The plan called for both of you to die in that ambush." He chuckled as though he had told some joke that only he understood. "Actually, I was to die there as well – or, at least appear so. There was a Yorax battlecruiser not far away and fully masked."

Anod remembered the suspicious activity that had triggered their patrol. She also remembered the beneficence of Alexatron. He had taken her to Beta. It was from that ambush that her life changed irrevocably.

"You said you did all this because you were bored," she paused. He stared at her as if to say, so. "You could have done other things to vacate that boredom. Why betray us? Why betray your people? Why become a traitor to the community that raised you?"

He smiled. "Those are too many questions. But, let it suffice to say, the Yorax gave me what the Society could never give me. I found sex. They gave me as much as my body could handle. They gave me the opportunity to create an entirely new race of humans born in my image. The original plan had me assuming a new identity, but you spoiled that part of the plan. Beta was to be the first of my colonies, but I needed to eliminate you first. Then, when you betrayed me to the Society and left Beta, the plan changed. We would first eliminate you then use this convenient population to create a colony of queens to produce my offspring. This is actually a much better plan." He waved his hand to dismiss the rest of their conversation. "I have had enough talk. This serves no purpose."

"Whom might I talk to in this condition?"

Zitger laughed hard. "Quite right. However, unfortunately for you, I still have a great deal of respect for your skills as a warrior. After all, you have managed to kill many of my soldiers all by yourself." He turned away from her. She found satisfaction in the contradiction of his words and actions. "So you see, I cannot allow you to live."

"Why have you punished my people?"

"Ah . . . the questions continue." Zitger turned back to Anod. He studied her eyes then scanned her tortured body. "I have time for a few more questions. Now, you want to know why. Well, it is because of you. I have to punish those who harbored you."

"None of them knew where I was."

"They would not help me find you. They would not betray you."

"As you betrayed me."

"To a higher calling, I am afraid."

"Why violate the women?"

"Also, a higher calling." Anod's puzzled expression spoke for her. "It is Yorax policy to assimilate the weaker peoples." He almost giggled. "It is my small part for the future. I have come to thoroughly enjoy the pleasures of the flesh, so I am all too eager to fulfill my duty. This is part of my commitment to the Yorax."

"But, young, innocent girls."

"Oh, but they are the best. I have planted many seeds, and I shall plant some more before I leave."

"You have done enough damage."

"I should stay and finish what I have started. My Yorax brethren will certainly think less of me for not finishing this lofty task, but I tire of this distraction you have become. The pleasure has gone now that I have you."

"You shall not have me much longer."

Zitger laughed. "How right you are," he said, and then turned to the door.

"Wait. I am not finished."

"You say that as though you are in control. I have decided to have one last coupling with you, and I shall finish you at the same moment I finish, so I can enjoy your convulsing body in a more intimate manner."

"Are you that much less of a man that you must have your women chained?" she spat.

Zitger stopped a few steps short of the doors and turned. "Are you trying to make me angry as your feeble humans call it?"

The question alone told Anod more of what she needed to know. "No, of course, not. I just want to know."

"Only the dangerous ones like you. Those two young ones were not chained, now were they? Most of these females are so passive, it is almost like they want me to take them – they want to be my seed pods."

"What has twisted your brain so much?" He took one step back toward her. Anger filled his eyes. Zitger started to speak but did not utter a word. "What has brought you to the point of violating these women?" she repeated.

"They want it."

"No, they don't."

"Then, why don't they fight? Why don't they protect themselves? They need me to impregnate them since their men are so weak."

"You are the one that is weak," she sneered. "They are strong. They shall survive long after you."

"Is that so!" he barked. Zitger stomped back to her, drew back his right fist, and hit her very hard at the corner of her left eye.

Anod saw stars as the world darkened and began to collapse. She was losing consciousness. She shook her head trying to hold onto awareness. Within seconds, a large quantity of ice-cold water shocked her back to reality.

"Oh, no. I am not going to let you take the easy way out."

Anod started to speak. She wanted to taunt him some more, but she could not hear any words.

"How was that for being weak?"

Anod felt the swelling of her left eye as it began to close against her will to keep it open. She also felt the river of blood flowing down her face. She tilted her head trying to keep the blood out of her eye to no avail. The tension in her arms meant her legs had given way. She struggled to regain her balance in a standing position.

"My, aren't you a brave man. Unchain me and let's make this sporting."

He laughed hard. "Unchain you. I shall soon have my satisfaction. There is no need to give you any satisfaction. I shall unchain your dead body."

"Honor."

"Honor, you say. You shall have no honor. You shall die on my terms like an animal to slaughter."

"What has caused you to lose your honor, Zitger?"

"The name is, Negolian. General Negolian."

"Like I said, Zitger, what has caused you to lose your honor?"

He turned and walked to the doors. "I am nearly finished with you."

As he pushed the door lock controls, Anod said, "Then, at least let me see your face when I die."

"So be it," he answered with the wave of his hand as he left the room.

Anod recognized the time. This was the moment she had been waiting for. The injury to her left eye was more than she wanted, but her actions were sufficient to make him respond in anger. What she needed now was just a little luck, and perhaps, if she was really fortunate, he might hold onto his anger. Anod knew probably better than Zitger that emotions clouded the mind and enabled mistakes. She needed just one or two openings.

As expected the guards returned. She examined them quickly. The first beneficial opening came to her. The trooper with the manacle key around his neck was one of the two Yorax sent to prepare her for the final insult and death.

The two guards worked the controls as they had done before. They moved her past the bench toward the U-shaped chair. Anod actually allowed herself the pleasure of a smile knowing her taunts had worked. Zitger intended to have her face-to-face. The tight chains and moving blocks positioned her in front of the chair.

Anod felt the chains go slack. The moment of action was now.

In a flash, Anod grasped the chain near her wrist and swung her right arm in a precise arc. The chain looped around the closest trooper's neck, and she jerked her arm back as hard as she could. The chain sank into the flesh on his neck. Terror filled the Yorax trooper's eyes as he foolishly tried to grab the chain imbedded in his neck. He tried to speak, but not a sound emerged.

Anod's cold stare watched the other trooper. His complacency allowed many seconds to pass before he recognized the scuffling sounds as something he should worry about.

Anod reached across her body with her left hand, grabbed the key and unlocked her right manacle without letting go of the tension she kept on the chain. The guard began thrashing as life ebbed from him.

With cold exactness, Anod tracked the foolish reaction of the other guard. He undoubtedly thought he could rescue his comrade and subdue her since three of the chains, and he probably thought all four chains, still restrained her.

The second guard swung his fist at her head. Anod easily ducked the blow. His angry energy caused him to lose his balance just slightly. Anod took instant advantage releasing the grip on the right chain, grabbing his shoulder bandoleer and pulling him toward her. As she had done with the other guard, now with his own weight holding the chain taut around his neck, Anod looped the left chain around the neck of the second guard.

Satisfied the first guard was no longer a factor, Anod held the chain tight and reached around his head gripping it as hard as she could and snapped his neck. Both guards twitched or thrashed as death came to them. They were still moving when Anod retrieved the manacle key from the chain around the first guard's neck.

Swiftly, she unlocked her remaining restraints. Once free, she stepped back against the chair that had been intended to be her final torture. Anod looked at the doors. The locks had still not moved. Both guards now hung limp, suspended by the chains around their necks.

Anod took just a moment to flex her joints. She knew what would be coming soon enough. She needed as much capability as she could attain. She squatted quickly and twisted her torso to regain as much movement as she could. Pain returned to her many wounds, but she ignored it – an annoyance.

Anod moved around the two dead guards when she heard the door locks move. She sprang to the doors but too late. They burst open for several Yorax troopers with weapons drawn and aimed as they entered the room. She froze not wanting to give them an excuse to fire. Even with a stun burst, she would be rendered helpless for several minutes.

Zitger pushed his way through the group. He smiled. He glanced at the two guards hanging by the chains then looked back at her. "It appears my caution was warranted. I cannot imagine how you managed this."

"The determination of a warrior."

"I suppose so. What shall we do now?"

Anod stood squarely toward them with her feet a shoulder width apart and her hands defiantly at her side. The sight of her bloody, battered, naked body to the side of two dead Yorax troopers hanging from chains had to give them pause. Zitger scanned the scene several more times.

"The determination of a warrior, indeed. Nonetheless, a simple command from me and this minor array of light rifles would end this once and for all."

"Yes, but you will not issue that command."

"Oh really? Then, what command shall I issue?"

"You will tell them to leave us and lock the doors behind them. We shall finish this ourselves."

"Now, why would I want to do that? An unarmed, chained woman managed to slip her restraints and kill two highly capable soldiers, apparently with her bare hands. Why would I want to fight that woman?"

"Because your morbid curiosity will want satisfaction."

"Why?"

"You must know whether you can beat me or not."

A grin washed across his face, then he nodded his head. He waved his hand for the guards to leave. One of them screeched out a response.

"It is all right. I shall deal with this swiftly." Apparently, Zitger had learned the Yorax language.

The troopers hesitated, and then did as they were told. The doors closed and locked.

"So, now you have your wish," Zitger said as he placed his hands on his hips as if to say, you must go through me.

Anod carefully assessed Zitger's condition. He was fully clothed in a suit similar to the Yorax. Only his hands and head were not covered. He also had a pistol and knife hung from his belt. He noticed her search and lifted both weapons from his belt and threw them across the room, sliding into a corner.

"You don't really think you are going to be successful, do you?"

"Of course, I do," she answered, not moving.

"Then, you shall know disappointment before death."

"We shall see."

Zitger moved carefully toward her. Anod remained perfectly still until he made his first thrusting move. She parried with a graceful stroke of her bent right arm and followed with an elbow blow to his ribs.

The first exchange moved sharply to a flowing dance of thrusts, blows, swings and kicks as their arms and legs blended together in a blur of motion. They each connected on occasion. The suit gave Zitger more protection against her blows.

The actions and reactions told Anod this would be a battle of attrition, in which Zitger would have the advantage in several ways. He was an expert warrior as well. She realized she needed to make an opening in some unconventional manner.

"Why don't you finish me off?" she asked as she jumped to place the bench between them.

"I will in due course."

"You have the advantage and yet you cannot take me."

Zitger moved to follow her. Anod kept the bench between them.

"What advantage?" he asked moving his head toward the two dead Yorax troopers without taking his eyes off her.

"You have protective clothing."

Zitger tried to dodge and weave in an attempt to make her miss. She countered each move perfectly.

"I suppose you want me to disrobe as well."

"Why not. It is only fair," she responded on the gamble he might actually give her that opening.

"I hate to disappoint you," Zitger said, then swung his leg over the bench.

Anod ducked. Zitger swung his other leg over rotating on his opposite hip. His angle was not sufficient. Anod thrust her fist hard into his groin. He collapsed to the floor in male agony. She kicked the heal of her right foot into his forehead. The blow stunned him, laying him out before her. Anod did not miss the opportunity. She struck him with a right-left combination to the bottom of his sternum. The stiffness of his suit lessened the severity of her strike but still knocked the wind out of him. Fear filled his eyes as he saw her pull her right hand back, coiled to strike. Anod hesitated. She could finish him.

"I will spare you if you will take these Yorax beasts and leave this place never to return." She remained poised over him as she watched him regain his control.

"Never!" he shouted with a coarse voice as he rolled and swept his left leg forcing her to jump away.

Zitger jumped to his feet and sprang to the corner where his weapons lay. Anod leapt after him catching his right foot just enough to make him stumble. Zitger made a mortal mistake of trying to crawl to his weapons instead of facing his assailant. Anod was on him like a tiger on a wounded water buffalo.

Anod struck him hard at the base of his head. She thought for a moment that she severed his spinal cord. Just as she started to move over him, he rolled and struck her hard in the ribs with his fist. She tried several feints and blows as he tried to sweep her off him. Her opening came when he tried to strike her groin. Anod coiled her left arm and fired. He managed to get another arm to barely deflect her thrust from his forehead to a glancing blow. His reaction left his most vulnerable spot exposed. Anod thrust her open right hand at his throat. She hit him hard, gripped as tightly as she could and snatched his windpipe from his throat.

Only gushing sounds and the flailing of his feet marked his final moments. Blood spurted from his opened neck like two throbbing geysers. Blood covered his face and began to quickly pool beneath his head. The rapidly pulsing spurts matched his pounding heartbeat. Life ebbed from him quickly as the flow changed to a bare trickle.

Anod stood over him, her chest heaving with her own exertion. "You evil bastard," she growled and struck him twice in the chest causing an additional spurt of blood from his neck with each blow. "You took my life and my family from me." She hit his dead body again, then fell to her knees and began an uncontrollable crying.

The memories of her children, Zoltentok and Sara, and the lively images of Bradley and Nick came to her. She cried for them. She cried for her loss. The retribution left a hollow, empty feeling that began to drain her strength. Zitger's life could not repay her loss.

The sound of the door locks shot a bolt of electricity throughout her body propelling her through the air to the corner and Zitger's pistol. She was not fast enough. The doors swung open allowing three troopers to burst into the room. The sight of Zitger's lifeless body surrounded by the large pool of dark red blood shocked them just enough for the moment she needed.

Anod grasped the pistol, aimed just as they followed her motion, and fired three times in rapid succession. Her shots found their mark. Two were dead before they hit the ground. The third was seriously wounded. Anod fired again to finish him.

Anod jumped to her feet and leapt to the door. She scanned the corridor in both directions. It was clear. She kept the pistol in her right hand and picked up one of the rifles in her left hand. Anod shot the two remaining troopers she found in the building.

Carefully checking a window, she determined her location. She was in the center building opposite the gateway. It appeared to be the control or command building. Anod had hoped to avoid a protracted battle where innocent captives might be injured or killed. Just as she was preparing herself to clear the other buildings, good fortune again came her way.

One of the silver star Yorax walked toward the center building. She quickly assessed his entrance point and what he would see when he entered. She did not have time to clear the bodies to draw him farther into the building. She would have to take him at the door. The best she could do was maybe a half step inside and hope he froze rather than recoil.

The assessment was precisely accurate. She waved him into the building. Anod pointed to the door. He closed it behind him.

"Do you understand me?" she said. He nodded his head. "Follow me," she commanded and began backing up with her pistol pointed at his chest. She went past the doors to her torture chamber and the pile of bodies. "Look in there," she said waving the rifle in her left hand toward the interior of the chamber.

The Yorax leader saw each of his dead comrades as well as his leader – the late General Negolian. He looked back to her as if to say what do you want me to do.

"We can do this the easy way or the hard way. It will be your choice. Do you understand?" He shook his head. "I can kill you and each of your friends until this peaceful planet is rid of your kind, or you can acknowledge that this battle and the war are over."

"I choose the last option," the Yorax trooper said in his squealing voice.

"Good. Then here is what you are going to do. First, you are going to recall any patrols you may have deployed on the planet. Then, you are going to notify your colleagues in the battlecruiser orbiting the planet that General Negolian is dead and the war is lost."

"What if they do not listen to me?"

"You will convince them, or you will die on the spot."

"Then, what?"

"You will depart this sector of the galaxy, and I will recommend to the Society that they not pursue you."

He stared at her then looked back into the room. He probably wondered how she had managed to get free and do all this damage. He looked back to her and bowed.

The Yorax motioned toward an adjacent room. Anod nodded her head in agreement. She watched him from a good distance. The trooper made a series of communications. Anod did not understand the Yorax language. Regardless, she would be able to deal with any attempt at counterattack other than a main battery projectile from the battlecruiser into the base camp. She could only hope her valor and boldness would produce the correct response. As troopers returned to the compound, they were transported to the battlecruiser that she guessed had probably picked up a stationary position over New Providence. The recovery and egress took most of an hour.

"That is the last of my people," announced the Yorax lieutenant.

Anod studied him. He stood before her. There were no signs of nervousness or impending betrayal. The vulnerable moment of disengagement was upon them. Anod did not have many options, but she could not allow him to think so. She had to take the risk.

"Do you want to take your dead with you?"

"We have no need for them. Dispose of them as you will."

"Including General Negolian."

"We have no need for him anymore either."

"So be it," she responded then waved the pistol indicating that he could leave.

His heals clicked together as he rendered her a traditional, open hand salute. She nodded her head in recognition but did not release her pistol or drop her aim. The Yorax trooper went outside and promptly decomposed for his transport to the battlecruiser.

Anod waited outside in the warmth of the late afternoon light. If the Yorax were going to counterattack, it would come now. She waited long enough for her to think they had complied with her instructions. With the caution of a warrior, she began searching the other buildings. She found no Yorax.

Anod opened the doors on the first large room of captives. Two dozen female faces turned toward her. There were gasps and groans.

"My God," came the voice of Naomi Gibritzu, "what have they done to you?"

Anod walked among them. Hands touched her shoulders and arms. Most of the women were clothed. Some were in various stages of undress. All of them were restrained in some fashion – some with one arm or one leg chained, and some with two or more limbs chained. A few, like Moma Gibritzu, appeared catatonic.

"We are free," Anod announced.

"By yourself?" someone asked.

Anod did not answer the question. "I need to retrieve the key," she said.

On her way back to find the manacle key, Anod checked the other buildings. They were empty. There were signs throughout the buildings that Yorax and Murtaurians had been there. At least there was no blood or other indications of injury.

As Anod released the captives, they touched her as though she was a deity returned to them in the flesh. The freed women tried to find clothes. A coat was placed around Anod's shoulders. A couple of them hugged her. Some cried from relief. As Anod unlocked the last of the manacles, she walked back through the crowd. They said words of praise, of encouragement, of sympathy, and of concern for her and her injuries. Those who knew shared with the others of Anod's loss.

Anod began to cry. Her muscles began to lose their strength. Her joints began to buckle. Hands held her up until the last of her control vanished. They allowed her to slump to the floor doubled up in an erect fetal position with her head between her knees. She wailed as the last of her adrenaline disappeared with her strength. The magnitude of her loss and those of her people overwhelmed her. They whispered words of sympathy to her. Hands stroked her back.

Naomi Gibritzu knelt beside her and placed her lips next to Anod's ear. "It is all right, Anod. You will recover," Naomi said softly to her.

Many hands touched Anod. She felt protected. Muffled words filled the background beyond Anod's cries.

"We are your family, now," added Naomi.

The outpouring of support amplified the intensity of the loss of her family and the combat of the intervening weeks. It was not that their sympathies made her loss more severe, but rather broke down the barriers she had erected to enable the battle. The open manifestation of her grief subsided with time and support. Anod slowly regained her composure. Several of the women helped her to her feet. They found some large, loose-fitting pants and an even larger shirt. Someone put a crude pair of sandals on her feet and tied them to her ankles.

As Anod recovered, the women began checking each other for injury. Naomi held her daughters in her arms. Other mothers held their daughters.

"Can we go?" someone asked.

"Yes. We are free," answered Anod. "The Yorax are gone."

"What did they do to you, Anod?"

"Nothing."

"It looks much more than nothing."

"It was part of the battle."

"And, you won. You won for all of us."

"I want to get back to my family," another said.

Tears welled up in Anod's eyes. She had no family to go back to. Some of the women would also discover they did not have families either, but Anod did not feel it appropriate for her to tell them. The more gradual the return to reality the better, Anod told herself. Several of the women used damp clothes to clean Anod's battered and bloody face. As her wounds appeared, there were more gasps and words of resentment for her injuries.

"Natasha and Anton are in hiding. I need to go to them."

"What about Otis?" another asked.

"I will try to get a message to Beta telling him to come home," Anod said.

"What should we do?"

Anod held her arms up against the pain she now felt everywhere on her body. "Listen," Anod said loudly and waited for quiet attention. "I know some of you have lost as I have. Others of you still have family to return to. For those who feel they can make the journey, you are welcome to leave. For those that live too far to walk, I suggest you wait here in New Providence. If we are lucky, Anton was able to save the shuttle and himself. I shall recover Natasha first, since she is the closest, and then take her with me to find Anton. If the shuttle is still working, I shall return to transport you home."

"Sounds reasonable," several of them answered.

"I suggest no one travel alone. We need to support each other. As soon as we can, we should all of us return to New Providence, perhaps in a few days, to assess the extent of the Yorax damage, and we can establish plans for our recovery."

"Yes."

"Agreed."

"Good," responded Anod. "I will go, now. I will contact you by one form or another within a few days. Those of you who remain here," she paused to calculate the time needed, "I should be back here by the day after tomorrow, perhaps earlier if I am lucky. There is a replicator in the center building of the compound and in several of the empty buildings in town. Everyone should eat."

"Who will go with you?" asked Cetia Gibritzu.

Anod smiled. "Thank you for asking, but it is best that I go alone. Only two will fit on a scooter, and I need to pick up Natasha Norashova."

"Will you be all right?" Cetia continued.

"Yes, I shall. You take care of your mother and especially your sister." Anod scanned the sea of faces watching her. "We have been through an ordeal. Let's take care of each other and make sure everyone is stable."

Anod walked outside. Local dusk was approaching. Many followed her through the gateway building. Words of horror filled the air as some saw the crucified men for the first time. Cries and wails burst forth as some of the women saw their husbands, fathers or brothers. Anod motioned for the survivors to tend to the grief among them.

The walk passed her first scooter, out of fuel, to the spare scooter hidden in the foothills took half the night. The pain and stiffness of her injuries made her travel considerably more difficult. The journey through the rugged mountains to the remote, lakeside camp and Natasha took the remainder of the night even with the scooter.

Anod reached her mountain hideout just before local dawn. She found Natasha sleeping peacefully in the small cave.

Anod wanted to join Natasha and sleep as much as she could. The let down after her combat made her fatigue even more pronounced, but many others waited on her. As gently as she could, Anod woke Natasha. She jerked awake with fear.

"You are safe. It is only me," Anod said with a strong, confident voice. "It is all over."

The early twilight and her rudimentary clothing hid most of Anod's injuries but allowed enough features for Natasha's recognition.

"You are hurt," Natasha said finally.

"Nothing to worry about. Are you all right?"

"Yes."

"Good. Can you go with me to find Anton?"

"Go with you?"

"Yes. I have a scooter. We might be able to make Horvak by afternoon."

"You need me?"

"Yes. You can help me find Anton."

"Then, let's go."

While Natasha readied herself for the journey, Anod found some food and ate as quickly as she could. Natasha wanted to eat more, but Anton's recovery was of greater importance. They left the mountain retreat. Progress was relatively slow until they were out of the mountains, then

Anod used the maximum speed of the scooter. Natasha did not handle the high-speed travel so close to the ground very well. She kept asking Anod, if she was sure she could see the obstacles ahead of them. The answer was the same every time. For most of the journey, Natasha buried her head in Anod's back, trying to ignore the precarious travel.

They arrived at Horvak. There were few people around to greet them. Those who did were women with tales all too familiar to Natasha and Anod. It took several hours to find the shuttle. The Yorax had not damaged it producing understandable suspicion for Anod. The craft could be booby-trapped or otherwise compromised. Anod tried several places that seemed appropriate for Anton to hide. Just when Anod was about ready to give up the search, Anton appeared from a small cave among thick, thorny bushes.

"Is everything clear?"

"Yes, Anton. The Yorax are gone. We are free."

As he approached, he saw the injuries on Anod's face. "What did they do to you?"

"Battle," Anod responded.

"They tortured her," injected Natasha.

"Those monsters."

"I am all right."

Anton nodded his head. "The shuttle is safe. They never came for me."

"Good. I will check it carefully to ensure it is clear."

"I can't wait to hear what happened."

"It will have to wait, Anton. We need to use the shuttle to move survivors from New Providence back to their homes."

"Survivors?"

"Like me," said Natasha.

Anton remembered what Anod had told her. "I am so sorry, Natasha."

"I know. There are others who are worse than me, like Anod," she said looking with hurt eyes to Anod.

"We need to go. There is much work to do to help the others."

Anod checked the exterior, and then the interior of the shuttlecraft. She nodded her head that it was clean. They loaded the scooter in the shuttle and all three departed for New Providence. The repatriation of the survivors took another twelve hours. When their immediate task was complete, Anton, Natasha and Anod found an undamaged house. The

Yorax had killed the Arquello family, all five members, early on during the occupation. Anod wanted to use the cleansing station and isopod to help her body heal faster, but she was too tired to work things out with Morgan. She needed to make sure everything was normal with Morgan, which would take more time than she could give. Anton and Natasha took turns watching over Anod as they allowed her to sleep as long as her body and mind would allow.

Chapter 16

When Anod woke up, the pain and soreness stiffened her body. She did not want to move. She just wanted to lie there until everything was better.

"How are you feeling?" asked Natasha.

Anod looked across the darkened room of the Arquello house to find her friend sitting in a chair. "Not so good, actually."

"I can imagine," she said as she stood and walked to the bed. "Your face looks like you were on the losing end of some brawl."

"The rest of me is worse."

"Oh, Anod. You have taken so much punishment."

Anod looked deeply into Natasha's eyes. Genuine pain and sympathy filled her expression. "It was mortal combat, and Zitger lies dead on the floor of his torture chamber."

"The communications among the citizens began before we arrived here. The people have raised you to the highest position in their minds. They are praising your courage, skills, commitment, and your sacrifice. There is no question anymore. You are our leader."

"I said this too many times, I do not want to be the leader," Anod responded. Tears formed and trickled down the side of her face.

"What is wrong?"

"I just wanted to be a mother," she choked out.

"You shall be again."

"I don't know," Anod said wiping away the tears. "I don't know if I can."

"In time, Anod, in time. Now, try to rest some more."

Anod glanced toward the covered window. The light coming past the edges told her it was daylight outside. She knew what she really needed. Anod slowly swung her legs out of bed and onto the floor then sat up. She was still wearing the same clothes the women had dressed her in after the release. As far as she could tell, every joint, every muscle, every minute portion of her body ached to one degree or another. Her head felt as if it was being squeezed by some circumferential vice. She held her head as though she was plugging some hole to keep her brain from flowing out.

"Anod, please, you don't have to get up. Anton and I are taking turns watching over you to make sure everything is as it should be."

"I need the isopod."

Natasha looked over her shoulder as if she might be able to check its status, but if there was an isopod in the house, it was in another room. "I don't know if it is working. It looks like the Arquellos never used it."

"I am of no use to anyone like this. My recovery will take too long without the isopod. I need to make sure Morgan is normal, and then have him evaluate the devices. I need the isopod," she repeated.

Anod stood only to stumble from dizziness. Natasha caught her. Her blood loss forced her cardiovascular system to work harder. "Where is Anton?"

"He is in another room sleeping. Should I get him?"

"No. I was just curious."

As her body adjusted and her dizziness passed, Anod shuffled toward the door. Natasha held her although Anod did not feel she needed the assistance. The main room was brighter. There was freshly prepared food on the table. Anod admired it, but did not feel like eating. She found the interface console for Morgan. She sat down heavily in the chair, and then scooted it to the position she wanted.

Anod examined the screens and controls. Everything appeared normal to her passive observation. She touched a series of spots on the center and right screens. At the bottom of the center screen came the words, STATUS NORMAL.

"Morgan," she called.

"It is good to have you back, Anod."

"It is good to be back, Morgan. I need to know if those measures instituted by the Yorax to monitor your activity have been removed?"

"No."

"Can you remove them?"

"No."

"Can you perform all your functions in your current condition?"

"My answer depends upon answers to two questions I am unable to answer. I have many indications that the Yorax have departed this planet. Can you confirm these indications to be true?"

"Yes, as far as we know."

"Does the existence of tapped monitoring devices affect your assessment of my performance?"

"No, unless they can somehow alter your conclusions and

performance."

"As best I can determine, they do not," responded Morgan.

"Excellent. Then, I need you to evaluate at least one of the isopods at this location as well as the cleansing station. I need the repair and regeneration capabilities."

"There are five isopods at your location – the Arquello residence. The family never used those devices."

"So, it appears. Can they be made operational?"

"I shall check." Morgan fell silent for a dozen seconds. "All devices are fully functional."

"Excellent. I shall use the cleansing station first. You will probably need two full scans to clean and examine, maybe more. You will note numerous injuries, both external and internal, over most of my body. I shall ask you to program the isopod for maximum recovery."

"As you command," Morgan responded.

Anod stood more slowly this time. Natasha had an arm around her just in case and guided her toward the room where the devices were located. As they shuffled along, Anton came out of another bedroom rubbing his eyes.

"I thought I heard voices," he said without looking.

"Yes, you did," Natasha responded, "and, it is your watch shift."

"Sorry. What can I do to help?"

"Anod is going to use the cleansing station and isopod to help her recovery."

Anton joined them taking the other side of Anod although his assistance was really not required. The devices were packed into what appeared to be a storeroom of some sort. Anod helped the other two wipe off the dust, cobwebs and other signs of disuse, and then moved one of the larger isopods away from the others. Anton cleaned up the general area at the center of the storeroom and the cleansing station, and then activated the isopod.

"Should we leave you?" asked Natasha.

"It is not necessary unless you will be uncomfortable."

"I would like to watch."

"Anton!" protested Natasha.

Anod held up her right hand. "It is quite all right. I have no particular modesty regarding my body. I must warn you, I am not a pretty sight."

"But, Anton?" questioned Natasha, meaning she did not think it proper for a man to see a naked woman he was not married to.

"It is all right, Natasha," Anod responded. "I truly do not mind. In fact, with the extent of my injuries, I think you both may learn something and witness the enormous recuperative power of these devices."

"Yes, sure," Anton responded.

They helped Anod out of her clothes.

"Oh, dear God," said Natasha as she saw Anod's damaged body for the first time in full light. "This is terrible and disgusting."

"They tortured her," Anton said.

"This is not torture. This is brutality and butchery. I have never seen injuries so severe."

"These will heal, perhaps not completely on the first cycle, but these wounds will heal much faster than you might expect."

What they did not realize and Anod did not want to tell them was her wounds, despite their current state, had already begun healing much faster than for people who had grown up on Beta. Her genetically engineered anatomy and physiology performed far more efficiently than other humans. The cleansing station and isopod would accelerate the regeneration process even more.

Anod creaked against her stiffness to examine her wounds. She still had bloodstains masking some of her injuries. All of her cuts were ugly gashes made more grotesque by the clotted blood.

Anod activated the cleansing station. She stepped inside and closed the clear door behind her. Anton and Natasha stood one meter away in rapt anticipation. Anod started the cleaning process. She closed her eyes and gave her body to the device. The deep heat and tingling over every centimeter of her skin relaxed her soreness so completely Anod nearly fell asleep twice. To her surprise, the cleaning and evaluation process took three full cycles. When the blue light disappeared and the hissing sound of the door released, Anod stepped out.

Both Anton and Natasha looked over her body. Amazement filled their eyes.

"That is incredible," said Natasha.

"That is beyond incredible."

Anod checked the results. Her body was completely clean except for the reddish cuts, the discoloration of the bruises and the swelling in places. All of the clotted blood, and other dirt and stains had been removed. She caught both sets of eyes. "I guess that was a good demonstration of the capability of the cleansing station. Now, if you can watch the isopod, you will see some of these minor wounds and injuries disappear, and even the more severe wounds heal substantially."

"Is it really that good?" asked Anton.

"It is. Watch for yourself," Anod responded as she moved to the isopod with far more grace and fluidity than before she went through the cleansing process.

Anod adjusted the isopod to the configuration and position she wanted then lay down inside. "Are you sure you can let me take another four hours for a sleep cycle?"

"Yes. Sure," answered Anton for both of them. Natasha just nodded her head still amazed at what she saw.

Anod winked at them as she closed the top. She pushed the start button and the isopod took control of her body and mind.

When awareness returned to Anod, she opened her eyes to see Natasha and Anton standing outside her isopod with almost child-like excitement all across their faces. With the restoration phase complete, the isopod cover opened.

"That was the most amazing thing I have ever seen," pronounced Anton.

"It was absolutely astonishing," Natasha added repeating their earlier pronouncement.

"We saw your cuts heal before our eyes."

Anod swung her legs out of the isopod and sat up. She glanced down at her body. As she expected, the minor wounds were gone. Many of the bruises and scrapes were gone. Only the more serious wounds remained and even they were only dark pinkish lines drawn on her torso and legs. With her left hand, she felt her left eye. The swelling was gone as well as most of the soreness. Anton and Natasha both nodded their heads wildly with large grins to amplify their excitement.

"We saw it happen," Anton said. "We saw your cuts close and disappear."

Anod stood. She worked all her joints and muscles. She stretched as much to evaluate her condition as to ensure her muscles were in readiness for the day, which as she noted was drawing to an end.

"I feel much better," Anod announced.

Natasha brought her some clothes that were more her size and liking, and clean. She dressed quickly.

"What has happened while I was asleep?" she asked.

Excitement returned to Anton's face. Natasha glanced at him, and then winked at Anod. She motioned for Anod to follow her. "You won't believe this," Natasha said without looking back as she walked to the front door.

Anod could hear an odd rumbling outside. She wondered what the sound meant. Natasha opened the door, and they stepped out onto a small porch. As soon as the crowd saw Anod, a raucous cheer reverberated through the group. Anod was overwhelmed. She swallowed hard to control her emotions – a sense of relief, satisfaction, gratitude, and deliverance. She heard her name, and words of encouragement and support. Anod held her arms up to quiet the crowd, but her action invigorated the group. Some of the smaller children ran up to touch her legs or arms, and then ran back to their parents. People jumped up and down as though they were possessed by some frenzied exuberance. Anod continued to wave her hands in an attempt to quiet the crowd. She pleaded in progressively loud tones for quiet. Then, as if by some switch, the frenzy passed, and faces concentrated on her.

When it was quiet enough for her to talk without shouting, Anod said, "I don't know what to say."

"You don't have to say anything. Your actions have spoken for you," someone shouted from the back, renewing the celebration.

Again, she waited for quiet. "I did what any of you would have done."

"You did what none of us could do," came the reply, followed by more cheers.

Anod wanted to refocus their attention from adulation of her to the future of their planet and community. She waited for the opening she needed. "Thank you all for your words of support, but we have much to do." They listened this time. "We need to bury our dead and assess the damage. We should take a careful census of our entire population. For those without homes, I trust others will welcome you into their homes. We must inventory our food stores and crops."

"Where do you want us to report this information?"

Anod glanced at Natasha and Anton. Both nodded their agreement, but Anod thought of a better idea. "Please report your information to Morgan. He can collect these details better than any of us. For those who are not comfortable talking to Morgan, please get the information to us," she said waving her arm to the three of them on the porch, "one way or another." She paused to observe gestures of agreement. "Can we meet back here in two day's time to evaluate this information and lay out our plans for the future."

Everyone agreed and that seemed to be the sign for the group to disperse. Several people added their own words of praise before they left. When everyone was gone, Anod joined Natasha and Anton in the Arquello house.

"What are you going to do?" asked Anton.

"I am going to watch over you two while you get a good night's sleep."

"Are you sure?" asked Natasha.

Anod chuckled. "Yes, I am sure. I will keep myself busy while you sleep. I need to work with Morgan on this census, and I need to contact Otis and the Society."

"I am going to use the isopod," said Anton.

"Me, too."

They disappeared. Anod turned to Morgan's interface console. "Morgan," she said.

"Yes, Anod."

"We are going to do a census of our entire population. I would like you to collect the information."

"As you wish."

"In addition to our living and dead, during the Yorax occupation, Zitger carried out an intentional campaign to rape our women and impregnate them. We need to know how many of our women are or may be pregnant from Zitger's actions."

"Yes. Do you know you are pregnant?"

The words stopped her cold. Her mind replayed events. Was it Bradley's or Zitger's child? She wanted to know, but she did not want to know. Morgan would be able to tell her since she had been through the medical screening of the cleansing station and the isopod, he would be able to pinpoint conception as well as other pertinent details including the genetic combination of the fetus.

"Actually, Morgan, I did not know, so thank you for the information."

"Do you want to know the length of this gestation?"

Anod recognized the significance of that information. She would know who the father was. Her conscience told her something different. She was pregnant with her third child. The father's identity would not bring Bradley, Nick or her children back to her. It would also not change Zitger's betrayal and treachery. She needed to focus on the new life growing within her . . . that was all that mattered now.

"No, Morgan, not at this time. Thank you though." Anod wanted her thoughts to go in other directions at the moment. "Have you notified the Society of our situation?"

"No. I was instructed to prohibit all communications. The Yorax monitoring devices could not be defeated. I considered the risk too great."

"Understood. Please contact the Society immediately, under an urgent priority. I would like to talk to Admiral Agginnoor, if possible."

"Please stand by," responded Morgan as he carried out his assignment. It could take minutes or hours depending on so many other factors.

Anod rose from her chair. She found a couple pieces of freshly baked bread to eat, more to occupy her body than for nourishment. Anod slowly walked around the room within sight of the console in case Morgan completed the call soon.

Hundreds of thoughts flooded her mind. What to do next? What did the future hold for Murtauri Four? What was she going to do about the child and starting a new family? Could she? What help could the Society provide? They had provided so much already and asked for so little. Images of her family brought tears to her eyes. She replayed the short time she had with Zoltentok in his little fort and the warm, flowing sensations of Sara at her breast. Why had all this happened? Zitger's answers were not sufficient. Personal gratification could not be the only or even principal reason for his treason. What could drive an accomplished warrior to betray everything that defined his life? The questions were endless – the answers few. Much would depend upon the information Morgan was collecting. The future would also depend on the Murtaurians, the Society and all the others who touched and surrounded them. What did the future hold?

"Anod," called the large central computer.

"Yes, Morgan."

"I have made contact with the Society. Admiral Agginnoor can talk to you, now."

Anod walked back to the console and sat down. "When you are ready," she said to Morgan.

Within seconds, the Society's Central Command icon appeared on the center screen. In a dozen more seconds, the image of Admiral Agginnoor appeared.

"Greetings," said the admiral.

"Greetings to you, Admiral Agginnoor."

"To what do I owe this pleasure?"

"I wanted to report to you that we had a major incursion by the Yorax."

"How major?"

"They occupied our planet for many weeks. They killed my entire family. They killed many of our men, and raped and impregnated many of our women."

"I am terribly sorry, Anod. What is your current status?"

"I killed Captain Zitger in personal combat and convinced the Yorax to leave us alone. They departed, I think, a couple of days ago. We are currently taking a census and conducting an inventory to assess the extent of damage."

"Congratulations, in a form, Anod. It sounds like you have done rather well on your own."

"We needed your help," Anod added as though the admiral could not arrive at the same conclusion.

"That explains many things," Agginnoor stated.

"How so?"

"We will need to complete our after-action evaluations, but we were significantly involved with a broad, offensive by the Yorax in the adjacent two sectors along the frontier. We did not hear anything from Murtauri Four or the Gamma Epsilon Sector. We wondered why your sector had not been hit, but we had our hands full dealing with the Yorax broad offensive. Then, all of a sudden, without explanation, the Yorax broke off the engagement and retreated immediately back across the frontier. Yesterday, they issued a general call for an armistice."

"We were prevented from calling for assistance."

"We must find a means to overcome that problem in case of future transgressions."

"Agreed."

"Should I dispatch a starship or a squadron to Murtauri Four?" asked Agginnoor.

"If you are able, I think a single starship should be sufficient and would be a beneficial sign for our people as well as anyone who might be watching."

"Consider it done. I will need to see who is closest and best able to respond. I will send a message back to you, once I have made that determination."

"Thank you, admiral."

"Anod, on a personal note, I offer you my personal sympathy but also the sympathies of the entire Society. We shall share your loss. Perhaps this tragedy can serve to strengthen our ties and relationship."

"We shall see. I should know more in a couple of days after we have completed our damage assessment and determine the will of our people."

"Please let me know when you are ready. Is there anything else?"

"No, Admiral Agginnoor. Thank you for your time."

"You are most welcome. Again, my sympathies, Anod. Good day," she said and immediately ended the transmission.

Anod stared at the screen as it returned to the routine symbols, annotations and information Morgan passed along regardless of whether anyone wanted or needed the data. There was some satisfaction for Anod that her tactical assessment had been correct – the Yorax had diverted the attention of the Society. To think, he was able to convince the Yorax to go to all that effort, expend all those resources and sacrifice all those people just to get her. How had he gained such a powerful position within an alien race? How did he convince them that hunting her down was worth the cost? Those were questions she did not get to ask Zitger. They were questions that would probably never be answered.

"Anod," Morgan spoke.

"Yes, Morgan."

"I just received a communication from the Society's Central Command. The Society Starship *Reliant* has been dispatched to Murtauri Four."

That meant Colonel Arkinnagga, captain of the *Reliant*, would be the senior representative. Anod smiled. "Thank you, Morgan. What is their estimated arrival time?"

"Seventy-eight hours."

"Excellent. That will give us time to complete our damage assessment. By the way, have you received any submittals?"

"Only six."

Anod's natural curiosity wanted to know, but she realized it would not be significant. "Do you have a preliminary assessment developed?"

"The best way for me to answer your question is to tell you what I do have, and then you can tell me if it is all I need to know."

"Very well."

"For the SanGiocomo family, I have the following information.

Murdered by the Yorax were Sebastian Nicholas SanGiocomo, Bradley James SanGiocomo, Zoltentok James SanGiocomo, Sara Jean SanGiocomo." Hearing the names of her lost family choked Anod causing her to swallow hard several times and wipe away the tears that burst spontaneously from her eyes. "Also, destroyed was Anod's personal android, Lornog. The SanGiocomo house was destroyed by fire. Anod Megan SanGiocomo is the sole survivor of the SanGiocomo family. She is recovering from injuries received from the Yorax during captivity. Her wounds are healing quickly at a rate consistent with her physiology. She is also pregnant. You have instructed me not to reveal the progenitor in your case."

Anod stood and walked around the room a couple of times to regain control of her emotions. The life she had grown to love had changed forever, yet again, and not in a way that brought her happiness. She wondered whether she would ever be happy again. At least she had a child growing within her. Regardless of paternity, she told herself as she placed her hands on her belly, this will be Bradley's child. She turned back to the console.

"Is that all?" she asked as she took command of the moment.

"No. I have five other collection elements."

"You can add to your collection of information that the interceptor stored at the hangar at Meganville was destroyed by the Yorax. I do not know the status of the Meganville crops. I suppose I should return to see what is salvageable from that field. Oh, also, all the food stores, other than the growing materials, were destroyed in the fire."

"I have added that information. I would suggest," Morgan continued, "it would be wise to inventory the crops at Meganville. If there is anything of value, the Murtaurians may need those foodstuffs."

"Agreed. I will try to do it soon." Anod stared at the screens. Her mind went blank. She needed some fresh air. "I would like to take a short walk outside. Can you manage in here for an hour?"

"Yes, of course."

"How are Natasha and Anton?"

"They are sixty-five percent complete with their sleep cycle. All parameters are nominal."

"Excellent, then I will return within an hour."

Anod rose from her chair at the console. She went to the storeroom. Inside, she could see the levitated, unclothed, motionless bodies of her two friends. Everything inside and outside both isopods was normal, just as Morgan indicated.

Outside, it was still nighttime. The cool air and light breeze felt refreshing. Lights had begun to return to New Providence. She walked down the street toward the main square and the Yorax compound. The death crosses had been removed, and the victims laid to rest. She stopped at the compound gateway, considered going inside, but instead turned left toward the foothills.

Away from the city, Anod found an appropriate spot and lay down on the slightly damp ground. Her mind's eye returned to that early morning when she floated on her back in the stream by her house. The blanket of stars above her detached the physical present. She kept asking herself the same questions. Why couldn't he just have left us alone? Why did he have to take her family? What had she ever done to him?

"No. No," Anod shouted as though she was commanding someone to stop.

She jumped to her feet. She needed to do something to keep her mind busy. She could not allow her thoughts to wander back in time or recall those memories, at least not yet. Anod knew she had to focus on the future. She walked slowly back to town with short and long glances to the stars above her. Anod would look up when she had a few steps of unobstructed, level ground in front of her.

There was a certain seductive attraction to the adventure of space, and all the worlds and peoples they had not yet discovered just in the home galaxy. Anod had heard of the new propulsion systems, or more properly travel systems, being developed for the journey to the galaxy Andromeda. Exploration beyond the home galaxy held boundless possibilities. The talk of travel to the next major galaxy seemed to deflect the lifetimes of exploration still needed just to map the home galaxy. Even during her time, Anod was keenly aware that Earth humans had only begun to see the far side of the home galaxy. It was a long way from being completely mapped. Perhaps, it was time for her to return to space and the warrior profession she had been banished from. If she could not do it as part of the Society, then maybe she could find another sponsor.

Mindful of the time and at the edge of town, Anod returned directly to the Arquello house. She looked inside. Everything was normal. She considered staying outside in the cool night air, however her two companions were probably nearing the end of their sleep cycle, anyway.

When she looked in the storeroom, both of her friends had begun the recovery process. According to the counter, they had another twenty minutes before the covers opened.

"Morgan, any news?"

"Anod," he said to acknowledge his recognition of her, "there has only been routine communications between various units. A message from the *Reliant* confirms their mission to assist us. Also, Otis Greenstreet is nearly home. He is a little more than a day out. He should arrive tomorrow morning."

"Excellent. Anything else?"

"The information from the census and inventory continues to come in."

"How many?"

"I now have thirty-two families or groups complete."

"Not quite half."

"Correct . . . forty-seven point one percent to be exact."

"Good."

"Anod, there is a concern."

She turned toward the console. "What is it?"

"Several families suspect there may be more than one of the families that were completely eliminated."

Blood drained from her body. Anod felt cold. Her body shivered. "Understood. Once we have all the data we can collect, you need to tell us who is missing. We will send out search parties to ascertain the situation."

"Yes, Anod."

Anod looked over her shoulder toward the storeroom. "Where are Natasha and Anton in their recovery from the sleep cycle?"

"They have another seventeen minutes, thirty-two seconds of recovery time. Do you need them brought out sooner?"

"No. They are perfectly fine." Anod's mind changed to other topics she needed to discuss with Morgan without alarming her friends. "What is your threat assessment?"

"External or internal?"

Anod thought the question a bit odd, however she was certain Morgan would see normal risks of life as an internal threat. "External."

"The external threat, based on all available data, appears to be low. All indications are the Yorax have indeed returned to their home planets on the far side of the frontier. Track information suggests the normal mercantile commerce traffic to Murtauri Four will return to normal within eight days time."

Anod's curiosity could not be contained. "What about the internal threat?"

"The monitors installed by the Yorax are the single greatest threat to my integrity."

"I will remove them with your help. Are there any specific tamper traps or other intrusion devices involved?"

"No."

"Have the Yorax tried to monitor your activity remotely since their departure?"

"Yes."

A cold chill shot through her body. "For what purpose?"

"It was a passive set of inquiries."

"Meaning?"

"I have no way to determine their intent. Their inquiries would be consistent with apprehension on their part as to what offensive action might be initiated from Murtauri Four."

Anod laughed. "Offensive action . . . how little they understand of us?"

"Quite the contrary, Anod. It indicates a very healthy respect for your skills."

"Perhaps. Anything else?"

"Yes, of course." Anod concentrated on the console. "I have been unable to assess the medical condition of our people. Of those I am aware of, we have several individuals with serious bacterial infections, two with viral infections and numerous wounds of various types. Based on the available data, our people are in serious health jeopardy."

Anod laughed again. "Thank you for your concern, Morgan, but you have only seen a small portion of the population. I suspect you have only seen the worst cases, not the majority or the best cases."

"I must trust your judgment."

"Thank you." Anod's mind kept churning. "Can you block any further inquiries by the Yorax or anyone else?"

"Yes."

"Do so. If there are any attempted intrusions by anyone, notify me immediately."

"As you command."

"Now, I would like to lay out a plan for removing those monitors."

Morgan and Anod examined numerous concerns as well as options to return the central computer to his secure state. The two veterans established a primary plan and two contingency plans based on what Anod might find once she began the process.

It was nearly time for the isopods to release her two companions. Anod went to the storeroom. She was standing just inside the door so that both of them could see her when they regained consciousness. Natasha was first.

It took the chemist several seconds to search the room around her and focus her eyes on Anod. She smiled at Anod as the sleep cycle completed, and Natasha was lowered to the bed of the isopod before the cover opened.

"Good morning."

"Good morning, Anod," responded Natasha as she looked to Anton's isopod.

Natasha tried to look unconcerned, but she moved quickly to dress herself as she glanced toward Anton's isopod several times. She was dressed before Anton opened his eyes. The sequence was repeated with Anton although more slowly and deliberately. Natasha left the room before he put his feet on the floor.

"Good morning to you, Anton."

"Good morning," he answered.

"Is everything all right with you?"

"Yes. I would say just about perfect," he said as he slowly began to dress.

Anod left the storeroom to talk to Natasha. "How do you feel?"

"Absolutely perfect. It is amazing how clear and crisp everything seems. I think I can say it is a perfect night's sleep."

"Good."

"Can I ask Morgan about my health?"

"Sure."

Natasha walked to the console as if Morgan needed her to be close for proper communications. "Morgan, this is Natasha Norashova."

"Yes, Natasha."

"I would like to know what you think of my health."

"Your health is excellent. No detectable abnormalities other than your pregnancy."

Anod started to respond, but Natasha beat her to it. "Pregnancy is not an abnormality."

"My apology," answered Morgan, which was a rarity for him. "I am still getting used to the ancient ways."

"Can you determine the length of gestation?" Natasha asked.

"With some degree of uncertainty, the fetus is fifteen days old, plus or minus two days."

Natasha stared at the screen. Part of Anod wanted to ask the same question about her pregnancy, but she forced herself to think of Natasha.

"Why did you ask that question? Didn't you already know Zitger impregnated you?"

Natasha turned to Anod. "I suppose out of some distant hope."

"Is there some chance it could have been your husband's child?"

She thought about her answer for several seconds. "No. I suppose not."

Anod thought about withholding her state but recognized it would become obvious soon enough. "I am pregnant, too," she said solemnly.

Natasha jumped up, hugged Anod, and gave her a kiss on both cheeks. "Congratulations. I am so excited for you," she said, and then her expression turned sad. "Oh, I am sorry. Did he do it to you as well?"

"He raped me several times, yes. However, I do not know if he contributed to this pregnancy, and I do not want to know. At this stage, it does not matter who provided the seed, I am pregnant, and to me, this is Bradley's child. That is how it shall be."

Excitement returned to Natasha's face. "Then, I am happy for you."

"What is all the commotion?" asked Anton as he joined them.

"Anod and I are both pregnant," announced Natasha with exuberant enthusiasm.

"Congratulations."

"Thank you," both women responded in unison.

Anton looked to Anod. "I can safely say that was the best sleep I have ever had," he said. "It is miraculous."

"Me, too," added Natasha.

"The more you use them, the more benefit they provide."

"Well, I am using that thing from now on," stated Anton.

"Me, too."

"What do we do today?" Anton asked looking to Anod for leadership.

"We continue collecting the information we need, prepare for the community meeting and begin the process of reconstruction."

"That is a lot," Natasha said.

"Yes, but it is our life," Anod answered. "Now, let us get something to eat so we can start the day."

Chapter 17

"I have collected all the information I am able to collect," announced Morgan by mid-morning.

The three Murtaurians stopped their planning discussion. "What are the results?" asked Anod.

"By my records, there were 68 families or groups on Murtauri Four, or a total of 404 human individuals, when the Yorax arrived. For those which I have confirmatory information, 58 people were killed, predominantly males; in all, 44 males to be precise. Five families were completely terminated. Of the survivors, Anod SanGiocomo's injuries were the most severe. Most injuries were minor, in the category of cuts and bruises. More significantly, I suspect, Zitger impregnated 31 Murtaurian women over the course of the Yorax occupation. Six women were previously pregnant, and four of those were raped anyway by Zitger."

The information delivered so calmly and without emotion by Morgan made Anod strongly nauseous. She considered running outside but decided to suppress the sensations. The news had an obvious effect on Natasha and Anton as well. The impact on Murtauri Four was more serious than Anod suspected. Anod could keep her mind from wondering whether she was one of those latter category women. She pushed the thoughts out. There were significant elements.

"That is fifteen percent of our population lost," Anod said.

"It is fourteen point thirty-six percent to be precise," added Morgan.

"My God, so many women raped. This is tragic," mumbled Anton.

Natasha began to cry, placing her face in her hands propped on her knees.

"I'm sorry," Anton whispered touching Natasha on the shoulder.

"These are facts," Anod said in a strong voice. "We cannot change them. Our task will be to survive and prosper for the memory of those we lost and in defiance of those facts."

"But, all those bastard children," said Anton mindlessly.

"No!" barked Anod startling her two companions. "They are children, simply that, children. We shall cherish these children as our next generation."

"But, Anod," protested Anton.

"No!" she exclaimed even more firmly. "I will have none of that talk. We must rejoice in our next generation. We cannot allow ourselves to succumb to the past or fall victim to our regrets. Our commitment must be to raise these children to be good, productive citizens – nothing else. We must place this horrific episode in our distant history, and we cannot allow these children to be tainted by our sense of propriety."

"But, he raped them," spat Anton.

"Our sorrow will not change that fact, now will it? We need the population."

Natasha had stopped crying. Both of them stared at Anod with expressions of bewilderment. Anod simply nodded to them then turned to the console.

"Morgan, you implied that you had not accounted for everyone. How many are you missing?"

"I do not have any confirmatory information for 27 individuals."

"We need to find them," Anod responded.

"So, we may have lost more," said Natasha.

"We do not know that until we have confirmed their status."

"We need to find them," Anton repeated Anod's direction.

Anod's mind kept working on the information. "Morgan, of those 27 missing, how many are males?"

"Twenty-five."

"They . . . have . . . been . . . killed," stammered Natasha.

"We do not know that" Anod replied. "We must assume nothing. They are simply unaccounted for at this point."

Natasha turned to capture Anod's eyes. Tears, sorrow and anxiety covered her face. She had already lost her husband, but her compassion for others carried over. "Anod, we know what they have done to the men."

Anod grasped her shoulder firmly but not hard. "I know Natasha, but we must deal with facts, not supposition." The widowed chemist nodded her head then let her chin fall to her chest. "We need to mobilize our citizens to find the missing or determine their fate."

The three concentrated their attention on several sketches of options based on the locations of the missing. Over the next half day, they sent messages, coordinated instructions and issued requests for assistance from those surviving Murtaurians closest to the last known location of the missing. One by one, the confirmation came to Morgan and the others. The process of finding their missing had a cohesive element for the community as though they were fights against some strange disease. Morgan reported the results of the search. Natasha's premonition was correct.

"Morgan, let me summarize the results of our missing search," said Anod. "Of the 27 you initially reported as missing, our people found 24 of those, all males and all dead."

"Correct."

Natasha began to sob softly as the words were spoken and confirmed. Anton walked outside.

"Three are still missing in that we do not have confirmatory information."

"Correct."

"The best we can do is third hand information that the two females and one male were probably killed. The two females were taken prisoner by the Yorax, and they were not liberated."

"Correct."

"I need to go back into the compound to see if I can find any signs of those three."

"That would be appropriate, Anod."

"Morgan, please confirm our community meeting tomorrow local zenith time for all our citizens."

"As you command," he answered.

Anod placed a hand on Natasha's shoulder. "I need to go back into the compound. I would suggest you stay here to help Morgan, if he needs it." Natasha nodded her head in agreement. "I am going to see if Anton wants to go with me. I should be back in an hour." Again, Natasha nodded her head. Anod stroked her hair several times then left.

She found Anton pacing outside in the warmth of Murtauri's light. Anod stopped several meters away until he acknowledged her presence.

"Why did they have to be so vicious?" Anton snarled at her.

Anod suspected the barbarity had been more to influence her than anything else. While the Yorax were a warrior culture, they were generally not indiscriminate in their violence. It was Zitger's acquired inhumanity that had done this to their people. Those views or impressions would not make the pain any less. This was not something she could discuss with the others.

"It is their way," she said simply, not wanting to get into the discussion.

"So sad," he mumbled.

"I need to go to the compound. Do you want to come with me?"

"What for?"

"There are two women and one man still considered missing."

"And, you think we might find some answers at the compound," Anton said.

"Yes. The two women were known to have entered the compound, but neither one of them apparently came out."

"Then, I will go with you."

They walked together through the town. Town's people and other visitors continued to shout words of praise and support. Some came out of their houses to greet Anod. She accepted the adulation and tried to show some appreciation, but this was not what she wanted.

The compound was open, as she had left it. They carefully searched first the left building then the right – the two buildings where the Murtauri women had been held captive. Additional destruction had been done, probably by some of the victims wanting their form of vengeance. The devices of their torture had been cut or broken, some to unrecognizable levels. Other than the damaged equipment, they could not find additional clues.

When they entered the third and center building, the biting, permeating, foul odor of death overwhelmed both of them. They staggered back as though they had been hit by a high velocity wind. Anod slammed the door shut.

"This is not good," she choked.

"Death."

"Yes. Some of the dead were not buried."

"What do you want to do?"

"We must search the interior. We cannot leave this as it is."

"How are we going to do that? I don't think I can stand it in there," said Anton.

"The only way I know is with masks."

They searched the town in the vicinity of the Yorax compound until they found a bucket, water, and some heavy cloth. They fashioned a couple of masks from the cloth and carried the bucket of water back to the center building. Outside the door, they soaked the masks and did not wring them out as they tied them to their heads covering their noses and mouths.

Anod opened the door again. The mask helped but did not eliminate the pungent odor. Anod moved quickly. Anton tried but could not follow her. She went first to her torture chamber expecting to see Zitger's bloated and discolored body. His corpse was not there, nor were the Yorax who died there that day. Other than the removal of the bodies, the room in which she had been beaten and raped was untouched. The smears of dried blood, the chains, the devices of her torment were the same as when she left the room. Anod thoroughly searched every compartment – nothing.

The adjacent or center room, the control room of the complex, was likewise untouched. The lights, displays, switches, all remained active. Anod would need Morgan's help in understanding some of the information as well as provide directions on extraction of other information. Perhaps, the Yorax kept a journal or other records of their activities on Murtauri Four. She could not do that now, not with this merciless stench. The water was evaporating, allowing more of the odor to creep through the mask. Anod considered going outside to wet her mask again, but she wanted to complete the search.

The next and final room was an odd combination of barracks, rest area and storeroom. When she opened the door, the assault on her eyes and nose stunned her. The smell seemed to come through her skin. Something was in there, but the abuse of her senses was too much. Anod closed the door, ran outside, pulled the mask off and vomited violently. Her body heaved until nothing came out. The smell from her clothing repulsed Anton.

"What happened in there?" Anton asked from three meters distance upwind.

Anod struggled to regain control of her body. "I don't know, yet, but whatever it is, it is not good."

"What do you think it is?"

"It could be many things," she answered, her mind racing through the possibilities, but she knew speculation would not be useful.

"What are you going to do?"

"As soon as this nausea passes, I am going to wet my mask and go back in there until I find the source."

"Why don't we just leave it?"

"First, we have three missing citizens and that may be them in there," she said waving toward the control building. "Second, I need access to the control room to gather information, and I cannot work in there under those conditions."

Anton nodded his head but did not move. Once the nausea subsided to a level she felt manageable, Anod thoroughly soaked her mask then tied it to her head still dripping water.

Anod reentered the building with a specific purpose. The smell seemed more intense, but the wet mask enabled her to continue. She methodically searched the room. Artifacts of the Yorax lay around the room – uneaten meals now moldy and rotten, drinks now dry, rumpled bedding of an odd metallic material. The main portion of the room held nothing extraordinary. The first compartment from the left held various supplies. The second compartment hammered Anod's senses.

She ran from the room, pulling her mask off as her gut convulsed so violently she stumbled each time as she fought with her body to get out of the building. Anod dove out as best she could. The violence of her nausea caused her to curl up in a ball. This time she resigned herself to letting the sensations pass.

Anton kept repeating himself. "What's wrong?" "Can I help?" "What can I do?" But, he kept his distance from her.

The recovery process took many minutes. Anod did not care how long. She just wanted these terrible abuses of her senses to pass. Slowly, a semblance of normalcy returned. She pushed herself to her knees. Anton kept talking to her, but she did not want to talk to him. After a few more minutes, Anod managed to stand on wobbly legs. She bent over with her hands on her knees. As each stage progressed, Anod eventually made her way to the bucket. She doused her face with water, found a crude cup and poured water over her head, wetting her hair thoroughly, and at least the shoulders of her clothing. When her convulsions began to subside, she stood straight and faced Anton.

"We need not look any further," she said.

A grim expression soured his face. "They are in there," he said.

Anod nodded her head as she swallowed hard, holding up two fingers.

"Could you tell what happened?"

"It is impossible to tell. There are too many possibilities. The fact is they are dead."

"Who?"

"Two women . . . the two missing women."

"No male?"

"Not that I can tell. It is not a pretty sight." Anton just stared at her. Anod felt compelled to say what her mind thought. "My guess is they were used by the Yorax. They probably had been confined in that storeroom, and my breakout dispatched their antagonists. If they were alive when I escaped, I did not hear any calls for help."

"Those cruel bastards."

Anod instantly regretted her conjecture. "The means of their demise does not change reality. If Zitger did this, he has paid with his life. If the Yorax did it, some of them have paid. The others will most probably not be brought to justice. The best thing we can do is bury them with respect and live to remember what happened."

"How are we going to get them out of there?"

Anod's mind saw the horribly distorted, naked bodies curled up against their pain at the moment of death. Seeing that horrific scene would not help others. The process of removal would rest with her. She must bear the agony to spare her friends, colleagues and fellow citizens.

She remembered the shuttle. There were at least two environmental suits to allow extravehicular movement in the vacuum of space. A suit would spare her further exposure to the disgusting stench, but it would not remove the grotesque sight.

"I need a suit from the shuttle. We also need a couple of large sealable bags or containers. I will remove the bodies if you and a few others can bury them."

While Anton went about the tasks she had given him, Anod returned to the Arguello house. She stripped off all her clothes outside, walked through the house ignoring the questions from Natasha and entered the cleansing chamber. She allowed the full cleaning process to work on her body as she forced her mind to concentrate on the beauty of the mountains and the slurping chatter of a waterfall.

"What happened?" Natasha asked as Anod exited the cleansing station.

"We found the two missing women."

"And?"

"We need to bury them."

"Is that why you had to do this?" she asked nodding to the cleansing chamber.

"Natasha," Anod said as she tried to find clothes she could wear, "you will have to trust me. You do not want to know more. Let it suffice that we found the two missing women. We only have one person missing now."

Natasha nodded her head in agreement. She helped Anod dress. Natasha's curiosity pushed her to follow Anod back to the compound, but Anod convinced her to remain at the house. By the time Anod arrived, Anton had repositioned the shuttle, collected the material she wanted and found two other men to help.

Anod instructed the group on the steps they would take. She withheld any of the details. Once everyone was ready, she put on the suit, activating all the systems before she donned the helmet and proceeded to the storeroom. Being inside an environmental suit on the surface of an almost idyllic planet made Anod feel odd, out of place, and strangely afraid – of what she did not know.

She used every gram of discipline to ignore the ugly scene and the thoughts of what these remains had once been. She sealed the bags of the two women and carried them outside. The men took the bags to a corner of the compound and buried them without ceremony. Anod tried her best to clean up the small storeroom. Fortunately, she was breathing clean air and did not have to smell the residual, but her mind filled in what her sense of smell could not detect. She fought her bouts of nausea against her own mind.

Through her suit communicator and helmet camera, Anod was able to confer with Morgan, and between them activated a smoke elimination system that would ventilate the interior. Anod decided to leave the system on for a day or so to make the building tolerable.

The three men waited for her outside. She nodded to them.

"Are you done?" asked Anton.

"Yes," she answered through her communicator.

All three men grimaced as the odor from the interior came out with her on the outside of the environmental suit. Death stuck to the non-porous material of the suit. She searched for clues of the wind direction.

"Where is downwind?" she asked.

They held their noses and staggered back from her. Anton used his free hand to point to her left. Anod moved two meters downwind from her assistants.

"I want you to throw several buckets of water on me to wash down the outside of the suit."

They did as they were told. Anod also washed her gloved hands as if it was her skin. Satisfied the suit was as clean as it was going to get with their crude methods, Anod extricated herself.

"I won't ask how bad it was," said Anton.

"Good. You don't want to know."

"What now?"

As she continued to pull the suit off, she said, "I activated the ventilation system. If we leave it on for a day, it should clear the residual odor."

"Why don't we just close it and leave it?" Anton asked.

"I need access to the control panel inside."

They stowed the suit. Anod thanked the men for their assistance, and then walked back to the house. Anton followed her. By the time they reached the house, Anod had already received several questions about what she had found in the compound. Natasha was waiting with more.

"I have received many inquiries from our citizens about what you found in the compound," Natasha said in a rather challenging manner.

"There are some things better left unsaid," responded Anod.

"She is right," added Anton.

"They still want to know."

"Is everything ready for our meeting tomorrow?"

"Yes. I think the entire planet is going to be here," Natasha answered. "What is left of it, at least."

Anod smiled – the entire planet, as if they had an enormous population. "Excellent. Now, I need your help," she said. Both of them looked at her like school children called upon by the teacher, and neither of them knew the answer. "I have a pounding headache, and my entire chest hurts from my vomiting. I need to go through the cleansing station again and take a sleep cycle."

"It is only early afternoon," responded Natasha.

"Yes, it is, but I am not in good shape. I need the recovery time." Anod did not need to examine her body to recognize some of her previous wounds had been aggravated by the morning's difficulties. "Anton, while I try to recover, please tell Morgan what we found and did as a result."

"I will. We can take care of things," Anton offered and waved toward the storeroom. "You go ahead and take whatever time you need. Everything will be OK out here."

Anod nodded her head and went to the room. She cried as the cleansing station worked its miracles. The release took her thoughts to the further example of Zitger's brutality, although she suspected Zitger did not know about the two women. The Yorax troopers were probably 'playing' with the two females, their play went too far based on the damage and injuries she saw, and the Yorax were trying to conceal their transgression from their leader. She held Zitger responsible as the leader, but then, that process would not change anything either. Anod knew it was important for her to erase those memories of the Yorax incursion, and it was important for her to focus her attention on the people for the future, or they might all lose the peaceful innocence that she cherished. This tragedy must not foul their peaceful nature.

Anod finished the cleansing cycle and went directly to the isopod. More than anything else, she sought relief from her thoughts, memories and the images storming through her mind. She pushed the correct buttons, watched the cover close over her, and turned her body and mind over to the machine.

Anod was alone when she returned to reality. She decided to use the quiet time. She touched the proper buttons to return to the levitated state as she allowed her mind to work on the upcoming community meeting. She wanted to say the correct things, but she really wanted someone else to take the leadership role. After all, she had a child growing within her, and she wanted to devote her time to the infant. Anod also wanted to anticipate the questions she would most likely be confronted with by some of the attendees. Levitation in the isopod offered a unique sensation. Nothing touched her body. She felt no forces or pressure. It was like neutral buoyancy in water or floating in space without an environmental suit. Her mind was active and ready.

Slowly, Anod removed herself from the isopod and dressed. She felt monumentally better than when she returned to the Arguello house. She splashed some water on her face and instantly thought of that unique feeling she had when she took her first water shower on Beta all those years ago. Anod smiled broadly although there was no one to see her grin. She saw those early days on Beta in her mind's eye when Nick had helped her adjust to being human. She had lived her entire life, until the ambush outside Saranon, in the controlled and perfect environment of the Society, and the warrior class of which she was a part. On Beta, she had her first experience of actually inhaling the scent of a real forest – feeling the rainfall outside SanGiocomo cave – her first pregnancy and childbirth. All those experiences brought her to this day. Despite the enormous loss in her life, Anod was thankful for all she had and for what lay ahead.

It was dusk outside when Anod returned to the main room. Natasha and Anton sat at the table. Also in the room were Naomi Gibritzu along with all four of her surviving children, Guyasaga with her surviving children and Mysasha. Her children remained with Hyoshi until the meeting time tomorrow.

"Well, good evening to you all, and to what do I owe this honor," Anod said in the cheeriest voice she could muster.

"We are here for you," said Naomi.

Anod was overwhelmed with emotion. She clutched her mouth as her eyes squinted and tears poured down her face. Her chest heaved with each sob. They gathered around her as if to hold her up and keep her from falling. Hands and arms embraced her, stroked her head, wiped the tears from her cheeks, and gave her the warmth of friendship.

"It is OK," said Mysasha. "Let it go. Nothing is going to hurt you now." Anod's emotions became a wailing as the pent up grief gushed from her uncontrollably. "You protected us, and now it is time for us to protect you."

Anod could not stop herself. Her muscles let go, but the hands held her. All Anod could make her voice choke out repeatedly was, "Why?" Their support leached the massive accumulation of sorrow Anod had forcibly held within her, and repressed for the fight she did not want. Anod had no idea how long this process went on. Their unqualified support, in spite of their own losses and wounds, made Anod's grief all the more poignant.

It was dark outside when Anod's control returned to her. It was Moma Gibritzu's cherub-like, innocent face that popped out at her. Anod reached for the girl's face and touched her cheek. As if by some miracle, she smiled back at Anod melting her grief into distant memories. Anod embraced Moma. They held each other as the group surrounded them. For Anod, the assaults during captivity had been combat – part of a battle against a twisted and determined adversary. For Moma, it was nothing but a crime – an evil act to take the innocence of a young woman. Tears returned to Anod wetting the point their cheeks touched. They held each other tightly. Anod cried in silence this time for the innocence lost.

They stayed together that night in the Arguello house. They shared their feelings and their innermost thoughts. They found ways to laugh, to find humor in the events of life. The healing process was a glorious tribute to the human community. In time, they slept in any available spot. Even Anod dozed with her head on the table.

The morning became a bevy of excitement, like some tremendous celebration. As the mid-day time approached, people gathered in the square of New Providence as they had done many times before. Anod greeted friends and received words of encouragement, adulation and praise with grace and humility.

It was time. Anod stood on the platform in front of the rock pile. The crowd rose in cheer with more shouted words of appreciation. Anod held her arms up in a futile effort to quiet the group. Eventually, it dawned on Anod the Murtaurians needed this collective sign. After many minutes, Anod pleaded for quiet. Over several more minutes, quiet began to come with intervals punctuated by shouts of support.

"Thank you all," Anod said when silence finally came to the meeting.

"Thank you," came the resounding collective shout back at her.

"We have much to discuss," Anod stated. All faces and eyes were on her. "We have come through a harrowing time. Many of us have lost loved ones, and for that, we collectively grieve. However, the best tribute we can possibly make to our dead is long life and remembrance of those we loved." She paused. The group remained silent although she could see tears and efforts to suppress their emotions among some. "We must think of the future. Our first order of business should be electing a new leader."

"We have a new leader," someone shouted.

Anod did not want it to be her. "I do not recall participating in an election."

"We didn't need an election," came another voice.

"We all want you."

The rumble began and rolled like waves through the group. A tension drew them tighter.

"You are our leader." They cheered.

Anod held up her arms signaling for quiet. She knew this was coming. "Thank you all. I am flattered and honored, but listen to me." They calmed. "I have lost my family as many of you have lost loved ones. I am pregnant, as many of you are," she said finding the eyes of those she knew were in the same state as her, "with my next child. I just want to be a mother."

"You can be a mother," they said. "You have saved us twice."

"You are a natural leader."

"We will help you with the children as we have in the past," another said.

"Please," Anod pleaded, "I have done my share. I just want to enjoy my future children." Anod liked the sound of her last sentence. She planned to have as many children as she could have.

"You can. We will help you."

"There are numerous others in our community who could be the leader," she said waving her arm over the crowd.

"Look, Anod," said Hyoshi Nagoyama as he worked his way to the front and joined her on the platform stump. "Nearly all of us have shared our views over the last few days and hours while you were doing more work on our behalf. We recognize your need for privacy, for a personal life, to be a mother, but we all feel the same. We have polled the entire community . . . every last one of us . . . and, we are unanimous. Unanimous! We want you to be our leader, to represent us. We have also agreed that we are your family, and we will help you in every way possible." There were shouts of support.

Anod felt that overwhelming feeling she felt yesterday evening. She did not want tears this time, and she kept them back. She did not want the job, but she also felt helpless to resist.

"You have not given me much choice," Anod responded.

"That was the whole idea," someone shouted.

Natasha moved to the front and extended her hand to grasp Anod's hand. "Please, Anod," she said softly. "We know this is not what you want, but it is very important to all the rest of us. There is no other choice for us," she added, motioning with her free hand and her head toward the group behind her.

Anod nodded her head, then said, "Very well, then," she whispered to Natasha. Anod straightened her back and held up her arms until quiet came. "I shall do my best."

The uproar deafened the individual words. Several of the people in front reached to touch her leg or her outstretched hands. Anod held up her arms, again, and quiet came more quickly than the previous times.

"Then, let us move on to the future." A series of affirmative words came from the crowd. "Let me update everyone to ensure we have the same starting point. The Yorax departed when their leader was killed."

"Thanks to you," shouted Guyasaga, causing the assembly to erupt in cheers again.

Anod immediately held her arms up. This is not necessary, she told herself. When calm returned, she continued. "I called the Society to report the incursion. They have dispatched the Starship *Reliant*, which should arrive tomorrow. I also called Otis Greenstreet. He is on his way back from Beta. He should arrive later today with the trading agreement between Beta and Murtauri Four." Clapping punctuated her words, this time. "As you know, we conducted a census and inventory. The stark reality is, we have one unaccounted for citizen, Jonas Murphy. If anyone learns anything about him, please let Morgan know immediately. Perhaps we can collect sufficient information to determine what happened to him. Also, we have lost twenty-one percent of our population."

Gasps told their surprise. "It is important that we join together to protect and nurture each other. Natasha, Anton and I are without family, and we have banded together. If there are any among us who are not living with someone for mutual support, please reach out. It is important that we protect each other . . . all of us."

"How many males?" came the painful question.

Anod stared at the back of the crowd for a moment as she chose her words. The truth was going to hurt, but they had to deal with the reality. "Sixty-eight males lost . . . mostly adults."

"Dear God."

"I didn't realize it was that bad."

"Isn't that most of our male population?" came the next question.

"To be frank, yes." More gasps. "It is eighty percent of our post-pubescent male population."

"They killed the males and raped the females," growled one of them.

"It was more than that," stated Anod. "This was a purposeful effort to subsume our population. It was not just rape as an act of violence against our women. He intentionally and methodically raped our women to impregnate them . . . to further his genetic string."

"Then, we should deny him his goal."

"What do you mean?"

"Destroy his offspring."

"No!" shouted Anod. "Survival is more important than pride or propriety. We must cherish this new generation. We need these children to ensure our survival."

The disagreement within the group started small then grew rapidly as smaller groups began arguing the point with each other. Factiousness swept the assembly. It took Anod several minutes to regain control. Several of the men started to leave.

"Wait!" commanded Anod. "You cannot leave." She waited for

the others to call them back. Anod held up her arms for calm. "I do not think we will find a more critical topic than this. How we handle this situation may well determine our very survival on this planet." The point reached all of them. "I would suggest we take some time to consider our options and discuss this crisis in smaller groups. Otis is due back this afternoon. The Society should arrive tomorrow. I recommend we adjourn for the day. Several of us need to brief the Society. I would like to seek their counsel regarding our options."

Most of the group nodded their heads. The expressions told Anod there was not a consensus. She could only hope logic and reason would guide them through the decisions that lay ahead. Even the adjournment proposal did not receive unanimous approval, but in the end, it was agreed. They would wait until after the conference with the Society to reconvene the community meeting.

The group disbanded. Several of the women who lost one or more members of their families gave Anod words of support and encouragement although none of them had a clear view of the direction. It was more to show their support and appreciation of the importance of the crisis.

Anod found Natasha and Anton. "I need some time alone . . . to think." Both of them nodded their heads. "I am going to the mountains," she said to Natasha, knowing she would know where. "I will return tomorrow by mid-day, before the *Reliant* is due to arrive. If something should happen, fly the shuttle through the lake valley," she said to Anton. "Natasha will show you where."

"Are you all right?" asked Natasha.

"Yes. I am fine," Anod answered although it was not entirely true. "I just need some time to think, to be alone with my thoughts."

"We will be here when you return," said Natasha.

"Please apologize to Otis when he arrives. I shall see him tomorrow. You can explain things to him."

Anod embraced them both, then went to the spare scooter and departed for her mountain retreat. She used the highest speed she safely could, forcing her to concentrate on flying the scooter rather than the questions before them. She would have plenty of time to consider facts and options. Anod arrived without difficulty. Everything was as she left it. The first thing she decided to do was go for a good swim without removing her clothes. The water always helped her. This occasion was no different.

Chapter 18

There was not much activity when Anod returned to New Providence. This time she rode the scooter directly to the Arguello house, deactivated it in front, and went inside. Natasha sat at the table stirring some food on her plate. Anton cleaned utensils from their midday meal.

"Welcome back," Natasha said as Anod walked through the door.

Anton turned and put his right index finger to his forehead in a pseudo-salute without saying anything.

"Thank you. It is great to be back."

"Did you figure things out?" Natasha continued.

"Some things seem clearer to me, but there are still more questions than answers. Did Otis return?"

"Yes," said Anton. "He asked for you but is checking on several friends."

"Have there been any changes from the Society?"

"No. They are due here anytime."

"What revelations came to you?" asked Natasha.

Anod sat down at the table and tore off a large piece of bread. Anton placed a large, hot, mug of tea in front of Anod, and then joined the two women at the table. Anod took a good bite of bread, chewed, swallowed, and then took several sips of tea. She nodded her head in appreciation to Anton.

"Well, it is clear to me that our first priority is security. Our present situation is probably acceptable for now, but we will need to work something out with the Society to prevent any reoccurrence of the violence or the invasion we just experienced. Second, we need to consider our future."

"What do you mean?" asked Anton.

"The male portion of our population has been decimated."

"We know that."

"We have elected to use biological interactive reproduction."

"So?"

"With only one side of the required pair . . . to put it bluntly . . . I think we are highly vulnerable to an unacceptable narrowing of our genetic diversity."

"What does that mean?"

"I need to consult with the Society when they get here, but I think it means we will be more susceptible to biological aberrations – less robust." Anod considered going into the disadvantages of a narrow genetic pool, but most of the Murtaurians were not scientists. The strengthening of their culture depended upon a healthy, broad mixture of the genetic material. It could be accomplished by several principal means. Some of those means would be less attractive to the Murtaurians. "We need their help."

"Do you need our help?" asked Natasha.

"With the Society talks, no, probably not, but you are both certainly welcome to participate. However, in an ultimate sense, yes; we will all be involved in solving this problem."

"We are ready," added Anton.

"The bottom line is, we must grow our population as quickly as we can, and we must enhance the diversity within our genetic pool."

Natasha and Anton stared at Anod. Both of them were beginning to see the picture but Anod was hesitant to draw the picture too clearly at this stage. She wanted to find another way, but that depended upon the Society and whatever assistance or sponsorship they might be able to provide. Anod felt quite odd with the seemingly endless string of requests to the Society with little perceived return. She felt like a beggar, or at least what she thought a beggar would feel like since the social phenomenon had been eliminated centuries before her existence. Neither of her compatriots wanted to talk as their concentration remained within themselves leaving their exterior devoid of expression.

"Morgan?" she said.

"Yes, Anod."

"Has the *Reliant* arrived in orbit, yet?"

"Yes."

"Has the captain requested a meeting?"

"No."

Anod noticed both sets of eyes blankly staring at her as if they had no idea what was happening. She could involve them in the initial meeting but decided it was not necessary. She left them in the house, walked outside in the bright light of a clear day and slowly made her way to the town square where the captain or her envoy would probably materialize.

She enjoyed the sounds of life as she intermingled the coolness of the shade tree with the warmth of the light from Murtauri. Several citizens stopped to say hello or chat about one thing or another. It was a peaceful way to spend the minutes until four bodies materialized six meters from her in the open area of the square.

Anod did not recognize any of the four, Society warriors. They were dressed in full battle gear with their weapons at the ready and arranged with their backs to each other reminiscent of the famous British squares of five centuries earlier. Anod could not tell whether they were male or female, and it really did not matter. She knew they were competent warriors, or they would not have been assigned to this task. They quickly scanned the surrounding features of the town. Satisfied the situation was safe, the other three warriors arrayed themselves behind their leader, who in turn focused on Anod, lowered his weapon and walked toward her.

The warrior saluted Anod who chose not to return the gesture since she did not feel like a warrior anymore. "I am Captain Althogorik, chief security officer aboard *Reliant*. I believe you are Anod."

"Yes, I am," Anod responded as she extended her hand to the leader of the security detachment who was about four centimeters shorter than her but appeared to be more stocky. The cold, gloved hand gripped hers firmly although it could have been the hand of an android rather than a female warrior.

"Is the planet secure?"

"Yes, as far as we know."

"Colonel Arkinnagga would like you to join her and the command staff aboard *Reliant* as soon as possible."

"I am ready anytime you are," Anod responded motioning toward the security officer.

"Then, if you will join my team, we will be off," Althogorik said, bowing slightly and sweeping her arm toward the other three members of the security team.

In an instant, she was standing on the transport grid aboard the starship with the four Society warriors. The only other person in the room, the operator, nodded toward them but said nothing.

"If you will follow me," Captain Althogorik said as she stepped aggressively toward the door.

For the first time, Anod noticed the unique clatter of the armor-plated suits the Society warriors wore in battle. It had been a very long time since she heard the rubbing and clapping sound.

The other three guards did not go with them. Anod had never been on this class of starship before. The passageways were straight and simple. Doors opened and closed without commands. Knowing Society security procedures, there had to be a sensing system that positively identified Althogorik, established her authorization to pass that point and operated the doors accordingly. The process intrigued Anod.

As they approached the next set of doors, Anod grabbed the security officer's arm. Althogorik responded defensively to the potential threat, but the doors did not open.

"May I ask what your intentions are?" she asked as she maintained her position, ready to strike.

Anod held up both arms in a gesture of surrender. "I was fascinated by the operation of your doors. I wanted to see if your systems would recognize an abnormal condition."

"They did."

"Yes. I am most impressed."

"Shall we proceed?"

Anod nodded her head. Althogorik turned toward the doors that opened automatically. As they stepped through the hatch, Althogorik said, "I take it you have not been aboard an *Intrepid*-class starship?"

"Yes, I have, but I was just curious about the security systems."

"There are many new features that might be of interest to you."

"Perhaps I might impose upon you for a tour later."

"I do not think the captain will have any objection."

Althogorik led Anod into the command conference room. She recognized Colonel Arkinnagga immediately.

"Good to see you, again," said the starship captain as she extended her hand. The two women were of comparable height and build although the colonel had silky gold hair pulled back tightly against her head into a round bun at the back.

"Good to see you," responded Anod.

"Let me introduce my staff. This is my first officer, Colonel Artomank," she said motioning toward the tallest person in the room. "This is my science officer, Major Ziikaar," she added regarding a male officer with medium brown, short hair and roughly her size and build. "You have met our chief security officer." Anod nodded her head in response. "And, this is our medical officer, Major Avyk." With the introductions complete, Arkinnagga motioned for them to sit around the table. "How much time can we have with you?" she asked Anod.

"I do not have much to go back to," Anod said with twinge of melodrama. "I can stay as long as we have something productive to discuss."

"Very well. Shall we begin?" Anod nodded. "What happened on Murtauri Four?"

Anod recounted the sequence of events with as much external, emotional detachment as she could project. She knew these professional warriors would see any emotional response by her as weakness . . . at best counter-productive and at worst negating. The various officers interjected questions as they came to them. Anod did her best to answer each and every one. There were some elements of information she did not possess. They wanted to understand Zitger's motivation, perhaps for different reasons and from a different perspective than Anod, but it was a common thread to their queries. Over the span of several hours, Anod brought them through the chain of events to the conference room and this debriefing session.

"So, it was biological subjugation," summarized Major Ziikaar, the science officer.

"I had not thought about it in quite those terms," responded Anod, "but, I suppose that is a reasonable conclusion."

"Nearly your entire adult male population has been eliminated and half of your female population compromised?" questioned Major Avyk.

"Yes."

"Did you examine Zitger's body?" asked Ziikaar.

"I do not think so. I was involved with other tasks. The bodies of Zitger and the other dead Yorax were disposed of in some manner, probably burial."

"Can they be recovered?"

Anod concentrated her eyes on Ziikaar. She wondered what he was searching for or worried about regarding Zitger's corpse. "If he was indeed buried, I imagine his body is retrievable."

"I would ask that we obtain Zitger's body."

"Yes," added Avyk. "We should conduct an extensive, forensic autopsy. Perhaps we can learn what caused him to defect and carry out such onerous reprisals."

"Can you comply?" asked Colonel Arkinnagga.

"We can certainly determine what was done with his body. If it was buried, it can be exhumed and delivered to you."

"Then, make it so."

Anod nodded her head in agreement. "My greater concern is the future, not the past."

"The biological compromise of your culture."

"Yes."

Reliant's officers stared at Anod as she searched each set of eyes. The science officer was the first to respond.

"As you know, Anod, we are not accustomed to the ancient reproductive methods. So, without researching the biology we have at hand, I cannot be precise. The infusion of a singular male genetic component into such a small population will substantially narrow the diversity of the gene pool. I am sure you recognized the potential consequences of this fact." Anod nodded in agreement. "Likewise, your population has been diminished to a precariously low quantity." Anod did not respond in any form. "At initial impression, it would appear the best option is gestation of the current embryos to add to your population numbers."

"And?" she interjected.

"You have two fundamental problems," began Major Avyk. "One is your population. You have little margin to tolerate further abuse from whatever process might threaten the population, which is why I think you need these new entities, first and foremost. The other problem is your genetic diversity. With your current male population, it would take several generations to reach a safe level of diversity. Your culture will be vulnerable for 50 to 100 years."

"That is an exorbitant risk," said Ziikaar.

"Can we encourage human male immigration?"

"Anod," said Arkinnagga. "You are at the farthest frontier of the Confederation and the closest to the Yorax Empire, a known belligerent culture. You are not on any established trade route. You have decided to remain an agrarian community. There are little incentives for anyone, male or female, to come here. Plus, most of the human species reproduce in a more controlled and stable environment. There is enormous uncertainty to life as you and your people have chosen to live."

"Are there any other alternatives?" asked Anod.

Ziikaar shrugged his shoulders then held his hand out as if to point to Anod. "As I understand these biological processes in the ancient form, you must mix your genetic pool as much as you possibly can. As I recall my human biology, you are constrained by a nine-month gestation cycle and perhaps a twelve to eighteen-month reinitialization term, although it could be as short as a few months as I understand the exceptions. However, I must say I have not studied this biology. I should take a few days research to properly form an opinion and provide sound advice. Further, it usually takes, by the old methods, twenty years to mature an adult."

"You mean mix partners?" Anod asked, knowing the answer but not wanting to face the confrontation with the citizens of Murtauri Four.

"Copulation partners?" asked Avyk.

"Yes."

"In that term, yes. That is exactly what I mean."

Anod laughed in uncontrollable fits. The image of standing on the meeting platform in the square at New Providence and explaining this to her compatriots staggered her sense of order. She knew deep inside that Avyk was precisely correct, and she had known for several days. She just hoped there might be some other way.

"I do not understand what is so funny," Major Ziikaar finally stated.

Anod held up her hand as she tried to regain control. "Let me see if I can explain this to you." She swallowed hard and rubbed her chin. "My people have lived for centuries since their banishment from Earth using the old ways. Families are formed around the nucleus of a male and female couple. They procreate for the purpose of producing offspring, who in turn established their own families. These matings are exclusive and perpetual." All the officers just stared at her as if to say . . . so. "You are suggesting we breakdown those cultural mores to cross-couple using our few remaining males to create a broader spectrum of genetic variations."

"Yes, precisely," answered Avyk.

"They will never accept that," Anod said, although she had considered the exact same thing.

"Well, then, you are resigned to accept the extended risk to your culture as you recover from this episode."

Anod stared at Major Avyk as though she expected the *Reliant*'s medical officer to wink at her. When the sign of Avyk's teasing did not come, Anod turned to Colonel Arkinnagga. "There must be other options."

"If there are, we will certainly try to find them. In addition to the detailed examination of Zitger's body, if that is possible, access to your central computer, Morgan is it?" Anod nodded. "Access to Morgan will undoubtedly give us more clues." Again, Anod nodded. "Is there anything else that might be of use in our investigation?"

Anod remembered. "Yes. Beyond the personal interviews with the survivors, if you deem it warranted, I managed to save the head and memory of my android, Lornog. I was able to open the memory. It preserves the last moments of my family. I would like to have that memory saved in the record to ensure no one forgets the brutality of what Zitger and the Yorax did here."

"If you will give us access to Morgan and deliver Lornog's head, we will ensure the information we recover is added to the permanent record."

"Thank you, Colonel Arkinnagga."

"Perhaps this would be the appropriate moment to adjourn."

"Yes," answered Anod.

Arkinnagga rose and extended her hand to Anod. With the respectful closing completed, Anod returned to the surface. She found Natasha and Anton where she left them, only this time eating supper.

"Did you visit the *Reliant*?" asked Anton.

"Yes."

"What did they say?" Natasha asked.

"They wanted to debrief me regarding the Yorax incursion."

"Did you discuss our future?"

"Yes." Anod was not ready to discuss the genetic crisis. "Do we know what happened to Zitger's body?"

"You mean, the Yorax leader you dispatched in the compound?" asked Anton.

"Yes.

"I heard he was buried at the backside of the compound in a mass grave with the other Yorax."

"We need to recover his body."

"Why?"

"The Society wants to do a full forensic autopsy to see if they can find out why he did what he did. They suspect, I guess, there may have been a genetic trigger or some such."

"Whew. That is not going to be a fun job."

"Anton, would you be so kind to find who buried him, where he is, and get some help exhuming his body. I would like to deliver it to the *Reliant* as soon as possible."

"I think I can manage that," said Anton.

"How long is the Society going to be here?" Natasha asked.

"I did not ask. I imagine they will be here until they are satisfied our situation is stable."

"Is there anything they can do for us?"

"Sure there is. They have already begun doing it. If we can turn over Zitger's body, they will . . . ," she stopped herself. Anod remembered nearly too late that Natasha was pregnant with Zitger's genes, and she herself might very well be pregnant by Zitger as well. Any discussion about their thin gene pool or possible defective genes in the male progenitor of so many developing babies would serve no purpose at this stage. Natasha looked at her as if to say, well . . . they will, what? "They will be able to help us close this episode."

"Somehow, I suspect there is more to this story."

"We have only begun the discussions with the Society. There is still much to be reviewed with them and a plan defined."

"Can I join you tomorrow?"

Anod knew she would not be able to shelter Natasha nor any other Murtaurian. Eventually, all these questions and concerns would be in front of the community. If she put any conditions on the dialogue with the Society, they would instantly know something was wrong.

"I would like to join you as well," Anton added before Anod could answer.

"As you wish. As soon as we transport Zitger's body to the *Reliant*, it will take probably several hours for them to complete their studies. We can all go up together to review their findings."

"Excellent," Anton said as he went to the control console and began his task.

Natasha and Anod went for a slow, objective-less walk. The dusk light reflecting off billowing clouds on the horizon suggested an approaching storm. Tomorrow could be rain. They talked about the happenings within the community. Most folks were recovering well. Some, like Moma Gibritzu, were still having difficulties. The gratification came with the mutual assistance they gave to each other, to help those in need of help. All of those hurt by Zitger and the Yorax would recover, including Moma. Natasha also made several attempts to glean additional information from Anod regarding the discussions with the Society. Anod carefully and successfully avoided answering her questions without a fib or obvious evasion.

The remainder of the day and night proceeded in a rather normal, almost lazy course. A routine was beginning to develop. Anod actually began to think of Natasha and Anton as part of her extended family although none of them really talked about it. They were settling into a comfortable relationship that none of them seemed particularly concerned about nor interested in altering. Communications using Morgan's services brought many friends to them as broken lives were mended and nurtured. They even talked to Otis who planned to return to New Providence in another day or two.

The next day clicked along as though each step was another tooth on an ancient cog rail system. Zitger's body was transported to the *Reliant* just prior to mid-day. Four hours later, Morgan informed them that Colonel Arkinnagga was ready to talk, which probably meant she had the results of their investigation. Anod acknowledged the information and indicated they would be in the square in ten minutes and that Natasha Norashova and Anton Trikinov would join her for the next visit.

Anod faced both of her friends. "You are going to hear some things up there that might be very disturbing. It would not be fair or appropriate for me to expose you to this discussion without forewarning you."

"Like what?" asked Natasha.

"There are two principal issues. One, our population has been seriously reduced, but more significantly, our genetic diversity and thus the inherent protection diversity gives us is well below acceptable levels." Both of them kept their eyes on her without expression. "There is also the possibility Zitger's treachery and aberrant behavior might have been genetically induced." Natasha gasped loudly and clutched her lower abdomen. "There is no benefit to premature conclusions. Let us see what the Society has turned up."

"Why didn't you tell us?" Natasha asked.

"I wanted to know the facts surrounding our situation, first. Speculation in the absence of facts is usually not helpful."

"But, Anod, I am carrying his baby." The fear in her voice sent a chill through Anod.

"Natasha, please be calm. I may be carrying his baby as well. So, we are both in this together." Anod's comments seemed to offer some solace to Natasha.

"Are we going to survive this?" Anton asked.

"Yes. The question before us is, how do we reduce the risk we currently face to ensure our survival and enhance our community."

"Is it really that bad?"

"I do not know. That is why I have asked the Society to help us understand the facts regarding our situation." Anod paused for head nods of agreement. "You do not have to go with me. I can do this part."

"No," they said simultaneously.

"I want to go," Anton added, and Natasha bobbed her head in agreement.

"Then, we need to go to the square."

Within seconds of their arrival in the open area of the square, a solo person materialized before them. The guard spread his arms as an invitation to join him. Anod nodded her head in agreement. They appeared aboard *Reliant*. Colonel Arkinnagga greeted them. They followed her to the command conference room. Natasha and Anton gazed in wonderment from start to finish. The two, new Murtaurians were introduced to the other officers before Arkinnagga motioned them to their seats.

"We have completed our investigation," Colonel Arkinnagga stated. "There is no need to interview your citizens unless you feel they might add to the record."

"Let us review the findings," answered Anod, "then, we can determine the necessity for further data collection."

"As a preface, based on the preliminary picture developed prior to and shortly after our arrival, the Confederation confronted the Yorax Empire. Their leaders claim they were duped by Zitger . . . they called him General Negolian . . . and, they desire only peace. A squadron of starships met with the Yorax at the frontier to conclude a treaty that should ensure your safety, henceforth."

"We truly hope so," said Anod.

"Now, the specifics of the situation on Murtauri Four present a more serious concern." Anod concentrated on Arkinnagga's face and eyes. The gravity showed. "The detailed examination of Zitger's corpse revealed a substantial string of genetic defects." The audible gasp and whimper came from Natasha as she covered her mouth and nose trying to suppress her reaction. Anod did not have to look at her to imagine the horror that had to be present in her eyes. "Several of these defects would most probably explain his behavior."

"Most probably?"

"We cannot be certain without a genetic reconstruction and interrogation. That capability only exists on Earth at this moment. The computational and projection requirements significantly exceed anything we could generate aboard a starship or even an outpost."

"So, are you going to take him back to Earth?"

Arkinnagga searched Anod's eyes for several seconds. "Do you think it necessary?"

"Before I answer that question, I would like to understand the impact. We think thirty-one of our women have been impregnated by Zitger, including Natasha Norashova," she said glancing down the table to her friend who still held her hands over the bottom of her face, "and, possibly me."

The last element changed Arkinnagga's expression. "Have you been examined?"

"I have used the cleansing station and isopod, so yes, Morgan has the information."

Arkinnagga looked to her medical officer. "Did we analyze that information?"

"Yes, ma'am, along with all the other survivor data that exists in Morgan's memory."

"Wait," Anod said strongly as she held up her hand to signal in case someone did not hear her. "I do not want to discuss those details just yet. We should know what you see as the implications, first."

"Very well," responded Arkinnagga. "Our analyses of the data we have retrieved and our research in the ancient reproductive processes tell us you have actually thirty-seven pregnant women of which thirty-one, as you indicated, were impregnated by Zitger. It is my misfortune . . . ." Natasha's muffled cry punctuated Arkinnagga's pronouncement. ". . . to inform you that Zitger's genetic mutations have been transferred to those embryos."

Natasha could no longer contain her terror and grief. She tried to stand then stumbled over her chair falling to the deck. Ziikaar and Avyk rose to help her. Anod joined them, embracing Natasha, who in turn latched onto Anod holding her very tight. Anod let her cry and moan into her chest.

With no signs of subsiding, Anod placed her lips next to Natasha's left ear. "Natasha, it will be all right. We will deal with this. It will be all right."

Without removing her face hidden against Anod's chest, she cried, "This is my first baby. Oh God, Anod. I have wanted a baby for so long. Why did this have to happen to me?"

"Life is not always fair, Natasha. We will deal with this."

Natasha lifted her head to capture Anod's eyes. Her reddened eyes and tear stained face amplified the grief. "How?" Her grief turned to anger. "How Anod? How do you propose we deal with this defective life growing within me?"

"And, others," Anod whispered to her.

The recognition she was not alone in this struggle calmed Natasha. Control returned to the accomplished chemist. She stood straight, wiped the tears from her face and eyes, and addressed the group. "My apologies," she said bowing with respect. "This is not an easy topic to discuss."

"Would you like to avoid this discussion?" asked Colonel Arkinnagga.

"No. No," she said waving her hand. "I want to hear this. I need to hear this. I am OK. I will try to control my emotions. Please, please," she added sweeping her arm around the table indicating for people to sit, "proceed."

After they returned to their seats, Anod looked to her friend and received a nod to go ahead. Anod looked to Arkinnagga. "What do you suggest we do?"

"Those decisions are not mine. All I can do is provide the information. You must make the decisions regarding your actions."

Anod nodded her head in agreement. "Fine. We shall do that. However, you must have a recommendation."

"This is not an easy topic given the conditions," Arkinnagga stated. "These genetic defects, because of their pervasiveness, are not likely to be correctable even with the best of our genetic manipulation capability. Further, these defects are likely to exhibit similar behavioral manifestations as these children mature." She paused to allow any questions or comments. When none came, she continued. "The consequences of so many defective humans in such a small population are incalculable, and to put it plainly, not advisable." Again, she paused. Anod motioned with her hand for her to continue. "You asked for a recommendation, and while I am reluctant to offer this, my duty demands it. I would recommend you terminate these pregnancies and start over."

Anod felt the nausea mounting swiftly with her gut. She had consoled herself to the acceptance with the new life within her as the innocent beginning she needed and Murtauri Four needed. The sensations mounted quickly. She felt like vomiting. Anod swallowed hard several times trying to control the urge. She glanced to Natasha who had buried her head in her arms on the table. As Anod gained the upper hand and suppressed her urge to vomit, she turned back to Colonel Arkinnagga.

"Do you know you are suggesting an action that is so completely and absolutely foreign . . . alien really . . . to our culture?" Arkinnagga did not respond. "Most of these women, young and old, have tolerated this violation of their bodies. It is their nature to give and cherish life."

"An honorable endeavor," said Arkinnagga. "However, the facts remain. These embryos are genetic mutations that possess aberrant, genetic, behavioral traits. Just as Zitger's aberrations overcame all his training, all his loyalty, all his commitment to his brethren, so to will these children, as they mature, overcome their training. We do not see a way to avoid the abnormal behavioral manifestations. They could become violent, illogical, and unpredictable. To be candid and blunt, these offspring present a real and expansive threat to all humans."

"Then, it was biological subjugation, as Major Ziikaar stated earlier," Anod said.

"Yes. He was attempting to spread his mutations to a larger group, to create a generation of mutants he intended to use to expand his influence and that of the Yorax. This was biological warfare at its most perverse."

Natasha could no longer control herself. She tried to stand but dove for the corner of the room. On her hands and knees, she vomited in the corner of the conference room. Anod went to her, feeling her own nausea returning. Anod stroked Natasha's back and shoulders until her convulsions subsided. The acidic, bile smell nearly pushed Anod over the edge several times. An android appeared and waited patiently for the two Murtaurian women to allow him access to the residue. The mess was cleaned up quickly. All eyes except Arkinnagga's were focused elsewhere.

"I am terribly sorry," Natasha said to the group. "Perhaps, I should leave."

"I will go with her," Anton said as he stood.

"Do you wish to go back to the surface?" asked Arkinnagga.

"Yes. I think it would be best."

"Captain Althogorik, would you escort our guests to the transport compartment?" Colonel Arkinnagga commanded as she rose to shake hands with Natasha and Anton. "I must apologize for this distasteful exchange."

"No need," answered Natasha. She lowered her head. "It is just that this news is very personal. Anod is right. This is not going to be easy for us."

Anod embraced Anton and then Natasha. "We shall surmount this obstacle as we have all others." Both of them nodded in agreement. "I must ask both of you not to discuss with the others what you have heard here this afternoon." Both stared at her not really comprehending the reason for the request. "I think it wise for us to understand what this means to us and lay out several proposals for our people along with a recommendation. We should not place this burden on them without a potential solution." Both of them nodded their agreement then turned to the double hatch.

Captain Althogorik led them out of the room and down the passageway. Anod and the others returned to their seats.

"I apologize to you as well, Anod."

"As Natasha said, it is not necessary. These are facts we must respond to."

"Unfortunately."

Anod's thoughts latched onto the life growing within her. She considered, for a brief moment, asking Major Avyk if she was included in the thirty-one. Knowing the answer now would not change anything other than it might interfere with her ability to concentrate and reason through the minefield. She could find out from Morgan in time.

Now, she knew she had to know the answer to the question. "What else is there?"

"Given the loss of this group of offspring, the vulnerability of your population becomes an even greater concern."

"Indeed."

"As I understand your culture, this may not be acceptable, but if you use our methods of reproduction and population maintenance, we might be able to help you reach a point of stability more quickly than you can do it by the ancient ways."

Anod ground through the elements of the suggestion. She knew precisely that Arkinnagga was correct. The Society's reproductive processes were precise and controllable, and boundless in scope. The uncertainty of procreation by their natural method could be eliminated using the genetic engineering features and efficient maturation mechanisms available to the Society.

"I know you are correct," answered Anod. "However, it was hard enough trying to convince my people to use a cleansing station, isopod and replicator. I will present this option to my people."

"What other options do you have?" asked Major Ziikaar.

"The ancient methods, as Colonel Arkinnagga calls them."

"But, that would take many generations, and even then might not be sufficient."

"In fact, the uncertainty of just gender determination could compound the problem rather than help it," added Major Avyk.

"I understand the reality of the science. I am just struggling with how to present this situation to the community."

"If there is anything we can do to assist you," said Arkinnagga, "we stand ready to help."

Anod's mind returned to Saranon, and those days prior to the ambush. Zitger had been pensive and perhaps even distant, but there were no indications or precursor events that could have foretold what he became. How did his genetic aberrations escape the medical screening systems?

Anod looked to Major Avyk then Major Ziikaar. "What happened to the cleansing station and isopod processes on Saranon that missed these mutations in Zitger's brain?"

"A question many of us have asked in the last few days," answered Ziikaar. "We have reviewed the recorded data from the week prior to the ambush for Zitger, Zarrod and you. While there were some abnormalities in Zitger, they were within the tolerance band of the systems. We must consider tightening the tolerances for those segments. However, the difference between Zitger's last scan on Saranon and what we found this morning is enormous. The mutations that led to his aberrant behavior must have occurred once he joined the Yorax."

"They could also have been induced by his removal from the genetic maintenance of the isopod."

"Yes, that is possible," Avyk said. "However, using you as a control, which is not entirely appropriate scientifically, but it is all we have at the moment, the natural mutation scenario you allude to is not evident. There are no abnormal mutations in your genetic structure."

"That is good to know, however, I have used a cleansing station and isopod."

"Indeed," Avyk continued, "but Morgan has not recorded any maintenance actions even remotely close to these abnormalities. I might take just a small sidestep to say for the record that the injuries you suffered at the hands of Zitger were some of the worst I have seen. I have reviewed the history of torment and cruelty from a millennium ago on Earth. The violence and torture must have been difficult to bear."

With her mind forced to recall those days, Anod felt the residual pain still with her from several sites on her body that had not yet completed the healing process. She could not deny the relief of knowing she was not apparently susceptible to similar mutations. "It was certainly not something I sought, nor would I care to repeat the experience. But, I survived."

"Yes, you did," said Arkinnagga. "You are an example for all of us."

"Thank you." Anod stood. "I think I should go. Natasha and Anton need me to help them come to grips with this tragedy."

"As you say then," the captain agreed.

They stood to conclude the meeting. Anod remembered one other question. She turned to Arkinnagga. "I asked you earlier if you were going to take Zitger's corpse back to Earth. Are you going to do the genetic reconstruction? Are you going to try to determine what went wrong with him and perhaps our systems?"

Arkinnagga stared at Anod as she considered her response. "Yes."

Anod motioned with her head and hands for the starship captain to continue her explanation. A longer silence persisted. The other officers looked out the large portal at the beautiful brown and blue planet with white smears across the lighted portion of the globe.

"I am sure you recognize the potential consequences of what we have found here. I have orders from Central Command to preserve his remains and transport them back to Earth by the fastest, priority means available. We must make every possible effort to understand what happened to him."

"I would like to know the outcome of your studies."

"It is not within my authority to grant you such access. However, I shall note your request and recommend fulfillment. I think you have a special right."

"Thank you, Colonel Arkinnagga. I want to know. I served many years with him, and who knows, their may be something within me as well."

"Within us all."

"Then, I shall endeavor to be as patient as I possibly can as we await the outcome of this investigation."

"You will not be alone."

Anod bowed her head, and then paid her respects and promptly departed. She stood in the square at New Providence. The storm clouds she saw in the morning were nearly upon her. She could smell the rain on the wind. Nonetheless, Anod remained where she landed and stared into the distance at nothing in particular. This was not going to be an easy subject to discuss, let alone resolve. Anod needed help to craft the argument that would enable her to lead her people out of this dilemma of threat and vulnerability.

Chapter 19

"Anod, I am so scared," Natasha said as their leader joined them in the main room of the Arguello house.

"I know, but we will overcome this adversity as we have overcome all the other obstacles."

"But, what I heard tells me I must," she shivered as she reached for the word, "destroy," clutching her lower abdomen, "this baby growing in my womb."

"We need to discuss options. There is no need to be hasty."

"What do you want to do?" asked Anton.

"It is time to present the situation to the community along with our options and a recommendation."

"When?" Anton persisted.

"Before I give you my opinion, let me ask you both some questions. What do you think of the facts you heard this afternoon?"

Anton looked at Natasha who could only shake her head. "Is it really as bad as they say?"

"Yes."

"Then, we must do as they recommend."

"No!" shouted Natasha.

Anod held up her hand. "I am asking for your views, your opinions."

Natasha Norashova placed both her hands in front of her hips. "Anod, this is an innocent life. What cause could there be for taking such innocence?"

Anod looked out the window. Rain began to spatter against the glass. The patter of drops offered a mesmerizing song. She eventually turned back to Natasha. "This is not easy. The assessment of Colonel Arkinnagga and her officers is accurate. The consequences of Zitger's deeds and defects are real."

"But, children are taught. They are not born with the knowledge of life. Maybe, Arkinnagga is wrong. Maybe, they can be taught our morals, our rules, our culture."

"The accuracy of the Society's genetic mapping and the results of the precise genetic structures are very well understood. If anything, they are probably understating reality."

"But, Anod. You are talking about destroying an entire generation of our children."

"No, Natasha. We must think of this situation in a different light. None of us wanted to be raped."

"I want a child."

"But, Natasha, is this the child you really want?"

"A child is a child, Anod," she protested.

"I understand your feelings, but these children have serious cerebral defects that Zitger intentionally wanted to spread among the human population as quickly as possible. He was using us as pods to grow his malignancy."

"These are just children," she whispered.

"These are children, Natasha, who will grow up to be just as abhorrent as Zitger and maybe worse."

"Maybe less."

"These natural processes are much less predictable, but yes. It could be less."

"There you go," Natasha added, feeling vindicated.

Anod knew this was just a taste of the debate for the citizens of Murtauri Four. If she could not persuade Natasha, she would not likely be able to convince the community. She also knew the outcome of this debate would probably decide their future. The unfortunate reality is, they had to make this decision soon to avoid damage to the women, and it would be based on what might happen one, two, five, twenty or more years in the future. Just Natasha's resistance indicated she was not likely to win the argument on what might happen in the future.

"We will be faced . . . all of us including Anton, Otis and other single males . . . with critical decisions to be made for ourselves as individuals, but I will submit, these decisions must be made in the context of the greater good – what is best for the community – or we are likely to cease to exist as a community."

"It is not that bad," grumbled Natasha.

"Yes, it is. The thought of having thirty plus maniacs like Zitger terrorizing our planet and this galaxy is staggering to the imagination and an unacceptable threat. The thought of his offspring procreating and multiplying among the other human populations is staggering. This is not a question of these being our only children." Anod felt tears well in her eyes when her mind went to her two precious children. "I lost two children to that madman. They were the most important elements of my new life among the Betans and now Murtaurians. I want more children . . . many of them. I want to immerse myself in the lives of those young people. I will have more children even if I must lose this one for the good of the community."

"Are you carrying Zitger's child as I am?"

"I still have not faced that. I am assuming that I am, and I face the exact same decision you do. I do not want it any other way. So, what I argue for you, I argue for myself as well."

"You could find out right now by asking Morgan, couldn't you?" Anton asked.

"Yes," Anod answered turning toward him. "However, it serves no purpose other than to bias my argument. I must look at this just as Natasha and the others must look at this." Anod looked back to Natasha and concentrated on her eyes. "I must advise and recommend with the full realization this decision applies to me as well. While my pregnancy is not as certain as yours, I cannot think my fate any different."

"I appreciate that, Anod, however it is possible, by your own words, that you are different."

Again, Anod needed to change direction. "Regardless of the result of Zitger's raping us, we are still faced with the population imbalance."

"In that," said Anton, "you are suggesting that the men couple with multiple women."

"I do not mean to be crude, but yes, that is exactly what I mean."

"That is revolting."

"I know it is not our way, but we are faced with a situation that threatens our very existence . . . in fact, worse than the Yorax."

"How so?"

"We could see the Yorax. We could see their actions. This population crisis is not so easily seen."

"But, the numbers are skewed," said Anton, "but why is that a crisis that would warrant abandoning our morals?"

"With such an imbalance and the uncertainty of natural procreation, we risk making the imbalance even worse. For example, the preponderance of our offspring could easily be female, making the imbalance greater. However, the most critical element of the population crisis is not the gender imbalance. To put a fine point on it, our greatest threat is the thin genetic pool. The lack of diversity makes us more susceptible to disease, injury and genetic malformations the ancients called inbreeding. We need far greater diversity to have a healthy population."

Natasha winced. "But, the thought of coupling with just any male for the sole purpose of diversity is disgusting."

"Thanks," Anton responded with lightness.

They all laughed. Anod was the first to turn serious.

"The worst part of this situation is, we will not see the consequences of our decisions until a generation or more from now, and by then, it could very well be too late."

Natasha and Anton stared at Anod. Then, as if some light had suddenly gone on, Natasha asked, "What could happen?"

"The more imbalance and narrower diversity in our population, the more vulnerable we will be . . . the more at risk. Somehow, I must make you and the rest of our community understand the gravity of this situation. We are not playing a game of chance. We are deciding the fate of our very existence. While I do not believe any of these decisions will affect us directly," Anod said circling her index finger to the three of them, "it will most assuredly affect the next and subsequent generations. We must think of our children and their children. We must think of the future of our entire culture."

"So," said Natasha, "you do not see the loss of these children," patting her belly, "as important as the population crisis, as you call it."

"No. I am not eager to end these embryonic lives growing within us, Natasha. I love children. I marvel in the miracle of birth, and I cherish nurturing my children. As I said earlier, I want many more, as many as I can physically produce. I wish we were not threatened in this manner. And, I am certainly not saying this is an easy choice. However, as much as my heart says do not do it, my mind says we do not want one more Zitger let alone thirty plus among us to terrorize our people even more. The best thing I can say is, think of what Zitger did to you, or to me. Think of that abuse amplified thirty or more times, that is what we face."

"I understand," Natasha said with a soft tone of resignation.

"We need to call a community meeting as soon as we can gather everyone up, probably tomorrow midday, I should think. I need your help to support those who will be confronted with this situation for the first time."

"They will be shocked," added Natasha.

"Yes, they will. However, the sooner we confront this predicament and resolve to overcome this obstacle, the sooner we can move into the future and settle our lives."

"You are correct," Anton said. "We know that, but it will not be easy."

"Indeed."

They set about issuing instructions and answering various communications. Several families wanted to postpone the meeting so they could attend to the immediate needs of their families or crops. It took some extra effort on their part, but they eventually convinced everyone. The meeting would be tomorrow at noon.

Anod's reunion with Otis Greenstreet occurred in midmorning. The ground and leaves were still damp from last night's rain. Anton and Natasha worked on some project at the house.

Otis walked around the corner of a building into the square. His chocolate brown, smooth, hairless skin over the strong, distinctive features of his face offered a delicate contrast to his sturdy build and confident swagger.

"Great to see you again, Otis."

"An honor to see you."

They embraced and kissed each cheek. They found a small table and chairs but the trees continued to drip. They stood in the open.

"Tell me about your journey back to Beta."

"It was good to see friends and our old planet."

"I'm sure."

"As I stated in my return message, I did reach a draft trade agreement with Beta. They want to improve communications as we do. They think they can support us in a mutual commercial exchange."

"What about immigration?"

"Ours or theirs?"

"Theirs."

"They are not against it. However, they asked me if any of our people wanted to return to Beta. So, why are you concerned about immigration?"

"I will explain later. We will go through all the details at the community meeting."

"The Yorax incursion was pretty bad, wasn't it?"

"Yes, Otis. It was very bad."

"This is never easy, but I offer my deepest and heartfelt condolences for your loss." Anod nodded her head and felt tears of remembrance filling her eyes. "I know those children meant so much to you."

"Thank you, Otis. Now, I must think of the future."

Citizens began to gather in the square. The trees finished dripping, for the most part. The brilliant light of Murtauri broke through the clouds. At the appointed hour, Anod motioned for Anton and Natasha to join her on the platform. Otis decided to join them as well. With four adults on the platform there was not much room to move.

As Anod readied herself, she saw Colonel Arkinnagga and Major Ziikaar materialized in the open square behind the assembly. She made eye contact and acknowledged their presence as observers – an obvious sign of the significance the Society placed on the decisions before the Murtaurians.

Anod raised her arms to quiet the cacophony of the crowd. She recounted the essential facts she learned over the last few days. As expected, gasps of shock and vehement protest intermingled with her words. It was not a pleasant discussion and debate. The conflict between their morals and their survival exploded within the community. The debate was vigorous.

As some of the raped and pregnant women – Naomi Gibritzu, Natasha Norashova, Guyasaga – joined Anod in front of the group. One by one, the women linked arms and began to convince the remainder of the Murtaurians. As the realization of their direction came into focus, one of the women shouted, "Lie still and think of England." The mythical advice of a Victorian mother to her daughter in preparation for the marriage bed conveyed the spirit. Several people actually laughed at the levity in an otherwise grave situation.

"You are genetically engineered. What about the Society fixing the genetic code of these children?" asked a male voice Anod did not recognize.

"Yeah, Nick . . . God bless his soul . . . told us he saw how fast your wounds healed," someone else added.

"Even Anton has witnessed this."

Anton Trikinov fidgeted a little on the platform as he was put on the spot. Anod knew this was an important part of the debate.

"Genetic engineering is impressive, but it is not that good."

"Why not?"

Anod glanced beyond the assembly to the two Society officers. Neither of them moved nor offered any indication they wanted to participate in the debate. "There are others who are more qualified to answer these questions," Anod began. "However, I will do my best. What you have witnessed with me is genetic repair. Errors that occur due to the normal aging process of replication degeneration or due to damage from some source can be repaired by the isopod. However, any genetic engineering must be done prior to the genetic code being released for replication as was done with the enhancements of my physiological capabilities."

"What does that mean?"

"It means the time to fix Zitger's defective or aberrant genetic code was prior to conception. I am not aware of any capability to alter existing genetic code in a living organism," she answered. Again, she glanced at Arkinnagga, who shook her head in agreement this time. "It is too late for these fetuses."

"You want to kill them."

"We do not do that!"

"We banned those procedures many generations ago."

Anod held up her arms to quiet the group. "We must put this in perspective. A contaminated and aberrant human male raped many of our women including me. We have his defective offspring growing in our wombs. We can pretend these are going to be normal children, but they will not be normal. We must think of these entities as a harmful virus planted in our bodies. Zitger did this for that very reason. He was planting the seeds of our own destruction and probably other cultures as well. If this virus were the Black Plague from Medieval times on ancient Earth waiting for the moment to consume us, would we have the same feelings? We are talking about our very survival as a culture."

"This threat from little children?" someone protested.

"These embryos will grow to adulthood. They are not and will not be normal. To be brutally blunt, this is a grotesque and evil contamination of our culture. We must rid ourselves of this adulteration and take the necessary steps to strengthen our community."

Natasha held up her arms like a sports victor. "As much as I have wanted a child, my first child, and many children," she said, "I am now convinced Anod is correct. The sooner we do what is necessary, the sooner we can move on to rebuild our fragile society."

"But, these are innocent children."

"We can look at this tragic situation in that light," answered Natasha. "Or, we can really see it for what it is . . . a perverse contagion within our bodies."

"Are you sure?"

"Yes," shouted Natasha. "It tears my heart out, but yes, I am absolutely certain."

Anod nodded her head in agreement with her friend. Most nodded their heads in agreement. Some remained stone still. Others joined the debate.

A resolute commitment grew within the assembly. Not only would they heed the counsel of the Society regarding Zitger's offspring, they pledged their support to enhance the depth and diversity of their population. The Murtaurian women would give birth to as many children as each of them felt they could support and each by a different male. No one would be forced or coerced into multiple donor couplings. A great deal of care was taken in defining a ritual for community acceptance to allow the execution of their plan without compromising the solidity of the family units, those that survived the Yorax crimes. Much to Anod's surprise, the Murtaurian husbands understood and accepted their roles as husbands and fathers in the new environment. They also allowed exceptions for intact family units, but even some of those couples joined the spirit of the future.

After four long hours of negotiations, the congress finally concluded. Anod knew there were hard times ahead. Despite the agreement of the group, she recognized the reluctance of more than one woman, or male, or family. The success of their plan depended upon unanimity of action. They had to feel the weight as well as the support of the community. They needed to protect each other.

As the meeting adjourned and people began the journey back to their homes, the usual joviality and levity that seemed to be so common among the citizens was missing. This was a grave and serious situation. The gravity was reflected in the mood and expression of her people.

Colonel Arkinnagga eventually joined the small group around Anod. "May I have a private word," she said.

They walked the twelve meters to the open area beyond the square, near the entrance to the former Yorax compound. Arkinnagga looked deeply into Anod's eyes then looked at the ground. When her eyes returned, she began.

"This is not easy for me, even as a seasoned warrior," Arkinnagga said. "In this task, I must appeal to your spirit as a warrior."

"I am a mother, now . . . well," Anod responding dropping her voice, "at least I will be again someday. I want my warrior days behind me."

"Understood, however I think you will see my meaning. The

Society has directed me to inform you they see Zitger's contagion as a direct, albeit delayed, threat." She hesitated keeping her eyes transfixed on Anod.

Anod knew where she was headed. "Your orders are to ensure the contagion is eliminated." Arkinnagga waited several long seconds before she nodded her head. "They must feel this threat, as you call it, is sufficiently great to overcome the non-interference axiom," Anod sneered.

"The answer is, yes."

Anod stared at the starship captain turned messenger. "While we share the same objective in this matter, I know your orders will not be acceptable to my people."

"Which is why I chose to confide only in you privately."

"What are your orders precisely?"

Arkinnagga studied her counterpart to determine whether Anod could be trusted with such information. "My orders are to use whatever means necessary to eradicate any and all of the live genetic material from Zitger, and to quarantine or isolate any non-living material, such as his corpse."

"That is rather extreme."

"Yes, it is. It is also a measure of how serious we see this threat. There is no doubt he wanted human hosts for his mutant progeny. He chose your community for two reasons. One, he needed to eliminate you, so your people were convenient. Second, you are the most remote human community in the Confederation and the closest to the Yorax frontier."

"So, my people suffer because of me."

"That serves no purpose, Anod, and you know it. Specific conditions and a touch of fate have brought us to this point. Not that it will change our actions here, but the entire Confederation is watching us. Zitger's treachery has killed many thousands of people. He wanted to grow others to carry-on his infamy."

"I understand all that."

"Then, you also understand why my orders are inviolate."

"Yes."

"Good, then what can we do to assist you?"

"The best thing you can do is stand clear. We must handle this in our way."

"Acceptable, as long as the outcome is the same."

"I am sensing a threat here, Arkinnagga."

"No threat. I have the utmost respect and regard for you, as a person, as a warrior, but I also have my orders."

"Then, do as I say. We will do what must be done."

"If so, we will have no reason to interfere."

"Good."

"Before I leave you, when will this ugly task be completed?"

Anod realized they had not agreed on a timetable for execution. "As soon as we can."

"I shall risk being rude, but that is not acceptable. It must not wait. This gruesome task must be done in the next day or two at the longest."

Anod felt resentment in Colonel Arkinnagga's words. Feeling a tension in her neck, Anod threw her head back and took a very deep breath, holding it to allow the surge to course through her arteries to her brain, and then released it slowly. She captured the starship captain's eyes. "This is not your planet, and I am not your lieutenant."

Arkinnagga stretched her arms out to her sides like the arms of a cross. She knew she had gone too far. "I did not intend to offend you or your people. I simply need to convey the severity of this tragic state of affairs." Anod, ever so slowly, bobbed her head to acknowledge the captain's statement. "Let me change the tenor of this exchange. What can we do to assist your effort to remedy this condition?"

"Leave us to our affairs."

The starship captain lowered her arms placing her hands on her hips. "You do understand my orders?" she repeated.

"Yes."

Arkinnagga studied her counterpart. The two warriors understood the meaning precisely. This was not an issue the Society was prepared to back down on, for the greater good. Anod saw the logic and rationale clearly; she just had to find the means to ensure success.

"As you say, then. We shall make a genuine effort to be patient. You have but to ask if you need our help."

"Thank you. Is there anything else you wish to discuss?"

Arkinnagga thought for a moment. "Yes, there is. As a personal note, I would like you to know your accomplishments as a warrior and a leader are becoming nearly mythical. The Society is diminished by your departure."

"Banishment."

The colonel nodded her head. "Unfortunately, yes, banishment. I have talked to Colonel Zontramani several times about you. We have all been impressed."

"No need. I am just an ordinary woman trying to live a decent life."

"Your humility is laudable but so out of place. You know perfectly well how extraordinary your achievements are."

"I did what I had to do. It was not like I had much of a choice."

"Anod, sometimes valor is defined by the courage a warrior musters up when there are few choices."

"Perhaps."

"Let me see here. After your ambush near Saranon, adrift and nearly dead, you found yourself virtually alone in a foreign human culture. When they were threatened by the Yorax, you flew a single, patched-together, Yorax interceptor against a division of Yorax battlecruisers and beat them."

"No. I would not have survived if the *Endeavour* had not arrived when she did."

"Fate often decides the battle. Nonetheless, you single-handedly defended Beta. Then, you led your people to this place, convinced them to accept items of technology that were foreign to them, and once again defended your people. Now, I know you did not testify as such, but it is clear you intentionally got yourself captured to get inside the Yorax compound, endured brutal torture and abuse, and manage to partially free a hand – one hand – to eliminate one of your guards. Even more amazing, you extricated yourself from the shackles and dispatched another guard. Then, you convinced a maniacal, and yet accomplished, warrior to face you in solo combat without weapons or any form of bodily protection."

"Again, I had no choice."

"Your courage and skills persuaded the Yorax without hesitation that they should leave. They should not incur more losses. A warrior culture with vastly superior numbers, weaponry and position knew when they had had enough. They could have decimated this planet and certainly killed all of your people, but they did not. They departed with their tails between their legs. If we could ask them, I am certain they would say they left out of respect for your valor in the face of those odds. They know, as we all do, when we are in the presence of greatness."

"Nonsense."

"You are entitled to your humility. You have earned it, Anod. I just wanted to convey my personal respect," Arkinnagga said, and then bowed deeply at the waist. "It is an honor to know you."

Anod quickly looked around feeling a little embarrassed. The others were absorbed in their own discussion. She had no idea what to say at this awkward moment. She simply extended her hand to Arkinnagga. They shook hands firmly.

"Now, if you will excuse me, I must return to my ship and leave you to your duty."

Anod nodded her head and waited several seconds before she turned to watch the starship captain and her science officer depart the surface. She slowly walked toward the small group – Natasha, Anton, Otis, Guyasaga, Naomi and Mysasha.

"What were you two talking about?" asked Anton.

"Our situation."

"How so?"

"They see our condition as both dangerous and precarious."

Natasha shook her head. "I am still having a hard time seeing how these tiny little entities not even big enough to distend our bellies can be such a threat to the Society."

"I agree with Natasha," said Guyasaga.

"I am the only one of us women who was not raped, and I am not pregnant," Mysasha added. "However, I am having a struggle with this as well."

Anod searched each of their faces. The concern was genuine and real. "Let us see if I can explain this in any better fashion." She placed her hands behind her head and leaned backward stretching her chest and abdominal muscles. "I think all of you know the Society has perfected genetic engineering to an extraordinary level. I am a living testament to their achievement. Our form of procreation is alien to them. Our ancient ways have been prohibited on Earth and among members of the Society for several centuries. Their ability to predict genetic outcomes goes down to the molecular and atomic levels. They know and can precisely predict hereditary results prior to replication of the DNA strings that are the gene sets. However, to them, we have become human incubators for a virulent contagion that threatens not only our culture but also all humankind. We are infected and must be cured as we would with any disease."

"But, these are living beings," replied Guyasaga.

"Just as a deadly virus is living. They view these entities as malignant tumors that may not claim the life of the hosts, however, from their perspective, these progeny of a defective male will certainly claim many, many more lives when they mature."

"It is still hard to think such things about babies we cannot even see, yet," Mysasha said.

"Believe me, I know. But, I know they are correct. This is reality. And, for our future, we must do the proper thing. We must protect our children and our future children. We have a responsibility to all humans, if not all living entities. We have no choice but to end these specific pregnancies."

"You are ready to do this?" asked Natasha.

"I do not know whether I am infected or not."

"You don't?" Guyasaga asked.

"Morgan does. He has done the full biological screening on me. I chose not to learn the results."

"Why?"

"I thought it might affect my decision-making process. I have assumed that I am infected, and I am prepared to take the same measures as I am recommending to each of the infected women."

"But, you don't know."

"No. We are at the stage, now, where I have no choice. I must know if I am infected. If so, I intend to carry out this procedure this afternoon. If not, then I shall carry this baby to term."

"So, it might be Bradley's baby," Mysasha said with an air of excitement.

"Yes, it is possible. I truly do not know."

"Let's go find out," said Natasha.

They all followed her to the house and gathered around Morgan's interface console.

"Morgan."

"Yes, Natasha."

"We would like to know if Anod is carrying Bradley's or Zitger's baby."

"I am unable to discuss another person's medical condition."

"Morgan," interjected Anod.

"Yes, Anod."

"I authorize your release of that information at this specific time," she stated. Anod felt a gripping tension turn her stomach upside-down and knot her shoulders. Several sets of eyes searched her face. Anod concentrated on the panel although that was not where the information was going to come from.

"Very well. The last five scans have shown consistent results.

The fetus within Anod is a combination of the genetic codes of Anod Megan SanGiocomo and Bradley James SanGiocomo."

Anod slumped forward then bent over at the waist covering her face with both hands. She felt concerned hands touching and stroking her back, shoulders and head.

"You are certain?" asked Natasha.

"Yes," answered Morgan.

"There is no chance of an error that Anod's child might have been fathered by Zitger?"

"None. The genetic codes for the two deceased males are substantially different."

"Congratulations, Anod," Natasha whispered at her ear, and then she kissed Anod's hand covering the left side of her face.

Anod felt the strength in her legs evaporate. The others detected the change and held her. She wiped her tears away before the others could see her reaction then stood straight up and took a deep breath. Both Natasha and Guyasaga needed her strength. She needed to maintain the empathy for her friends who had not been so lucky. They all hugged and kissed each other with words of encouragement.

"What do we do now?" asked Natasha.

Anod surveyed the group of faces looking to her. "The best way is to command Morgan to terminate the virus and remove the infection," Anod said, intentionally avoiding any reference to Zitger's contamination.

"Right now?"

"If you wish. We can carry out the procedure as soon as you are ready, or you can wait until you enter your next sleep cycle."

"If I am going to do this, I need to do it now."

"Me too," said Naomi Gibritzu. "I need to get my girls here as well. They are on the other side of town with friends."

"As you say, then," Anod responded.

Naomi left them to find Cetia and Moma. Natasha slowly walked toward the storeroom. The others looked around to find something to keep them busy. Guyasaga touched Anod's shoulder.

"I must go to Samuel and my children. I will be with them, and I will probably take care of my infection, as you call it, tonight with my family."

"That is a good idea, Guyasaga. You need to be with your family."

"I shall talk to you tomorrow," she said. They hugged, kissed and separated.

Anod watched Guyasaga walk back toward the square to find her husband and children.

"Will you help me?" called Natasha from the storeroom.

Anod nodded to the others that she would take care of her. Natasha stood in the middle of the room still fully clothed. Anod shut the door behind her.

"I know how this must be done, but I need someone with me, and you are the best friend I have."

"I will be here."

Natasha prepared herself. She sought Anod's embrace. "This is not easy."

"I know, Natasha. I know."

They kissed, and then Natasha gave the appropriate commands and entered the cleansing station. They maintained eye contact until the process began, and then Natasha closed her eyes until it was complete. When she opened the door and stepped out, Anod wrapped a robe around her.

"How do you feel?"

Natasha looked to Anod. Sadness filled her eyes. Tears descended her cheeks. "I should be in pain. I should feel an agonizing pain, but I don't. I feel no different."

"Natasha, we are here with you." Anod took her bowed head in her hands and kissed her forehead. "I would suggest you use the isopod, now."

"But, it is early."

"We can tell it to give you an extended sleep. Twelve hours would be sufficient."

"It can do that?"

"Yes. The system was originally designed to place humans in hibernation for long space travel. You can tell it to suspend you for however long you want. You will wake up tomorrow morning fully rested as if you had only gone through a normal four hour cycle."

"Yes, you are right. It will probably help me forget what I have just done."

"I think so as well."

Again, Natasha took Anod's embrace then entered one of the isopods. Once she was into the sleep mode, Anod joined the others.

Naomi had returned with her older daughters, Cetia and Moma, as well as the younger two of her surviving children. Anton and Otis instinctively knew their task as they entertained the younger children. Without words, Naomi guided her older daughters to the storeroom. Between Anod and Naomi, they helped the two girls through a full cleansing cycle. When they were complete, Anod found robes for them and wrapped an arm around them on either side of her. They watched as Naomi completed her process. The Gibritzu women did not want to use the isopods, yet. They dressed and returned to the main room. Otis and Anton kept the younger children content and prepared a light meal. It was a quiet, solemn evening.

A good portion of the evening was spent communicating with various people around the planet. Anod gave everyone a step-by-step checklist for the disinfecting process. Some reported back their completions. Others wanted to talk some more about the moral dilemma. Anod coached, supported, encouraged and empathized with the other infected women. They shared their mutual pain.

In a few hours, only Anod and Otis remained awake. "Was it really that bad?" he asked.

"Yes, it was. It has not been easy for any of our women."

"I cannot imagine."

"They need our support, all of them."

"And, they shall get it."

"It is good to have you back."

"I am glad no permanent damage was done to you."

Anod looked deeply into his dark eyes with an odd mixture of frustration and burgeoning anger. "But, there has. I have lost my family, my children, that is permanent, and that loss will be with me until I take my last breath."

"I am sorry, Anod. I did not mean to bring up your tragic loss."

"I know."

"I am here for you, if you need me," he said with confident, caring, soft words.

"As you have been all those other times."

They retired as well.

Chapter 20

Action began before Anod rose, and she was the first to rise at the Arguello house. She was thoroughly engaged with Morgan at the console when Otis joined her, followed shortly thereafter by Anton and the others. They took turns gathering up bits and pieces to make a meal. Everyone seemed to be in good spirits despite the emotional trauma of last night.

"What is the problem?" asked Natasha as the last to rise.

Without looking away from the console, Anod answered. "Most of our women have fulfilled their obligations."

"That is a rather harsh way to put it."

"Perhaps. If so, my apologies."

"But?"

"We have seven we have not made contact with, two who are pending and four who so far have refused to comply."

"Has anyone talked to them?" asked Naomi.

"Yes . . . in a gentle way. However, I think we will need to visit each of them. We simply cannot allow this virus to survive."

"Anod!" protested Natasha.

Without looking back, she held up her hand. "Again, my apologies, but the facts remain."

"Do you really think such pressure is necessary?" asked Otis.

This time she swiveled in her chair and faced the gallery behind her. "Have you been raped?"

"No, but they have."

"Were you tortured by that madman?"

"No, Anod, I wasn't. So, what is your point?"

"He killed the majority of our men just because they were males and might interfere with his grand design. Not only did he violate most of our adult women and many of our older girls, he was able to impregnate most of them. I have lost my entire family. Natasha lost her husband. Naomi, Cetia and Moma lost their husband and father along with two brothers. There are many others who have suffered. Just one or two of his offspring would have a lifetime to wreak havoc on our community as well as spread to other cultures. Please do not forget the destruction and death he caused on Beta. He forced us from that planet and nearly succeeded here. Whether we like it or not, we are once more at the front lines in a battle for survival. The sooner we are rid of this virus, the sooner we can think of a more pleasant future. We must get on with what we must do."

The group stood stunned by her onslaught. She recognized too late that she had laid it on too thick. Anod spun around and made herself busy at the console. She heard more than one of them leave the house for the outside. She was correct. There was nothing that was not precisely true. Anod wanted this ugliness done so they could put it behind them and move on to brighter tomorrows. She felt a hand on her shoulder.

"We all feel the pain in one way or another," whispered Naomi. "But, we must have compassion for those who have suffered and continue to suffer from this travesty." Anod nodded her head as if some huge weight was pulling her chin to her chest. "We will help you, but we must understand the anguish of each individual."

"I know."

"Good. Now, make us a list of who has not completed and we will visit them . . . each of them . . . personally."

Naomi did not wait for an answer. She went outside to gather up the others. Anod did as Naomi suggested. They agreed Anod should remain in New Providence to coordinate their efforts. Each of them took their assignments and departed.

Anod lost herself in images and thoughts – some happy, some sad. She regretted letting the stress get to her. These were the only people she had and the only people she wanted. Her mind for the first time turned to the as yet unfelt new life growing within her. Anod remembered the joyous experience of carrying Zoltentok and Sara. This was another opportunity to enjoy the pleasure. Anod also knew the intensity of these events would not be beneficial to her unborn child – Bradley's child.

A knock on the wood of the door jam broke her thoughts. Anod turned to see Colonel Arkinnagga standing in the doorway.

"May I come in?" she asked.

Anod nodded and motioned toward a chair near her. The starship captain moved the chair and sat so they faced each other one meter apart.

"We have monitored the situation," she began. "Can we be of any assistance?"

"What do you propose . . . taking them by force?"

"No, Anod. However, using our forecast and projection capabilities, we might be able to help the doubters see what could be in store for them and all of us."

"An interesting proposition." Anod's thoughts turned darker.

"What if that does not work?"

"You know the answer," Arkinnagga said without the slightest change of expression.

"Yes, I suppose I do."

"It is sad that it has come to this, that these women who have been violated by an intruder must endure yet one more violation."

"We hope it does not come to that. For your information only, I have reaffirmed my orders with Central Command. I might also tell you the Yorax are prepared to make substantial consolations in an attempt to achieve a lasting peace."

"Good. At least something good has come from all this damage."

"More good than you think, Anod."

"Like what?"

"We will talk when this situation stabilizes. At the moment, I think our best efforts must remain focused on the task at hand. Your people will need healing as well."

"Yes, they will."

"I thought I would carry out a brief visit to show my support, offer whatever assistance you feel might be appropriate, and make sure you are doing well."

"I am fine. I suppose you know I am not carrying the infection," Anod said.

"Yes, I do. Although this is not something I am familiar with, as you know, I suppose congratulations are in order."

"Thank you," she answered bowing in recognition.

Arkinnagga departed before any of the others arrived. Anod stared at the door for several minutes, her mind a blank, before she turned back to the console.

She received reports from Morgan as the process continued. As specific tasks were completed, they shifted their efforts to help each other. Anod intentionally did not interfere as she monitored the team's efforts to persuade the dwindling resisters. A couple of women, encouraged and supported by their husbands, left their homes and hid to avoid the termination of their pregnancies.

The process of finding the last of the infected women took several more days. The two families, both childless couples who had struggled to have children, were brought to New Providence, not as prisoners but as friends who needed the intervention of friends. Anod and others spent another couple of days talking to them and explaining the data available through Morgan. In the end, they resorted to the offer from Colonel Arkinnagga. Anod and Natasha joined the two couples for transport to the *Reliant* for the forecast simulations to help them see the potential outcomes. They ran the most probable as well as several variations. None of them were particularly pleasant to watch. The inherent distrust of the technology made the effort to convince them more arduous. Even Majors Ziikaar and Avyk joined the education sessions. Finally, the husbands removed their objection as they recognized the importance of eradicating Zitger's infection but also with the cross-fertilization initiative they were collectively embarking upon, they would gain the families they sought. The reality of the greater good took the dominant position.

Anod called a community meeting for the following day. The citizens gathered as they had all the previous times they had been summoned. Anod took her position and raised her arms.

"Citizens," she said waiting for quiet. "We have successfully endured our latest trauma. To all those who have suffered this cleansing process, I offer my humblest and sincerest sympathies on behalf of all of our community. This has not been easy, but it is complete. I can report to you that we are finally free of the last vestiges of an evil entity. It is time that we look to the future and a flourishing community on M4."

"What do we do?" asked an anonymous voice.

"We live our lives the best way we know how." She wanted that to be her succinct answer. No one else spoke. "We have begun the long journey to repair the damage done to our community. As some of you know, Otis Greenstreet returned with the draft trade agreement with Beta. Our brothers and sisters on Beta have offered to help us."

"With immigration?"

"No. They want to stay on Beta."

"Maybe we should go back," said another.

"I want to go back," added a man.

Anod held up her arms again. "We, each of us, are free to do what we must. For those who wish to return, we can arrange transport. However, I would like to concentrate this meeting on those who wish to stay."

"Here, here."

Anod scanned the crowd. Faces looked quietly to her. "Now that we are rid of the infection, it is time to continue the healing process. We must build our population, and it is imperative that we strive for a balanced diversity. Although this task will not be easy either, it is vitally important that we agree on the rules for achieving diversity."

A vigorous discussion and debate ensued. They needed more males to replace the enormous percentage lost during the Yorax incursion. They traded ancestral techniques passed down through the millennia. In the end, they agreed to use whatever means they could find without using the Society's DNA manipulation technology. Several couples continued to have difficulty with multiple couplings to achieve the broadening of the genetic pool. They also resolved this question by allowing families to choose their means as long as the result was the same. Some wanted only natural couplings. Others could not come to grips with the social risks, so they chose artificial insemination using multiple and different donors. A few were prepared to try implantation of genetically engineered ovum from the Society if the transportation means could be worked out. They collectively created table of exchange to keep track of their progress and maximize their efforts.

Anod felt a sense of pride and rejoiced in the cohesion that came to her community. Despite the risks, obstacles, misgivings and uncertainty, everyone began to feel the communal protection of the group as they threw their efforts into the rebuilding process. Diversity and the variations it brought became a common theme of dialogue and discussion. Most of the Murtaurians celebrated and reveled in the broadening spectrum of humankind. Their slogan became, DIVERSITY WILL PROTECT US. Signs began to show up around the towns or on houses. People believed.

Anod began to relax just enough to enjoy the thought she held part of Bradley within her – the SanGiocomo line would not be broken, at least not yet. She eagerly awaited the first kick and the roundness of her belly, filling with her growing child. Anod wanted to set the example, to show her commitment to rebuilding their community.

The *Reliant* made several short patrols but stayed in the vicinity of Murtauri Four. The officers and crew rotated to the surface for liberty periods to relax. The interaction was good for the starship personnel to enjoy themselves, and it was good for the Murtaurians to become familiar with their skills and commitment to their profession.

On the *Reliant*'s last visit, the Society Starship *Endeavour*, captained by Colonel Zontramani, joined in the recognition. The two captains came to Anod and asked her to take a walk with them. They meandered among the rocks in the shade of the forest between New Providence and the mountains.

With the amenities and ancillary topics behind them, Arkinnagga opened. "First, as we said earlier, we are emissaries from the Society and Central Command. Admiral Agginnoor sends her regards." Anod acknowledged the greeting. "Second, we would like to convey the sincere appreciation of the Society for your leadership in eliminating Zitger's infection, as you call it."

"We have all heard of extraordinary heroism in finally bringing that traitor to justice."

"Thank you, Colonel Zontramani. I just wanted to stop the bleeding."

"We have petitioned Central Command to place your accomplishment in the record of the Kartog Guards."

"But, I am no longer a member."

"As you say, nonetheless, you were a member and some are proud to call you a member today."

"Thank you."

"To say the least," continued Arkinnagga, "Central Command was quite concerned about Zitger's activities and took a big sigh of relief when we reported your eradication of his infection."

"We are glad as well."

"How are your people handling the trauma?" asked Arkinnagga.

"Rather well considering that termination of a pregnancy is virtually non-existent among these people."

"It had to be done."

"We know, but it did not make it any easier."

"We are most grateful for your sacrifice," Zontramani added.

"Thank you. It helps to know others recognize the sacrifice."

"You advocated cross-fertilization to enhance your population," said Arkinnagga. "Are they accepting your recommendation?"

"Yes. We have agreed to a set of rules. Each woman including me will have as many babies as they feel they are able to have, and each baby will have a different male donor."

"Excellent."

"Extraordinary," added Arkinnagga. "The resiliency of your people is truly extraordinary."

"They have learned from their ancestors how to survive. They will do what must be done."

"So we learn," said Zontramani.

Arkinnagga stopped to face Anod in a small flat spot of ground with massive gray boulders towering above them. The sweet, earthy aroma of deep green trees growing from just about any available crack cast them in shade verging on darkness.

"We have one other assignment," Arkinnagga began. "On behalf of the Society's Council of Elders, we have been asked to extend an invitation to you, as the leader of the community of Murtauri Four, to visit Earth."

"Earth?"

"Yes."

"I have never been there."

"Neither have we," said Zontramani.

"This is a supreme honor, Anod."

Her mind asked immediately – why? Why was she being invited to Earth, a place she represented and served her whole life until her banishment and a place from which her predecessors had come from centuries ago? Why now? Then, she thought about being separated from the place that had become her home. She was slowly returning to happiness. She knew as soon as her child was born she would feel a sense of focus, a sense of being, a sense of purpose.

"Please tell the Council of Elders I am grateful for their invitation, but I would rather stay here." She knew as soon as she said the words the refusal would not be appreciated. Just a half dozen years ago, she would not have considered refusing such an invitation. Anod had grown up with an almost mythical attraction to Earth, as most of her compatriots had as well.

"Anod," they both replied.

Arkinnagga continued. "You cannot refuse such a prestigious invitation. This is important for them to honor you as well as for them to know a true hero."

"I was banished from the Society. I made a life and a family as the Betans and now Murtaurians have done since their ancestors were banished from Earth. My family died here," she said as she pointed in the direction of Meganville. "I have no reason to leave this place."

"Anod," said Zontramani. "Let me see if I can explain. You are a genuine hero. Your courage saved countless lives in this generation and probably many generations to come. We are trying to strengthen the alliance for your protection and ours. I am not sure how the Council plans to honor you, but I am willing to wager it is substantial, perhaps reinstatement in the Society."

"I do not want to be a hero, and I do not want to be reinstated."

"Anod," protested Arkinnagga.

"I know you mean well, and believe me I am honored by this gesture. To be candid, there is an element of curiosity and fascination to see the place from which we have come and is the object of all those stories we have heard over the years."

"Now is the perfect time for you to see Earth in all its glory," Arkinnagga said. "You have all those questions I am sure you have held like the rest of us."

"Let me talk to my friends to see what they say."

"Very well. We will stand by awaiting your reply."

They walked back to New Providence. The two captains returned to their ships undoubtedly to report their less than satisfactory outcome to Central Command. Anod joined the reduced group – Natasha, Otis and Anton – back at the house.

"What did they want?" asked Anton without even a greeting.

"They wanted to thank us for eliminating the infection."

"They want to thank you," he answered.

She ignored the slight. "They also invited me to Earth."

"Why?" asked Otis.

"Some gibberish about being a hero and the leader of our people."

"All true," Natasha added.

"Are you going?"

"At first, I said, no. I did not want to leave this place."

"Why?" asked Otis again.

Anod stared at him with incredulity, and then glanced at the others who seemed to share his question. "My family died here. My only friends are here."

"Sounds like you have other friends in very high places," Anton said. "You should go, Anod. You should go for all of us."

"Some of the rest of us would like to go, too, but we will be content with your stories of the visit."

"I don't know if I am going."

"Anod," said Natasha. "You must go."

"I am pregnant."

"So, does that prevent space travel?"

"You have done it before in an interceptor," added Anton. "You will travel like a dignitary this time. You are a hero and the leader of an entire planet."

"But . . ."

"No, buts," interjected Otis. "You must go for yourself – for all of us."

"Do you really think so?"

"Yes," came the enthusiastic and simultaneous reply from all three of them.

"What do you think the others will say?"

"What others?" asked Otis. "Our Murtaurians?"

"Yes."

"They will say represent us well," Natasha answered.

"Do you really think so?"

"Yes," again came the simultaneous answer.

"If it will make you feel better," Otis said, "we can call a community assembly to provide you with that affirmation."

"That might not be a bad idea."

"Don't you want to go?" Natasha asked.

"As Arkinnagga and Zontramani pointed out, I, like many others, have maintained a fascination with Earth. None of us have been there, but we have heard the stories. So, yes, there is part of me that wants to go."

"All of us have the same fascination," Otis said.

"I do not think I can go and make it back here in time to deliver my baby."

"Then, deliver it there," said Anton.

"No," barked Anod. "I want to deliver it here with the help of my friends. Mysasha has helped me both times and Guyasaga has nursed both children when I needed her help."

"How long will it take?" Natasha asked.

"Perhaps two to three months each way even at hyper-light speeds."

"Then, you should wait."

"Maybe. Let us call an assembly. I want to make sure if I am going to do this that I am representing all our people."

The assembly was called. The overwhelming response she received confirmed the opinions of Natasha and the others. To her surprise, the community basked in her honor and wanted her to represent them on Earth.

Anod formally replied to the starship captains. She agreed to go, but only after her baby was born. The Murtaurians understood. The starship captains thought they understood and could convey to the Council of Elders the necessity of delay. Once the appropriate arrangements were made, the *Reliant* and *Endeavour* departed for other parts of the galaxy.

The Murtaurians settled into a routine and sense of community brought even closer together by adversity. Anod withdrew from daily political activities so she could enjoy her pregnancy and ready herself for her next birthing. All was right with the world. A bountiful future lay ahead. There were truly a myriad of reasons to rejoice, and they rarely failed to do so. Justice had been done.

Cap Parlier

Author of *Anod's Seduction* and *Anod's Redemption*

Cap and his wife, Jeanne, live in Andover, Kansas, along with Cap's mother, four dogs and a bowling ball with legs otherwise known as a cat. He is a graduate of the U.S. Naval Academy, a former Marine aviator, Vietnam veteran, experimental test pilot and successful manager who currently serves as engineering manager for an aerospace company. Cap is a former director of the National Marrow Donor Program and director emeritus of The Marrow Foundation. Cap helped a Soviet test pilot who was a hero of the Chernobyl disaster and needed treatment for his radiation exposure obtain a bone marrow transplant in the USA, and Cap told the story of these heroes of Chernobyl in his book, *Sacrifice*. He brought his aviation, engineering and intelligence experience to *TWA 800 – Accident or Incident?* when he joined Kevin E. Ready to co-author the detailed assessment of the 1996 tragedy. Cap has numerous other projects completed and in the works including screenplays, historical novels and a couple of history books. He has remained an outspoken and fervent advocate of manned space exploration, as well as inner space exploration.

Interested readers may wish to visit his website at <http://www.parlier.com> for his essays and other items, or subscribe to his weekly on-line "Update from the Heartland." Cap can be reached at: cap@parlier.com.

Printed in the United States
23260LVS00004B/91-153